Haunting Me

By Nikki LeClair

To A.F one of my soulmates, and E.Z, and all the girl's nights that we rely on.

To my real life Clara, after twenty years of friendship, I can't wait to see what else is in store for us.

And lastly, to my husband, who I threatened never to dedicate a book to.

Chapter One

"There is a clause in the contract that states I have the right to post whatever I want about the bastard if *he* leaves me. And he did. He left me!"

"What my client means to say, is that she was within her right to post what she—"

"—It's defamation of character!" The deep voice booms around the room. "Yes, the contract stated she was legally able to post whatever she wanted to on her Profile in the event my client left her, but it also stated slander would void the entire agreement."

That's my boss, Terrance Meyers. Dressed in a black suit and yellow tie, big wide hands gesturing profusely as he asserts our case to the judge sitting fifteen feet away from us. He's an obnoxious man; he rarely smiles and wears too much aftershave. He had recently replaced his black comb over with hair plugs and to everyone's horror he doesn't look half bad. Next to him stands our client, Calvin DiRusso a mousey, baby-faced man dressed in a polo sweater and designer jeans. He's barely said a word all day, practically the last six months.

The opposing council retaliates and my mind begins to meander.

Sometimes I wonder if I landed in the right profession, if I jumped into this career field too soon. But if you knew me and my story could you blame me? My brother is an editor at Hughson Publishing House, and my sister is a contemporary artist, whose work has been featured in galleries around the world. My sister Addy married young. I am the oldest and was teetering on academic probation in university because I wasn't sure what I wanted to do. It was by chance I chose to major in Law; I met and fell for Preston Brant. He was majoring in Law so he could one day take over his father's new law firm. Of course, only my closest friends know the story of how I decided to study Law.

I even tried to follow Preston to Meyers and Brant. Of course he was accepted and I was not. Meyers and Brant were slowly making something of themselves at that point and they only wanted the best of the best, or anybody directly related to a partner. When I ran into Preston three years later he introduced me to Terrance Meyers; and he urged me to reapply. I was having trouble with my boyfriend Dylan, at the time. He had a harebrained idea to invent a 2-in-1 pen/pencil product which sounded exactly like its name. At the time he had a prototype created and it didn't look half bad, but he needed money. I was stupid enough to take out a twenty thousand dollar line of credit when he asked me to. The idea sank.

So, reapplying to Meyers and Brant seemed like a sign at the time. Getting a job there would insure a decent salary and freedom from the calls of my Bank. This time I was hired as Terrance's legal assistant. Preston quit a week later. He claimed in a company email that he found his real purpose in life, breeding sheep dogs in a ranch down south.

Life in a law firm changes you rather quickly; you have little time for a personal life. Dylan and I grew further apart until he just left without paying me back. His leaving had an upside though; I needed to put most of my energy on my new job, and making sure I could prove to them I would one day be an excellent hard working lawyer. I mean, you have to be focused, serious and invest years of your life to it.

I've devoted almost three years of hard work. Three years of no vacations, only a handful of girl nights, and missed holidays. Three years of being behind in paying back the twenty thousand. Minimal payments each month kept the bank from blowing up my phone. The rent in this city is high, and turns out Legal Assistants don't get paid much.

Three years and I still find myself drifting into other thoughts as the proceedings go on. It's not that I don't *want* to pay attention; it's only that sometimes the case is so boring.

I'm aware that not every case can be as exciting as an episode of Crime Report. Though it seemed everything that either came across the desks at Meyers and Brant were last will and testaments, land disputes, and pre-nup variances, including the new age pre-nup; the Social Media Pre-nuptial agreement. As you can imagine, it is exactly what it sounds like. Both parties agree to what can and cannot be posted on their social media accounts during the marriage, and if the marriage should dissolve. It's what we're sitting through right now.

The room is empty; except for the judge sitting at her bench across from us and the court transcriber sitting near her left typing away. The opposing council is at our right side and she's appointed Douglas Ferris. He's a pompous overweight lawyer with a habit of making sexual remarks towards any woman within ten feet of him. As annoying as he was, he was one hell of a lawyer and had a win ratio of ninety percent.

"Everyone should know what a cheating loser he is!" the soon to be ex. Mrs DiRusso shouts over at us. She is a stunning ex-model with legs up to her neck and long, wavy light hair. "He's lucky I didn't post more so our friends can see it!"

As the room erupts in an outburst between both sides and the judge smacks her gavel angrily, I feel a jab in my side from an elbow. I glance over at Greg who works with us. His glasses are slipping slightly off his pointy nose as he motions down at his hand. He's offering me a piece of gum, which I assume is to stifle my yawns. I take it with a grateful smile. I like Greg; we have been working together for the last three years and he will without a doubt be an incredible lawyer someday.

Whenever Terrance lets he and I schedule the bar exam that is, it seems like the two of us do less research and more coffee runs or dry cleaning pickups. I have noticed that over the last six months I have been the one getting the coffee and Greg was doing most of the legal work.

To say Terrance isn't fond of us is an understatement. He loathes us. He over-works us, verbally abuses us at times and forgets to pay us overtime every time we clock in the extra hours. So why do we stay? Because getting your foot in the door in any of the city's top law firms is virtually impossible, and we both knew it would all be worth it in the end. Plus I need the money, and the hope of a raise in the near future to pay off that stupid twenty thousand dollars.

I notice the room has become quiet and the judge is starting her concluding statement.

Thank God, I don't think I could stand this case any longer.

Behind the typist is a small round clock and I sit up to see the time, as I unwrap my stick of gum. It is twelve-thirty exactly. Pushing the piece of mint gum inside my mouth. my feet begin to bounce up and down slightly.

This was supposed to be over at noon, and now I am definitely going to be late.

I can feel myself begin to sweat through my white blouse, the grey suit jacket I have over top is much too heavy for this type of weather. What was I thinking? It's May.

Nice job Phoebe.

Riley Barret, my sweet, handsome, charming boyfriend of just over a year has reserved a table for us at his favorite restaurant for lunch. Something he has done numerous times but only twice has he invited his mother and father along. His father is rarely off his cellphone, he's a stock trader. His mother? I don't think she's ever thrown a kind word my way or given me more than ten seconds of her attention.

I am determined to win her over. I have to. Riley is the best boyfriend I have ever had. He isn't a couch surfer like Dylan. He doesn't shy away from serious talk like marriage and kids. He never misses an opportunity to tell me he loves me. In fact, he is way too good for me and I have a feeling most people in my life knew it too. The fact that he comes from a well to do family means little to me. Although I suppose if people found out about my large debt they'd question everything.

"...in the case of DiRusso versus DiRusso, I find that the bonds of the pre-nuptial agreement have been infringed upon by Mrs. DiRusso and therefore construe that she is no longer entitled to the country home and ski lodge as was previously stated in the document—"

Mrs. DiRusso lets out a loud gasp that ripples through the Judges words and the Judge throws her a look as she goes on. "She will be entitled to the five million dollar divorce clause from Mr. DiRusso however, an alimony of fifty thousand a year."

"That's insane!" Our client stomps his foot, "She broke the terms of the contract!"

"So did you, Mr. DiRusso," the judge shoots back raising her eyebrows, "By cheating on your wife. May I suggest that when you decide to marry for the fourth time you make sure you have an iron clad pre-nup in order? Case dismissed."

8

She hits her gavel once and both attorneys thank her for her service and time.

"That was intense eh?" Greg says to me as we both stand up, "Glad it's over."

"Right," I fake a smile, "Me too."

Five minutes later Greg and I are outside the court house, waiting for Terrance on the steps and I keep checking the watch on my wrist.

It is twelve forty now and that leaves twenty minutes to get across town, which I know is impossible during a Monday at lunchtime. I begin fishing through my black tote for my phone and once I have it I quickly begin to text Riley that I may be late by fifteen minutes due to traffic.

"Something wrong?" Greg asks me,

"No, well yes," I sigh, "I have lunch with Riley and his parents and I'm going to be late."

"Court ran late, they'll understand."

I hit send on my message and throw my phone back into my bag. "I just hate being late for lunch when his parents—"

"—I hate to break it to you Miss. Mercer, but if you decide to indeed buckle down and throw your life into this rat race then there will be many lunches and dinners you're going to miss."

I turn around to see Terrance behind me, face down at the phone in his burly hands and a frown over his large face. He stands over a foot taller than me and three inches wider. I could hide behind the man if I ever needed to.

"I know." I try to back track quickly, swallowing my gum. "It's just that—"

"Greg you have lunch plans?" Terrance doesn't bother looking up at us.

"Uh no, was just going to eat at my desk when we got back to—"

"—Excellent. Let's make headway on the Sears case. Call the stepson in to interview him about what he saw at the pool house and get me any background information on him you can."

"I can do that," Greg nods like a good little soldier.

I watch Terrance put his phone in his pocket and hoist up his expansive leather bound briefcase. We make eye contact and I smile.

"Don't you have a lunch to get to?" Terrance asks me with a frown.

"Um yes, just wondering if there is anything else you'd like me to do?"

His face softens and I feel a spark of conquest come over me when I realize that it most likely won't be anything dry cleaning or coffee related. "On your way back to the office, stop by and place an order for ten cases of that red wine I like and five cases of the white my wife enjoys. I need it for my birthday party this weekend. It's very important that you get the right order, Phoebe, hear me?"

Well, at least it's not coffee right?

"Right," I feel my voice hit a low. "Okay, I will do that."

"This is a very important party," Terrance wags a finger at me, as if I have already screwed up. "Significant people will be there. Including McFadden and I *need* his case."

I've heard all about McFadden. In fact everyone who has read a newspaper lately has. He's a billionaire going through his first divorce from his wife of fifteen years and looking for a killer lawyer to represent him in the court room. He's been shopping around over a month, and rumor has it, he has set his sights on someone at Meyers and Brant. Terrance badly wants the case; I've never seen him ache for a client this badly.

"Right, okay," I nod just like Greg had before, "I know."

"Stop doing that," Terrance grumbles, instantly annoyed. I watch him pull up his briefcase and pop it open as he holds it in one hand. He pulls out a stack of papers stapled together and shoves them at me. "You may as well send these off by carrier for the Sears case. It has to get to his lawyers by tomorrow morning. Send them off *before* three o'clock you hear me? Don't mess this up."

"Yes, I will do that."

I take the papers and fold them neatly into my tote. Terrance makes a face as he watches me cram the papers in but says nothing else. He brushes past me, his aftershave stinging my nostrils, and Greg lags behind him.

Al Fresco was Riley's favorite place to eat; it was a vegetarian restaurant where everything they served was organic. Honestly if it wasn't for Riley I may never eat anything healthy at all. He is an inspiration really; six months ago he became a vegetarian and has been going strong.

Sometimes I miss steak or lobster or even tacos but eating more greens gave me heaps of energy. Seeing people eating all that greasy food doesn't even bother me anymore.

Except that it does. More than it should.

There was a pizza party at work last Friday for a partner and I managed to sneak a slice into the office I share with Greg. I couldn't even eat it because Riley showed up minutes later for our annual Friday lunch date. I remember just staring at the baked olives and crispy pepperoni and all that melted cheese...and *that* smell...

Oh God, I'm starting to drool.

I catch a whiff of the passing hot dog cart behind me and my mouth waters a tiny bit. I find myself wondering if I should just get a small dog after this lunch, since the meals here never squish my hunger. I shake that feeling away quickly deciding ten minutes is late enough.

I wipe my mouth quickly and look back into the restaurant.

I can see Riley and his parents' right before I enter the restaurant through the solar reflective doors. Riley looks right at home in a pair of khaki shorts and a blue t-shirt buttoned up to his collarbone, his light brown hair styled to the side and his sky blue eyes focused on the menu. His parents look absolutely ridiculous in the restaurant. His father in a grey designer suit, his salt and pepper hair styled identically to Riley's and his head burrowed into his phone. His mother sits perfectly still in a pink Chanel suit, her dark greying hair pulled up into an elegant beehive, holding the menu as if it had been cased in mud. She is so intimidating; I get goosebumps if I look at her too long.

I pull the doors open, adjust my pencil skirt and pat down my long auburn hair as I walk towards them. The restaurant is chic-modern with hanging energy saving lights that look like orbs, light green tiles at your feet, a steel bar running along the side for single patrons to sit at. There is no hostess at the steel green podium so I pass it with ease.

As I near the table, Riley looks up from his menu and smiles. His blue eyes give me a once over. "Wow, serious Phoebe today I see."

He stands up and pulls out a chair next to him, while I sit he gives me a peck on the cheek. I can smell his ivory soap on his skin still, and his hair shines from under the orb light as he sat back down. Another thing; Riley had fantastic hair, and I was always envious of it.

"Mr. and Mrs. Barret," I nod their way. Riley's father looks up with a smile at me before taping back away on his cellphone, his tightly wound face suddenly imploding in wrinkles. Riley's mother just threw me one of her pierced lip smiles. I've come to know it as a smile she doesn't want to give but does for the sake of it. "I'm so sorry I'm late. Court ran late and the traffic was horrendous."

Mr. Barrett snorts. "Tell me about it."

"Phoebe has been in court all month mom," Riley throws his arm on the back of my chair as he proudly smiles from me to his mother. "My busy lawyer!"

Mrs. Barrett's thin eyebrows rise at me, "So you are finally a practicing attorney?"

I should lie; I really can't stand her giving me any attitude about still being an 'errand girl'.

"No," I end up saying slowly, seeing her face drop. "But I think my time is right around the corner."

"Isn't that what you said six months ago?" she shakes her head slowly as she looks back down at her menu. "Still just an errand girl."

I keep my composure but find myself smiling just as tautly as she had when she first saw me moments ago. I drop my tote bag on the floor and pull my chair up against the table as I look down at the menu on my plate. "Everything is so yummy here. I don't know what I'll get."

"You'll get what you always get," Riley laughs next to me. "The spinach greens with extra fat free ranch on the side, and no tea or coffee. So don't ask."

I look up to find him smiling at me. It's been four
months since he went on his anti-caffeine crusade and cut it out,
which really was for the best in the long run. Too much caffeine
was horrible for your body. Riley showed me some videos on
YouTube on what a mere three cups of tea or coffee can do to
your body.

He's so endearing, he's so *perfect*. For me anyway. For
my old friend Clara he was 'too good', but a nice change from
my past men. Faye and Satine, who I met in college, thought a
boy scout would do me some good. Of course two turbulent
years with Dylan the fraudster would see everyone in my life
agreeing with Riley as my new choice. Just thinking about
Dylan's name in my head has me tensing up uneasily. You could
say that it was Dylan's fault that I ended up with Riley. If Dylan
hadn't screwed me over in the end and made me so desperate
than maybe I wouldn't have jumped on Riley the way that I did.

"You know me so well," I lean over and brush his lips
with mine quickly. As I turn back to my menu, Riley shifts in his
chair and clears his throat to get our attention.

"I was going to wait until after we ate but," his hands are
glued to his legs and he bursts out into an eager grin. "I am just
so excited that I can't wait any longer!"

"Excited for what, dear?" his mother eyes me
suspiciously for a moment before looking at her husband.
"Maxwell! Pay attention."

Mr. Barrett looks up from his phone but keeps his head
down. I wonder if he ever gets stiff neck from being in that
position all the time. Riley turns fully around to face me and his
hand slips into the pocket of his shorts.

What is happening—oh.

Oh. My. God!

He produces a small brown box and my heart launches
against my chest so hard I begin to breathe heavily. I can no
longer feel the menu in my hands as I watch Riley gently open
the box in his hands.

I'm staring down at a magnificent, princess cut, clear
diamond that had to be at least 2 carats. The band was thin white
gold which made the diamond look even bigger than it actually
was. I can hear his mother gasp and his father chuckle.

"I want you to marry me. You make me so happy, you have been a constant support the last year and I don't know what I would do without you. I am so proud of the man you help me be. I love the life we have together and I want you by my side as time goes by. Please, say you'll marry me."

I don't hear what his mother mumbles beneath her breath. The only thing I can focus on is the pounding in my ears from my heart beat. I think my hands are slightly shaking, although at the moment they feel a tad cold.

I don't believe this. I'm being proposed to. Right now. This is it. This is it.

Riley's smile is contagious and soon I burst into my own.

"Yes! Yes of course I'll marry you!"

By two thirty we have finished lunch, and Riley's parents had paid the bill. I could barely touch my salad despite being incredibly hungry. Riley spent the whole time discussing his plans for our future, moving out from our loft into a condo, having kids within a year or two, growing his advertising company and opening up a division in L.A.

We said farewell to his parents in front of the restaurant after their town car pulled up. Riley and I parted ways shortly after since he had a meeting and I made my way down to the FedEx store around the corner.

My ring sparkled like crazy in the sun, and my hand looked so small now.

I was a fiancée.

An engagee.

Is that a word, engagee?

I sent one mass text, to Clara, Faye, Satine and my family.

I'M ENGAGED!

I stop in the middle of the busy sidewalk and feel myself frown through my elation. What was I doing again?

Oh right! The contracts for Terrance.

I spot the Fedex store at the corner and pull out the contracts from my purse as I continue walking. Every once in a while I glimpse down at my ring. It's blinding!

I'm greeted with a familiar smell a second later, the grilled greasy hot dogs from before.

I may as well pick one up, Riley isn't around and what he doesn't know won't hurt him. I glimpse away from my ring and don't know how I missed people yelling or moving out of the way.

Or the general eruption that was happening around me.

"Runaway cart!"

I was too late to move before it hit me straight in the chest and legs.

I'm knocked to the ground fiercely. I land on the curb of the sidewalk so violently my entire left side numbs, after mauling me with aches that cause me to yell out. My knees burn beneath me and around me papers go flying like ceremonial doves.

I can taste something metallic in my mouth, so much of it, and I know its blood.

I struggle to sit up on my aching elbows and fight to get my eye sight back to normal.

Through the blurriness I can see the contract papers around me, already dirty and smudge with sidewalk grime. Hotdogs crowd around me and my skirt looks like it's either stained in my blood or ketchup.

My head feels suddenly very heavy as a headache crashes against my temples, and I lean my head back against the flopped over cart behind me.

Chapter Two

I awake to a white ceiling. My vision is distorted and black spots move every time I feel my eyelids open. I feel like everything I see is a puzzle.

Then I sense it.

Complete agony in my entire body. From my head to my toes, I feel heavy. As if my limbs are concrete. I want to let out a groan to match the level of pain coursing through my veins but my mouth is too dry.

Can I move my arm? Am I moving it?

I blink a few more times until gradually the black spots disappear. The blurriness is slowly diminishing enough for me to see that I'm in a single bed with a metal bed frame at the end, a clipboard hanging over the side. There is a green curtain drawn around me drooping from rods attached to the ceiling.

I hear beeping every few seconds, but am nervous turning my head may hurt too badly. There's an IV running across my left arm into the top of my left hand. I squeeze my eyes shut and whence a little.

I *hate* IV's. It's not the needle or the prick you get when they attach it to you. It's the small tube coming out of a small hole in your skin. It's the way blood can creep up into the IV. I want it out, *now*.

I can see that I'm in a light green hospital gown and that to my right; ugly tan curtains cover the windows. It's also extremely cool in the room. Against my bed is a table with a green tray on it, covered by a lid, and a matching green plastic cup.

My mouth is dry, so much so that it makes that 'smack' sound.

"Please stop doing that, it's very irritating."

The voice comes from behind the hanging curtain to my left. It hadn't crossed my mind that I might have a neighbor in this room. From the sound of the woman's voice I take it she wasn't a spring chicken either.

"Sorry," I apologize between my dry lips. As I speak my bottom lip stings and I make a sucking noise as I lightly touch it.

I hear my neighbor gasp, "You can hear me?"

I frown as I'm about to tell her that of course I can hear her, a curtain isn't exactly a wall but the curtain opens before I can. Two people stomp into my side of the room, a tall male and a short female. It's my brother and sister; they both share the same look of concerned displeasure. My brother Tom, almost at six feet with jet black hair and pale skin stood in a jogging uniform with the new smart watch glistening on his wrist. My sister Reese has pulled her black hair into a tight bun and her oversized glasses sit perfectly on her small nose. She's in a pair of jeans and a bulky grey sweater. When I tell people she's a contemporary artist they are never surprised.

"Oh good," my brother lets out a breath as he walks closer. "You're awake."

"We stopped mom from coming, thought it would stress you out more. Addy sends her regards; she says she hopes you can forgive her for not showing up. She has back to back meetings with Brain."

Addison is the youngest of us, and just as successful as Reese and Tom. She married out of college and her husband Brain is a State Senator. She runs two different charities and we rarely see her or Brain, except at Christmas.

"And Dad?" I blink at Reese.

She exchanges a look with Tom and shrugs, "Tom sent him an email. Last we heard, he was down in Mexico somewhere."

"I told him his presence was not needed," Tom adds, boredom filling his tone.

The thing with my Dad is, he doesn't do well sitting in one place too long. The disappointment the four of us felt long ago as kids has now turned into resentment and relief of his absence most of the year.

Reese walks over to the table next to my bed and grabs the cup. I watch my brother shut the curtain behind him before coming to my right side.

"Have a drink," Reese puts the cup my way; she has now folded a straw into it. "Doctors said the pain killers will dehydrate you so the quicker you drink water the quicker that IV is out of you."

My family knows of my revulsion towards IV's.

I slowly lift my heavy hand and take the cup in it. They both watch me as I put the straw into my mouth and drink it in long sips. Soon I've reached the bottom of the cup and the water slurps.

"That is not polite," says my neighbor in her raspy tone.

I repent without much care, happy she can't see me as I say it, "Sorry."

"How are you feeling?" Tom narrows his brown eyes at me.

"Alright," I shrug handing Reese back the empty cup. "I feel sore all over and tired." I see them exchange a look and find myself frowning, "What happened to me anyway?"

"You don't remember?" Tom questions.

"No... I mean I remember lunch and Riley and leaving Al Fresco and—" my face fills red as I recall the hot dog cart. Slowly I bury my head in my hands, "Oh my God. I was run over by a hot dog cart."

"Apparently so," Reese smirks loudly. "Everyone jumped out of the way and you just kind of kept walking in its path. That's what the witnesses said."

I was run over by a hot dog cart.

"The concussion happened right after."

I look up at Tom as my hands drop to my sides. "I'm sorry, the *what*?"

"Apparently you had a minor concussion," Tom goes on. "Right after it hit you." He bends over slightly to his side and pushes a button on the side of my bed. It begins to move upward with a loud thunderous noise and soon I'm sitting up right.

Reese wheels the table with the tray over my legs. She slowly removes the lid and picks up the fork and knife sealed in plastic. "The Doctor said it was a minor one, and that you probably smacked your head off the side of the metal cart instead of the pavement."

I look down at the tray she shoves my way and make a face. I can see yellow mash potatoes, dull peas, carrots and some kind of white meat on the plastic pink tray.

"Eat something," Reese places the fork and knife down next to the tray. "It's chicken."

18

I poke the piece of meat with the fork. It certainly doesn't look like chicken; nothing like the chicken I had at the shawarma place, last Wednesday. Again, what Riley doesn't know can't hurt him.

"It's dead," Tom declares, "Don't worry."

"Tom and I can get you something better if you want," Reese offered.

I don't even have to think hard about what I want.

I've been craving it over the last few days.

A cheesy, greasy slice of city pizza.

"She wants pizza," Tom smirks suddenly. "That's her pizza face."

"How did you know?" I ask, surprised.

Reese smiles, "We know. After Riley gets here we can run down and get some for you. I could use some pizza too."

My heart jolts at Riley's mention and the machine behind me beeps loudly, "No! Don't bring up pizza. Riley will kill me."

"I cannot believe you are still on that preposterous green trend with him," Tom frowns as he derides me. "It is unlike you and—"

"—It works, I'll have you know," I interrupt proudly. "I'm down a few pounds and am bursting with energy."

Tom blinks at me. "Then why do you have black circles under your eyes?"

"Don't get her riled up Tom," Reese gives him a quick look.

"I'm just saying, her blood sugar was low, she probably isn't getting enough protein," Tom says offhandedly with a shrug. "The Doctor says every test came back normal despite the low blood sugar, and the CAT scan was fine. You'll need to be monitored the next few nights at home."

"I'm sure Riley can do that."

It suddenly comes to my attention that neither of them has congratulated me. I did mass text them only hours before, telling them I was newly engaged. "Speaking of Riley," I go on as I clear my throat. "Did you guys get my text message?"

"Of course," Reese's mouth twitches and she produces a smile. "Congratulations."

19

"Mom will be thrilled," Tom adds.

"Won't she?" I smile at him. "She loves Riley doesn't she? Check out the ring!" I throw my hand towards Reese and gasp when I find it bare. "My ring! Where is—"

"—I have it," Tom pulls something out of his jogging jacket and thrusts it my way. "They took everything off you when they changed you from your clothes."

I take my ring slowly, admiring again the giant, glistening stone staring back at me. I slip it back on the finger it belongs on and lean back against the upright bed. "Wait a second, where's Riley?"

"He's on his way," Tom answered. "He was in a meeting and I had to leave a message with his secretary. She gave it to some person named Jamie."

Jamie. Riley's partner's girlfriend who also works at the advertising firm.

"They gave you my bed you know?" my neighbor calls out to me with a huff. "Shafted me aside." Before I can apologize again to my nosey bed neighbor, my sister speaks to me,

"The Doctor said you could leave tomorrow morning. You have to take it easy though, no work for the next week or so. Just in case. He should be in soon to talk to you about what happened."

We hear scuffling at the door of the room and before Tom can open the curtains to see who it is, they are thrown aside in an exaggerated fashion. Riley appears and lets out a loud sigh when he sets his eyes on me. "Honey!"

"I'm alright, honestly," I let him know. He reaches my bedside and sits down next to me on the bed. Tom looks annoyed at the way he was tossed aside but says nothing as he walks around the bed to where Reese stands. Riley has cupped my hands in them and kisses my raw knuckles,

"I can't believe this happened. I'm sorry I wasn't able to get here sooner," his face bellows with concern and it makes me smile slightly. "My meeting went later than expected and Jamie couldn't give me the message until the very end," he stops short after his eyes catch the tray at my side and he makes a face. "That looks revolting. I bet none of it has any nutritional value whatsoever. I'll zip back down to the nearest grocery store and snap you up some greens. You need it now more than ever."

Tom and Reese gather towards the other side of the room as they watch us.

"I'm glad to hear you're alright," one of Riley's hands touches the side of my face. "I just can't believe you got a concussion" his face turns at the word. "A *concussion.*"

"She was run over by a hot dog cart," Tom speaks up. "She's lucky she didn't roll into traffic."

Riley ignores his comment which I'm thankful for; I'm embarrassed enough by that part of the story as it is. I mean *a hot dog cart.* Who gets run over by a hot dog cart?

"Didn't you see it?" Reese asks crossing her arms over her chest. "Eye witness reports say you just kind of kept walking in its direction. Zombie like."

"Do you think it was the proposal?" Riley suddenly remarks, his eyes widening a little bit. "Did that distract you? Make you feel out of it?"

"No," I say quickly. "I was thinking about work; you know how work has me stressed out at times. That's why I wasn't focused on what was ahead of me."

"Well," Tom intrudes. "You decided for whatever reason to be a lawyer."

I hear a croaky laugh from the other side of the room. "In my day when a woman had an accident like that after she was proposed to, it was because she needed a quick get away from that relationship."

"That's rude," I snap.

"Phoebe," Tom frowns, "it was a joke."

"No" I tell him, "Not you, what—"

"—Ms. Mercer?" I hear a strange man's voice from behind the curtain and a second later it's brushed aside. A short, stubby balding man in a white coat enters. He has a small name tag pinned to the white coat and the initials of the hospital above that. He gives me a smile as he looks at me and puts his hands into the pockets of his coat. "It's nice to see you awake. My name is Doctor Grier; I've been monitoring your case ever since you came in this afternoon."

21

"Tell us Doctor," Riley gets up and turns full spin to face him. A tad dramatic, but I appreciate his concern and ignore the smirk Reese and Tom exchange with each other. "How is she?"

"She's fine. In fact, she's better than fine," Doctor Grier continues to smile my way. "The tests we did when you were sleeping came back great. Your knees are badly bruised and there are some cuts there we bandaged up but they should heal within two weeks. Now, in regards to the concussion—"

"—Are you sure it was a concussion?" Riley interrupts using his hands as he speaks. "Aren't those pretty difficult to determine?"

"It was most definitely a concussion," Doctor Grier tells him confidently before he looks back at me. "A small one, but without a doubt a concussion."

"So what do we do Doctor?" Riley asks him. "Keep her on bed rest? Legs elevated? Should she take a leave of absence from work?"

"A woman should never let a man speak for her," my neighbor quips through Riley's words and I feel my jaw clench a bit. Who does this woman think she is? My mother? She should really be minding her own business.

With my jaw still clasped I speak to her, hoping her words didn't make Riley feel bad. "I *can* speak for myself."

Riley looks over his shoulder and frowns at me, "I know you can speak for yourself. I was just asking the doctor, in general."

Before I can tell him that I wasn't talking to him the doctor goes on. "No need for bed rest exactly. I would advise taking it easy however, and a short leave of absence from work should be taken. Two weeks, four tops. Your brother told me you are a lawyer, and that kind of stress isn't good for you right now. If you have any of the following symptoms; sudden headache that doesn't go away with over the counter medications, numbness of the arms, legs or hands, a heavy feeling in your chest, you must come to the hospital right away. I'll be discharging you tomorrow morning and you'll take home some information to look over that lists all these symptoms and more."

I cannot take any time off work. No way.

"Doctor Grier? I actually can't take any time off work right now," I say. "I work at a very busy law firm and if I took any time off, even a day, my boss would kill me."

Or he wouldn't, he'd be thrilled and replace me with a snap of his fingers.

I can't risk either.

"If you must, I suggest you go part time," Doctor Grier sighs taking his hands from his pockets. "The moment you mentioned your job, I saw your heart rate go up exceptionally."

I glance over my shoulder at the machine I'm attached to and can see that my heart is beating at 110 right now.

"A normal heart rate clocks in around 60 beats a minute," Doctor Grier clarifies.

"Phoebe I very much doubt your boss would care if you took a week or two off work," Tom addresses loudly to the room. His brows came together in a very serious expression as he stared at me. "For Pete's sake you just had a *concussion.*"

"If you really can't leave your job then maybe you can work from home?" Reese suggests.

Riley bends over somewhat so he can put a hand over mine and give it a squeeze. "I don't think you should work at all right now. Let's talk about it when we get home alright?"

The doctor agrees that part time can work if I *absolutely* need to return to work, but strains the importance of destressing myself whenever I feel overworked or overwhelmed. Then he tells everyone to leave me be, so that I may get some more rest. Slowly my brother and sister file out, promising to give our mother an update and swearing they will convince her to stay home. Riley leaves last, whispering tenderly how he hates sleeping alone in our loft and will be back tomorrow morning to get me.

When they finally leave I'm left staring at the green curtain around my bed with my hands at my sides. I should have asked them to leave me something to read at least. The clock hanging on the wall said 8:50 pm and I realized it had been a while since I was in bed at this time. Terrance had a habit of giving me the most tedious tasks of a case, when he gave me real work to do, that is. Most nights I didn't get into bed until well after midnight.

23

"I thought they would never leave!"

I jump slightly in my place, realizing I forgot about my nosey neighbor on the other side of the curtain.

"Yes well they did," I tell her. "If you don't mind I would really like to get some sleep." I manage to reach behind me and pull the hanging cord from the florescent light. It instantly shuts off and half of the room is engulfed in darkness. I lean back into my bed and shut my eyes slowly.

Maybe I could try this going to bed early thing.

It can't be as hard as it seems, tons of people go to bed at a reasonable hour.

"He didn't even bring you any flowers!"

My eyes tear open and I find my neighbor standing right at my bedside. She has her hands on her hips and her eyes are small as she glances around my side of the room. I notice her strawberry blond hair first; it's super short and impressively curly. She's definitely older than I intentionally suspected. Her face is colored in wrinkles but there's fineness about it. She's stocky but dressed impeccably well; a pair of white baggy trousers and a golden blouse that ties right under her neck.

"What kind of man do you have that doesn't even bring you flowers?" she gazes down at me now, lifting one of her light eyebrows.

"It would have been a waste," I defend frowning. "I leave tomorrow morning."

I don't want to tell her that I suddenly wish he had brought flowers. It would have been a nice gesture. Come to think of it, when was the last time he brought me flowers?

"It's not proper," she tells me and gracefully crosses her arms over her chest. "So what's your name, girl?"

"Phoebe," I answer. "If you could just let me have some sleep I'll be eternally grateful."

"No dice sugar-pie," she snaps her fingers in front of my face as I shut my eyes and I jolt my head back at her action. "You can see me. You can hear me," she gestures at my ears, "so we need to talk."

"Can't you bug a nurse to talk to you or something?" I beg her. She was slowly getting on my nerves but I told myself to remain calm. Last thing I need is to have a stroke after this concussion.

"Ha," she laughs, and it's as raspy as before. "You don't think I've tried?"

"Maybe they think you're obnoxious," I mutter as I adjust the blanket at my waist.

"Excuse me?"

"Never mind," I smile up at her. "Maybe you should try again to speak with one of them? They may enjoy the company since they are on night shift."

"You don't get it do you sugar-pie? They can't see me."

I stare at her, "What do you mean they can't see you?"

"I mean," her hands come on her hips again, "They cannot see me."

I have no idea what she's getting at and in actuality it's bothering me a little bit. Couldn't this woman just wait for her family to visit? She could talk their ears off then.

We stare at each other for a moment and I watch her become frustrated.

Loudly she sighs and drops her hands to her sides. "I'm a ghost darling."

I frown in confusion and shake my head as if I'm hearing things, "I'm sorry, *what?*"

"G-H-O-S-T," she spells out with the same irritated tone as before. "A spirit, an apparition."

As in the living dead? As in Casper?

I swallow, "A ghost?"

"Don't you know what a ghost is!" She suddenly exclaims my way.

"Yes I know what a ghost is!" I cry back gripping the blanket that's covering my waist. "I have seen Casper and Dead like Me."

"I don't know what that is."

This woman is crazy. She is nuts. Why isn't she strapped to that bed over there?

"I'm not crazy," she remarks as if she read my thoughts.

"So you believe that you're a ghost?" I ask, slowly my eyebrows raise with the question.

25

"I don't believe it, I *know* it," she folds her arms over her chest again and shrugs. "I have been a ghost for a while now."

"How long is a while?" I may as well accommodate her.

"About a month, and nobody has been able to see or hear me," she points a finger my way. "Until now, until you."

I blink at her.

"Hello!" She waves her hands in my face. "Have you gone into a shock of some kind?"

"No, sorry it's just that, this is the first time that anybody has ever told me that they might be a ghost," I inform her with a shrug. She leans over, so close that she's inches away from my face.

"I am a ghost. There is *no* might. My name is Edie Edwards and I died right there in that bed that you are lying in, a mere four hours after I was admitted to the hospital, a month ago."

She seems so certain and I pity her. There is obviously something wrong with her. Could it be Alzheimer's?

I look down and spot the 'call' button against the side railing of my bed in bright red. I look from it to her and take a slow breath, "Okay. Well I'm just going to call a nurse in here so she can escort you back to your room, and maybe after a good's night sleep you'll be back to your old self."

I watch her let out an irritated grunt as she stands back up and glares around the room. She snaps her fingers and points to the curtain dividing the two beds. I watch her give me an uneven smile, "You want me to prove it?"

"Look lady, I'm not really in the mood for these games," I breathe. "In case you hadn't heard? I had a small concussion."

"By being run over by a hot dog cart," she adds with a smirk.

I feel my eyebrows drop in a frown. "In any case, I was injured and I would like to get some sleep before I return home tomorrow."

"Just humour me," she orders.

I fold my arms over my chest and motion for her to continue. Sluggishly, dropping her hands to her sides and taking a long breath she steps up to the curtain. I watch her hesitate and then shut her eyes. She mutters something but I don't hear her and just as I open my mouth to ask her to repeat it, she walks into the curtain.

Or should I say through, *through* the curtain.

She walked through the curtain.

It didn't even move.

No breeze from her body, nothing.

It was like she melted into the ugly green fabric.

The room is utterly silent.

At that moment I realize that I forgot to breathe and gasp out, it echoes around the room.

A second later her head appears, this time it pokes out from the curtain and her body seems to be behind it. She looks towards me and smiles big. "See? Told you. I'm a ghost."

"I think I'm going to throw up."

It's true, all of a sudden my stomach turns into knots and something crawls up my throat, something acidic, sour and just plain foul. It burns as I attempt to swallow most of it down. It's followed by a crippling panic, the kind you get watching horror movies by yourself. Coldness brushes my covered and once warm backbone. I can feel the hairs on my arms gradually raise and my heart beats with thuds against my already aching chest. It feels like it's about to beat out from my chest again and I place a hand against it as if that would somehow stop its misfire.

Something beeps behind me and the woman looks away from me, her face suddenly on edge. She bites her bottom lip. "Oh dear, your heart rate is at 100. You should try to relax, take deep breaths."

I watch her step out from the curtain, her whole body appearing just as it was dressed before, un-phased from the mysterious curtain walk through.

"Okay, okay," the woman takes a single step towards me, her hands extended outward. "I'll leave you for now. So you can calm down. I need you to not die on me; you're going to help me. I'll be back tomorrow," she puts her hands down in front of me and makes a settle down motion with them. "Just…just calm down."

What is happening here?

Chapter Three

When I woke up the next morning, she was gone.

I ate my dried out scrambled eggs and picked at my burnt toast alone, constantly looking up and around the room to see if I could spot any movement. Nothing moved and nothing made a noise the entire time I sat in my bed.

Riley came to pick me up a little after eleven a.m. and that woman was nowhere to be seen.

What the hell was wrong with me?

I must have hit my head harder than the doctors intentionally thought.

Here I was, imagining a woman who thought she was a ghost, for crying out loud!

Never mind, I told myself firmly as we drove back to our loft. Whatever that was yesterday, whomever I managed to conjure up is gone now. It was a momentary lapse from the trauma I went through, and I obviously used it as a scapegoat. That's normal right?

Of course it is. Hundreds of people experience weird events after they've been through a scary health affair; some of them wake up a completely changed person from before, some can't will themselves to get out of bed anymore and some, like myself, summon up imaginary women who believe they are ghosts. Perfectly normal.

I will myself to put last evening's weird event out of my mind the second Riley and I enter our loft. It's not really our loft, more like *his* loft but we live in it together and split on the rent. I moved in last month when my lease on my old apartment with Clara went up. Riley jumped at the chance for us to live together, so Clara found a nice one bedroom on her own.

It's a gorgeous space, ceilings over fifteen feet high and exposed brick all around. The loft door is an old warehouse sliding door made of metal so it's incredibly sound proof. The windows have been updated to vertical casement but we rarely open them since the wind ratio six floors up is pretty high on most days. Our living room was styled by Riley's mother when he first moved in and I hated that I enjoyed her décor.

A set of white sectionals sat attached to each other in the middle of the room, underneath a fine flat woven beige rug. The square coffee table was made from pine and there was a yellow daisy and white carnation bouquet sitting in a vase upon it. The sixty inch television sat on top of a pine TV stand about ten feet away from the sectionals. To the immediate right of the living room was a single white door which led to the bathroom and near it was our kitchen. The cabinets where designed with pine wood as well and the appliances had all been purchased from some independent furniture store Stella told me she was sure I had never heard of.

On the other side of the living room is a seven foot high wooden partition made again, with pine, and designed to have each slab of wood entangled into the next piece. Our bedroom was on the other side of the partition.

Once inside, I let Riley move around me so he could set my purse and information from Dr. Grier down. Today he opted for his sweats and matching grey t-shirt informing me he would be working from home so that he could take care of me for my first day back.

"Now in a few minutes I'm going to go fill your painkiller prescription," Riley threw my purse and the pamphlets down on the sectional he had walked over to. "I'm also going to pop by the office to make sure everything is running smoothly." He motions at the coffee table then, "those flowers are from Addison and Brain."

I give him a small smile and feel overshadowed by his large one. "You don't have to get my pain killers Riley, I honestly won't need them. All I have is a small headache."

There's a rustling sound to my left and I turn my head to see two figures pop out from behind the partition. They are holding a 'Welcome Home' party sign between the two of them and are bouncing it up and down. Faye and Clara.

Faye, in her black slacks and a grey sweater that said 'Sweater Weather is Better Weather' in a clever font; she works as a personal shopper at several big name department stores. Over the years she's told us stories of countless celebrities. She had, at one time, been asked out repeatedly by one of the members of a very popular boy band but she wouldn't disclose who. Her short black hair rests on her shoulders and her glasses sit atop of her head; next to Clara she's tiny, with an almost opposite complexion.

Clara stands at almost six feet in jeans and a simple green skin tight t-shirt. She has the same olive skin as I do, but I have a curvy frame; she has a thin one. And while I have long barely layered auburn hair she has rich highlighted blond hair. I often wondered why she hadn't gone the model route instead of becoming a booking agent to musicians. Not that she isn't great at her job; in fact she's one of the top agents at Wayward Records.

"Welcome home!" they exclaim together with big smiles.

"Guys," I walk over to them as they tread towards me. "That is so sweet. Thank you!"

We exchanged a dance of hugs, but they both keep holding on to each one of my hands.

"We wanted to get wine and take out but weren't sure if you would be up for it," Faye smiles brightly. "We decided to wait until you got back here."

"Satine is going to FaceTime with us later," Clara tells me squeezing my hand, "She's still in Japan, closing the deal with that Soda company."

Satine also has a fabulous job. She worked in an advertising company and was a supervising manager in their international department. It meant she got to travel the world at least four times a year, sealing deals with major companies to promote their products over here. In fact, she was the reason Riley decided to give up on his sports agent career and make an attempt in advertising, eight months ago. Her stories of travel and perks made his eyes glisten. When I met Riley, he had left his personal training career behind, and was just adjusting to a career as a sports agent. Now he had his own advertising firm; his ambition knows no bounds.

"How are you feeling?" Faye asks as she lets go of my hand and takes the other end of the Welcome Home sign from Clara. She begins to fold it as I answer.

"Yesterday was awful but today I feel normal," I drop my hands to my sides. It's true too; despite a slight headache creeping up on me that Doctor Grier told me may last a few days, I felt fine. My body aches were gone; I had slight pains in my knees but no throbbing.

"Well that's a good sign," Clara tells me, "So what do you feel like having? Sushi?"

"It is the healthier option," Riley calls out from the kitchen.

Clara makes a face and I ignore it as I nod, "He's right. I should be throwing myself further into this eating healthy thing."

"I'm pretty sure you have been already," Clara whispers.

If only she knew what I snuck behind everyone's back.

"Sushi is perfect," I disregard her comment and smile at Faye as I answer.

"Okay so you stay here and unwind," Faye tells me as she gestures to the sectional. "We'll go pick up some food and some *organic* wine. Then later we can discuss my birthday dinner at Pre-Fab Burritos." I make a face at her but she just motions me to be quiet with her hand.

"I brought you some of that lavender bubble bath and rose mud musk thing you like from Lavish Looks," Clara gestures to a small brown bag on the coffee table I hadn't noticed before.

"Thank you!"

I absolutely adore their products; even if they are a tad on the pricey side. I rarely splurge on them unless they have one of their discount sales and even then, I spend a couple hundred on them. I let Clara usher me to the couch where I fall down onto the smooth fabric, leaning back into it and throwing my feet up across from me.

"Isn't Pre-Fab Burrito known for cooking everything in bacon grease?" Riley asks Faye as she walks towards the door and reaches for a pair of blue runners. "Do they have anything on their menu that won't cause a heart attack?"

I can see Clara roll her eyes as she turns her back on him.

"I'm not sure actually," Faye replies grabbing the tote and slipping on her shoes, she gives me a quick look as she slips them on. "Anyway it's my birthday Riley; you can eat greasy grub once, it won't kill you."

31

"She has a point there," Clara adds, joining Faye at the door. I watch her slip into a pair of yellow flip-flops gracefully. "Or maybe we can all just meet up before hand and eat somewhere."

"Don't even dare," Faye threatens. "Is Mark coming?"

Mark Devers has been Clara's on and off again boyfriend, going on two years now. He owns Wild Wonders, a chain of camping and fishing department stores. They met when she had to set up a venue for a musician with an outdoor theme. Despite their issues, when they are together, you wouldn't think there could ever be trouble in paradise. But Clara was tenacious, and Mark was easy-going. The slightest argument between them, no matter how small, often led into a break up.

"No he is not," Clara clears her throat and focuses on her shoes. "And he will not attend anything with me ever again."

"Oh, Clara" Faye sighs, "I'm sorry."

I nod my head slowly; "I thought last time would be the last time. I'm sorry."

"I'm not," Clara throws a hand up. "I've wasted two years on him and I am not wasting more time talking about it now. So let's go."

I watch them leave the loft in a hurry, promising to be back within an hour. Once gone, Riley turns around and smiles down at me. "Okay I'll do most of my work in the kitchen as to not disturb you girls. Are you sure you don't want me to get your pain meds?"

"Positive," I nod.

"Okay then," he turns and takes a few steps away from me then backtracks. "Almost forgot. Last night some files came for you by carrier. I put them on the desk over there. We should talk about your work at some point, I don't mind you doing small stuff but I think you know it isn't good for you to go back to work." He points over me to my only piece of furniture in the whole loft; an antique roll top mahogany desk I had picked up at a flea market before moving in. It really is beautifully refurbished and seal coated. There were five drawers on the right side, only one cabinet on the left, and a cozy space for your legs.

I stand up from the couch and walk towards the desk, "I'll just do this and then take a week off, I promise."

Behind me Riley makes his way towards the bathroom and I hear him enter and close the door as I get to my desk. The files from the carrier are right on top of a stack of old magazines. I pick up the big folder, sealed with special tape, and pull the chair out from underneath the desk.

After sitting, I pull out a hundred pages worth of interviews for the Sears case with a sticky note attached to the front page. It says *'highlight each victim's claims'* in Greg's handwriting. Beneath the words is a smiley face and I smile as I pluck the sticky off. In a red mug I use as a cup holder, I pluck out a yellow highlighter and pull off the lid with my lips, spitting it out on the desk.

"Should you really be working already?"

The voice startles me so that I push my chair backwards and let it fall to the ground behind my feet. I find myself staring in the green eyes of the woman from the hospital room. She stands next to my desk ,with her hands on her hips, giving me a scolding stare in the same golden blouse tied at her neck and white pants.

"Oh my God," I pant feeling my heart skip a few beats as I stare back at her.

"Surprised to see me?" she puts both hands out in front of her as if she's expecting applause after a performance, "I told you I would be back."

I shut my eyes and take a long breath; my hearing has deafened and I can hear ringing. When I open them she is still there, in the same position, hands out in front of her. I close my eyes tightly, feeling my face constrict as I wish her away. I feel my lips part and whisper, "You're not here. There is no way you are here right now."

I peel my eyes open slowly and see her scoff at me,

"I most definitely am right here sugar-pie, as plain as the greys in your hair."

I grab the top of my head, "I do not have any greys!"

"I can see three," she points at my head, "Just around your hairline here." She then indicates at her own hairline at her forehead. "I'd get my colorist on that if I were you."

I drop my hand and glare at her, feeling my eyebrows dip, "How did you get in here? The door was closed."

"Hello?" She's sarcastic to me, "Ghost remember? It wasn't exactly problematic to slide through your front door."

"Stop saying that!" I hiss, my hands going to my ears.

"Saying what?"

"That word 'ghost'. You are not a ghost," I throw down the highlighter and it bounces off the files towards the back of the desk. "You are just some crazy woman who has broken into my apartment. A crazy stalker woman."

"How dare you," she jerks in disbelief and frowns at me. "I am not crazy. And if I broke in, then why didn't you just hear me open the front door? That thing sounds like a freight train!"

"It does not sound like that!" I shoot back balling my fists at my sides.

She throws her hands up at me frustratingly and turns away. I watch her walk slowly from my desk, scrutinising the wooden partition that divides the loft and the hibiscus plant against it.

"Okay, you need to leave now," I order her, pointing to the door behind me. "You need to get out of here before I call the police."

She begins to laugh and twirls around to face me, her hands coming together at her pelvis. I watch her shrug, "Go ahead and call the police. See what happens."

We stand facing each other again. Neither of us makes a move, we both only blink until she finally sighs and comes towards me. "Look, do you want me to convince you that I'm a ghost again? Do you want me to walk through your dull couch? Or waltz through that tacky partition into your bedroom?"

I don't know what to feel exactly; insulted at her dig at our furniture or trepidation at the fact that she may show me, again, just how she can walk through things.

"No! Don't do anything," I order, "Just—just stand there."

The door to the bathroom opens and I swing around as Riley leaves it.

Riley! I forgot he was here.

Purposefully, I move out from in front of the woman and watch as Riley looks up at me with a smile, slipping his smart phone into the pocket of his sweats.

34

Does he see her? Of course he does! He has to.

"Okay I'm off to the office. I won't be long, and I'm picking up the pain killers just in case so no arguments," Riley bends over at the door and grabs his runners.

I watch him in horror. He can't see her?

"Riley," I stammer, "Do you notice anything?"

He puts on his last runner and stands up, looking around the loft. Slowly he frowns and is about to say 'no' when I signal towards the partition and to where the woman is standing. He then nods and gestures where I had motioned to, "Yup I do. The hibiscus plant needs tending."

The woman lets out a laugh so close to me, when I turn I notice that she's standing right next to me now.

I hear the front door thud open and screech as it's pulled.

Wow, I never noticed that sound before. It makes the hairs on my arms stand.

Riley smiles again at me as he steps on the other side of the door and grabs it with both hands to close behind him, "Be back in a jiffy."

He leaves us in silence. The street below us is the only noise drifting through the loft and the sound of the elevator in the hall pinging open. It pings shut a second later and we can hear it canter back down to the lobby.

"Well now we can talk in peace, without interruptions."

Riley hadn't seen her. In truth he looked right *through* her, like she was a phantom.

Like she was a ghost.

Okay, so maybe she *is* a ghost. Maybe she is telling the truth about having died and then being, reborn? Is that the right word?

I fiddle with the idea for a moment as I watch her walk around the sectional to have a better look at the rest of the loft. I draw in a breath as she walks through the end of the couch as if it wasn't even there.

I have a ghost in my living room.

I'm staring at a woman, who was probably a very hip, stern grandmother when she was alive. She had just walked through my couch, and may walk through my coffee table. A stylish, dense being standing with her hands on her hips judging the modern lamp lanterns hanging from the loft ceiling a few feet above her head. A spirit that only I can see.

How hard had I hit my head? I should Google 'concussions and ghosts' later on. In fact I should Google 'Ghosts' in general.

"Okay," I let out a deep breath, "So he didn't see you."

She turns her head my way and raises her eyebrows as if to say 'told you so.'

"I'm guessing if my friends return right now then they wouldn't see you either?"

"I very much doubt they would," she slowly turns to face me. "Now, are you ready to listen to me?"

"How is it that I can see you? And nobody else can? I have never seen ghosts before," I place a hand to my forehead and look at her. "I'm not even sure I believe in ghosts!"

"Does it matter now?" she asks me, "Because here I am. A ghost." She opens her arms as she speaks, "In the flesh, or rather ghost flesh." She is getting annoyed with my dawdling conclusion because she drops her hands and sighs at me. "Look, people have accidents or die and come back to life claiming they have supernatural powers or see ghosts all the time. For heaven's sake, they make movies of it, write books about it, television shows. All which I might add are strikingly accurate I now realize, except possession. That is entirely over-blown."

My mouth hangs open, "You saw a possession?"

"Few days after I died," she answers wearily and looks down at her blouse. I watch her adjust the ruffles at the bottom as she goes on. "Visited a poor possessed girl in Italy. Not nearly as interesting as you would think."

"What was she possessed by?" I ask, immediately intrigued and hating it.

"Didn't think to ask," she shrugs. "The second the priest started throwing around holy water I high-tailed it out of there. I didn't want to be forced into the land of the peaceful until I concluded my unfinished business."

"Which is?"

"To catch my killer, and find something of mine that was lost and is very important."

She tells me this as if it's a normal thing.

36

"Someone murdered you?" I gape.

"Well, I'm not sure," she sways in place for a second then stops and looks serious again. "But I certainly know someone caused me to have that heart attack and die hours later. I have a suspect in mind. And you," she points to me with flare, "are going to help me."

"This feels surreal," my hands sit in front of me at my thighs and I shake my head a bit, "This is so surreal."

"Look sugar-pie, if we could just get over the whole dramatic epiphany of you realizing that you can actually see ghosts that would be wonderful."

I want to tell her I don't appreciate her snarky attitude when my phone rings inside of my purse. She watches me like a hawk as I walk over to my purse and fish inside for my cell phone. When I finally find it, the ringing has stopped and the screen says I have one new voicemail. I recognize the number as that being from the office and quickly dial into my voicemail. After setting in my passcode, the message begins,

'Phoebe? It's Greg. Listen, I hate to bother you when you're resting but I overheard Terrance tell people that he was going to look for someone to step in while you were gone. I have a feeling he plans to replace you. Give me a call as soon as you get this.'

I let out a shriek as the voicemail ends.

I cannot believe this!

Although, I can believe this, Terrance does hate me after all. This is the perfect opportunity for him to have me replaced. I cannot lose my job, not now. Not that I'm engaged to Riley. Stella has already shown her distaste towards me and if I'm unemployed, it will be way worse. At least with this job, the prospect of taking the bar soon and maybe receiving a permanent placement at Meyers and Brant, may help Stella soften up on me a little.

"What's the matter?"

"I'm sorry," my face scrunches up as I try to remember the ghost's name. "Edna? I have to run into work for a second."

"It's Edie," she corrects me visibly annoyed, "and you're not supposed to be working."

Panicking, I throw my phone back into my purse and throw the bag over my shoulder, "It's an emergency."

Chapter Four

Less than thirty minutes later I leave the elevator of the skyscraper Meyers and Brant is located in and make a sharp right, approaching a set of glass doors that lead to that firm. I pull them open and enter the cool bright lobby to find all the chairs full with waiting clients.

Edie is gone. She never followed me out of the loft and she didn't make an appearance in the cab on the way over. I figured she was waiting for my return or she had given up and moved on to someone else. I secretly knew it wasn't the latter but I could hope, no?

There is only one receptionist desk at the front but it's a big one, entirely black and stocked with three Mac computers and impeccably well-dressed secretaries behind them.

I'm still in my clothes from last night I suddenly realize as the blond secretary throws me a stare. My skirt is tattered at the ends and smudged with dirt from the street. My suit jacket has a few stains on it, I assume from the mustard and ketchup. How could I have left the house like this? And secondly, why didn't Riley bring me any fresh clothes this morning?

I make a beeline down a small hallway that ends up splitting four ways, and turn to the left. It's where Terrance's office is located and his private boardrooms. Each room is divided by glass walls that are soundproof and blinds that give you privacy if you need it. It always smells like coffee and I deduced it was because there were at least four coffee machines on the go at once.

Terrance's secretary, Annie, doesn't even look up at me from her desk. She chatters into her headpiece and sits with her long legs on the desk, her black heels visible for everyone to see. As I pass her in that enormous wooden desk, she laughs loudly at whoever she is speaking to. It was obvious to anyone that she wasn't hired for her law experience but more so for her toned legs.

I walk through our individual empty lobby and just as I'm about to walk past our small private coffee room, Greg rushes out of it. He nearly runs straight into me and grabs my arms to stop from knocking me over. He looks distressed, his wavy dark hair is falling over his forehead and there are visible bags under his brown eyes. He's in a dark suit, bright green tie. "Phoebe! What are you doing here?"

"You called me about my job," I remind him frantically, "so I came in here to make sure Terrance doesn't replace me."

"I didn't think you'd show up right away," he takes his hands off of me, "I thought you'd call at least. You should be in bed, taking it easy."

"I'm fine, really," I let him know with certainty, "just a small concussion."

"Well don't let him hear you say that. That is total grounds for putting you on sabbatical," Greg warns me quickly. He then takes a step back and looks me up and down with an uneasy look, "You look horrible."

"I know, it's from the accident," I take a look down at myself. "I forgot to change before I ran out of the loft."

"What the hell are you doing here?"

Greg turns on his heels and I step to the side so I can see Terrance heading our way. He struts angrily, his suit flapping at his sides as he holds two pale folders in his hands. He's frowning so intensely at me I feel a bit rattled and have to swallow it down.

"I um, just came in to check on everything," I answer standing still and clenching the strap of my bag on my shoulder. "To see if you needed anything else from me."

"Aren't you supposed to be off work for two weeks?" Terrance demands. He reaches us and shoves the folders from his hand towards Greg, who fumbles a bit as he struggles to keep the papers inside of them.

"I was given the okay to do part time work," I shrug. Which is the truth, in a sense.

"And you decided to come dressed for work like a homeless person?" he shoots back with his hands on his hips. "Don't think I don't know about the contracts either. They called this morning threatening legal disorganization because you failed to send them in yesterday."

"I—um I don't—"

"—Did you finish the work Greg sent for you yesterday?" Terrance cuts me off, his hands unmoved from his hips.

"Yes, almost," I backtrack, and watch him look increasingly annoyed at me. "I will get it done by tonight and send it over by fax right away."

"Good. I'll have Greg email you a check list of everything that should be ordered and ready to go for Saturday," Terrance tells me as he reaches into his suit jacket and pulls out his phone. He frowns as he looks down at it. "I assume you can at least accomplish that?"

I nod sternly, "Yes I can."

"YOU!"

I jump in my place at the shriek in my ear.

I peer over my shoulder to see Edie standing right behind me. Her face is contorted into an absolute look of hate as her eyes stay fixated on my boss, who hasn't looked up from his cellphone.

I look away from Edie as Greg throws me a look, mouthing 'something wrong?' and I manage to slow my racing heart enough to mouth back 'never-mind.'

"He did it," Edie accuses harshly. "He did it. He killed me."

She cannot be serious right now.

She's pointing at Terrance and I try my best to ignore her as he looks up straight at me. I give him a smile and he just frowns. "Is there anything else you want?"

"Oh, no," I declare, "unless, you have some more case work for me to do?"

"Mercer I'm dealing with something very important and the Sears case is slowly taking precedence. You have work I need you to do for it already." His tone of aggravation is strong and I find myself nodding to it.

"He's talking about my case," Edie suddenly whispers as if he would be able to hear her. "He's talking about the case of my missing will, that's what he's dealing with. Bastard."

What?

It's hard for me not to look over at her and question her as to what she means. I see Terrance eyeing me and I realize he expects me to answer him,

"Yes, okay. Then I will just focus on highlighting the interviews."

"Good."

He brushes past me and Edie moves out of his way. In a panic she turns to me, "Stop him! Stop him and ask him to help with what he's doing!"

"*Stop it,*" I hiss under my breath making sure neither Greg nor Terrance can hear me.

I am being haunted by a crazy ghost.

A ghost who thinks my boss, whom is a complete stranger to her, has something to do with her death and this missing will of hers.

Edie spins away from me and looks back at Terrance, who has turned the corner and walked out of sight. Exasperated and showing it by throwing up her hands, Edie looks over at me. "Great. Now he's gone."

"So you want me to walk you down?" Greg asks.

I turn around to face him and shake my head at him. "No that's okay, thank you. Just do me a favor and keep me updated with whatever is going on here okay? I don't want to lose my job."

"Of course I will," Greg nods, "We're a team. You'd do the same for me."

I can hear Edie snort unladylike behind me, "He likes you."

I want to tell her that he most certainly does not and that at our first all-nighter for Terrance he turned me down after I had had too many glasses of wine. It was utterly embarrassing and the next morning when Greg brought it up, I pretended I didn't remember it happening.

"I'll see you later," I tell him with a small smile,

Quickly I turn away and head back down the hall. I can hear Edie tramping up beside me. "Why didn't you ask your boss to help? Furthermore why didn't you tell me that this was your boss?"

"What are you even talking about?" I mutter trying to hide my moving lips with my hand. Nobody is around but I don't want to risk it. The woman's bathroom is coming up to my left and I make a sharp turn into the door, pushing it open. There's only a stall and sink in it, generic with white tiles lining the walls and dim lighting from above the mirror. I lock the door quickly and turn around to find Edie looking straight at me.

"You can't talk to me when I'm in front of people," I tell her sternly, "it distracts me."

"Your boss is—*was* my attorney. The attorney of my estate anyway," she ignores what I said and rambles. "He was hired by my husband and my nephew. He did my will four months ago. I ended up firing him and demanding that the will be thrown away. I hired a new attorney, Herman Puckett who did my new will and now that will is missing. I left it in my safe and now it is gone and it's ruining everything I had planned to leave behind. I don't know how Terrance got it from my safe but he did."

"Hold on a second," I throw up a single hand and shut my eyes briefly. "I have to catch up. Terrance is your lawyer?"

I hear my phone vibrate and chime inside my purse so I raise a hand at Edie to pause. The display says Mom and I draw in a breath.

"If I don't pick up then she'll just keep calling," I say out loud, "I knew she wouldn't listen to Tom." I take the call placing the phone to my ear and see Edie raise her eyebrows impatiently. "Hi mom."

"*Jitterbug! Are you alright? How are you feeling?*"

Jitterbug. Something my mother and father have always called me, ever since I could remember. To be honest it's getting annoying. What future lawyer wants to have that as a nickname? You want a strong nick name like the Pit Bull or the Shredder. Or like the one people call Terrance, the—actually it's too R-rated to think about it.

"Mom, I told you to stop with the jitterbug—"

"*—Tom told me to leave you alone,*" she cuts me off, "*he said to leave you be. I told him to just wait when he has kids how he will feel if—*"

"—Mom, mom. I don't have much time to talk right now, I'm in a...a meeting."

"*A meeting? With who? Why? You have a concussion! You should be home in bed! Where is Riley? Why isn't he taking care of you?*" She gasps as an idea jolts to her. "*Oh

43

jitterbug...I'll pack my things and be there tomorrow. I can come in on the morning train—"

"—No!" I don't mean to shout but a slight panic is drawing in. "No mom, please. I'm fine. Honestly, I am feeling much better. I mean it was hardly a concussion."

"But you need someone to take care of—"

"—I have Riley, and Clara and Faye. Tom and Reese live in the city too, remember? Please stay home, I promise if I get worse then I will get Tom or Reese to call you. Alright?"

"But—"

"—Alright mom?" I look up and find Edie tapping her foot at me, arms crossed over her chest and one eyebrow raised. "Now, I have to go. I'll call you later. Love you, bye."

Edie nods in approval as I end the call. "Now, where was I? Oh yes, that scum sucking devil...He was recommended by my nephew before my husband died last year. He wrote my husband's will and divided up the assets. He did a wonderful job attending to my husband's wishes but he thought me a fool and kept trying to confuse me and take advantage."

"Terrance wrote your will?"

"Yes, but then I fired him when I discovered what a weasel he was."

"Then you hired a new lawyer, drafted a new will and put it away for safe keeping."

"Yes. My nephew went to retrieve it a few days after my funeral and it was gone."

"Didn't your nephew contact your new lawyer about your new will? He would have it on file."

"He doesn't know about my second lawyer! I never got around to telling him, nobody knew," Edie explains. "Old Herman is retired, he runs a part time firm from his home and his niece is his secretary. Each spring he vacations in Europe and he left just before my death. The only copy of my will was in my safe and I don't know how he got into it, but Terrance did. He took it and he hid it."

"Okay, well what good would that do him?" I ask.

"He's having an affair with my maid and in my original will I left her fifteen thousand dollars, and a small stake in my company. He's a money grubbing parasite and he's trying to steal from me. He hid the new will, I'm sure of it; I overheard him tell my maid that he would insure that she would get more than what was entitled her. "

I didn't want to argue with her against this; Terrance was money grubbing. He even clocks his clients for his time when they call to make an appointment to see him. He always worked to get his clients more than they asked for because it meant he received more than he asked for. Yet to think he would hide a client's will behind their family's back is outrageous. That could ruin his career, put him behind bars. That I know he would never ever risk.

"Okay, this is insane," I inform her. "It's bad enough that you are haunting me but to claim that I work for your ex-attorney? The world can't be that small. He would never do what you accuse him of. He's greedy sure, but Edie, he would never do that. Not in a million years."

"Oh please," Edie rolls her eyes at me, "of course he would. He's a lawyer. Lawyers are horrible."

"Hey, I'm a lawyer."

"No you're not, you are a secretary."

Her label puts me back into a foul mood and I frown at her. "Well I will be one just as soon as Terrance gives me a chance."

"He will never give you a chance," Edie chuckles, "because he likes you as his personal assistant. His maid."

"Stop!"

We're both silent to each other, and Edie is the one who breaks the stare first by taking a quick breath. She puts her hands out at me, "We shouldn't be arguing about this. It's futile. Let me tell you the whole story. Last year my husband's health began to deteriorate, we have no children. My sister and her husband have long passed and we have a nephew over in England, who we contacted to inform that everything would eventually be left to him. He flew down to make sure we hired a good attorney, who could be trusted, and we hired Terrance Meyers. I was never fond of him, he was too rigid, and has an unpleasant face," she adds motioning to her own. "Anyway the will he created for my husband was iron-clad, so I hired him to put the finishing touches on mine, as well. Then I caught him, shortly before I was to sign my new will, being handsy with my maid."

"Are you sure? Because he's married," I inform her. "Even though he can be a pig at times he wouldn't cheat on his wife. She's an heiress to some produce company."

"I know what I saw," Edie says sternly, "and that's not how a married man should be acting. I confronted him about his unprofessional behaviour and fired him. He promised me he got rid of the will as I requested. Four weeks ago he attended the extravagant birthday party I threw for myself. He was very angry with me that I cut out his girlfriend in my new will. He threatened to sue me but what grounds did he have? I paid him for his time and fired him because he was being improper."

I shake my head, "I didn't know any of this. He never said anything to me about this case."

"Shocker there," Edie sarcastically quips.

It was hard to believe Terrance hid this from Greg and I. He usually made us take over cases like this because he found them mind-numbing. How had this happened right under our noses?

"He also pushed me into the pond and let me drown."

"Hold on a second," I'm firm with my tone as I raise a hand, "*what?*"

To accuse my boss of hiding legal documents is one thing but to accuse him of murder? That's something entirely different. I can already see this playing out in my head and it isn't any good. What does Edie expect me to do? Say, *'oh morning Terrance, I was just wondering whether you've hid a legal document and possibly shoved an old lady to her death? No? Okay, thanks.'*

"I can tell you don't believe me," Edie breaks my thoughts as she wags her finger at me. "I can see it engraved on your face."

"Of course I don't believe you!" I cry, "Why would you even think I would? For Christ's sake I barely believe that you are a *real* ghost here, let alone that my boss murdered you and hid your will."

"I am a real spirit!" Edie proclaims loudly. "Do I have to prove it again to you?"

"No, just don't walk through anything anymore," I implore with a breath.

"So you'll help me then?" Edie raises an eyebrow at me.

"I don't understand what or how you think I can even help you. My boss won't divulge anything to me, not even if I was to get him drunk," I let her know, "in case you haven't noticed? The man hates me."

"Oh I've noticed," Edie places her hands on her hips and looks around the small bathroom. She makes a face at everything and gradually looks back at me. Her face drops when she notices my blasé expression. She must know that there is no possible way I could help her.

"Edie, I cannot help you," my purse slips from my shoulder. "It would ruin my career."

"What career?"

I ignore her jab and go on. "My *budding* career then. Furthermore, you don't have any proof do you? You are just assuming that Terrance hid your new will and that he pushed you into your pond."

"It's the last thing I remember before waking up attached to tubes in the hospital," Edie's voice rises to a screech and I grimace at it. She suddenly looks very menacing, her face contorts and shadows over. Her normal body colour becomes almost grey and she stiffens up. "I couldn't accuse him because I had tubes down my throat, do you have any idea how it feels to wake up in that state?!" The bathroom light begins to flicker violently as she yells and my eyes flutter from surprise. It suddenly becomes very cold in the room, and I quiver. "I was a healthy sixty year old woman and I wake up strapped to an uncomfortable bed in an ugly gown with plastic tubes coming out from my mouth before I die hours later from a heart attack."

Not being able to stand the bizarre flicking of the lights I scream, "Alright, fine!"

There's no more flickering and Edie's posture radically changes back to what it regularly is along with her complexion. Whatever shadows and greyness there was, is now gone. She stops breathing heavily and straightens herself up, retying the bow at her chest line that had come undone by her outburst. I

47

catch sight of something against her chest, purple in color but the bow tie hides it from view again.

My heart beats hard in my chest from what I just saw and I can feel my body temperature slowly rising back up. "What was that Edie?"

"I don't know," she shrugs as if it was no big deal, "obviously I am unable to control my emotions while dead."

I was starting to think she wasn't good at controlling them when she was alive either.

"So you'll help me?" Edie holds no regard for my startled appearance.

Feeling pushed into a corner I say, "If you can get me some proof, any proof that Terrance did this then yes. I will help you, on the condition you leave me alone right after. I don't have room in my life for a ghost."

An unstable ghost I want to clarify.

She seems to think about it for a moment and dramatically looks up at the ceiling as she does. After a few seconds she carries her eyes back to me, "Alright. You have a deal."

Chapter Five

For a few moments after waking, I forgot the events of the last few days. It's Friday morning and I'm blissfully wrapped in my white duvet cover with my head nestled into a 320 thread count pillow. I even make an 'hmmm' sound after I realize I don't have to jump out of bed and rush into the office. It's a heavenly feeling.

That is, until I realize that there was probably a ghost staring at me right now.

An impeccably well dressed, self-entitled, badgering ghost.

Slowly I pull the cover off my face but remain still. My dark brown eyes scan the room and I see nothing out of place. Our white armoire stands against the brick wall, closed. Our dresser rests against the wall across from the bed, completely clean and void of any beauty products.

I edge up, resting on my elbows as I glance around the room some more.

Edie isn't here.

She didn't show up all of yesterday either.

My God, could I have really been imagining her the last few days? I mean, she could have been a figment I created from the stress of the concussion, no? After all, I haven't seen her since Wednesday after leaving the firm and now it's Friday morning.

Please, please let this all just be a form of stress I created.

I finally manoeuver myself from the king sized bed, not without effort though. It was Riley's insistence that we get such a large bed, I was quite content with the queen size he had prior to this.

When I leave the bedroom, my black robe tied around me snuggly; I find the loft empty, and the bathroom door wide open. I walk through the living room, catching sight of a bright orange post-it on the Sears file I dove into Wednesday night after Clara and Faye left, and all day yesterday.

It had been a good Wednesday afternoon, the three of us sat around the living room just having wine and eating over-priced sushi. Riley ran in just to change into his workout clothes

49

before joining his running group at the park. I badly wanted to confide in Faye and Clara about Edie. I almost did twice, but each time my words fell short.

What was I supposed to say exactly?

'Guys, you wouldn't believe this but I have a ghost haunting me. She says she was murdered and wants me to investigate. Also, the accused is Terrance, my boss. Surreal right?'

I would sound absolutely looney.

I hadn't even thought about what Edie said once, when I got home. I shoved it from my mind and went on with Faye and Clara, face-timing with Satine shortly afterwards. Then later on when Riley returned and they left, I submerged myself into the Sears case for the rest of the night until I was too tired to function. I never left the loft yesterday either; I finished my work and faxed what I needed to.

I read the post it without picking it up,

Lunch @ 1 with mom and me. @ Al Fresco.

Lunch with Stella? A wonderful way to get me feeling inferior. I wonder for a moment if I can cancel or if I can come up with a legit excuse to be pardoned from it. Who am I kidding though? If anything, Riley will just have it rescheduled to a time that is convenient for me which would be anytime really since I'm part time now. Something I forgot to mention yesterday.

I get to Al Fresco at twelve forty-five, presuming I'll be early enough to have some caffeinated tea without Riley telling me it's bad for my system. I could really use a strong cup of it to down before I even speak with Stella. So when I see her tapping her long manicured nails on the table, speaking sternly to Riley about something, my heart sinks a little bit.

Of course she's early. Of course they're *both* early.

She's in a crème colored suit with ruffles at the sleeves and around her boney collar bone. Her hair pulled back tightly into her signature bee-hive. Riley wears a crème colored dress shirt with his jeans. This isn't the first time they've accidentally dressed alike either.

Next to them I'll look completely out of place but it's not like I can change now. I'm in a pair of skinny jeans and a simple red t-shirt which I have paired with a string of fake pearls. My hair is pulled into a messy bun because I gave up half way of trying to make it look decent.

As I approach the table Riley stands and pulls out my chair with a smile. Stella gives me a lingering once over, only smiling when I have sat down.

"Interesting pearls," she says and I realize it's her way of complimenting me.

"Thank you, I got them at a flea market."

Her face drops and Riley chuckles as he places an arm on the back of my chair "Don't worry mom. It was before she met me, no more flea markets for her."

I want to remind him that I like flea markets but it's futile because he always has good points why we should never go to one. Like fleas, and bed bugs and people ripping you off.

"I'm pleased that you're up and about, Phoebe," Stella goes on relaxing into her metal chair. "You had Maxwell and me in a worry over your accident."

I doubt that. She was probably hoping it would put me in a coma.

"Well I'm alright, just a minor concussion and a few scrapes," I let her know. "The doctor gave me pain killers for the headaches but I haven't taken any yet."

"Good news," Stella pushes a smile then drops it as quickly before she leans over and fiddles for something in her purse. "Now I was speaking with Riley yesterday evening." When she reappears she has a miniature black binder in her hands. "And we both agreed that we should do this as quickly as possible and more importantly, as stress-free as possible."

"Do what?" I look from Riley to Stella.

"The wedding of course," Stella blinks at me unimpressed. "You do recall accepting Riley's proposal don't you?"

"Of course I do." I hold back my frown.

What does she think happened to me? I lost my memory or something? I'm clearly wearing the diamond on my finger hand in front of her.

"Wonderful. Riley and I thought the long weekend in July would be nice," Stella opened up her binder and sighed delightedly at the page before her. "The Saturday afternoon. We were thinking of doing it at the golf and country club. As you know we are members and the fee is greatly discounted if we agree to use their caterers. The food is fantastic," she looks up with a serious face, "their dessert menu alone is divine."

Independence Day weekend is what, a month and a half away?

That can't be nearly enough time to plan a wedding. How will I be able to plan a wedding that quickly while working at Meyers and Brant?

"Uh," I clench my jaw a little bit as I look from Riley to Stella, "isn't that too little time?"

"No its not," Stella simply states, throwing me a sharp smile and then flipping a page in her wedding binder. "Now I thought today we could make a firm decision about whether or not to do it at the Golf and Country club, and a decision on the menu of course. Next week we will do a bit of dress shopping."

"I like the club," Riley interjects, and then casually looks my way. "It's where mom and dad had their twenty fifth wedding anniversary party."

Isn't the bride supposed to plan her wedding with her *own* mother? Or her bridesmaids? I don't even have bridesmaids yet! Isn't there supposed to be an engagement party beforehand?

This is too much; my mouth is getting dry. Where's my water?

"You haven't seen it yet," Riley places a hand on my arm and gives me a squeeze, "but I know you'll fall in love with it. Mom says that they will work around us and our healthy lifestyle choices. I've already researched some vegan wedding cakes."

"Vegan wedding cake!"

Edie's voice bellows around us with a snarly laugh and I try hard not to turn my head at her. I know she's standing over me, I can hear her laughter vibrate around me. "What a horrendous idea! Nobody eats vegan cake."

I want to tell her that plenty of people do and it's healthy for you and chalk full vitamins. Instead I look away from Riley back to Stella and force a smile. "My only concern is that the club may be just a tad out of our price range."

Stella chuckles at me and swats at me with her hand. "Phoebe, dear? I thought Riley had informed you that the wedding would be entirely paid for by Maxwell and me."

What?

My body tenses, a signal that this would end badly for me. One thought matches it; bad idea, bad idea, bad idea Phoebe.

"As a gift, from us to the both of you," Stella adds, brimming with a self-righteous smirk before looking back down at her binder. She runs a finger down the page she is looking at and I glance over at Riley; who gives me a quick grin. Can't he tell from my expression that I'm uncomfortable?

Oh God. What do I do? How do I reject this gesture? If I say no, she'll hate me even more won't she? And Riley? Look at him. He's so happy. So excited.

"This won't end well," Edie sings over my head, "just letting you know. In case you actually think this is a good idea."

I scream at Edie in my head. *Of course I don't! I'm not a lunatic. I know what Stella is like; if she pays for the whole wedding then she'll own me for life.*

"Exactly, I know women like her and that's all they aim for. Hoisting someone in the palm of their hands as if they are God," Edie sighs loudly. "So kindly decline the offer and tell her you'll do it your own way. I've seen their golf and country club and trust me sugar-pie, you can do a whole lot better."

As nice as it feels to know Edie is on my side I don't think I can actually—hang on a second. How did she—how did Edie know what I was thinking?

She steps up on my side, and I swat my head her way, my eyes narrowing at her. The expression makes her frown at me and cock her head back a little bit. "What?"

Gone is her golden blouse from the past two days. Today she's in a flowy sheer flowered blouse, a loose shirt beneath it and a pair of white slacks again. Her strawberry blond hair sits pinned around her face in loose waves. A casual 1930's look.

"Phoebe?"

I dart my eyes off my ghost and crank my neck Riley's way. His eyes rest upon mine but his brows are slightly lowered, "Yes?"

"Did you hear what mom said?"

"Oh, no, sorry," I look back at Stella. "I was distracted by something. Go on."

Of course Edie didn't hear my thoughts, that would be absurd. She's a ghost, not a mind-reader. She can walk through walls and couches and hospital curtains but she cannot read people's minds.

"If I could read people's minds I would have read Terrance's long ago, found out all of his dirty secrets and somehow figured out how to air them out to dry."

I shoot my head in Edie's direction and my mouth falls open a little bit.

Holy hell! You can read my thoughts!

It takes Edie a moment but then her expression matches mine.

"Son of a—" Edie snickers after a moment, "I can read your thoughts!" She slaps her hand against her leg in triumph and looks around the room. "I wonder who else's I can read."

"Phoebe!"

We both look at Riley but he's only looking at me.

"Sorry, so sorry," I look from him to Stella who wears the same expression as her son. In fact they look identical whenever they appear annoyed. The same sunk dark eyebrows, creases around them, and curved lips, one side slightly more dipped than the other. I never noticed that before.

"I was just telling Riley," Stella's mouth slightly twitches as she speaks to me, "that I'll be taking you and your bridesmaids shopping next week, so I will be emailing them. Is the Wednesday alright? Or the Thursday better?"

"Bridesmaids?"

"Yes," Stella looks taken aback again, "*bridesmaids.* You have bridesmaids yes?"

"Well," Edie snorts. "There's no need for her to be hostile."

"Yes I do," I ignore Edie and attempt some humour in my tone, "my bridesmaids. I think, well I can try to get my bridesmaids together next week. Thursday morning should be good."

"And how many are there?" Stella has a pen in her hand and has it set on the page in front of her in the binder. I wonder for a second if it's a solid gold pen or not. She looks up at me expectantly. "Well? How many are there?"

"Oh umm…"

Definitely Clara, Faye and Satine. Well, if Satine can get the time off of work, also would my sisters agree—it's no use. I can't focus. Not when I know Edie is somewhere in the restaurant reading my thoughts.

I mean this is *huge*, she can read my thoughts! Maybe she can read Riley's thoughts and Stella's? Oh I would love to know what Stella thinks. Could she possibly put thoughts into people's minds?

I suddenly feel ashamed for even thinking it. I could never ask her to manipulate a person like that. Edie is absent from my side so I gaze casually around the restaurant to see if I can spot her anywhere.

"Phoebe! What is going on?"

Riley's voice cuts through me and I look back over at him. I don't think I have ever heard him speak to me in that tone before. He was more than annoyed, he was angry.

"Will you please be present in this conversation?" Riley asks, removing his arm from my chair and sliding up against the table. I watch him pout at his mother.

"I'm sorry, really I am," I say suddenly feeling sheepish under both their eyes. "My head is just not in it today. I'll try harder." I take a breath and look squarely at Stella. "I don't have my bridesmaids yet. I haven't asked anyone—"

"—You haven't asked anyone yet?" Stella looks startled at my confession and she exchanges a look with Riley. "Nobody?"

"Well no, I haven't really had the time," I answer.

"You didn't ask the girls the other night?" Riley probes, frowning at me again, "Why not?"

"My God, is this a lunch date or an interrogation?"

Edie pops up next to me and crosses her arms over her chest. "Are you sure you want to marry into this family? I've known the mother in law for only ten minutes and even I can tell she's horrid. And your fiancée? I don't see it. He's very good looking but," she sticks a finger in her mouth and mimics throwing up, "he's too…blasé."

I didn't ask for your opinion.

"You didn't have to. I always give it," Edie replies wistfully. "Anyway, wrap this up. It's making me sick. I have the proof you required."

What? How?

"I listened to Terrance's phone call last night; his flirtatious secret phone call to my maid."

"Phoebe clearly isn't able to focus today," Riley says loudly looking over at his mother, "maybe we should reschedule?"

"There isn't time to waste," Stella glares from him to me. "The wedding is less than two months away. We have nothing yet. No flowers, no band, no—"

"—No, it's alright," I put my hands out over the top of the table and look at the two of them. "Let's keep going. I can focus; I think it's just a small headache coming on, that's all." I hate to lie but I don't see any other way to go about it. I don't want Riley angry with me. With the mention of a headache his stance softens a bit and he picks up his glass of water to take a drink.

"Excellent then," Stella leans back into her seat, paying me little regard as she looks back down at her binder and flips a few more pages. "Now for the bands, Riley has compiled his list of favorites. He says you won't mind if he chooses so I thought we could go through the list and make appointments to see each one."

"I think we should break into your boss's office and find more evidence," Edie has leaned over and begun whispering in my left ear. Immediately I'm tuned out of what Stella is saying. "I think he's hiding some things in there. He has a locked cabinet and I know where he keeps the key."

Are you out of your mind? I'm not breaking into Terrance's office! That's a crime.

"He was also on the phone a week before I died with Herman telling him he was calling to inform him that I had rehired him as my lawyer and Herman's services were no longer required. Herman thought it was a prank, bless the old boy. I forgot to tell you that tidbit."

Okay, that is a tad suspicious.

"See!" Edie practically screams in my ear, "He's guilty I'm telling you!"

Stella is gesturing at me and I panic just a bit. What did she say? Is she still talking about the bands? Or has she moved on to something else?

"She asked which day is better for you to watch the bands audition. Next Saturday or Sunday," Edie tells me, her tone full of annoyance.

"Saturday," I blurt out at Stella, and smile for good measure. "Definitely a Saturday."

"Saturday," Stella sighs as she begins to write something down in front of her, "it is…"

"There is more I have to tell you. I can't do it when your focus is split down the middle," Edie goes on and I watch as she steps in front of me, blocking Stella from my view and standing in the middle of the metal table. I draw in a sharp breath and next to me Riley sits up,

"What's wrong?"

I can't do this. I can't focus on the wedding with Edie constantly in my ear or walking through objects. Or reading my mind.

"I—I'm sorry, I have to go."

I push my chair back before Riley can say anything and I watch his mouth drop a little. As Edie walks out from the table I can see Stella's contemptuously glare at me.

Riley begins to stand up, "Phoebe what is—"

"—It's just a headache," I motion for him to sit back down as I begin to back away. "I'll be fine. I'm just going to go home and take my pills. I'll be okay in a few hours. So sorry, really sorry!"

Twenty minutes later I've slammed the loft door shut behind me and fallen against the cold metal. The entire ride over here in the cab was horrible. All I could think about was lunch and what a disaster it had been. Riley had yelled at me. Stella had thrown me more dagger stares then I have ever received from anyone in my lifetime and a ghost can now invade my personal thoughts.

What a nightmare.

Why hadn't I just kept my eyes forward a few days ago? If I had just been paying attention none of this would have happened. I wouldn't have been run over by a hot dog cart.

"Took you long enough to get here."

I open my eyes and find Edie standing in my living room.

"Edie."

"Shall we continue?" she asks. "Now, we have to get to my house right away. Before five o'clock. There's an auction going on and dozens of my pieces are being sold, my revised will could be in one of those pieces. Terrance has a few buyers there on his behalf too; he was on the phone with them this morning."

"Edie." I'm sharp with her and she gives me a glare. "Did you not notice how awful that lunch was? It was horrible; Riley got angry with me. I couldn't focus with you jabbering around me and walking through tables!"

"I am sorry about the lunch," nothing in her tone suggests she is truly sorry. "But it wasn't horrible just because of me you know," she says straightening up her posture. "It was awful because of your future mother-in-law, and your future husband."

I want to argue with her but realize I don't have the strength right now. That it would just rile her up and then she would never leave me alone. She'd always intrude on my thoughts.

"You're right," Edie quips hiding a smile, "I would definitely intrude on your thoughts and never leave your side."

"Okay, stop doing that." I order angrily.

Before she can retaliate, my phone goes off inside my tote bag and I reach in to grab it. Riley's name and office number flash on the screen. I don't know why but my nerves shoot up as I place the phone against my ear,

"Riley?"

"Phoebe. What the hell was that?"

"I know. I'm sorry," I push away from the door and drop my bag on the floor. "I didn't mean to be so rude at lunch; my head was just not in the right place."

"My mother is appalled Phoebe," Riley goes on, *"and frankly, I'm a little bit hurt, here. Our wedding seemed to be a hassle to you."*

"Riley please don't say that," I beg him as I turn my back on Edie. "It means everything to me. It's just been a few days since the accident and I'm still all over the place."

"Tell him you have a ghost haunting you," Edie jokes, "He'll understand."

"Sssh!" I shot at her as I stomp my foot.

"I didn't say anything!" Riley exclaims.

"No, I wasn't talking to you," I tell him quickly, "I meant—never mind. I'm sorry."

I hear him sigh on the other end and I can just imagine him shaking his head, contemplating our relationship. I know I would, if I were in his shoes, if anyone had treated my mother the way I treated his today.

"Maybe I can come by now and we can talk?" I suggest, trying to break whatever train of thought he may be having. Maybe I could even tell him, about Edie? He would understand wouldn't he? I'm being haunted and it's making me crazy.

"Ha!" Edie laughs loudly, "He'll commit you to get tested, more like it. He won't understand, nobody will, sugar-pie. Just say it out loud to yourself and see if even you believe what you are saying."

I hate that she's right. I can only imagine Riley's face if I tell him about Edie. It would be the end of our engagement for sure.

"I have a meeting in an hour," Riley finally tells me, *"but I have time before that."*

"Okay, great," I feel myself perk up, "I'll come right over."

He hangs up without a word and I turn to look over at Edie who has crossed her arms over her chest to show her displeasure with me.

"Not a word," I say to her as I walk back over to the door and my purse.

"Fine. I won't say anything," she throws her hands up as she promises. "But if I don't say anything then you have to go to my house and stop the auction."

"Edie—"

"—I just want you to *try*," she appeals clasping her hands together. "Just go and look around and see if you can try to stop some of my things from selling."

"Fine."

Chapter Six

Riley's advertising company was still putting together the odds and ends. It was only six months old and was still operating out of a strip mall plaza next to a real estate office and a nail salon on the west side of the city. Even though it had only five employees and used tattered cubicles it still had a progressive kind of atmosphere about it when you entered.

It was named R&J, after Riley and his school mate James. James had put up most of the money for the company and had the connections to other media firms. He needed Riley because Riley had the charisma James lacked. Where Riley looked like a J-crew model, James had a slight resemblance to a skinnier, dweeby Mr. Clean. James had brought along his girlfriend Jamie to be their assistant; she had hired the other three employees whose names I did not know.

Edie was at my side as I left the cab and clicked her tongue when she saw my heavy tip.

I shut the cab door and back away as he drives off, keeping my back to the glass doors of R&J behind me.

"Don't talk to me here, alright?" I tell her after making sure nobody was in earshot of me and my ghost. "I don't want to be distracted again by you. It was embarrassing and I couldn't focus on what was important."

"Your wedding is not as important as my death."

I don't even try to argue with her at the moment. "Just be quiet while we're here, okay?"

"As long as we keep our bargain, my silence for your attendance at the auction."

I look over at Edie and find her eyes fixated on me; the look she's giving me says 'all or nothing' and it's adding to my foul mood. I've known her for only a few days and it was enough to know if I did not agree she would probably scream in my ear this entire visit.

"Alright, fine," I give in and turn around. I keep my mouth as closed as I possibly can as I walk towards R&J. "But if I hear one word from you, everything is off."

"I'll do you one better and wait outside," Edie nods as she begins to follow me towards the glass doors. "The carpet inside that building looks questionable."

"You're dead," I remind her keeping my lips as still as I possibly can. "What is it to you?"

"I can still smell," Edie reveals, "better than when I was alive. I can smell the fungus all the way over here. So no thank you, I will wait outside."

I roll my eyes at her and pull the glass door open to R&J. I have to tug it pretty hard to get it to open further than two feet but I manage to do it. I stumble inside, stepping over the air bump in the grey carpet at the door and hear the door behind me swoosh slowly closed. Nobody even looks at me as I enter the room, except Billy the receptionist, who gives me a casual smile before looking back down at his cross word puzzle.

Beyond him are three cubicles, a small hallway that leads into the offices of Riley and James and a shared bathroom. Glancing over my shoulder I see Edie on the other side of the glass wall, her hands sideways against the glass and her eyes peering into the room. I shake my head at her as I move past Billy and the cubicles, towards Riley office.

His office is the one on the right but before I can get to the door, it pops open and Jamie waddles out. She sees me and smiles largely,

"Phoebe, hi! I'm so happy to see you," she reaches me and throws her arms forward so I can come into a hug. She smells like herbal incense, earthy and dark. It was something I had to get use to but it came easy since she was such a fantastic person. Her short black hair was thrown atop of her head loosely, and held back with two pencils. She wore a long flowered peasant skirt and a brown tank top, matched with a wreath style belt around her waist.

"Hi Jamie, it's great to see you too."

"I'm happy that you're feeling much better," she pulls away from me, holding her million dollar smile. "So scary what happened to you, I'm happy it was nothing in the end. I even told Riley he could take a few days off, I know about all our clients, mock ups, the works. I would have been happy to step in."

"I'm glad you're so happy," her smile is infectious and I feel mine growing,

"Oh I'm sorry," she laughs so hard she snorts a little and hits my arm lightly. "I should explain. It's my new mantra. I'm Happy. I'm happy because of this, or because of that. I really feel it strengthening my inner core." She makes a grabbing motion with both hands at her stomach. "It's really brought my cheerful attitude from here," she signs her hand at her chest then moves it above her head, "to here. Powerful stuff. You should try it."

I can only imagine what Edie would say to that if she were here with me.

"I just may Jamie, thanks," my face is starting to ache from my smile and a wave of relief washes over me when the door to Riley's office opens. He comes out, bumping straight into Jamie, "Sorry Ja."

"It's okay" she laughs and backs away from us, "I'll leave you two to it. Phoebe? Come back to my yoga class with me soon. Riley mentioned you are off work so some yoga will do you some good," she takes a deep breath and raises her hands slowly, "to relax."

"Oh, I'm not off work," I declare slightly shaking my head, "I'm back part time."

"What?" Riley's face dips and I find him frowning at me, "Since when?"

Drat. Telling Riley completely slipped my mind; this could not have come at a worse time.

"Is that a good idea?" Now Jamie makes a scrunched up face, "You did have a concussion."

"It wasn't that big of a concussion, I mean I really am fine," I tell her then bring my attention to Riley, "and since yesterday. I'm sorry I forgot to tell you, they need me on a case, so I agreed to stay on part time."

"You just had a concussion! You were complaining of a headache at lunch with mother," Riley exclaims running a hand through his hair, "Phoebe, you promised me you would take time off. Use your head; they don't need you that badly."

Part of me wants to tell him that he's right and that I stupidly volunteered but that wouldn't help this moment. He wouldn't understand why I had to go back; even if I told him there was talk of replacing me. He'd suggest threatening to sue or something and that could ruin any chances at a decent career in law.

"They do kind of," I feel my defenses weakening, "Terrance won't hire a replacement—"

"—Terrance," Riley spits his name out like old milk. "That guy is such an idiot."

His digital watch beeps and he looks down on it, drawing in a breath through his teeth as he looks up at me. "Babe I totally forgot. The client just bumped up the meeting, it's in fifteen minutes. We'll have to talk later."

"I can hop on over for you Riley," Jamie calls eagerly, "it's no trouble. I know the client."

"No thanks Jamie; James needs your help with a client proposal," Riley gives her kind grin and she nods then smiles my way,

"See you soon, okay Phoebe?"

I bob my head and watch her back away with a dance in her step into James 'office.

Riley gives my arm a squeeze as I look back at him, "We can reschedule this talk right?"

"Sure," I can't help but feel a tad disappointed, "I can just go home, wait for you."

"Perfect," he leans forward and kisses me hard against the forehead with little conviction. "I'll stop by and get some groceries. I'm making the switch to vegan starting tomorrow so I need to be prepared."

"Vegan?"

Oh no.

"Yes, vegan," he leaves my side and goes back into his office calling out the rest of his answer to me. "Remember we talked about it last week? I want to make sure I have less than four percent body fat by the wedding."

"Oh, okay."

"We can do it together; it'll be good for you to take the step with me. Don't worry; I hear it's not as scary when you have the right recipes."

"Vegan, eh?"

I say nothing to Edie as I get into the cab Jamie called for me. I shut the door behind me and within a second Edie moves through it to sit next to me. She wiggles her nose at the smell of the cab, Korean bbq would be my guess, and peers over at the white guy behind the glass partition.

"Tell him we're going to Cedar Springs. 33 Lundy Lane."

My mouth caves when I hear the destination.

"Cedar Springs!"

" 'cuse me?" the cab driver glances at me through his rear view mirror, "Cedar Springs?"

Edie gives me a nod and begins to adjust her curly bob, feeling the tresses.

"Yes," I tell the cab driver as I watch her, "Cedar Springs please. 33 Lundy Lane."

"You got it."

I could easily just have given him my address and said to the hell with Edie. But we did make a deal and she kept up her end of the bargain. Besides, I felt I could use the distraction.

Riley, a vegan? I hated the idea because I knew it was my future. My only enjoyment when we ate out was when I could convince him to go for sushi or seafood. Now we wouldn't even be able to do that! What do vegans eat anyway?

"They don't eat anything from animals," Edie tells me with a sigh, she leans back into the seat and stares out the window as we move down the city street. "Only things planted into the ground. Waste of a life if you ask me."

"Well I didn't ask you." I set my purse on my lap as I drop against the tattered leather seat.

"Sorry?" the cab driver looks back at his rear view mirror at me again,

"Oh, nothing. Just talking to myself. Could you put the music on? And kind of high?" I don't feel like answering Edie in my head, and if I have to talk to her, I may as well do it normally.

"I sure can," he tells me with a smile. "Very rare I get a passenger who tells me to blast the music." He laughs, an obvious smoker's laugh, and hits a series of buttons on his console until the music turns on and I find myself listening to an

80's rock band. Next to me Edie makes a twisted face and I roll
my eyes, confident the cabbie can't hear me I speak to her,

"Let me guess? This music is *horrid*."

"I happen to be a fan of White Snake," Edie shoots my
way as she glares at me, "*Here I Go Again On my Own* happens
to be one of my favorite melodies."

I let out a small giggle, picturing this prim and proper
woman dancing to White Snake at a beach party in the 80's. I
doubt she was the girl in the spandex with crimped hair and pink
streaks.

"You'll never last, you know," Edie tells me. Her lips
pierce together and her eyes become small as she looks at me.
"As a vegan I mean."

"I can do it," I go into defense mode, "I know I can. I'm
a vegetarian aren't I?"

I can feel Edie's eyes peer into me, "Are you?"

Don't think, just answer.

"Yes, now drop it."

"Do you like that girl?" Edie suddenly asks me.

"What girl?" I lean against the window of the cab,
placing my elbow against the door and casually covering my
mouth with my hand so the driver can't see me.

"That girl, that works with your future husband?"

"Jamie? Yes I do. She's a bit out there but I like her.
Why?"

"No reason," Edie dramatically tosses her head towards
the window on her side and looks out. She side-eyes me a
moment later, obviously fishing for me to elaborate on what she
is getting at.

Fine. I'll bite. Why are you asking about Jamie, Edie?

"Well," her head spins back my way and she moves her
body to face me "Reason is because, I don't like her."

I smirk, keeping my body pointed towards the window,
my mouth hidden behind my hand, "not surprising. You don't
like anyone. You barely like me."

"True," she admits hardly embarrassed, "but what I
mean to say is I don't *trust* her and I don't think you should
either. How involved is she with that firm of Riley's?"

My face contorts and I drop my hand as I look over at her. Just what the hell is she getting at?

"I don't mean to be accusing of anything," Edie puts both hands up in the air. "I'm just sharing a feeling. And my feelings are usually on par. I have a feeling Terrance is involved with my missing will, and I know I'm right."

"*Allegedly. Allegedly* involved," I remind her coarsely, the frown completely taking over my face. "And Jamie would never backstab Riley or James, her boyfriend."

She shrugs and leans back into her seat, "she just seems very involved with things being a secretary and all."

I can't help but feel offended; after all, Terrance treats me like a secretary as much as I hate to admit it.

"No more talking," I tell Edie sternly as I turn my back on her. "Conversation is over."

"Miss?" the cab driver turns down his music and I see him look at me over his shoulder quickly, "say somethin'?"

"No, I didn't say anything."

I still don't quite believe what I'm standing in front of.

I was barely able to pay the cab driver once we pulled up in front of 33 Lundy Lane.

This was Edie's house?

I was standing in front of a three foot high iron fence, encasing what I assume is the entire property. There is one opening to my left to let a paved driveway reach the front of the house; a gate is closed a few feet before me. The driveway is full of cars, each more expensive than the one behind it. BMW's, Porsche's, limited edition Hummers and Bentley's. As if the golden driveway wasn't impressive enough, Edie's house was one I had only ever seen in films and read in novels.

Two story's high, the home was more like a manor.

Just how rich was Edie?

Against the iron fence, from which I stood a mere five feet away from was indeed a faded stone plaque that read Edward Manor circa 1790.

It was breathtakingly beautiful.

Obviously modeled after the homes in the French Quarter in New Orleans, it was purely white and the pillars on the wrap around porch were a faded sandy tone. A Victorian revival home with three section slider windows on the first floor decorated with white curtains on the inside. A small porch on the top floor sheathed a pair of French doors and wrapped its self-half-way around that floor. A set of curved steps led up to the bottom porch, the black French doors closed firmly with a large sign hanging on them that read 'auction in garden'.

"You have a garden?"

"Beautiful isn't it?" Edie walked up to the iron fence and leaned in with a happy sigh. "This was built over the original Edwards House in 1875. My father remodeled it again in the 40's, then my husband and I remodeled again about ten years ago."

"Edie," I step up next to her and look at the small front yard, decorated with luscious hedges and bushes of bright flowers I have never seen before. A handful of lavenders line the front porch neatly. "This house has got to be worth millions of dollars."

"One point five exactly, it's mostly the land that holds the value," she takes a breath, "but I'm not talking about it. It's tacky to discuss money."

1.5 million? No wonder Terrance kept this from Greg and I. Edie is worth a small fortune; and I've learned clients like this he tends to keep to himself.

If he was involved in some way of course, which I still doubt.

Next to me Edie chuckles as she glances at me quickly, "We'll see. Come on, the auction should be starting soon."

I half expect her to walk through the iron fence but instead she walks around me and begins a slow trek up the paved driveway, around all the cars crowded into it. As I followed her I wonder how they would all get out, and when the time comes it could be a traffic jam.

"Merida! That wench. She would be here the moment I drop dead."

I look away from a BMW to find Edie in front of a vintage, yellow Porsche parked almost at the front of the driveway. She's pointing at the rear view mirror where a pink air freshener bikini top hangs from it, swaying from the light breeze.

"Look at that," Edie tells me when I reach her, "the woman is almost sixty for God's sake!"

"I take it you two were best friends?" I snicker as I look from the impressive car to Edie.

"We were actually," Edie tells me seriously, "although I always suspected she had a jealous streak in her. This just confirms it. I'm surprised she could afford such a car, seeing as her late husband left his insurance money to their three children, and not her."

"Edie, she could be here to pay her respects. She could be crying in a chair watching all your stuff be given away and begging them not to."

"Ha," Edie blurts sarcastically, "I'll drop dead again if that's what I see. Come on."

I follow her out of the driveway, around the large closed garage, down a stone pathway lined with yellow pansies on both sides of it. When we finally get to the end of the pathway and come out from the side of the garage, I see a whole slew of people before us.

The property stretched out as far as my eyes could see; was that a lake an acre or so down?

It's beautifully decorated with hedges and rose bushes every few feet. The cluster of people have gathered in the middle of the green yard under a large white tent. The pathway we stood on led to the tent, which was set up over a stone section I assumed was meant for big events like this. Everyone was dressed impeccably well and in my cheap pearls and red shirt I couldn't even blend in as one of the waiters. Even they looked better than I did.

"Edie!" I whispered, "Why didn't you tell me to dress up!"

Edie howls loudly, "Nothing you own would have suited this, believe me, I have looked. Now come on."

What is she expecting to happen here?

"Edie wait," I whisper again and watch her stop. I motion for her to follow me behind the nearest green hedge so I could hide behind it. She rolls hers eyes and places her hands on her hips as she watches me run behind it. "What exactly do you think we are going to do here?"

"I told you," she appears next to me and drops her hands at her sides, "you're going to stop my things from being sold!"

"How exactly?"

Her face drops, "I don't know."

"Edie. You need a plan! I can't just demand this auction be stopped."

I watch Edie bite her lip and after a few seconds she looks back into my eyes, "Okay. Just follow my lead when we get in there."

I pull my hair out of its messy bun and run my hands through the strands in an attempt to look somewhat nice. I pull my shirt down and brush off my jeans as if they were dirty; then I rush out from behind the green hedge and follow Edie down the pathway.

So far no one has even noticed me; not even the waiters.

Everyone at the auction is undeniably older than I am, except the waiters, and better dressed than I intentionally thought. There are labels everywhere; Gucci and Prada purses swing left and right as I enter the tent in my three year old Nine West black heels. A waiter passes me with a tray of red wine and I scoop one up.

I wonder which one of these people was hired by Terrance.

Music plays from somewhere I can't see but I recognize it as one of the Rat Pack singers. I skim the crowd to spot Edie and can't find her anywhere. There isn't a place to sit either, no tables or chairs; just a podium towards the back of the small tent and a white screen next to it.

"Merida, this must be *so* awful on you."

I spin around when I hear the name and peer through the standing guests around me. Then I spot her, the woman I assume is Merida.

She's dressed in a pink dress much too young for her aging figure and a big pink floppy hat. It has a Gucci strap placed upon it. Her blond hair is in tight curls at her shoulders, and her matured face is caked with makeup, complete with a shade of pink lipstick. The skin around her eyes was exceptionally tight and I know no woman aged sixty looks that wrinkle-less.

There are a few people surrounding her, and she's drinking from a champagne glass. There are no tears behind her eyes and her posture is far from depressive.

"It is extraordinarily dreadful," she answers the man to her left; her voice sounds like honey. "I cried myself to sleep. She and I have known each other for over twenty five years; we were, as you all know *inseparable*." She takes a long sip of her champagne and a bit of it drips down her chin, she responds by giggling like a school girl and wiping her chin. "Whoops...as I was saying, we were peas in a pod. I know Edie would never want me mourning her death like I have; she would want me up on my feet, going on with life, living it to the fullest."

Somehow, I doubt that.

Somebody asks her about the auction and she smiles, "Of course I will bid on a few things! I was a little sad to find out that she didn't leave me even an album of our trips together but I understand the cause," Merida nods sympathetically. "She wanted to donate what was raised to charity, she had a kind heart like that."

I sip my wine as I begin to look around for my ghost, but Edie is nowhere to be found. It wasn't like I could call out her name either; everyone would here would think me crazy. Besides I don't want to make myself known just yet, I'd like to stop this auction with as little attention brought onto me as humanly possible.

"And who are you?"

Somehow Merida had caught sight of me and waddled over as I looked around for Edie. Now she was standing two feet away from me, her thin eyebrows raised and her one hand cupped around the elbow of the arm that held her champagne glass.

Oh no. How do I even answer this?

"This," Merida's voice is high now, "is a private event with a guest list. Who are you?" The posse that had surrounded her was beginning to glance over and my nerves bounced about.

Think of something Phoebe!

"Uh, I'm related to her."

That was what I came up with? Oh God.

"*Related*?" Merida isn't buying it. "If you were related to her I think I would know."

Edie! Where the hell are you? I could use some help right now!

"You can't just waltz in here you know?" Merida goes on, and then looks around at the guests, "I'm calling security."

Chapter Seven

"No, no you don't have to do that!"

Wine spills out from my glass as I motion at Merida, and this only causes her eyebrows to raise even further. Her blue eyes run me up and down slowly, but before she can say anything else someone steps up next to her.

He's young, a few years my senior would be my guess, standing at well over six feet. His dark blond, almost brown-red hair is cut short and he has brown eyes that are fixated on Merida. Creases on his forehead signal a serious demeanour and the navy blue suit he's in only added to it. It's a fit suit, and you can see he keeps himself in decent shape if his arms are any indication. He was unmistakably attractive, in a brooding type of way.

"Merida, we are starting the auction," he tells her kindly. His accent was odd; a definite mix of American and British. I watch Merida gesture at me with her empty hand,

"Porter. This woman claims she was related to our dearly beloved Edie but I suspect she's a party crasher. Look at those pearls, they aren't even real."

My mouth drops a bit as she insults my necklace. Why couldn't Merida just forget me and go bid on the auction?

The man turns to face me and his eyes narrow as he looks me over. His heavy gaze gives me slight chills and I can feel goosebumps treading up my back.

"You're related to my aunt?"

This is Edie's nephew.

Now that I've realized the fact, I can see her in him. Almost the same color of hair, but definitely same deep eyes and the same kind of intense forehead.

"Oh for Pete's sake, you said you were related to me?"

I have never been so relieved in my life. My shoulders slump right away and I feel my breathing get light again at the sound of Edie's voice. She steps up next to me and shakes her head; I try not to gape at what I see her dressed in. It's a bright teal dress that ends delicately at her feet and cascades down her back gracefully.

"Gorgeous, isn't it?" Edie takes a step back from me and twirls slowly, "I just had to change. Everyone here is in their brunch best and I looked frumpy."

Across from me, both Edie's nephew and Merida frown, clearly confused as to why my attention has drifted to a trio of men lighting up cigars near us. Edie begins to swat away the smoke that floats our way.

You left me to change Edie? Are you insane? Help me!

Edie stops at hearing my tone, and drops her hands, she then glances over at her nephew and Merida and gestures at them. "Tell them you are my late husband's sister's son's daughter. My husband cut ties with his side of the family years ago and they won't question it."

"Related through marriage," I finally say placing a smile over my nervous mouth, "I'm her late husband's sisters' son's daughter. The youngest one."

Both Edie's nephew and Merida blink at me, then they exchange a look and I can tell they don't believe me at all. Edie must catch it too because she tells me to add,

"You are from Canada, the west. That's where Clinton's family was from. Let them know that I reached out after Clinton's death to make amends. That nobody wanted to speak with me because they still blamed Clinton about the maple syrup incident."

Maple syrup—

"—Just say it," Edie interrupts me, "trust me that will do it."

"I'm from Canada," I say smiling at her nephew and Merida again, "from the west. Aunt Edie reached out to us after Uncle Clinton's death but nobody wanted anything to do with her. You know," I step up closer to them and whisper, "because of the maple syrup incident." They both raise their eyebrows in unison and I take a step backwards again. "But I decided to let bygones be bygones. It was ages ago anyway, and it didn't involve me. Aunt Edie was always kind enough to send us birthday gifts and Christmas presents, money to help with our college. She seemed so genuine that I called her back and we became close."

"Oh bother," Edie gags next to me, "what a load of crap, now that? They won't believe."

I suddenly realize how ridiculous what I said was; but I ran with what she gave me.

"I had no idea of any of this," Edie's nephew frowns at me again. "Aunt Edie never mentioned any of this to me or my father."

"Porter, my nephew," Edie introduces into my ear. "He's the one we have to be careful for. He's like a hound-dog, always suspicious, never smiles, serious."

Great. Just what I need. He's probably a lawyer too isn't he Edie?

"No he's not a lawyer," Edie tells me, "he owns a company over in England. Does well for himself but he can be as serious as the plague so just remember that. Tell him that I said he might be suspicious and if that was the case, then he is more than welcome to check my phone records and bank statements."

He won't find anything there!

"Yes he will," Edie sounds annoyed with me now. "I sent money out west to an old friend and would call her twice a month. He never knew that; it wasn't important."

"She said you might say that," I finally say to Porter, keeping my tone civil, "and told me to tell you that you can check her phone records and bank account as evidence."

"As evidence," Merida repeats into her glass as she glares at me, "my, my, my…"

Next to me Edie gasps and attempts to hit me in my shoulder but her arm slides through. I follow her panicked stare and see a few people gathered around the podium. "They are starting the auction!"

She sashays away from me and I hold in a gasp.

Edie! Edie get back here!

"No need," Porter says and I realize that he's speaking to me so I give him my attention. "I know Aunt Edie has relatives out west and I believe she would have been generous to her less fortune family."

"If I may ask," Merida speaks up, "why didn't you come to the funeral?"

Damn it.

"Oh I paid my respects afterwards," I answer grimly, hoping I look somewhat real with this emotion, "I can't attend funerals. Emotionally, they just destroy me." I lie with a sombre tone and bring the wine back up to my mouth. I take a long sip all the while aware of Merida and Porter's eyes on me as I look around the tent.

Please go away, please go away…

"Do you plan to bid on anything of Edie's?" Merida probes, raising a thin eyebrow my way as her means of letting me know she was still apprehensive of me. "Is that why you are here?"

I don't have the money to bid on this stuff. I can't say yes. Think of something Phoebe, think of something…

"I'm here," I take the wine from my lips, "because…"

"You're here to stop the auction that's why! Tell them!"

Edie has reappeared and now stands between me and Porter and Merida.

I can't say that Edie! I don't have a reason why to stop it, you never gave me one!

"Why are you here?" Merida pries, swapping another look with Porter.

"Tell them I hired you, to be—to be my new maid!" Edie snaps her fingers at her idea. "That I hired you to start this week but then I died."

I don't have time to argue with her.

"She hired me," I blurt out, "to be her new maid. I was supposed to start this week, but then Aunt Edie passed away. I thought I would come by anyway, in case I was still needed. I owed Aunt Edie that much, at least."

"She has a full staff," Porter tells me, clearly unmoved by the sentiment of my last line.

I look to Edie and she nods at me,

"Tell him I wanted Rosanne to go retire. Her eye sight is failing her and she's slow."

I can't help but frown at her stuffy attitude. "Edie wanted Rosanne to retire; I was supposed to take her place. She wanted her to get a nice severance package though."

Edie gasps loudly, "I did not want that!"

"Ah," Porter draws out the word and slowly nods as he does, "I see. Strange she didn't communicate any of this with me, or Rosanne herself…"

"He thinks he's so clever," Edie smirks shaking her head at him. "Tell him the reason I didn't tell him about the hire was because it was a small matter, and he was busy dealing with his psychopathic ex-girlfriend."

I feel myself chuckle inside and stifle a smile for fear of showing it. Instead I step up around Edie, closer to Porter and Merida as I speak, "She didn't want to burden you with that. She said you were dealing with your crazy ex-girlfriend and that was stressful enough."

I step away to find Merida looking up at Porter, whose eyes are glued onto me. I wish I could read him but he was illegible.

"Porter!" Merida exclaims, "You didn't tell me you were single. You knew my daughter was interested."

Slowly Porter takes his eyes off of me and says, "Merida, I apologize I had no idea. Aunt Edie never mentioned it."

He's lying isn't he? I scan his face trying to catch a hint of emotion.

"Course he's lying!" Edie tells me with a snort, "Her daughter is a plastic gold digger. We laughed about it when I told him Amanda was sniffing around for him after the New Year's Eve party."

"I'll set something up, Amanda will be just thrilled." Merida laughs jabbing Porter in the chest with a long nail before taking a drink of her bubbling champagne. I wish I could say I feel a little bad for the guy but I get the feeling he isn't someone who's going to make my job any easier.

"Excuse yourself," Edie orders, "and follow me. I have a plan. Don't drink all that wine."

"Excuse me," I say to Porter and Merida, I don't know why I curtsy but I do before I spin around and hurry away from them following Edie.

"*What*" Edie grumbles, "Was that?"

I don't know. They make me nervous.

"So you bow as if they are royalty?"

What's the plan Edie?

I only hope she can sense the aggravation in the tone in my head. I am so over this event, this day. I just want to go home and hid away in my loft waiting for Riley to return. Wait to start my new vegan lifestyle.

I wait for Edie to respond but she doesn't, instead she keeps walking, moving through people as if they aren't there. I cannot believe I am getting use to watching her stroll through objects in this world as if it's no big deal. As if it's a normal thing.

She stops near the screen projector, rested atop a table. Next to it are pictures of furniture, desks, chairs, bookcases, lamps. Each one catches my eye for its seamless detail and expanse. There are pictures of clothing sealed in clear bags, jewels like diamonds, rubies and emeralds. A cameo locket made from pure gold is listed at well over five thousand dollars. A picture of a gold rose pendent, rubies encased throughout, catches my eye. It's a gorgeous piece of jewelry and looks old, older than any other piece of jewelry I can see.

Whoa. This is all your stuff? Edie, some of this is gorgeous.

"Most worthless," Edie sighs, catching me looking at the jewellery. "Now, hurry up."

I follow her closer to the black projector and she motions at it,

"Spill your wine over it."

You must be joking.

"Just spill it, hurry. Nobody is looking."

I can't believe I'm doing this. I cannot believe I'm doing this.

I tip my glass over slowly as I pretend to be caught up in looking at one of the pictures on the table. I hear a few drips and then Edie mutters an ecstatic 'Yes!' as I pull my wine glass up. Before I can say anything, Edie orders me to follow her again. I finish what is left of the wine, which is not much, one gulp precisely and set it down on the table as I scurry away.

We exit the tent; Edie stopping for a moment to make sure no one had spotted us, or rather me, then jets it towards a line of round trimmed hedges. I can't help but giggle as I watch her run; she jitters back and forth completely off balance. When she gets to the bright green hedges, she beelines around them and I hurry to follow her. Once around, I find her pointing down to a large pipe that escapes the ground and has a small box attached to the top.

"Open it," she orders.

I flip open the grey plastic lid and stare down at three metal switches.

"Flip them," Edie tells me pointing at them, "The sprinkles will go off."

"Edie," I let out a breath, "are you sure about this?"

"Yes. I need time to find my will! It could be in one of the desks that are going up for auction."

"I'm sure your nephew cleaned out everything."

"There are hidden drawers in the desks," she tells me her tone slightly more irritated. "He doesn't know that."

I shook my head at her. "Edie, hidden drawers? Could you be anymore cliché?"

"Turn them on!"

I flick all three switches up. Edie and I watch as all over the gardens, small black cubes raise a few centimeters from the grass and begin to spray water. Not just around them, but from the top of the cubes as well, making each sprinkler look like it was producing a work of art. Screams exploded from the tent, both male and female. Suddenly my back was littered with the cool spray I had had a hand in turning on, and even I gave out a small yelp. Next to me Edie begins to laugh as she watches everyone in the tent scurry out, and I rush to join them.

Minutes later, the sprinkles have been turned off and all the guests now stand drenched, visibly upset on the back porch of the house. Again, a beautiful wrap around white porch layered with decorative pillars. Antique outside tables stand on the porch with pots of flowers on top of them, a few matching chairs are filled by guests of the auction. Everybody drips with icy water; and not one person looked pleased. Especially Merida, who stands by the back French doors on her cellphone screaming into it about what had just transpired.

I sit on the edge of the porch fence with Edie next to me, the entire time she chuckles as she spots one of her old friends dripping in displeasure. My jeans are clinging to my legs in an annoying way and my red t-shirt sticks against my torso as if it will squeeze me like an anaconda. I can't even imagine what my hair looks like now.

"Look at them," Edie continues to laugh next to me, "They look like sewer rats!"

That's not a nice thing to say about your friends.

"Bah! They aren't my friends," Edie scoffs. "I couldn't stand half of them; they are all here to reap the benefits of my death. They'd be quick to sell your soul if they could get above asking price."

A few seconds later a very wet Porter calls out to everyone at the steps of the porch, "I apologize for the inconvenience and the debacle with the sprinkles. The gardener has assured me that they were turned off before he left this morning, and we have concluded there must have been a short circuit somewhere. That being said, we will have to postpone the auction at this time."

Nobody makes a sound, except Merida. "That's foolish Porter. We could do it inside!"

Instantly Edie and I perk up, eyes on Porter as we watch him consider her suggestion.

"Postpone it!" someone yells from the crowd, "We are all soaking wet."

"Yes," a woman interjects, "I want to go home and change!"

Soon everyone shouts the same thing and Merida throws her phone into her oversized Chanel bag in a huff. Porter raises his hands again, "Alright everyone. We will postpone the auction. Please accept my apologies and check your emails this week, for the new date and time."

I let out a sigh of relief with Edie as everyone slowly starts to file off the porch.

"That was a close one," she states, "now we have the whole weekend to find the will."

Weekend? Wait, today is Friday?

"Yes today is Friday!"

Oh my God!

I jump off the porch fence and land on my feet. I open my bag and rummage inside for my cell phone, thanking the universe that nothing inside my purse was damaged from the water.

"What's wrong?"

My boss's birthday party is tomorrow! I completely forgot.

"I doubt he expects you to attend, you just had a concussion," Edie reminds me.

It's not that, I was supposed to confirm everything with the caterers and the wine people and—

"Uh oh. Phoebe."

I find my cellphone just as Edie says my name and I look up. A shadow has loomed over us and as I turn my head I find Porter staring down at me. Again, an indecipherable expression over his face as he looks from my phone to my face,

"I suppose you and I should speak then, since you are now under employment of the house."

What? Wait—no.

"Yes! Yes you are," Edie gets frantic against me, "it's perfect! You can search the house for my wills while you work."

I am a bloody lawyer Edie do I have to remind you? I can't moonlight as a maid!

"You're not a lawyer! You're a lackey and you're barely part time."

"Porter Burroughs," he extends his hand and I take it in a firm shake,

"Phoebe Mercer."

"I suppose I should show you where you will be staying then." His arms drop to his hands. "I'm afraid the maids have the weekend off so they won't be here to train you until Monday."

He beckons for me to follow and I panic slightly. "Um, I can't stay right now."

"What?" Edie barks, "I beg to differ."

Porter frowns at me and I swallow down the nerves that had erupted with this lie.

"I have some loose ends to tie up this weekend," I explain, "It's a long story really."

I only hope he doesn't ask exactly what it is.

81

"That may be for the best anyway. Let's have you back here Monday then," he says after a moment and rolls the sleeve of his wet suit-jacket up so he can check the time on his watch. "Now if you excuse me I have some business to attend to, see yourself out with the guests? I'll see you nine a.m. Monday morning."

"Great," I smile with relief at him, "Monday morning it is."

He nods his farewell and stalks away from me.

Edie is gone too.

"You did what?"

It's hard for me to take Riley seriously in his skin tight grey running suit with yellow strips down the sides. His brown hair falls over his forehead as his eyes grip mine and he looks dumbfounded, confused; as if I just spoke to him in another language. I know the way he looks at me is justified. If he had told me he had taken a job cleaning houses in another town I would have borne the same look.

"I took a job as a maid, for a client."

"A client?" he shakes his head now, "A maid?"

The story I was able to make up on the way home that was semi-believable, was that a client needed my help cleaning her home; she was an elderly lady I had grown close to.

"It's only temporary," I remind him with a shrug.

We stand across from each other, the kitchen island between us, three plates upon it, full of Riley's first vegan meal. Sautéed, saggy, lettuce leaves on one plate with roasted walnuts, badly burnt tofu on the other covered in some kind of pink sauce and fried vegetables on the other. There's a recipe book near us, opened to a page that shows this meal and Riley's end result doesn't look anywhere near as appetizing as what is in the book.

"Phoebe," Riley says my name as if I were a child, "You are a lawyer. Not a maid."

"It's only to help her out."

"That doesn't—" he runs a hand through his hair as he looks from me. "I can't believe you would do that. You aren't supposed to be doing anything except relaxing at home. You had a concussion three days ago!"

"I know I did! I just can't stay home and relax though," I tell him. "I will go crazy! And cleaning can be very therapeutic."

"Why are you all wet!" he suddenly demands to know.

"I uh, was caught in a flash rain storm," I lie as I tug at my red shirt.

"I just don't understand what's going on with you," Riley shakes his head again; "do you know that my mother is still expecting a call from you? So you can apologize to her and we can go on planning the wedding?"

In hindsight maybe I should call her and apologize for my rude behaviour at lunch, but in truth I wasn't in the mood to hear her voice. Or talk about her plans for the wedding. For *our* wedding. I mean shouldn't we be planning our own wedding? Why is she even taking the wheel?

"Riley," I speak softly hoping it will affect his mood in a positive way. "I wanted to talk to you about that; your mother and the wedding."

He crosses his arms over his chest and begins to tap his foot, visibly annoyed at me. I have to hold back a chuckle as I wonder if he knows how funny he looks in that suit in that position. Instead I go on.

"I love that your mother is so gung ho about this wedding. I love it, I do…"

He doesn't have to know that's a lie.

"…but I think it's a tad weird she wants to do everything. I mean, it's our wedding isn't it? Shouldn't we be figuring this stuff out?"

I watch him wheeze and drop his hands, "You want to figure this stuff out? You want to figure out what to put on the menu, schedule cake tastings and wine tastings," he begins to count down his fingers. "Plan out the venue at the country club, order six different types of flowers, arrange the guest list, the seating list, the song list—"

"—Six different types of flowers?" I frown. "We only need bouquets for the bridesmaids, and centre pieces. And I already know that I want chocolate cake, red wine—"

"—What about the flowers on the end of the aisles during the ceremony? " Riley interrupts with frustration. "Or the flowers in the flower girl's hair? In her bouquet? What kind of red wine? Merlot? Cabernet Sauvignon? What about the whites? Chardonnay, Pinot Grigio? Do you know which goes best with a vegan dish? And chocolate cake? It *has* to be vegan. There may not be any cake at all, Phoebe."

No cake? But it's a wedding!

I stand dumbfounded as Riley grunts annoyingly and swats at me with his hands as he turns around, "I'm going to jog. I need it. Don't wait up. Oh, and before I forget," he motions to the coffee table in the living room as he pulls open the loft door. "I got you some of that Sweet Orange soap from Lavish Looks you like."

And now I feel horrible, noticing the paper bag on the coffee table.

I realize I could chase after him and beg him not to be angry, but after today I just didn't have the energy. Instead, I lean against the kitchen counter resting my elbows on the cool counter top. I pick up the fork left on the plate of fried vegetables and swoosh them around on the dish. I stick the fork in a carrot and hoist it into my mouth.

Maybe Riley is right about his mother planning the wedding? I mean, do I really want to figure out cakes that have to be vegan? Or all the flower arrangements? I mean I never knew you needed that many flower arrangements before—

Chewing once is enough; the sour explosion that follows makes me gag and I turn around quickly to spit it out in the sink behind me. I spit three times before the taste begins to finally subside. How could Riley eat any of this?

Chapter Eight

Riley came home late from his jog, showered and went straight to sleep. When I woke the next morning, he had left a note saying he was going into the office with James to prepare for a client meeting Monday, and would be home late. So I spent most of Saturday by myself, dodging phone calls from Reese and Tom.

Edie made an appearance during the mid-afternoon to tell me the two dresses I had chosen for tonight's party looked drab. When I asked her what she was doing she was secretive about it and I figured it was something to do with her missing will. She made me a promise not to intervene tonight at the party.

It was now almost five o'clock and the party starts in an hour. I was sitting on the bed fully dressed in a knee length black pencil dress with lace trimmings at the chest line of a sweetheart neckline. Clara sat behind me on her knees, with my curling iron, putting the finishes touches on my hair. Faye stood at my dresser a few feet away pulling out a pair of silver chandelier earrings and then deciding on which bracelets went with them. On top the dresser sat my open laptop. A petite, black haired woman on the screen with bold green glasses watched us work as she sipped her latte, overseas.

"That is a bummer man," Satine says from the screen, "I'm sorry I'm not there."

I spent the last hour telling them my issues with Riley and his mother. The only thing I didn't tell them about was Edie.

"It's alright," I speak loudly so she can hear me clearly from across the room. "It's not like you could do anything about it anyway."

"While I do think it's weird that you took a job as a maid," Clara says behind me, "I do get the therapeutic nature of cleaning. Whenever I'm mad it's what I do, I pull out the bleach."

"It is a de-stressor," Faye adds nodding with her back to us.

85

"I never heard of this old lady client before," Satine says to me, her voice bounces a little bit from static, "you usually spill the beans on all your clients."

"She's pretty boring," I answer with a shrug, "she just wanted some stuff done with her will." I catch Satine eyeing me and I frown at her. I'm pretty sure I sound convincing don't I? "What?"

"Nothing, I didn't say anything," it's Satine's turn to shrug as she drinks her latte.

"All done," Clara states and I feel her pull the curling iron up over my head. Then she slides towards the edge of my bed. I push myself up and pat my hair feeling the cooling warmth of the tresses. "You sure you just want to leave it down?"

"Yeah," I nod running my fingers through it, "it's a classy but casual party. To impress Steven MacFadden."

"He was in the paper today," Faye turns back around walking towards me with earrings and silver bangles she's picked. "Dating some model about twenty five years his senior. Fifth model he's been out with since his separation newspaper said."

"Wonderful" I sigh, "I suppose she'll be there this evening."

"Here," Faye hands them to me and smiles, "Tiffany's. Limited Edition. Don't you dare lose them or scuff them. I'm dead if you do."

"I promise I won't." I smile gratefully as I take the pieces and walk over to the standing mirror to put them on slowly. "Thanks so much Faye."

"Remember to plug me at this thing." Faye drops down on my bed next to Clara and sighs, "I could use the work."

"Slow?" Clara asks her.

"No, but my building is not rent controlled," she lets us know. "At the rate they keep raising it I may need to find a new place within six months."

"I can kick my sub-letter out," Satine offers from the screen with a smile. "I don't like her anyway. She's burning incense and that's against one of my rules."

"How do you know that?" Clara asks her with a laugh, "Please don't tell me you have a nanny camera somewhere in your place."

Satine winks at her, "I may have…"

"Thanks for the offer," Faye says, "but if anything I could just come crash on Phoebe's couch. I'd score some wicked vegan meals out of the situation."

"Ha ha," I tell her as I place in the last earring, "please don't say anything to Riley about it. You know how serious he is with this stuff."

"You are marrying a vegan," Clara makes a face at me; I can see it through the mirror, "do you realize you will no longer have steak?"

"Or sushi," Faye adds snapping her fingers.

"Or anything remotely yummy," Satine says into her latte.

"Okay, enough, I get it." I slip on the bangles and turn around to look at all three of them as best as I can with Satine on a screen. "Looks good?"

They all give me thumbs up.

Terrance has hosted his party at the law firm, in the large conference room Brant and Meyers often use for seminars. It's located off the front lobby of the firm; really an exceptional area. One wall consists of nothing but windows to the gorgeous city skyline, and the ceiling is made of mirrors with escaping pod lights that dim the room. The large table has been moved out, along with all the leather chairs, and replaced with several tall serving tables. There are waiters in simple black trousers and white shirts, carrying golden trays of champagne flutes and small hors d'oeuvres. If there is music in the room coming from the speakers above, I cannot hear it.

I recognize most of the guests as other lawyers in the firm, a few other partners, some clients and ex-clients of Terrance's as well. Many faces are strange to me and I begin to feel overcome in it all.

"Phoebe?"

I turn around to see Greg standing behind me, confusion over his freshly shaven face. He's in an Armani suit and I know its Armani because it's his only designer suit. He wears it at firm events or in the court room if we have a large case. His brown hair is combed elegantly to the side.

"Hi Greg," I move closer to him. "I was starting to think I would have to mingle with clients or the partners."

He gives me an unsettled laugh and then leans into my ear; I'm hit with his strong, minty aftershave. "I didn't—we didn't think you would be coming tonight."

"Why not?"

"I don't know," he shrugs at me and puts his hands in his pockets as he leans away from me, "maybe because you just had a concussion a few days ago?"

"I'm feeling like a million bucks," I let him know. "I told you that the other day."

"I know that, it's just that Terrance…well he threw a fit when word got out that you had been hit by a hot dog cart. He was really embarrassed about it; said it made him look bad that his intern could be that stupid."

I wince, "How did he find that out?"

"Riley called in the other day to demand why he made you come back."

What the hell was Riley thinking calling Terrance?

My eyes flutter shut and I place a hand on my forehead, Greg can see my panic and he reaches for the nearest waiter carrying the champagne. He hands one to me and quickly sips his own.

"I guess you didn't know he called in eh?" Greg asks me.

"No," I snap, "I did not."

"I should have called and told you."

"No," I frown kindly at him, "no you couldn't have known that Riley didn't tell me."

I begin to glance around the room; a few partners and co-workers catch my eye. They look away, snicker or exchange a few whispered words with each other.

Wonderful. Now I'm known as the girl who got run over by a hot dog cart.

I put the glass to my lips and take a long drink of the bubbly liquid.

"You look really nice," Greg tells me a moment later and I smile at his kindness.

"Thank you," I acknowledge with a small smile, "so do you."

"Ms. Mercer?"

Terrance approaches us slowly, setting his empty champagne glass on the nearest table. He's in a dark suit, complete with a bow-tie and eye-brows that are trimmed for the evening. His black hair was combed backwards giving him the greaser look that in my opinion suits his personality.

"Happy Birthday Terrance," I put on my best smile but it's lost on him.

"I didn't think you would be here," he says straight away, "after that *matter* with your fiancé. I didn't think you would show your face here ever again."

"I'm so sorry about that," I immediately apologize, "I had no idea he called to talk to—"

"—Talk?" Terrance places his hands into the pockets of his trousers and smiles arrogantly, "No Phoebe, he did not talk. I talked, he yelled, and then he said some obscene words. To tell you the truth it was quite an eye-opener for me when I realized that was the type of man you chose for your husband."

I'm going to kill Riley. He's ruined me.

"I'm so sorry," I say again, "that was inappropriate of him and he will never do it again, I promise. He won't ever call here or show up here or—"

"Terrance? I'm afraid I must be on my way."

I know that voice.

I look up at the man that interrupts us and he automatically meets my dark eyes. Dressed in black pants and a grey suit jacket, a thin black tie to match his black dress shirt, is Porter Boroughs. His dark eyes run over me and when they set upon mine again he slowly frowns.

Oh God. This cannot be happening right now.

"Phoebe?"

"Phoebe," Terrance repeats my name and looks from Porter to me back to Porter. "You two know each other?"

"I just hired her," Porter puts his hands in his pockets, his suit bunching up as he does. "Or rather, I should say Aunt Edie did."

"Excuse me?" Terrance swings his stare my way, "Edie Edwards?"

I find all three of them looking at me; Terrance, Porter and Greg, who mouths *what is going on?'* as he stands slightly behind Porter.

"Oh, yes I am a distant relative of Edie Edwards," I finally say, my words spongy in my throat as I look back at Terrance. "Related through marriage."

Edie!

Where is she? I could really use her right now.

"I'm here sugar pie."

Her voice floats in my ear and from the corner of my mouth I can see her appear next to me. She's in a black suit, white trim on the collar and hem of the pant leg. The buttons are large and studded with fake diamonds. Her strawberry blond hair sets in its usual short wavy style against her head.

"I've been here the whole time," she tells me, "across the room. Keeping my distance as promised. My, look at the situation we are in."

"You never mentioned being related to an Edie Edwards," Terrance says his arms crossing his chest, "and hired for what may I ask?"

He's seething. His brows have come together and his lips are twitching. His eyes dart from me to Porter and I can't help but wonder if maybe he's a tad nervous. But why would he be nervous? Unless, Edie is right?

No. That's ridiculous.

"Is it?" Edie raises an eyebrow as she looks my way, "Or is it sane?"

"My Aunt hired her to be a maid just before she passed," Porter explains to Terrance. "She's set to start this Monday."

"Is that so?" Terrance puffs up slightly and his stare deepens. "I assume that would work, since you are only here part time now, or possibly not at all."

Great. He's threatening me with my job.

I nod slowly feeling my mouth go cotton dry, "That's exactly it. I will be able to juggle both perfectly. Cleaning can be very therapeutic."

"Ms. Mercer here must have informed you of her recent health debacle then?" Terrance looks over at Porter and fakes his concerned expression. "No?" he asks when he sees Porter's frown. "She was run over by a hot dog cart and had a minor concussion. About four days ago."

"Four days ago?" Porter looks back at me, confounded by Terrance's words.

"Reassure him you can do the job!" Edie cries in my ear, "He may fire you if he thinks you can't handle it. Or if he thinks you're crazy."

"But I can do it," I say, with confidence I hope I fake well. "Trust me, I can. It's just the diversion I need, the healing I need after my minor concussion."

Porter doesn't look very convinced and I can feel my heart beating against my chest. My back has begun to get all sweaty and my mouth is getting drier by the second. Drinking the champagne does little to relieve it.

"Terrance! I hear this is the hot dog girl!"

Steven McFadden walks up to us and stands between Terrance and I. He's a short man, only a few inches past my height in heels and teetering on extremely over weight. He is smartly dressed though, in a black suit and white dress shirt no tie but a whimsical turtle brooch on his lapel.

"This is Phoebe Mercer," Terrance is cool in his introduction of me, "my assistant."

"Hot Dog cart girl is your assistant?" Steven barks with a laugh, "If this little lady was my assistant I'd be in some trouble, know what I mean?" he winks at me and roars with laughter. "I'm just kiddin' miss. I heard all about your hot dog cart accident and don't you worry," he wag's a stubby finger at me, "happens to the best of us. I had my foot run over once by a carnie pushing a cotton candy trolley."

I fake a smile and Steven McFadden hits me once hard on the back.

Edie steps away from me, "He is a repulsive man."

Terrance moves quickly and places a hand on Steven's back, motioning across the room. "Steven, how about you and I step away for a moment to discuss—"

"—Ah, no, no Terrance Meyers." Steven pushes his hand off, "There will be no work talk tonight. This is a night to enjoy ourselves, it's your birthday!"

Terrance looks instantly annoyed and next to me, Edie delights in it.

"Wants him badly doesn't he?"

Yes he does. The man is a billionaire; signing him could set Terrance for years.

"I should ruin everything."

No! No, Edie, I beg of you please don't. This night is already a mess; I look like a complete fool in front of my boss, and your nephew. I just want the rest of this night to go by with as little drama as possible, alright?

Edie is looking at me, and after a few seconds she lets out a huge sigh. She then disappears.

"I must be on my way." Porter breaks the silence around us and I watch him shake Terrance's hand firmly before looking back at me, "Ms. Mercer." He shakes his head once at me, bids Greg goodbye and quickly walks away.

Suddenly Edie appears and I jump a little, catching Greg's look.

"Trouble at his company," Edie answers me, "nothing he can't handle. Now ask the man where his accident happened."

Why? Where did you go? Did you know your nephew would be here tonight?

Edie rolls her eyes and lets out a breath. "Just you never-mind where I went, and no I had no idea Porter was invited to this thing. Now do as I say and ask the man that question."

"Where did it happen?" I ask Steven quickly, I can feel my hand gripping my champagne glass now. "Your cotton candy accident?"

Steven chuckles, his belly jiggling. "County fair in Texas. I was eighteen years old, trying to impress this girl from my class and got my toes broken in the process. She ended up going with my best friend the rest of the summer."

"Ask him if that was the summer he met his wife."

Edie, I don't think that's a good idea. He's in the middle of a bad divorce with her.

"Just do it," Edie retorts.

"Is that when you met your wife?"

Terrance gives me a look, one that I have received many times whenever I asked him a question he expected me to know the answer to. I look back at Steven, who is still smiling at me.

"I certainly did, met her that summer. She worked at the ice cream shop and I must have gone in three times a day for a solid month just so I could see her. When I finally got the courage to ask her out I was surprised she said yes. We married a few months later and had our first daughter a year later."

"Tell him that's lovely," Edie begins to orde. "How hard it must be for him to be going through this, and how from what you've read about him it was not deserved."

"That's a lovely story. I'm so sorry to hear about the divorce, from what I have read you're a generous man, and don't deserve it."

"Why thank you my dear," Steven smiles at me and reaches forward to pat my hand. "Can you believe it? That woman is throwing away twenty five years of marriage for her yoga instructor? And she has the audacity to tell everyone that it's me who had the affair!"

"That's horrible," I nod along with him, "but the truth will come out. It always does."

"I wish I could get the ball rolling." He chuckles again giving me a wink.

"I have a friend who is a personal shopper to a very prestige department store in the city and she loves to gossip." I shrug, smiling deviously, "perhaps I could tell her a tale or two for you?"

His laugh is so loud, that a few people around us end up throwing him a malodorous look; he doesn't even notice as he looks back at me. "I would owe you a mountain of favors for that!"

Steven doesn't give me the chance to respond; instead he turns to Terrance, who quickly swipes off his aggravation for a bogus smile. Steven grabs his arm, "I like the way you operate Terrance. You have a good team here, honest and refreshing."

He motions to Greg and I. "Let's finalize this shall we? I'll be in Monday afternoon to sign the papers."

I feel Edie's cold breath on my ear, "you're welcome."

I fly home to Riley. There was no way I could have stayed at the party after that. It went from a miserable failure to an absolute success! I must have thanked Edie a thousand times over in the cab ride home in my head. I don't know how she found out that information about Steven McFadden and his wife, but I expected it had happened when she disappeared for those few seconds.

Finally, having a ghost is coming in handy.

I pull the door to the loft open, making a face at the thunderous noise the door creates, and rush inside. I find Riley lying on the couch, eyes on the television screen, in grey sweats and a blue t-shirt. Once he sees me he hits the mute button on the remote and sits up, watching me as I slide closed the loft door. I kick off my heels and turn around to face him.

For a moment I'm reminded of how he had called Terrance and yelled at him but I won't spoil the moment yet.

"You won't believe what happened!" I squeal with a smile. "I managed to charm Steve McFadden into signing with Terrance! You should have seen Terrance's face when Steven praised his choice in a team. I thought Terrance was going to blow a fuse. Hopefully he'll put me on the case."

I bounce over to the couch and sit down next to Riley. Lines gather around his eyes and his look is concentrated, even his smile is barely there. I can feel my heart drop into my stomach and my body slumps when I realize something is off.

"What's wrong?"

"Nothing is wrong," he tells me setting the remote down on the coffee table. "I just want to talk to you about something."

"Okay?"

"He's going to end this outrageous relationship," Edie's voice appears behind me and I peek over my shoulder to see her standing near the partition in the room. She's watching us sternly with her arms crossed over her chest. "Best thing he could possibly ever do for you."

I pass over what she says and look back at my fiancé, "Riley?"

"My mother stopped by while you were at the party," he places his hands on his knees, "we talked about some things. The wedding, the business, the stuff going on between us."

"You talked about us to your mother?" I feel myself irk back from him.

Behind me Edie laughs, "Of course he would, he's such a momma's boy."

Riley gestures at himself, "I just needed some advice."

"Why didn't you go to James, or Jamie?"

"They don't know what's going on," Riley explains, "I don't want to tell them about the stuff that's been going on with you."

He sees my expression and lets out a sigh, "Phoebe, come on. It's been four days since your concussion, and you've went back to work when you shouldn't have, taken a job as a cleaner, and it's as if you are in another world or something. You just haven't been yourself."

I don't really have anything to say to him. In a way he's right, even I know that. If I was on the outside looking in, I would be just as concerned. Yet it's not like I can tell him that I'm seeing a ghost? Or that I need to help a ghost solve the case of her missing will?

"I don't mean to come down on you with all of this," Riley goes on after seeing my expression. "And mom told me that maybe I haven't been as understanding as I could be with everything you're going through."

I blink at him. Stella didn't tell him to immediately dump me and find someone more worth his time?

"Probably because she knows you're as good as he'll ever get," Edie mutters, "he's lucky."

"So," Riley continues slowly smiling at me, "she suggested something that I think will work wonders for us, and especially you."

"I'm afraid to ask what it is." I truthfully say.

Riley smirks and reaches for my hands. He grabs them and squeezes them in his clammy palms, "She recommended we go see her shrink, Doctor O'Dell. She specializes in couple's therapy and I really think it could help us, mostly you, with what has been happening."

"Couples therapy?" I make a face. That kind of face you make when you step into a field of cow dung. He can't be serious, can he?

"Even you have to admit things are a bit out of the ordinary between us lately and you maybe aren't dealing with the accident as well as you should be?"

"This is ridiculous!" Edie exclaims as she appears on the other side of the couch looking down at us. "Couples therapy, bah! In my day you dealt with problems within the home. You sat down, had a shot of whiskey, cried and got over it."

"Mom said she's going to make us an appointment. Doctor O'Dell is pretty booked up but mom thinks she can get us in in a week or so," Riley gives me a comforting smile and rubs my shoulder with one of his hands. "We'll give this a try. I'm sure it will help." He leans in and kisses me softly on the cheek. As he pulls away I give him a small smile,

"Alright, okay. We can give it a try."

"Great," Riley's smile grows and he lets me go, jumping to his feet and snapping his fingers my way, "I'm going to make us a healthy snack. I've been drying out avocado as an experiment so it should be done by now."

I watch him hurry away from me into the kitchen and drop back against the couch. I can sense Edie standing over me, hands on the back of the couch.

"Sugar-pie," she tells me. "I have a feeling this won't go well at all."

Chapter Nine

"He's not here. He won't be here till end of the month. What do you want?"

If I ever answered Terrance's phone like that he'd kill me.

"I was wondering if by any chance he had a copy of Edie Edwards' will in his office?"

"Who?"

Next to me Edie sighs, "She knows me. Describe me."

"Uhhh...she was about five ten, light reddish curly hair, in her sixties," I crinkle my nose as I glance over to her. "She was kind of high maintenance."

"Oh, I think I know who you're talking about. She was here a few times yeah. Hold on a second..."

I hear clicking and I look over at Edie. She's in a lime green suit with a matching lime green headband in her hair. We're are in a cab heading to her house this sunny Monday morning so I could start my new job.

When I suggested calling Herman's niece, his secretary, she told me I would be wasting my time. Yet I couldn't ignore the fact that if the niece did find the will in Herman's files, *if* he did by chance ignore Edie's request to destroy any copies, then I would be home free.

"Sorry her name isn't in any records. You must be confused."

"Told you," Edie smirks, looking out the cab window.

It was worth a shot Edie.

"Are you sure? I mean if you remembered her then—"

"—Sorry, no. I have to take this incoming call. Bye."

I hear the call drop just as the cab begins to slow down. I look across the seats to find Edie has departed and we've arrived at her house. I paid my fare, all the while skeptical as to whether Porter would even let me in the front door. After all, he was already suspicious of me and what happened at Terrance's party certainly didn't help matters.

All day yesterday Edie was in my ear; telling me of places she thought Terrance may have hidden the will. Riley had spent Sunday running in and out of the loft getting ready for his client presentation this morning so the topic of seeing a couple's counsellor was never brought up again. I dodged a call from my mother at some point in the afternoon and blew off drinks with Reese and Tom. I wasn't in the mood to leave the loft.

This morning I wasn't in the temperament to venture outside either but here I was, an hour away from the city standing in front of elegant, strong French doors. I knocked on the doors once, and then rang the doorbell. As I waited I glanced around the porch I stood on; it was empty. Not a decorative chair or bench not a potted plant. The porch disappeared around the bend and I arched backwards to see how far it actually went.

I didn't get very far because the doors opened in front of me.

Porter stood before me, dressed in a grey t-shirt and pair of dark jeans. He looked mystified to see me.

"Morning," I say slowly.

"Good morning," he then shook off his expression and pulled the doors wider, "I'm sorry. I thought you would have changed your mind about this job."

"Nope," I smile and give him a small shrug as I drop my hands to my sides, "here I am!"

"Right, come on in then."

He moves out of my way and lets me pass him into the house. I clutch the strap of my purse as he closes the doors quietly behind me. I'm standing in a front hallway with walls embellished in gorgeous vintage wooden panels. A dazzling antique chandelier hung from the ceiling with fake candle lights dimly lit. Twenty feet away was a large wooden staircase that winded up against the wall leading to the second floor; it was painted white, the railing matched the dark wood of the steps.

To my left was a large hanging mirror with a gold frame. In front of it, a beautiful long buffet table, vintage candles sat upon it with two crystal vases, each stocked with lavender. I could smell them, so fresh and light.

There was a door way beyond the mirror and from where I was standing I could see a beautiful grey couch with flower patterned throw pillows. A fireplace rebuilt to its formal 1940's brick glory was behind it. Small vases of lavender stood on the mantel along with picture frames. An oval antique hanging mirror hung over it.

"The house is beautiful," I say as Porter steps up next to me,

"Yes it is," he then lets out a sigh, "Let me show you where you'll be staying then we can go find Rosanne. She runs the house."

"Welcome to my home!"

I look towards the staircase and find Edie standing in the middle of it. She has her hands in the air as she greets Porter and me.

"Well? What do you think?" she asks beaming down at me.

I haven't seen the rest of it yet.

She rolls her eyes at me and slowly begins to descend the epic staircase. "Just wait till you see the rest of it, it's a dream."

"Come along," Porter says motioning for me to follow him.

There's a doorway beyond the stairs and I follow him through it, taking a look at the portraits we pass on the wall. There's one large one of Edie dressed in a long white gown in the back gardens. We end up entering a glamourous teal toned kitchen with large bay windows overlooking the garden, beneath them a quaint little breakfast nook made up of an oak table and cushioned benches.

A sweet, rich, but sensual scent gets caught up in my nose and I recognize it as the aroma of a freshly brewed pot of coffee. There is a large island in the middle of the kitchen; a great sink sits in the centre for the dishes. The cabinets around the room are wood, painted teal; the counter tops light grey granite. The fridge has three doors and is stainless steel, sitting to my left. The stove has eight burners and two oven doors. This room was as incredible as the front hall; I was anxious to see the rest of the house. "Beautiful kitchen."

"Isn't it?" Edie asks with a happy sigh as she walks in behind us, "I wasn't sure about the teal at first but it works doesn't it? Suppose it's the windows that do it."

"Through here," Porter stands to my immediate left in front of the fridge, pushing open a swinging white wooden door, "is the dining room. Hardly used."

"Maybe *now* it's hardly used," Edie quips shaking her head at him.

I peek through and take a glimpse at the dark room, from what I can see it's a dining room with dark walls and an exquisitely long dining table. Before I catch a glimpse of anything else the door swings shut and Porter motions for me to follow him again. We cross the kitchen to my right leaving through another swinging doorway that leads into a rather small white hallway. There is simple white tile at my feet and we pass an open nook to our left which houses a large washer and dryer, almost industrial style.

There are four doors in the hallway, two on the left and two on the right. All four of them are shut. Porter leads me to the single door on the right, turning the glass knob and pushing the door open. I find myself looking into a small room, painted all white with a dismal white three drawer dresser and no closet. There is one rectangular window with plastic blinds drawn over it, and a double bed against the wall. There isn't even a back frame to it, just a simple bed frame housing it off the floor.

"This is where you will stay," Porter says. "I know it's a bit bland but I assume it won't be a problem seeing as you may not be staying here often, if at all."

I catch his tone and look at him, "Right. Look I'm sorry that I didn't tell you about working with Aunt Edie's ex-lawyer. I realize I probably should have."

"Yes," Porter agrees lifting his eyebrows, "you should have." He looks over my head then, "Ah Rosanne, there you are. This is Phoebe Mercer the new maid my aunt hired before she died."

I turn around to see a middle aged woman standing at the end of the hall; she has a white laundry basket in her hands full of linens. She's in a white button up dress; her dark thick frizzy hair is pulled back by a butterfly clip, hair greying her temples. I guess she's either Spanish or Portuguese; her skin is darker and there is has a beauty mark above her lip. Her dark eyes run over me a few times.

100

"Hello" she finally says, her accent thin but I recognize it as Spanish.

"Rosanne will take over for now," Porter walks around me and heads down the hallway, "if you have any questions you can direct them to her."

Thirty minutes later I'm following Rosanne around the house in a matching white button up dress that goes to my knees. The uniformed dress I wear is a bit baggy but I realize comfort and style isn't what Edie was going for with these. She wanders behind me, critiquing everything Rosanne instructs of me.

The second floor of the home is just as glamourous. The walls where wooden white panels; bright portraits of landscapes hung on invisible nails. It was a wide hallway with dark wooden floors that require a special wax once a month made from organic oils. A series of large wooden white doors run up and down the hallway, none of which Rosanne lets me see just yet.

At the end of the hallway on both sides are three foot wide, seven foot tall bay windows that let in incredible amounts of light during the day Edie tells me. It was why each table stand in the hall, the railing and even the pictures, needed to be dusted every three days.

"We will start you slow on your first day," Rosanne tells me warily glancing over her shoulder at me. "Dusting is on the schedule for today and it is light work, but in this house takes up most of the day."

Wonderful.

"I caught your sarcasm," Edie says next to me.

It's not like I was trying to hide it and by the way? Don't you think I will be cleaning your house forever alright? Find a way to get rid for Rosanne so I can start searching for your will.

"It's not that easy," Edie reminds me. "It's not like I can force thoughts into her head or anything. Believe me I wish I could."

A door opens at the end of the hall and Rosanne stops in front of me. Edie draws in a slow dramatic breath as a young woman walks out carrying a blue bucket and mop. She's in the same uniform Rosanne and I are in but hers hugs her curves sultry. She has dark hair just like Rosanne, including a beauty mark along the side of her right eye. The same dark eyes but smaller and fuller lips painted with a light pink lipstick.

"That's Marta," Edie whispers as if anyone else can hear her, "She's Rosanne's niece."

Is she the one you think is having an affair with Terrance?

"Not think, *know,*" Edie corrects. "Benedict Arnold, that one. I'm sure she watched Terrance with me on the deck. Once she found out I put her in my will then she sided with that greedy bastard boss of yours."

Is she the reason you don't trust Rosanne?

"Obviously," Edie sighs, "Apple can't fall that far from the tree."

"Marta, meet Phoebe," Rosanne introduces as the young maid approaches us. It's then that I realize the young girl can't be more than twenty one years old! Good God, if Edie is telling the truth and Terrance *is* having an affair with Marta then he'd better have done a background check. He's old enough to be her father!

"Hi," Marta grips both the handle of the bucket and the mop.

"She was hired by Mrs. Edwards before she passed," Rosanne explains.

"Mrs. Edwards never mentioned hiring a new girl." Marta looks at Rosanne and frowns.

"It's a long story," I tell them both, Marta still doesn't look my way.

"Look at her!" Edie wanders behind the young maid and snarls at her, "She plays the innocent card so well don't you think?"

"Phoebe will be starting in the library today," Rosanne says to Marta,

Marta shrugs her shoulders and walks between Rosanne and me. "Mr. Burroughs is working in there again."

Great.

"Try to be quiet as Mr. Burroughs works," Rosanne begins to walk again; I watch her move right through Edie's right shoulder.

"I'm going to follow Marta." Edie spins and glides after Marta. "Try not to tell anymore white lies while I'm gone." Before I can answer the ghost she disappears.

Rosanne stops at a door not far from where we stood and pulls it open. It's a small linen closet and under the last shelf is an assortment of cleaning supplies. Dusters, dust pans, small brooms, wipes for shining up the wooden railings and more. She reaches down and picks up a black duster and hands it to me,

"Mrs. Edwards liked these. They are organic fibre and don't push any dust into the air, leaving behind a lemon scent."

"How long did you work for Edie?"

"Mrs. Edwards," Rosanne corrects as she shuts the door with both hands, "and for about fifteen years."

"That's a long time. I suspect you and her where close?"

Rosanne doesn't answer me; instead she motions for me to follow her back down the hallway. It's obvious she's guarded, and if I were in her shoes, I would be too. She probably thinks I came back for money.

"Was she always so, eccentric?"

Rosanne raises an eyebrow my way so I clarify,

"You know, so lively and—and dramatic?"

I watch a small smile spread over Rosanne's lips and she gives me a small nod, "Mrs. Edwards was definitely a spirited lady."

We stop at the last door to our left next to the staircase and Roseanne knocks once before opening it. She sticks her head in and I hear her asking if it would be alright for the room to be cleaned. I can hear Porter murmur something to her and Rosanne steps back, pushing the door open for me,

"Go on. I'll be in the kitchen when you are finished this room."

"Great, thanks."

I clench the duster and walk towards the room.

Look at me, a lawyer and a maid. How did this *even* happen? I can picture how ridiculous I look at this moment and how much of a laughing stock I must be at the firm now.

I enter the library quickly and Rosanne closes the door quietly behind me. I find myself standing in a room that looks like the old law library I used to study in, only smaller. The walls are made up entirely of bookshelves and each shelf is stocked to the brim. There is a small stone fireplace to my left and placed in front of it is a three seater brown sectional. There is another set of bay windows across from the entrance; the curtains have been pulled to the side and clipped back. There is a wooden roll top desk, much larger than the one I have at home, in front of the windows, and I see Porter standing behind it. His back is to me and he is on his phone.

I don't even know where to start. I wish Edie where here to tell me.

I suddenly realize that I have wished for Edie's presence more times than I would like.

Walking towards the nearest bookshelf I start dusting the shelf closest to my height. I'm done in less than five seconds and move to the shelf below it. Again I'm done fairly quickly and kneel to reach the bottom shelf. How can this be therapeutic? It's *so* boring.

"You have to tell the board I need more time, a few weeks tops. I am positive we can find a more appropriate buyer."

The Board? This must be the trouble Edie mentioned earlier.

I stand up to reach the next shelf, extending my arm slightly so.

"Lavish Looks is a major company, and once people hear it's on the market there will be numerous companies stepping up to the plate. I'm positive I could find one more suited to take over."

Lavish Looks?

I turn around and find Porter leaning over the desk, his phone to his ear and his shoulder is arched to keep it from falling from its place. He's shuffling through papers on his desk.

"I know my aunt would roll over in her grave if she heard Merida wanted full control. Tell her to give me a call when she is free, understand?"

He doesn't say goodbye to whoever he is speaking to and instead stands up, grabs his phone from his shoulder, ending the call. He looks up quickly and catches me staring at him.

"Sorry," I immediately apologize, "I didn't mean to eavesdrop, but did you say Lavish Looks?"

104

"Yes I did."

"Aunt Edie owns it?" I guess slowly.

"She and Merida, they started it up twenty five years ago," Porter tells me as he sets his phone down, "I take it you have heard of it?"

"Are you kidding?" I can't help but exclaim. "It's one of the best beauty companies out there! I just used their Sweet Orange soap this morning, it's divine. I love their lavender bath foam and salts. Their rose mud mask is amazing. I mean I don't buy it often because it's expensive but I love it, all my friends do too."

Edie is worth more than a small fortune! It's not just her land that is valuable. No wonder Terrance was gung ho to seal her as a client. Here I thought she was worth a small handful, but she must be worth a few million if she owns Lavish Looks.

"Quite," its clear Porter doesn't share my enthusiasm for the line.

Suddenly Edie appears next to me and I'm grateful for Porter looking down at the desk again; he didn't see me jump. Edie's face is all red and she begins to pace,

"I told you she was going to contact your low-life penny pinching boss!"

Err, what happened?

"I don't know exactly what he said but she promised that she would keep an eye on you and I quote 'I'm sure she isn't here to find it' unquote. Then I heard her tell him 'I am trying my best but it's hard with Porter around all the time'."

No way. I knew Terrance was greedy and a tyrant, but to actually hide a will?

"That's what I wasn't finished telling you the other day!" Edie barks at me. "He hid my old will in that desk over there where Porter is working. I found it the day of my party and before I could throw it out, I hid it."

Then where is it? Edie you haven't known where this will is the whole time, have you?

"That will is the old one!" Edie snaps looking at me gravely. "I want that one destroyed before Terrance claims it as the only testimony left behind by yours truly."

There are two wills missing? You couldn't have mentioned this earlier, perhaps when you critiqued my outfit choices yesterday!

Edie ignores me as she sashays away from me, "I just need to remember where I hid it after I found it…"

"What?" I gasp.

You don't remember? How can you not remember Edie!

"Did you say something?" Porter tilts his head at me and I become stone.

Edie seems to ignore my panicked stance, "I don't know why I forgot. I can't explain it."

"What um, is going to happen to Lavish Looks now that Edie is gone?" Luckily I'm quick on my feet and Porter doesn't suspect me of communicating with his dead aunt.

Side note Edie; I can't believe you didn't tell me you own Lavish Looks!

"I mentioned it once I'm sure," Edie shrugs.

"Merida plans to buy it all," Porter answers me as he pulls the chair out from under his desk and sits down. "She plans to either sell it or have her daughter run it so she can retire."

"She's *what*?" Edie's 'what' comes out jagged as she glares at him. "Her daughter is a joke!"

As Edie stomps over to the desk and begins to peer over her nephew's shoulder, I decide I should step up my cleaning game and head over to the end table against the couch. I launch into dusting when Edie lets out a shriek so loud I almost drop my duster. I look up to find her hands against her face.

"That twat!"

Edie. Explain.

"She's threatening to sell her shares to Bold Beauty if Porter doesn't sell her my half of the company…ohh I could just ring her botox infused neck!" She makes the strangling gesture with her hands and bits of her hair fall out of place.

I know of Bold Beauty; I have seen their products in all the major beauty outlets. I also read that their new bath and beauty line was failing, so it made sense that the company would be interested in Lavish Looks.

"Tell him he has to stop the sale! Right now," Edie frantically looks at me as she points to Porter.

That would be stupid of me Edie considering I have no idea what is going on, remember?

"He can't sign off on the sale," Edie walks over to me just as panicked as before, "she'll ruin Lavish Looks; Merida doesn't care about what they do, this company is her ATM. I've been the brains behind the whole operation for the last twenty years. "

Well I don't see what I can do about it. Maybe it's for the best?

"It's not for the best!" Edie screams at me, "I've worked hard for it! I have made that company what it is and it's practically my child. She can't sell it!" I'm about to tell her to settle down when the lights above me start to flicker. Slowly at first then wildly. "I knew she was going to do this when I dropped dead. She kept bugging me the last few years to retire and sell and we fought about it. She was so angry with me. I bet you she had something to do with my missing will and my death too!"

Porter has brought his attention to the hanging lights on the ceiling and I can see him frowning at them, "Must be the wiring. I will have to call somebody in. We plan to sell the house so I can't have that be an issue."

Edie knock it off!

"Sell the house?" Edie twirls around to face him. "Tell him over my dead body is he selling this house! This is my home, it stays in my family and it doesn't get handed over to some moron who plans to bulldoze it down to use the land for a shopping centre!"

The lights continue to flicker and Porter slowly rises from his desk. I watch him walk over to the nearest hanging light and look up at it, "First time this has ever happened…"

Edie stop!

She vanishes, and the lights stop flickering.

Both Porter and I hear a loud sizzle then the sound of something snapping. The lights burn out and were left in dim light from the bay window.

Chapter Ten

"Can you believe it? If you rub lemon on the faucets of the shower the hard water stains come right off. It really is crazy. I will never buy those chemicals again. Save us some money."

"We don't need to save money, Phoebe. We are not poor," Riley lets me know,

My tone dies down a bit, "No I know that, I was just thinking since you are vegan—"

"—Can we please talk about something else now?" he sounds annoyed and I even hear him click his tongue on the other end.

"Yeah, sure."

I suppose nobody wants to talk about cleaning products really; I feel foolish for getting excited about the lemon thing Rosanne showed me this morning. Of course Riley doesn't want to hear about it, his fiancée was a lawyer last week, now she's a maid?

Three days have passed since Edie's little tantrum in the library. I've worked here for three days already, always returning home to a displeased Riley. He doesn't want to hear about my work and when I try to bring it up he shoots it down right away. I was surprised I got into it as far as I could today.

It's noon, my scheduled lunch break and I'm in the kitchen sitting in the nook next to the gorgeous windows. Rosanne always makes us lunch and today she made chicken wraps with tomato soup. I haven't told Riley any of this, and I haven't told Rosanne that I'm technically trying to be a vegan.

The thing is, I'm pretty sure what Riley has cooked the last three nights is not what Vegan meals are supposed to look or taste, like. Last night, his couscous was watery and the chickpeas tasted like rubber.

"When will you be at the office? Has Terrance called you back?"

Monday night I called Terrance and I called Greg. Asking both of them to send me over any work that needed to be done and neither of them returned my call. I called again this morning and got both their voice-mails, again.

"No, I have the morning off tomorrow so I'll stop by the office."

"Good. I'm not a fan of you working when you should be home but I'd rather you work at the law office then as a maid."

I can't help and squirm a little bit in my seat. I understand that to him, and most people, it's better to be a lawyer than a maid but there's a smudge of guilt creeping up in me whenever I look over at Rosanne. She's standing at the island sink doing the dishes and minding her own business. Behind her brews a pot of coffee for Porter.

"Don't forget dinner is at 5 tonight," I remind him.

It's the day of Faye's birthday at Pre-Fab Burritos.

I hear him sigh now, *"I don't know what the two of us will eat there."*

"They have salad on their menu," I tell him as I swirl my spoon in my soup.

"I don't know if I trust their salad. Alright I have to let you go. James and I are on our way to pitch to Mountain Shoes again. You have a check-up with Doctor Grier Thursday at eleven a.m., his secretary called to confirm it this morning."

"Oh right, I forgot that's Thursday. Good luck with Mountain shoes."

"Thanks, see you at five."

I hear him hang up and then set my phone down next to my plate.

"If a man ever spoke to me like that I'd throw him into the bay."

I glance up to find Edie sitting across from me. She has placed her chin in her palm as she leans against the table. She's dressed in a white garden dress with a matching floppy white hat. I can finally see the necklace she usually tucks underneath her clothing. It's a small glass orb stuffed with purple petals that I guess are lavender and it hangs off a vintage chain half way down her chest. It's quite lovely.

I haven't seen much of her over the last three days; she appeared twice yesterday to tell me to search the den off the back of the kitchen. I searched it top to bottom yesterday. The den was packed with old furniture and the windows where all closed. I sneezed a million times from the old dust.

"I think we should search the library today."

Edie, Porter has set up shop there again.

"Maybe we can get him out of the way. That desk was where I found my old will. The one Terrance had assured me had been thrown out," Edie explains.

What was on your new will?

"I left everything to Porter, I changed it drastically after I fired Terrance. A few days after my funeral Porter goes into the safe in my room and finds no will."

How could Terrance get into your safe? Did you give him the code?

"No don't be silly," Edie scowls leaning back into the booth, "nobody knew the code but Porter and I."

Could Porter have something to do with it?

"Never," her word is sharp and so is her look.

Sorry. I was just entertaining an idea; forgive me for hoping my boss wasn't involved in this confusing mess.

"Well he was, and still is and you should just accept it."

If nobody knew the code but the two of you then how did Terrance get your new will?

"That's just another thing we have to figure out," she gives me a sly smile and crosses her arms over her chest. "What is Rosanne still doing here?"

What do you mean?

I begin to dig back into my soup realizing my lunch break will be over soon.

"I wanted her fired. Why hasn't Porter done it yet?"

I don't know, but maybe he knows there is no reason to fire her.

"Ha! I don't trust her any more than I can throw her; she is related to Marta after-all."

One bad seed doesn't make the whole ground rot Edie.

I watch her roll her eyes at me as the door to the dining room swings open and Porter comes through. He carries a mug in his right hand and walks over to where Rosanne stands at the sink; he awkwardly places it into the water and turns to leave when Rosanne calls out to him,

"Mr. Burroughs? The man interested in buying Mr. Edwards sailboat is still at the boathouse."

Porter stops in his tracks and places a hand to his forehead, "I completely forgot. Alright, I'll head down there right away then."

You have a boathouse?

"Not my idea, my husband's. That wretched sailboat is not something I am sad to see go." Edie suddenly draws in a breath, "library is empty! Forget the food, let's go."

But I—

"Just forget it, you shouldn't be eating it anyway remember? You are a *vegan*," Edie smirks as she slides out from the breakfast nook.

Annoyed, I push away my half eaten soup and stare at the chicken wrap that I had only taken one bite out of. I force myself from the breakfast nook and begin my walk through the kitchen,

"Thanks for the lunch Rosie but I'm going to cut it short."

"Not hungry?" she asks looking up from her dishes.

"I'm hoping to cut out early; I have a friend's birthday dinner tonight."

I leave the kitchen and trek up the stairs towards the library. The door is propped open a little bit and I pause when I hear some shuffling going on in there. Could Porter be back already? Is it Edie making noise?

I step up to the door and peer through the opening; but I'm not looking at Edie or Porter. I'm looking at Marta. She's standing at the desk in front of the window, frantically searching through the papers on the desk. I watch her as she starts pulling the drawers open to comb through whatever was in them, by the third drawer she slams it shut in anger.

"Be quiet! Do you want to get caught?"

I know that voice. That deep, critical, bear like bark coming through Marta's phone.

"I can't find the damn thing!" Marta's exclaims towards the desk where I assume her phone is set, "How do you know he didn't find it already?"

"Because he would have said something, use your head."

Marta says nothing else and continues looking through the next drawer.

I don't believe this...I mean I believe it. I just don't feel as traumatised as I should. I don't feel stunned hearing Terrance's voice on the other end ordering young Marta about.

"Probably because you knew, deep down, what I told you was true." Edie's voice swims in my ear. I look over to find her at my right side, "You knew your boss was capable of this treachery, and murder."

"Hold on a second here," I whisper, "Murder is entirely different. That part of your story is definitely insane."

"*You're* insane," Edie snaps. "You're the one engaged to a space cadet!"

My mouth drops a tad, "Space cadet! What is that supposed to mean?"

"Forget it. Just get in there," Edie orders pointing at the room, her finger skates through the wooden door and I make a face when I see it. "Stop her before she finds it."

"I thought you said it wasn't in the desk," I recall in a murmur.

"I said it was where *I found* it, but maybe I hid it in there thinking Terrance wouldn't look in the same place he hid it in?" Edie suggests.

I blink at her, and stand up straight. Outside the door is a bucket that I assume Marta left, with a duster and a rag inside. I bend over and pick up the used rag then take a breath and begin to push the door slowly open; thankful it creaks as it opens wider. Marta freezes and throws her head my way, her eyes bulge a bit as she sees me and she slams a drawer shut.

"What do you want?" her tone full of irritation,

"Oh, I was told to clean in here, again."

"I'm cleaning in here," Marta quickly professes, "so go clean somewhere else."

"Clever little hussy," Edie stated frowning intensely, "go over there and drag her out!"

Don't be ridiculous! That's assault.

"Well think of something," Edie stomps her foot at me. *You are such a child.*

"Tell her to go clean my bedroom, I bet she would jump at that suggestion."

"Rosie doesn't want you in here. She wants you to tidy up Edie's bedroom."

Marta stares at me, after a moment she glances down at the desk and I can tell she's looking at her phone since Terrance is still on the other line. Listening. Spying.

"Alright, fine," Marta picks up her phone and I watch her slide it into the pocket of her uniform dress. She begins to make her way towards me, and I notice an obvious bounce in her step now. I move out of her way and wait till she has left the library, shutting the door behind her before I make a move towards the desk.

"What are you doing?" Edie demands. "Don't waste your time over there, it's obviously not in the desk otherwise she would have found it."

"Edie," I clench my jaw thinking about our hallway conversation moments ago, "You are *so* frustrating do you know that? First you say it could be in the desk now you say it isn't." I bite my bottom lip and look around the room. "I could check one of these books?"

"Ridiculous," Edie tells me, "I didn't read any of them."

Not surprising.

"I heard that," Edie snips.

I wander over to the desk anyway, glancing down at all the papers Porter has scattered over the gorgeous desk. There are file folders on top of file folders and a stack of business cards. I pick one up; it's simple, white and black with Porter's name on it and the title 'Advertising Media Director' beneath it for a company called Media Gate.

"Wait, Porter is in advertising?"

"Among other things," Edie brushes herself along the bookcase slowly, "he's multi-talented. Like his father. Like me."

I don't say anything else as I set down the business card slowly, "Where is the secret drawer?"

"It's on the left side, bottom drawer, in the back. You should be able to pop it open."

I bend down and pull open the drawer; there is nothing inside of it but hundreds of faded receipts. I push them aside as I yank the drawer out further and knock on the back panel. It echoes a bit; signalling its hollowness.

I do as she says, popping it open with my fingers and sink further to the floor so that I can see inside; it's empty.

"Empty, Edie."

"Long shot," Edie tells me with a sigh, "Come check here, in one of the end tables."

I pop the back panel shut and slowly get to my feet, "Edie, I don't think that is where you would have hidden your wills. Now think, didn't you have a place that maybe was just for you that nobody knew about?"

Edie makes a face at me and before she can answer she whips her head over her shoulder and stares at the door. I hear it too; the sounds of muffled feet before the door and then the handle turning. I slam the drawer shut with my feet and spin around to face the window. I tug the rag off my shoulder and beginning to pat the spotless window with it. I hear the door creak open and Edie behind me let out a breath, "It's just Porter."

"Oh, I didn't realize you were cleaning in here again."

I turn around and give Porter a small smile as he walks over towards the desk, "Rosie said she noticed the windows were a bit smudged and I told her I would do a quick clean before I head home early today."

Edie snaps her fingers at me, "I'll be right back."

He doesn't say anything else as he reaches his desk and turns his back to me, I watch him go through the papers on his desk, shifting some of them to the other side and vice versa. Just as I intend to turn back to clean the rest of the windows I notice a slip of paper with a familiar embalm printed in the top right end cover. A monogram of the letter's R&J.

Riley and James.

I would recognize that symbol anywhere; I hated the design and recall Riley getting in a fit because I said it looked too feminine.

"Riley and James."

"Sorry?" Porter looks my way with a slight frown and then he looks back down, noticing the paper I have caught sight of. "You know this advertising firm?"

114

"It's my boyfriends—I mean my fiancé's firm. Riley, he's my fiancé," I explain. "They just started it up a few months back. I didn't know you were a client."

"No, not a client," Porter shook his head at me. "They pitched to us."

"They pitched to another media firm?" I frown.

His mouth twitched and I wondered if that was perhaps the start of a smile, "No. Not to Media Gate, to another company that I'm dealing with."

My instinct is to pry, "How were they?"

Instantly I regret asking him the question and as he looks up at me to answer I put up a hand, "Actually no. Don't tell me, I don't want to know, conflict of interest and all that."

"I wasn't going to tell you," Porter lets me know. He slowly stands up from the desk and slips his hands into the pockets of his trousers, "You and he have been together for some time?"

"Over a year," I answer proudly.

"How did you meet?"

"His father needed a lawyer, and so he came to Meyers and Brant. He hired Terrance as his lawyer and we met one night as we briefed his father."

Before our conversation could continue Porter's phone rang and he reaches into his chest pocket to retrieve it. He gave the ID a quick glance, "Excuse me."

"Sure," I move away from the window quickly and walk away from him realizing that he was waiting for me to exit before he began his conversation.

Faye had managed to book the only patio table at Pre-Fab Burrito for her birthday. I didn't know half of the people seated with us but I did recognize them as her coworkers. The table easily sat fifteen people and stretched along a dimly light patio with colorful hanging sombrero lanterns coming from the wooden roof top. The patio panels where painted different colors and in the corners stood tikka torches for light. Lively Spanish music blasted over our heads and I always found it put you in the best of moods. It was a casual, fun place which I had attended with Faye, Clara and Satine numerous times because the food was cheap and the drinks even cheaper.

I sat between Riley and Faye tonight, dressed in a simple black dress, hair in a ponytail while Faye dressed in a blue skater dress with grey strips that accented her torso finely. Next to her I looked frumpy, but Riley had rushed me when I got home. He sat next to me, leaned back in his chair engrossed in his menu but wearing an annoyed frown as he read through the choices.

"So how is the new job?" Faye practically had to shout in my ear.

"It's not too bad, tedious but easy," I shrug as I answer her, "Of course I'm only a few days in."

"Who exactly do you work for, if your client is dead though?"

We both look across the table and see Clara leaning over as best as she can to hear our conversation. She's in a green off the shoulder top and dark jeans, her wispy blond hair curled loosely for the evening.

"Her nephew," I shout to both of them, "he's from England. Nice guy. Serious though."

"Is he cute?" Clara asks with a smile, "Because you know I'm looking."

"Well," Riley interrupts us as he sits up in his chair. We watch him set down his menu, "At least I can have boiled rice for dinner."

"Yummy," Clara says sarcastically, "I, on the other hand, will have the macho burrito with extra cheese."

"Do you know what that *does* to your body?" Riley makes a face at her and I can't help but smirk at Clara's expression,

"Heck yes I do. And I'd have it every day if I could."

"I don't know *how* you can stand him," Edie's voice bellows over me and I pretend not to take any notice. "Boiled rice? Has the man ever heard of *living*?"

Edie, not now please. I don't want a repeat of what happened at lunch with Stella.

"Nobody would even notice with this dreadful music blaring," Edie shouts, "and anyway, I've come to tell you what I found out!"

Tell me later.

"I got an email from Satine today," Faye says loudly. "She says she should be home by the end of June, maybe even earlier if things go well with this contract."

"No, not later," Edie retorts, "Now. I found out some interesting information about Merida and Lavish Looks." Edie is now standing behind Clara her hands firmly on her hips.

"For real?" I ask Faye directly, "I thought this was a major account."

"She says she wouldn't miss planning your wedding," Faye turns to me now and smiles, "she's trying to hand over her account to another team-mate."

"Did you hear me?" Edie demands.

Go away Edie. I'll talk to you tomorrow.

"Phoebe doesn't need help," Riley perks up and places a hand over mine. "My mother is doing all of the planning. We don't have time for it, and she loves that kind of stuff."

I don't hear it but I see Edie chuckle behind Clara as Clara gives Faye a silent look. I know what they're thinking. I hate that I'm thinking it too but really, in hindsight this could be the best way to go about the wedding. If only my gut could agree with that statement.

"It's for the best," I find myself shrugging, "I mean it's stressful to plan a wedding and I don't need the stress after my accident."

"Which reminds me," Riley looks from me to Clare and then to Faye, "my mother told me she emailed you both about dress shopping tomorrow and none of you replied."

Dress shopping? That was tomorrow?

Clara's mouth caves, "Uh—"

"Wait, that's tomorrow?"

Riley frowns at me, "Don't you remember? You scheduled it with mother last Friday."

Oh God. I forgot. I completely forgot.

"You don't have time for that," Edie reminds me, "we have to get into Terrance's office tomorrow morning."

"Could we maybe reschedule?" I ask Riley with a smile, "It's just that I'm needed at the office tomorrow—"

I'm interrupted by a colorfully dressed waiter who steps right through Edie and forces her to vanish. A second later Edie pops up right next to me, halfway through my shoulder and Faye's.

"Phoebe. I don't mean to ruin this night out with your friends but we are on deadline here. I have to find my wills before Terrance does, and before Porter sells everything. If Merida sells Lavish Looks to Bold Beauty, they will liquidate it. That's what I have to tell you. She's been speaking with the board and I don't think Porter knows it. She has secret plans behind everyone's backs!"

Edie, I hate to break it to you but that's what happens these days, especially if there is no family to take over the company. Maybe it's time to let Lavish Looks go.

"Never!" Edie stomps her feet as she stands, "It's my baby! You have no idea what it means to me, it's everything. That spiteful cow is doing this on purpose."

Edie—

"Phoebe," Riley cuts off my thoughts and I look over to find him frowning at me, "What would you like to eat?"

"Oh," I glance back at my closed menu realizing the waiter has been waiting for me to order, "I'll just have a taco, the house taco or whatever."

"Phoebe," Riley puts a hand out to stop the waiter from writing down my order, "That has meat in it." Clara mutters something from behind her wine glass and I can see Faye throw her a look. "Maybe you want some plain rice? Some salad?"

"Umm, okay…"

"I founded Lavish Looks when I was eighteen with my father," Edie suddenly states, "my mother died when I was young and with her went our fortune. She left behind a lavender farm that was our only source of income, my father's wood shop never succeeded. When she was alive she would make teas with it, mud masks and soaps. My father and I started Lavish Looks from the ground up over thirty years ago and it's all I have left. Twenty five years ago, Merida and I decided to launch it nationally. I have no other family except Porter, but he and I were never that close. I own sixty percent of it, Merida owns only forty. She sold her shares piece by piece when she came into some money trouble. I remember that in my new will; I state what I want the future of Lavish Looks to be."

Her story has thrown me off track. I can hear Riley say my name again but it's overrun by Edie again,

"I've made a lot of enemies in this world because I stuck to my guns. Merida is one of them, so is Terrance. Now I realize I am not the easiest person to get along with and that I may be overbearing and loud and unconventional at times…but I am grateful for your help. And more than that, I *need it*. I won't be able to rest unless I do something, and I need you to help me."

Oh God. Edie, I am trying-

"For god's sake Phoebe!"

At this point Riley shakes my arm and I look over at him, "Sorry. I don't—I was somewhere else just now."

Riley slumps back in his seat, his demeanour that of a child's, "You're always somewhere else."

I can feel myself redden a little bit, sensing both Faye and Clara stare at me. The rest of me begins to get warm, and I'm suddenly very uncomfortable. I need to take a breather, talk to Edie somewhere else, and make her go for the night. "Excuse me."

I slowly push my chair back and stand up, making my way around the table to the bathrooms.

The bathrooms are located in the basement of the restaurant and the females only house two stalls, both of them empty as I enter. The washroom is painted dark pink, and the décor matches the colorful hats and lanterns outside of the patio. The Spanish music still plays only at a decent volume.

I find myself standing in front of the semi-foggy mirror over the orange sink. I'd splash water on my face but it would ruin my make-up.

"If you ask me," Edie suddenly appears behind me, standing against one of the stalls, "your fiancé is lucky he has someone like you, who puts up with his absurdity."

"Edie," her name leaves my lips sharply. "I really could use some space right about now, alright? I'm sorry about Lavish Looks, the story you told me was lovely but I really want to be without you at this moment alright?"

"Fine," a pout ensues as she points to me, "but just so you know I'm not the one you are angry at. You're angry at yourself."

She vanishes just as the door to the bathroom swings open and Faye and Clara tumble in. They stand together as the door shuts behind them, watching me as if I may run into the stall and hide for the rest of the evening.

"Riley left," Faye let me know, "He said he wasn't up to tonight."

I find myself okay with hearing this news.

"Are you alright?" Clara asks, she steps up behind me and puts a hand on my shoulder, "You seem kind of, all over the place, according to Riley."

"Yeah, and we didn't want to say anything before but it was kind of weird you took a job as a maid," Faye adds sheepishly.

"Something is going on with you and I don't think it's just the concussion," Clara says crossing her arms over her chest. "Tom called me and said you where avoiding him and Reese. Riley says you seem scattered."

Scattered? That's the perfect way to describe me.

"You know you can tell us anything right?" Faye says stepping up to me as I turn around to face them, "We won't judge you."

It would be great if they knew about Edie; I wouldn't feel so alone dealing with Edie's problem. Or Edie herself. I'd probably feel way better too.

Oh God, here it goes.

"Okay. Ever since my concussion something happened to me and my brain."

They are silent, waiting for me to go on.

"I woke up and I could see things. Well not things, *someone.*"

Clara frowns, "Someone?"

"An older woman. Her name is Edie. Edie Edwards. She died in the room that I was admitted to and she's a spirit."

They both blink in unison at me,

"I'm sorry, a ghost?" Faye repeats.

"I know it sounds crazy," I go on, "but it's the truth. She's a spunky sixty something year old lady who lived in Cedar Springs and owns this beautiful huge house…it's not a client I work for. It's her."

"You work for a ghost?" Clara's eyes go small as she tries to understand.

"Her will went missing, and Terrance use to be her lawyer, but she fired him. Now he's trying to find her old will because in the old will Edie had left a good amount of money to her maid Marta, who is having an affair with Terrance. When Edie found out about the affair she fired Terrance and rewrote her will to cut off Marta. Both wills are missing. I have to help her find it so she can, you know, move onward with her death. So I'm undercover as a maid at her house trying to search for it."

"I think I saw this on an episode of Ghost Whisperer," Faye murmurs.

Clara's eyes scan my face and I can tell she's trying to decide whether or not to believe me.

I was a fool to think they would believe me, lord knows if things where the other way around I wouldn't have believed them. I would have thought they were crazy, suggested seeing a shrink or taking a sabbatical from work or getting a cat scan at the hospital to see if the concussion caused damage—

"I believe you," Clara sucks in her words and nods slowly at me, "I totally believe you."

I swallow, "You do?"

"People experience all sorts of things when they suffer a traumatic incident," Faye jumps in. "There are tons of records of people having heart attacks or dying and being revived waking up to seeing dead people or visions of the future."

"It would totally explain why you've been acting so out of character," Clara adds.

"I wouldn't say it's out of character," Faye touches Clara's arm and gives me a quick look, "it's more like she's become more, vigorous? I mean look at her. The bags under her eyes are gone and she has a slight complexion, again. "

Clara crinkles her nose, "She's right. I recognize this Phoebe from before Meyers and Brant."

I frown at them, "I don't feel any different from before the accident, other than the fact that I can see a dead woman."

"Either way," Clara throws up her hands and places them on my shoulders. "We believe you. And I know just how we can help you. We're going to take you to see a medium."

Chapter Eleven

The next morning I awoke at the loft, finding it empty, and feeling torn from yesterday's drama. I didn't even apologise for it. I felt the crippling ache of guilt creeping up in me when I thought about how frustrated Riley got again, but it was followed closely by another feeling. It was my own level of annoyance and I couldn't figure out why or who it was aimed at.

I showered quickly and went about the schedule for the day. The first part of the plan was to break into Terrance's office at work. I would have done it at night but I didn't have a key to enter the building. I figured I had an hour to get to the office building and search it without being late in meeting Stella, Faye and Clara for dress shopping at eleven a.m. I decide on simple grey palazzo pants and a black t-shirt; something easy to get in and out of when trying on dresses.

The ride to Meyers and Brant wasn't long and because I left after nine there was almost no traffic. I rode the elevator up to the firm quietly, my hand gripping the strap to my blue tote bag. Once the doors to the elevator slide open I found myself looking into Edie's blue eyes. Today her choice of outfit was a bright yellow sundress, and a matching headband with a side flower. She stood with her hands on her hips and a bright smile over her lips.

"Morning," Edie greets with a nod, "I trust you slept well."

Why are you so chipper?

"Because," Edie moves close to me as I leave the elevator and begin my walk towards the glass doors. She starts to play with the lavender filled orb hanging against her chest. "Your boss was called into court an hour ago so his office is empty. Should be easy to get in there and mess around."

I still don't know what you expect to find.

"Something, anything that incriminates him."

Yes but, whatever I find in his office is inadmissible in court you do know that, right?

I pull open the glass doors and shuffle inside the main lobby. The two secretaries glance up at me before exchanging a look with one another. I mutter an over enthusiastic 'good morning' and hurry around the desk towards Terrance's side of the firm. Once I'm waddling down the quiet hallway, Edie reappears at my side,

"This is exciting isn't it? Like an episode of Charlie's Angels. Only there are two of us. And I would be Charlie." She tells me, "So really it's more like Charlie's Angel."

We reach Terrance's office and find the door closed; but not locked. I twist the metal door knob further and push the door open. The office is dark and there is only a faint sign of light appearing from the computer screen across the room. I hurry inside, shutting the door quietly behind me. I know the light switch is right next to the door so I run my hand across the cool wall until I feel it. I flip it up and the room ignites in a bright florescent shade.

"Not much of a decorator is he?" Edie remarks as she wonders into the room.

"He doesn't believe in wasting time with such things," I say glimpsing around the large room. The carpet beneath my feet was a dark grey like most offices in the firm. The glass walls where hidden behind large black blinds and against the plastered wall sat several tall black bookcases; filled with nothing but law textbooks and cases. One blue tall filing cabinets sits next to the bookcases. There was a pathetic looking plastic tree in the corner of the room and two black leather arm chairs across from Terrance's large metal desk. Not one picture of his wife, or children, sat on the dreadful bureau. Only a picture of him, shaking the hands of the state senator.

I'm walking towards the desk when Edie floats to join me,

"Check the drawers first. Then the filing cabinets—"

"—You just go keep look out," I order motioning towards the door as I drop my purse down on the desk, "If he catches us I am definitely fired. There goes any hope of finding your will."

I push back the computer chair until it hits the wall and pull open the first drawer. I find nothing but post-its, pens, pencils and a few paper clips. I shove it closed and move down to the second drawer beneath it.

"I don't know what you think we're going to find in here, he's not dumb enough to leave any evidence around his office."

Edie never responds, and I look up to find the room empty.

It takes me five minutes to go through all the drawers and find nothing of value. The only thing that surprised me was finding a drawer full of candy bars; I even snagged one. I moved on to his computer, which was password protected and after ten minutes, I gave up. Opening up the candy bar and walking away from the desk, I stood in the centre of the room biting into the chocolatey gooiness.

I spot the filing cabinets but know they are locked; he has the only key and never let Greg or me into them without his supervision. If he has anything about Edie then it has to be in there.

I can hear my phone vibrate inside my purse and I resist the urge to go to it.

"Any luck?"

I glance over my shoulder at her. She's standing half way through the office door. I shake my head at her,

"Nothing. If he has anything about you it would probably be in the filing cabinet but he keeps it locked at all times and has the only key. Sorry Edie, looks like we are out of luck."

"Not necessarily," Edie stays put but cocks her head towards his desk, "look underneath his desk."

I slowly take another bite of my candy bar and head over to the desk again.

"You shouldn't be eating sweets when you're going dress shopping."

Ignoring her, I reach the desk and set down the chocolate bar next to my purse. Getting on my knees and bending down, I twist my neck so I can see under his desk. Instantly I spot a key attached to a magnetic strip and my mouth caves a little. "He is so sneaky."

I yank the key off the magnet and jump back on my feet, hurrying towards the filing cabinet. It fits perfectly into the top keyhole and I only need to turn it a little before I hear a popping sound to indicate the three drawers are open.

I don't bother with the first drawer; I just move onto the second marked for E-O and open it. I flip through the files until I find the only one marked 'Edwards' and push it open so I can look inside. I expect to find only a few sheets of paper since he was Edie's lawyer for such a short while, but instead I find hundreds. Some papers clipped together, some single and some stapled.

How do I even go through this all?

"Sorry to interrupt, sugar-pie, but he's on his way."

Over my shoulder I can see Edie's head peering through the door, "Where is he?"

"He left the courthouse, he's in a cab."

Damn it.

"I just found your file."

She disappears and I look back down into it. Cursorily I grab the file and throw it open on top of the drawer. If the calculations in my head are correct, and there is no traffic, Terrance will get here in about twenty minutes. That leaves me ten minutes to go through everything before I can safely depart without him spotting me.

That isn't enough time.

I find myself looking at newspaper articles about Edie's husband, and Edie herself. Most of them dated from the nineties or early two thousands printed off from the internet. I skim through them, noting they couldn't be important; most headlines had to do with their charity benefits, their grand Christmas parties or Lavish Looks. There are so many of them I'm about to toss the folder aside when I come across some pictures.

Pictures taken from a distance of Edie and her husband, pictures of them on the street, or through the window of their kitchen. There's even a picture of Edie in the garden on the telephone. I find two pictures of Porter as well, one taken at the airport and one taken through the window of the kitchen as he sat with Edie.

All dated about a year ago, and definitely taken by a private investigator.

After the photos I find bank statements, Lavish Looks account statements more like it; the percentage of the company's stock and the share of each board member. Next is a bank statement of Edie's personal account, numbers well into two million. All dated after Edie had terminated him as her lawyer.

Edie was right.

It takes a few seconds for the thought to sink in.

Edie was right about Terrance; in hindsight that is. There was still no proof that he hid her new will or he's trying to pass off the old one as the only will. But then again, if he *was* innocent why did he hire a private investigator for a standard will drafting case?

"Not to put pressure on you, but he's only a few blocks away," Edie tells me.

"But I'm not done."

I look down, realizing there is so much more to her file that I need, *I want*, to go through. Frustratingly I close the file folder in my hands and lift it to put it back where I found it, when something slips out. It's a small piece of paper, square shaped, and it falls onto my feet. I bend over to pick it up and find myself holding a white business card.

There's a Private Eye logo on it, and the name William Geller beneath it. His card proudly boasted the fact that he had been in the field for almost twenty five years. I keep the card in my hand as I shut and lock the filing cabinet. Quickly I put the key back in its hiding place and grab my purse, throwing the business card inside of it before I bolt from the dark office.

Edie doesn't appear again until I'm in the cab heading to Betsy's Bridal; a chain of bridal boutiques owned by one of the city's most famous socialites. I don't even want to focus on the fact that I won't be able to actually afford a dress from there, instead I hold the private eye's business card in my hand. Never has Terrance had to hire a private eye to investigate a client unless it's a divorce case.

"So now you believe me don't you?"

Alright, I sort of believe you. There was a lot of information in your file for a standard Will and Testament case. I admit that it's shady of Terrance to have had you followed, and to have somehow got hold of your account statements after you fired him. But Edie, this doesn't prove that he hid your new will and that he is looking for your older one.

"Or that he killed me," Edie added with a sigh.

Again, very doubtful he murdered you.

"So what do we do now?" Edie asks ignoring my tone, "You said there was lots in there, we should plan to go back."

I don't see how I can do that.

Edie exhales, "We should go see this Private Investigator. Where is he located?"

On the east side I answer, reading the address in my head.

We both sit quietly the rest of the way to the store.

Once were there, I'm greeted at the front doors by Clara and Faye. I was expecting them to have expressions of anticipation over their faces, but they look less than pleased. Faye must have come straight from work since she was dressed to the nines in an expansive grey tailored suit and white blouse, while Clara was in a simple pair of ripped jeans and orange t-shirt.

The shop was exquisite; dazzling crystal chandeliers hung from the ceiling, lighting the place up brightly. The carpet at our feet was a sandy tone to match the painted walls and white border trim. The walls to my left and right are covered with racks of beautiful white dresses of different designs and snowy shades. There are several mannequins on carpeted platforms, dressed in ball gowns or empire waist dresses, complete with veils and diamonds. To my left and my right are two large doorways and I don't know what's beyond them.

When I look back at Clara and Faye, the beauty of it all was frayed from me by sensing some obvious tension.

"Didn't you get any of our messages?" Clara asks me right away, "We've been trying to get a hold of you."

"Why?"

Faye's brow crinkles and she lets out a sigh, "We were just about to leave."

I frown, but before I can ask why, I hear my name,

"Phoebe? Finally, you've joined us. Come along now."

Stella stands to my left in the doorway. She's dressed herself in another cream colored suit jacket and a black pencil skirt that ends swiftly at her knees. Her signature beehive looks brighter in this light and her wrinkles look diminished.

Faye and Clare rope their arms around mine as we walk towards the doorway.

"Forgive me for over stepping my boundaries but," Faye whispers loud enough for Clara to hear, "If I were you I would seriously reconsider this engagement if this is your future mother in law."

Again I frown at her, but say nothing since we've reached the doorway and have entered a room smaller than the one we just left. One side of the room has three tall mirrors and a platform in between them. There are several beige arm chairs around the room for guests and only one dressing room divided from everyone by a white curtain with glistening gems in the fabric.

There are two women in black suits standing near the mirrors, one of them significantly older than us and one of them about our age. Both of them have clasped their hands in front and smile at me largely. Stella stands next to the dressing room, motioning at two other women roughly my age who stand near her.

"Phoebe, this is Amelia," she gestures at the taller of the two women. A blond with beautiful sleek hair dressed in a tight green dress, with a tan only attainable by a tanning booth. "And this is Kennedy."

Kennedy is the shorter of the girls, but equally as stunning. Her blonde hair sits just at her shoulders, streaks of brown throughout, and she's dressed in a pair of running shorts and tight tank top. Her arms are exceptionally muscular, and so are her legs. I think I can even see a six pack beneath her tank top.

"These are Riley's cousins. They will be your third and fourth bridesmaids."

My what?

"So nice to meet you," Amelia approaches me first, smiling brightly as she grabs my hand to shake it, "I can totally see why Riley asked you to marry him. You are just *so* cute."

129

Was there—did I sense a tone there?

"Aunt Stella told us you have literally nothing planned for the wedding," Kennedy doesn't even greet me, she just gestures, "and she told us of your attack. But don't you worry we can totally help Aunt Stella with everything while you relax."

"It wasn't an attack." I frown, "It was a small concussion."

"Same difference," Kennedy laughs lightly and pulls open the dressing room curtain.

Inside the dressing room hanging from a long metal rod are at least ten dresses. All of them big, all of them puffy. Pairs of white shoes sit beneath the hanging dresses as well.

"Look Phoebe," Clara's voice is full of sarcasm, "they picked out the dresses for you. *All of them.*"

"It was no trouble at all." Amelia flicks her wrist at me, "Aunt Stella had Riley text a picture of you to us and we knew what kind of dresses would suit you."

"You'll look like a giant cream puff," Clara states.

I half expected Stella to scold her, but she simply sat down in the nearest arm chair.

"Your friends are *too* cute," Amelia laughs, gazing at Clara. "They helped pick out some of the dresses, too."

Faye crosses her arms over her chest, "Everything we picked out you vetoed."

"So *cute,*" Amelia repeats before she turns her back on the three of us. "Let us show them to you. Excuse me? Could we have some champagne please?" I watch the attendants nod at Amelia and scurry from the room.

"Now some of these dresses will probably be tight. They are 'as is' of course, taking them in will cost a fortune, and really is a travesty considering they are designer…" Kennedy gazes from the sea of white back to me. I watch her slowly run her eyes up and down my body so I attempt to cover my torso with my arms. "But we have a month and a half till the wedding and I can whip you into shape!"

I look down at my body. I guess my stomach could be flatter, and my arms could be a little bit more toned—

"She looks fine," Clara can't help but snap,

"Of course she does," Kennedy back tracks in a serious tone. "I just mean, every bride wants to look her best don't they? I'm a personal trainer. I *know* what I am talking about. Starting tomorrow we'll meet up for three hours every night and this weekend I'll pop on by to help you cook smarter meals. I know Riley is all into becoming a vegan, but he did mention he thought it was hard for you so I thought I could bring over my fail safe recipes."

The thought of having to see Kennedy every day for the next month and a half was starting to give me a headache. "I'm sorry, stop."

Kennedy frowns at me and Amelia turns around gracefully.

"Look, I'm so sorry but I don't have time to work out three hours a day until the wedding," I say kindly to Kennedy. "I appreciate the offer. I don't like big dresses like that, and I was thinking maybe an off-white color dress instead of a very white dress? And I have a third bridesmaid; she's just overseas on business."

I won't even mention how I don't need them as my bridesmaids.

"They are eggshell," Amelia mutters giving the dresses a look. "Very white, also known as linen white, is last season." From the corner of my eye I see Stella's stance has stiffened and her eyebrows have lowered in aggravation. She opens her mouth slowly,

"Phoebe. Amelia and Kennedy are only offering their *assistance;* don't you think you should be more open to their suggestions?"

"We have a problem."

Edie appears before Stella and I realize I hadn't even noticed that she was gone until now. "You left a half-eaten candy bar on Terrance's desk and he knows *you* were in the office. He's heading to the house now to tell Porter you broke into his office and demand he fire you."

Oh God. I forgot about the candy bar!

"You cannot get fired, Phoebe," Edie's tone is threatening.

I'm aware, Edie.

131

"Phoebe?" Stella's voice interrupts us and I jerk my head to the side to see Stella frowning at me. "Is something the matter?"

"I have to go," I tell her. "I'm sorry. I know this is sudden, but I have to go. We'll have to reschedule. It was nice to meet you." I nod at Kennedy and Amelia as I back away from them all.

I can hear Faye and Clara behind me, and they are silent until we reach the store doors.

"That was so funny!" Faye laughs, "Stella looked like she was going to blow a gasket."

"I'm sorry but if those girls are your other bridesmaids," Clara opens the door for us and we stumble into the chilly May air, "then I bow out."

"They won't be my bridesmaids, don't worry. I don't want them part of anything." I head to the street and throw up my hand to hail down a cab. "I'll talk to Riley tonight about it."

"Is there really an emergency, or did you just need a quick escape?" Clara asks as a cab pulls up alongside of us.

"There is, sort of," I open the cab door, catching the look Faye and Clara exchange, "What?"

"Is it, you know," Faye shrugs slowly, "that ghost lady?"

I forgot that I had told them about Edie. I pause for a moment to feel them out, wonder if continuing to be truthful with them could back fire on me. They could chalk it up to me being crazy, and tell Riley to have me committed. Maybe I could act like I was joking?

"We don't think you're crazy," Clara jumps in as if reading my thoughts. "If you say you see this lady then you see her. End of story. I just, wouldn't tell Satine."

Less than an hour later the cab driver pulls up to Edie's house, and I have rehearsed what I plan to say to Terrance and Porter at least a hundred times. I spot a black sports car in the driveway that I recognize as Terrance's. I pay the cab driver, leaving a hefty tip and bolt out from the cab as Edie appears on the front porch. She's motioning for me to move along faster, and once I open the front gate, I jog up the pathway to the grand house.

132

"He's in the dining room with Porter," Edie tells me. "You should hear the lies he's telling my nephew. That you broke in, stole from him, went through his private things—"

"Edie!" I cut her off as I join her frantic state. "Those are all true!"

"That's our secret," Edie reminds me with a huff, "to everyone else you did not do those things. He's giving reasons for Porter to fire you."

"Do you think he will?" I bite my lip as I glance at the closed French doors only feet away from where I stand.

"Course he will! If he thinks you're a thief. Terrance has been here for almost thirty minutes having coffee with Porter and spewing all these lies about you. I can't even repeat some of them!"

The curtains in the windows behind Edie move slightly and I back away from sight. The last thing I need is to be seen talking to nothing on the porch of this manor. I beckon for Edie to follow me as I head towards the French doors, slowing opening the right one and walking in quietly. There's nobody around, and I shut the door behind me, tip toeing towards the kitchen when Edie appears in my path and stops me in step.

"Get into the dining room and stop what's going on in there." She points at the wall.

I follow her command and head into the kitchen but make a sharp left to the dining room door. I can hear muffled voices and one of them bellows so loudly I instinctively know it's Terrance.

Adjusting my posture and running my story again in my head, I knock twice on the door. I then push it open with both hands, stopping my purse from sliding off my shoulder. This is the first time I've stepped into the dining room.

The wall to my right is replaced by a gorgeous bay window from ceiling to floor and the rest of the walls are paneled with dark wood. There is a crystal vintage looking chandelier hanging from the ceiling and the table in the room seats almost twenty people from the quick count I do in my head. There are three long buffet tables against the wall; fresh flowers sit in vases and gold frames of different shapes and sizes sit around them.

"Wonderful isn't it?" Edie asks me as she parades around the long table. "Forgive the mess Porter made." She swats at the end of the table near the window, which is littered with papers, old boxes and numerous file folders stack atop of each other. "I used to throw many dinner parties when my husband was alive. I was known for them actually."

"And there, is the culprit."

Somehow I had overlooked both Porter and Terrance, who sat at the dining room table near Porter's mess of papers. Terrance stood first, daunting in a jet black suit and red dress shirt sans tie. With his black hair wispy to the side with exceedingly high amounts of gel that shone in the light from the window.

"Did you have an eventful morning, Phoebe?" his tone is ice as he re-buttons his suit jacket and his eyes fixate on me.

Okay, here goes nothing.

"I did yes, be it a dramatic one." I answer with a small smile as I glance over to Porter who has now stood from his chair. I can't read his expression but it looks like one of curiosity, his eyes scaling mine as if he thought he could catch a lie from me.

"I can imagine," Terrance snaps placing his hands on his hips. "Even more so *dramatic* is the thought that you assumed you could get away with it."

Edie appears next to me and swiftly kicks the air towards Terrance, "I could just kick him in his apples!"

"Get away with it?" I master a decent frown as I look from Terrance to Porter. "Porter knew I had the morning off."

Terrance takes a step forward and his mouth whips open. "Taken the morning off to break into your boss' office, go through his personal property and steal!"

"Steal indeed!" Edie shouts in his ear as if he could hear her. "She took a measly candy bar you Fatso, she did you a favor!"

"Break into whose office?" I hope my expression looks as confused as the tone that escapes my mouth. "I was out dress shopping with my mother in law, and bridesmaids."

Terrance scoffs loudly and shakes his head, turning to Porter who has placed his hands into the pockets of his grey pants as he watches us. "Do you believe this fabricator? Lying even though she was spotted going into the firm by secretaries?"

"Oh I went into the firm," I nod watching Terrance spin my way again, "but only to check to see if you had any work for me. When I realised you and Greg were gone, I left to meet with my mother in law and bridesmaids. I didn't break into your office or go through your things. I wouldn't throw my career away like that. And if you don't believe me then you are more than welcome to call Betsy's Bridal. They'll tell you I was the bride whose bridesmaids chose puffy dresses for her to try on, and that she got very upset and left early to come back here."

It's silent in the room and I don't know how much longer I can stare down Terrance for. His stance has blown up and his frame looks wider than before. Suddenly I begin to wonder what the man would say to me if Porter wasn't in the same room with us.

"You can make damn sure that I will be contacting Betsy's Bridal the moment I leave here, and if your story doesn't add up? You can forget about waltzing into Meyers and Brant ever again."

He adjusts his posture and dusts off his suit as if this argument had dirtied him, then he slowly turns to Porter, "I trust you will deal with this matter once I'm gone?"

Porter's raises his eyebrows at me and the breath he lets out is definitely one of annoyance.

Oh God, Edie he's going to fire me. Look at him.

"Shh don't say that," Edie hisses behind me. "Just because he looks like he doesn't trust you, doesn't mean he doesn't."

Yeah, right.

"Terrance it seems to me that there isn't a matter to be dealt with," Porter places his attention to him rather strictly. "I don't believe Ms. Mercer has broken into your office and I may be jumping to judgement on her character, but based on what I have seen it isn't likely she did. If you do somehow find evidence of her breaking into your office then bring it to my attention, and I will deal with the matter."

Terrance's face flushes a little and he clears his throat, "Fine."

I move away from the door as Terrance walks towards it. It swings shut behind him and Edie vanishes from my side; no doubt heading after him. I'm left alone with Porter, and after a while the door behind me stops swinging.

"You didn't have to do that," I say finally.

Porter takes a sigh and keeps his hands in his pockets, "to tell you the truth I'm not a fan of the man. He's an exceptional lawyer, but that is where it stops. The last thirty minutes with him were a complete nightmare, and I had a sense half of his accusations towards you, were lies."

I make a face, "What did he say?"

"That you have a drinking problem, and have numerous times been caught in theatrical office trysts."

I can't help but gasp. "He's the one having an affair!" quickly I realize my misstep and shrug my shoulders. "Or so I have heard."

"Indeed," Porter's mouth twitches a little at the corners before he turns away from me, and walks back to the head of the table where he had been sitting.

Did he just, sort of smile? The man who never smiles as Edie puts it, smiled?

I watch him sit down in his seat and he speaks without looking back up at me, "I won't keep you from your work, but Ms. Mercer? I really hope you were not lying about breaking into your employer's office, I would be disappointed if I knew it was true."

"I promise," I nod smartly at him, "I do not do that kind of stuff."

"Good, no lying. I don't have the time to deal with dishonest people; I have important work to do and a very tight deadline."

I nod my head, "I promise."

I felt the confidence in my words but I also felt something else, and I knew exactly what it was.

Shame.

I felt guilty for lying.

Chapter Twelve

"How can you *not* like my cousins? Everyone likes them! They're helpful and caring, and were hurt when you tore down their suggestions for dresses. They sent me pictures of them and I can honestly say that each one looked better than the last! You didn't even give the dresses or them a chance, you pre-judged."

"Riley, they were so obnoxious and one of them basically called me fat! Faye and Clara hate them, and I know Satine will loathe them. It's my wedding, I'm the bride. I choose my bridesmaids, not your mother. By the way, you aren't supposed to see my dresses, its bad luck."

"You need four bridesmaids Phoebe!" Riley calls out from the bathroom and I can hear the cupboards being opened and slammed shut. "I've chosen James and my three cousins. It needs to match up perfectly. You also know I don't believe in luck."

"It doesn't need to match up," I make a face I'm happy he can't see as I put on my shoes at the door. I'm in a black V-neck jersey dress with little color to me, except for the red hairband in my hair.

I stayed at Edie's longer than expected last night, because Rosanne had me working on all the bathrooms, much to Edie's dismay. When I finally did get home Riley was asleep, and this morning all we did since we awoke, was bicker.

He stands in the bathroom doorway with a towel around his waist and two jars in his hands. "I'm not un-asking them Phoebe. What's done is done. They are going to be your bridesmaids. I don't know why you are so upset. Mom thinks it's purposely directed at her."

"Well she is being controlling."

"She doesn't mean to be. Come on Phoebe, you know that!" Riley steps back into the bathroom. "She doesn't have a daughter; she is excited. She wants us to have the best wedding possible and she wants to make sure it's our dream wedding. Don't you see that? Why are you so defensive?"

I would retort angrily, but my cellphone vibrates in my hands and I give it my attention. A text from Greg pops up on my screen, one I have been waiting for since Terrance left Edie's yesterday.

Terrance made calls to the store, they confirmed your attendance so you're in the clear ☺. *Although, they did mention to him that you seemed 'bonkers'.*

I can't help but smile as I reply back with,

You have to be to work at Meyers and Brant, right? Keep me updated on any case work.

"Phoebe!"

Riley's scream echoes around the loft and I tear my head up from my phone to see him standing in the doorway of the bathroom. He's shirtless, but immediately I notice his skin is a shade darker. He wears a clear shower cap and through it I notice white foam spread through his hair. It's his face however, that floors me. It's covered in a dark green mask and is drying to mud.

"Riley, what are—what is—," I giggle a little bit and watch his expression harden.

"It's a homemade seaweed mask, and a homemade baking soda, coconut hair mask. Your Lavish Looks mango hair wrap dried out my scalp last night."

I'm glad Edie isn't around to hear that.

"You look darker too…" my nose crinkles as I look back at his six pack.

"I'm tanning; I want a nice complexion for the wedding. I bought you a package too. It's in the kitchen, you should start going," he points to me and then gestures up and down his own body. "You don't want to be pale in a white dress."

"Faye said my complexion was nice the other day."

"She was just being nice. You need some color."

Tanning booths? Barbie bridesmaids? Bulbous dresses? This isn't my wedding. The thought pops in clear and loud.

There's a burst of laughter next to me and from the bright red dress I can tell its Edie. She's bent over in laughter as she points at Riley. "You cannot be serious about this man!"

"Riley," I keep calm as I disregard her, "I have to go to work but can we talk later?"

"Fine, go to *work*." He shrugs me off and re-enters the bathroom, slamming the door behind him but not before adding, "Go clean houses."

"I don't feel right about this Edie."

"Stop being such a baby. You broke into your bosses office so what's the difference breaking into her room? And by the way, we should go question the Private Investigator later on, when you're finished here."

Rosanne had Marta helping her with the cleaning of the spare rooms upstairs. I was instructed with the laundry and the ironing, which gave Edie the idea to badger me into going into Marta's room down the hall and snoop through her things.

So now I follow my ghost, quietly down the hall. We pass my room and Rosanne's, before we reach the one at the end of the hall; Marta's.

I turn the knob, not surprised that I find it unlocked.

Porter's words fly into my mind and I cringe a little, gripping the handle.

"What's wrong?" Edie demands, her voice a whisper for some reason.

"I feel bad," I turn to face her, "about doing this. When I told your nephew I didn't."

"What?" Edie's face turns, "What are you talking about? Just go in for Hell's gates!"

I bite my lip and look back at the plain white door.

Why do I feel so guilty about lying to him? There was no guilt when I lied to Terrance, or when I hid my eating habits from Riley.

"Because Porter is decent, Terrance is a horse's ass and Riley is a piece of work. Now open this door, and go look for anything that ties Marta and Terrance together!"

"Edie," it's my turn to snap at her, "even if I find evidence what does it prove? Porter already knows Terrance may be having an affair because I let it slip, so he won't care that it's with Marta. He may be creeped out, but I doubt he would care."

I watch her as her eyes glaze over mine. I can tell she's thinking about what I said, whether I had a point or not to this.

"Wouldn't it be better to just keep looking for one of the wills?"

Again, she seems to reconsider breaking into Marta's room, and she even smiles which has me believe she would agree with me. "No I don't. Now she left her cell phone on the charger before running upstairs, so you can search it to see if you she has anything on there that links her to Terrance."

"Number one? Terrance would instruct her to delete their messages, or emails right away. And number two? Whatever we find is without a warrant, which would be thrown out in court."

Edie groans loudly and exclaims, "Just do it! You could find something of value!"

Deciding it meaningless to argue with her, I push the door open furiously and walk into the room. It's as empty as mine except for a messy twin bed in the corner, and a dresser with clothes escaping from each drawer. The top of her dresser is scattered with perfume bottles and make up brushes, even old magazines.

"It smells like a candy factory in here," Edie holds her nose up to the air and makes a snooty face, "vulgar."

Marta's cell phone is resting next to her bed on the night-stand, the indicator light blinking to imply that she has a new message. I walk over to her bed and sit down slowly, lifting the phone from its place but keeping it attached to the charger.

"Go upstairs and make sure they don't come back down here," I tell Edie as I spot her shaking her head at Marta's perfume collection. "I don't want to be caught."

"Fine," Edie turns to face me, "the smell is turning my stomach anyway."

She disappears and it occurs to me that I have become used to watching her float in and out of rooms and vanish like a magician. Now my stomach twinges a little bit too.

I swipe the screen of Marta's phone and hit her messages icon. There are over twenty subject lines and I scroll down finding only one name that jumps out at me. Terrance. She didn't even give him a code name or nickname. She used his real name, and I couldn't help but chuckle.

I hit the messages and read the last sentence sent from Marta. A simple '*I miss you*' which Terrance received but never replied to. The message above that was Marta asking '*when will*

I see you? It's been over a week' and again, Terrance received it but never replied.

Most of her messages to him are lovey dovey, and there are minimal responses to them from him but as I scroll up things get interesting.

A message sent from him the day after I began working at the house read,

I don't know what she is up to but I can tell you she is not related to Edie in the least bit, not even through marriage. I'm working on getting rid of her at the firm and over there, so just keep up your end of the bargain.

Marta's reply was simple,

I'm trying but Rosanne is constantly on my ass. It's hard to search for them!

Terrance's response came quickly,

Don't worry about her; we'll deal with her too.

Marta sent an emoticon of a smiley face with devil horns before asking,

And your lawyer girl? She already caught me snooping.

There came no response from Terrance which had me feeling grateful.

I had to acknowledge everything now, didn't I? Terrance really was involved, the evidence was only growing. Whether or not he had plans to do away with Edie was another matter but it was clear enough that he was after her new will. He's greedy but he's not a murderer...is he?

Their conversation is too long for me to read through so I copy it all. I'm lucky Marta left her email open so I can quickly paste the entire conversation on a blank page and send it to myself. I'm working on deleting any trace of my email in the send folder when Edie appears in the middle of the room.

"Rosanne is coming down!"

I place the phone back in its place, making sure it sits exactly as she left it before we both hurry towards the door, closing it quietly behind me.

Edie walks behind me as I head towards the laundry room down the hall,

"And? What did you find?"

"Just lots of mushy talk. I haven't read all of it, but it's suspicious."

"I knew it!" Edie squeals behind me in delight, "I just knew it!"

The laundry room is small, made for only the large washer and dryer and a long counter top table attached to the wall for folding any clothes. I have left a pile of whites that needed to be folded on the counter and that is where I head to.

Edie bops up to me, leaning so that her elbow goes right through the countertop. "What kinds of things do they say?"

"Umm, something about a plan to do away with Rosie, Terrance doesn't believe I'm related to you through marriage." I pick up a cloth placement and begin to fold it. "How is there this much laundry when only Porter lives here?"

"Anything about the wills?"

"I don't know, I didn't read it all. He hasn't been responding to Marta much now". I give her a look as I move onto the second placement. "I'll read it all tonight."

"We should check my room after you're done in here, Marta has the afternoon off and Rosanne will be cooking Porter's dinner. We can get away with going through my things."

"How is it you don't remember where you placed the old will?" my mind goes back to that issue, which has been plaguing me since she admitted the truth to me.

"I don't remember much from the day I fell into the water, I told you. I vaguely remember arguing with Terrance, and I barely remember taking the old will from my desk," Edie reminds me with a breath.

"You didn't throw it out?"

She pauses and her face scrunches up. After a few seconds she begins to shake her head,

"No, I didn't. I recall thinking I should burn it, being it was a once a legal document but I know I never did because..." She snaps her fingers, "Because as I went to burn it I got ash on the sleeves of the dress! I was scared to ruin the dress more by the sot and smell of fire."

"Okay?"

"You should see the dress I wore. A beautiful yellow sundress with gold embroidery along the collar and sleeves, it had a matching vintage black and gold sequin headband. I looked like a star," she begins to daydream at the wall, grasping the lavender orb necklace at her chest.

"Edie, where is this going?"

"Oh right," she spins to face me again. "I didn't want to smell like ash so I may have hid the will in the stack of wood and paper near one of the fireplaces! To burn it later."

"Do you remember which fireplace it was?"

"Could be any of them, but the living room one is the one I use the most. And the one in my bedroom," Edie tells me, "and neither has been lit since it's the spring."

My cell phone vibrates in the pocket of my uniform dress and I slip my hand in to retrieve it. There are three text messages flashing on the screen one from my mother, one from Greg and one from Reese.

I check the one from Reese first,

Phoebe, text me back. Or call me. Tom and I would like to see you.

I make a mental note to respond as I swipe to the next message from Greg.

Terrance wants you in tomorrow morning, to discuss things with you. Ten a.m. he says.

Great. My firing, I just know it.

I don't bother to dwell on that right now, as I suddenly feel today could be a very bad day, and move on to my mother's text message.

JITTERBUG. PLEASE TELL ME WHY I WAS TOLD TO KEEP MYSELF OUT OF MY DAUGHTERS WEDDING AND THAT I AM A 'GUEST' AT HER BRIDAL SHOWER???

What is she talking about? I don't even have plans for a bridal shower. I've barely spoken to her since my concussion. Quickly I reply with,

Relax. There must have been a misunderstanding. There isn't a date set for the shower.

Her response comes even quicker than mine and again in all capital locks,

THEN WHY WAS I TOLD TO KEEP THE SUNDAY OPEN IN THREE WEEKS FOR A BRIDAL SHOWER? AND I

WAS TOLD MY INVOLVEMENT WAS NOT 'NEEDED' FOR ANY 'ASPECT' OF THE WEDDING.

Stella.

Mom, stop replying in cap's please. I don't know why you have been excluded, but I will figure it out and get back to you.

I put the phone back into my pocket and my irritation must show because Edie stares at me, "What's the matter?"

"I don't know," I answer turning to the laundry, "something about my bridal shower and my mother being excluded."

"I don't mean to step over the line," Edie walks over to me slowly, "but don't you think you're allowing a little too much of your future mother-in-law?"

I bite my lip as I think about what Riley said earlier. His mother doesn't have any daughters, and she really only means the best, in her own messed up way. Perhaps I could talk to her? One on one? Maybe that would help calm things down a bit?

"I've been around women like her my whole life sugar-pie," Edie sighs. "She won't take what you have to say to her lightly."

"I'm sure she will understand if I explain everything to her. She seems rational."

We both look down at my phone as it starts to ring and Edie watches me take the call from Riley. Before greeting him I frown at her nosiness and turn my back to her.

"Hi," I say into my phone.

"Phoebe. Please tell me why your mother called my mother and gave her a 'piece of her mind'?"

Oh God.

"When did she do this?"

"A few minutes ago. Apparently she told my mother to back off from planning the wedding, that you are not her daughter and that she has no right to interfere. My mother got so upset she had to go lay down because her anxiety went through the roof. You know she's prone to stress related illnesses, Phoebe."

"Riley, I don't think my mom meant to be rude to her, she's just been so frustrated because Stella isn't keeping her in

144

the loop," I explain. "I'll call my mom and get her to apologize to your mom. I'm sure they can come to an understanding and work together."

"Ha! Fat chance," Edie snips, "his mother deserved what she got."

I wave her to silence as I hear Riley continue, *"Good, I hope so."* He takes a deep breath, *"So, how was the appointment? What did the doctor say?"*

I frown at my reflection in the window, "Appointment?"

"Your check-up, with Doctor Grier."

Oh no.

"Damn it!" I exclaim into the phone, "I forgot."

"You forgot? Phoebe! How could you forget about that? I told you the other day!"

"I'm sorry I've just been so—"

"—Distracted, I know, you're always so distracted." His tone is sarcastic and stone like. I get the chills, as it reminds me of his mother. *"From the wedding, from my mother, hell even from me and I've just about had enough of it. Do you have any idea how it makes me feel when you seem a million miles away all the time?"*

"How about she just had a concussion, you knob-head!" Edie shouts behind me.

"Riley," my voice cracks a little, "I know I seem distant and weird lately but I really—"

"—Distant and weird and defensive and unloving."

"Unloving?" I repeat creakingly.

"Yes unloving! It's a bit selfish if you ask me."

Selfish?

My hand falls from my ear and balls into a fist, "If I'm being selfish it's because I had a concussion last week that's why! If you ask me, you aren't being a very understanding and loving fiancé. It's been 'do this and do that Phoebe' the entire time without any consideration as to whether I *want* to actually do it! Do I actually want your cousins as my bridesmaids? Do I actually want a rush wedding?"

"So you don't want to get married, then, is that it?" he cuts me off with a shout.

"I never said that!"

"Well you certainly implied it, didn't you? Fine, you don't want to get married then let's not get married. Forget it."

I hear a click and he's gone.

Did we just—did we just break up? Was that a break up?

I expect to feel broken, overcome with a wretched sinking feeling of once again being single. I pause for a second, there's a slight stinging behind my eyes but that's all there is; no tears, no heart dropping into the pit of my stomach.

Just silence, and confusion.

I hear Edie clear her throat awkwardly behind me, "If you want my opinion that was positively for the best."

"I didn't ask for your opinion," I can't help but snap. I place my phone back into my pocket but not before setting it on silent.

Why did I fly off the handle like that? That isn't like me. I feel a slight pounding in my head and take a few breathes hoping it goes away. I need to distract myself.

"Distraction is the key," Edie sings clearly intruding on my thoughts again.

"Alright, okay. Let me finish this," I turn around to face her again and gesture at the laundry on the folding table. "Then we'll go look through the fireplaces."

I finish the laundry about thirty minutes later and begin to rummage through the fireplaces with Edie. All of them had been emptied; the wood and paper piles held nothing but small branches and old flyers. I had one fireplace left to check when Edie decided to follow Marta on her afternoon off, believing she would be meeting with Terrance.

Not that I minded being alone; especially after what happened earlier today. Each time I checked my phone I found no missed calls and no text messages. Every time it angered me; shouldn't Riley be reaching out to me? Shouldn't he be in a panic that he would lose me?

With Porter out for the day, and Rosanne busy with a duck in the kitchen, I was confident I didn't have to peer over my shoulder in the living room. I forgot how splendid the room was, the antique furnishings and grey modernist couches set in the centre of the room. There was a large white armoire between the two bay windows in the front of the room and I wondered what was inside of it. As I entered the room I notice the gorgeous white liquor bench and cabinet to my left against the wall stocked with vodka, gin, rye and numerous bottles of fine wine.

Edie must have been a drinker.

I crossed the light carpet to the enormous white stone fireplace, and noticed right away that it hadn't been cleaned like the others.

Next to it, the wood pile was stacked high and the paper bin was almost filled to the top.

It has to be in there, the will has to be in there.

I knelt down in front of the papers and began to lift them from the box. So far there were only flyers and old newspapers. I lifted stack by stack, setting them onto the ashy stone floor of the fireplace.

I suddenly got to thinking about what would happen if I actually found this will. Would Edie have me burn it? It still didn't solve the case of her missing revised one and that's the one that truly mattered.

"Oh, I didn't know anyone was in here."

Porter's voice startles me and I move on my knees to face him. He only gives me a glance before he turns and walks towards the impressive liquor cabinet against the wall. "Continue with your work, I'll be out of your hair in a minute."

He's dressed in a dark suit and I can smell his cologne, a smoky yet sweet aroma. From the way he stands as he pours his drink, I got the feeling he had a rather stressful morning. I hear his phone ring and watch as he takes it out of his pocket, looks at the screen, hits a button on the side and slides the phone onto the counter top away from his drink.

"Rough morning?" I can't resist asking.

"In a way, yes," he answers, keeping his back to me as he adds ice into his drink. Sensing the end of the conversation I edge myself back to the paper bin and keep shuffling through; I was half way through the pile already and there was no sign of any legal documents.

"May I ask you something?"

I look over my shoulder to find Porter watching me.

"Sure," I nod.

"Why does a woman with a promising career decide to shaft it aside to clean houses?"

"It was a favor to Edie," I remind him, slowly shrugging. I look down at the papers in my hand, shuffling through them and finding nothing but flyers. "And it wasn't such a promising career anyway."

"Hard to imagine, at Meyers and Brant." He takes a slow drink and watches as I place the papers to the side.

"I'm just a legal assistant; I still have to take the bar. And if you haven't noticed, Terrance is not my biggest fan." I make a face which causes Porter to smirk and shake his head as he looks down at his drink.

"That I did notice yes," he pauses as he looks up at me. "So why did he hire you?"

"He said that he wanted to hire an underdog because he wanted to 'try something different'," I air quote his words. "Don't get me wrong, the man can sell ice to an Eskimo, but he's not very easy to get along with."

"I quite agree," he nods again and takes a quick drink.

This talk of Terrance reminds me of what's in store for tomorrow; my ten a.m. firing. I'll be unemployed and un-engaged, all within twenty four hours.

"Could I have tomorrow morning off?" my voice is heavy as I ask. "I need to go into the office for a meeting."

"I don't see why not," Porter turned around setting his empty glass back down on the table, "take the whole day. There isn't much to do around here until next week."

"What happens next week?"

Porter slowly refills his glass, "We prepare for the auction again. Merida has been on my back since I cancelled the last one." He hesitates and draws in a breath, "I suppose it's time to get rid of most of Aunt Edie's possessions."

I open my mouth to protest, knowing that if Edie where here she'd throw one of her lighting flickering tantrums but nothing comes out. What exactly can I say? I have no reason for him to postpone the auction, at least none that comes to mind. "When is the auction?"

"Next Thursday," his glass is full as he turns back around to face me. "Is it unreasonable to ask you work into the evening that day?"

"No, I could work."

Something tells me Edie would make me anyway.

Chapter Thirteen

When I got back to the loft nobody was home, so I took the opportunity to call the Private Investigator since Edie had pestered me the whole ride home. It was not a good conversation.

"Will Geller," he greets. His tone was husky, rough and unfriendly.

"Uh, hello. My name is—"

"—Don't give him your real name!" Edie hisses as she stands over me.

"My name is Florence," I lie awkwardly, pressing my phone against my ear as I sink into the bed. "And I'm calling about my sister, Edie Edwards."

There's heavy breathing on the other end, *"and?"*

"And I understand that you were hired by her lawyer Terrance Meyers to—"

"—I wasn't hired by anyone," he suddenly states with a grunt. *"I don't know anybody by those names. What did you say was your name again?"*

Damn it. I should have known he wouldn't give up information on a client, especially Terrance, who brought him boatloads of work I imagined.

"It's Florence. I was just wondering if you could give me some information about why you had been hired—"

"—Listen lady, if that person was a client, I wouldn't give out information. You're wasting my time."

I hear a dial tone and drop my phone on my lap, looking up at Edie who stares at me with wide eyes, "What a beastly man."

"He would have to be, to be working for Terrance."

"Should we break into his office?"

"No," I point a finger at her. "No more breaking into people's rooms. My nerves can't take it anymore."

"You could bribe him!" Edie suggests with a smile.

"With what money?" I chuckle as I think about that looming twenty thousand dollar debt. "Even if I did, it's not like you could pay me back."

"I could give you one of my valuables?"

150

It was tempting. Knowing that some of her jewellery was priced near, or over, the amount required to obliterate my debt, I still couldn't agree to it. Something about taking Edie's valuables felt nasty.

For the rest of the evening I read Marta and Terrance's text conversation, finding nothing incriminating, before falling asleep.

When I awoke the next morning, it was clear that Riley hadn't come home the entire night. Part of me worried; where was he? Where did he stay last night? Did he maybe come home and sleep on the couch and then leave before I awoke? Were we even together now?

The other part of me felt relieved. I had nothing else to say to him after our phone call yesterday. In hindsight, maybe I should apologize for being not committed to this wedding but in truth, the wedding didn't feel like my own. My stomach turned at the thought of Stella planning everything without my consideration.

When I checked my phone I found only two messages, one from Dr. Grier's office insisting I call to reschedule my appointment, and one from my brother. His was simple to the point, a 'call me back as soon as you can' voice mail. Nothing from Riley.

"Maybe that's a good thing," Satine quipped on the phone with me as I got ready to head into the office. *"I mean do you really need his kind of hysterics before this meeting?"*

"Hysterics?" I frown as I do up the buttons to my dress. A black dress with grey strips fashioned to look like a suit, a modest v-cut at the chest. If it was my last day at Meyers and Brant then I was at least going to look good when I leave with my box of stuff.

I hear Satine sigh loudly on the other end, *"Look. I love you; you're one of my best friends so I feel I need to tell you that maybe this fight with Riley was a good thing. I mean he's very dramatic and flighty. Maybe he's not the best match for you. This whole Vegan thing too, he shouldn't be pressuring you to do it if you don't want to."*

I frown, aware she can't see my expression. "Wait a second," I pull my hair out of the butterfly clip that held it up. "Do you all think this way?"

She's silent and I realize she's given me her answer. They hate him? I caught the frustrating remarks about Riley from Clara, but I never thought she could *hate* him.

"I know you three have your issues with him," I frown as I pick up the phone from the dresser, "but I didn't think you all hated him."

"*We don't hate him*" Satine quickly retorts, *"We hate his mother."*

"Well nobody likes Stella!" I exclaim, "You can't punish Riley because of his mother."

"Nobody is punishing Riley, Phoebe. Where is this coming from? You just finished telling me you can't understand why you aren't more upset about your fight yesterday."

"I'm just—I'm just confused lately," I place a hand to my forehead as I warm up. I have been confused lately; before the concussion I was mad about Riley. He was a good man from a good family, and yes he could be dramatic but he cared for me.

Realizing that Satine was still waiting for me to speak I went on after the brief pause. "I didn't expect you all to let me allow a guy like Riley to slip through my fingers. I have to go or I'll be late."

"Don't be angry," Satine chimes in before I can hit the end button, *"if Riley makes you happy then that's all that matters to us."*

I think about my conversation with Satine the whole ride to the office. Then I think about my conversation with Riley yesterday, again. *Distant and weird and defensive and unloving* he had said. I get the distant thing, that I am able to blame on this Edie, but unloving and defensive? Was that really true?

I scrunch up my nose as I try to think about that. I come to realize that since the concussion last week Riley and I haven't even hugged, or kissed, or had sex. Oh God, I had become unloving.

As we reach my building and I pay the cab driver my cell phone goes off. I quickly leave the cab and stand on the busy sidewalk searching for my phone inside of my bag. When I reach it I see the name Clara flashing and I answer, "Hi."

"Hey. Satine told us about your conversation this morning. Thought I should call to make sure you're not angry with the three of us."

I sigh, pushing the strap to my purse up my shoulder, "I'm not angry with you guys, I'm just annoyed."

I hear her clicking away at her desk, *"At us or at how Riley treated you?"*

"He treated me fine!" I can't help but shout into the phone.

Jeez, maybe I am getting more and more defensive.

"You don't have to shout, Phoebe."

"I'm sorry," I run a hand through my hair and walk towards the building, zig zagging through the passing side-walkers. "I've been having a rough couple of days."

"I know," comes Clara's calm voice, *"and I'm sorry. I'm just calling to tell you that if the wedding is off, were here for you."*

"Thank you," I yank open the big doors to the building and hurry inside, "but I doubt the wedding is off. I've had time to think rationally, and have decided to go see Riley after this meeting talk to about things. I love the guy. He's perfect for me."

"Is he?"

I frown as I cross the large lobby, passed the sign in desk to the row of elevators, "What do you mean?"

"I think you're wearing rose coloured glasses, I think because he looks good on paper you assume he is good for you. I'm not saying you don't love him exactly, but there is a difference between loving someone and being in love with someone. When Tom called he and I talked about how—"

"—You and Tom talked about me behind my back?" I snap, I reach the first set of elevators and push the floor button. "Clara, you know nothing of my relationship with Riley, you don't know what goes on behind closed doors."

"Don't shout...and Tom's just worried about you," Clara's tone is full of apprehension you couldn't miss. *"You're right, I don't know what goes on behind closed doors but I know what you tell me. I just don't want you jumping into a marriage*

153

because you're convincing yourself that he's perfect. He definitely is not perfect; a perfect man wouldn't try to change your entire lifestyle, appearance—"

"—That is not fair, Clara. He does it because he's health conscious and he cares about me."

"You don't think that maybe, just maybe, you're trying to convince yourself of that? I think you're ignoring those feelings that are popping up that tell you, something isn't right. All because you think he's the best you've had, and will ever have."

I stalk into the elevator as the doors swing open, squeezing through the exiting people.

"No offense, Clara, but I don't think *you* should be giving advice on love or relationships. Things have been hard on Riley since the accident."

"Hard on Riley? I'm sorry, who had the concussion? It's always been 'Riley thinks this' 'Riley suggests this' 'Riley, Riley, Riley' and I think the reason you guys are fighting is because you are finally, deep down, realizing that you've been the only one doing all the changing!"

"I'm sorry I have to go," I cut her off angrily; "I'm losing you in this elevator."

I end the call and throw the phone into my purse as the elevator's doors close.

As if my mood couldn't get any worse.

It took the short fifteen second ride up for me to realize that Clara had made some great points. I hated her for it. Did I love Riley? Of course I loved him, but did I love him enough to marry him? He hasn't listened to a thing I've said about the wedding, that I can't deny. But is it worth throwing away? Why is part of me so relieved after yesterday's fight? And the other part is so, so confused and torn?

I need a plan; after this meeting I will head over to Riley's office and force him to listen to me, with no interruptions. I'll tell him everything I'm feeling, this relationship could work with some effort from both of our parts. After all, we are adults, this was real life and this was how relationships worked. It's not always raw and passionate.

154

I look down at my phone and send Riley a quick message,

I will be at your office in about an hour so we can talk.

I hit send and throw the phone into my purse confidently.

Once I was inside Meyers and Brant I make a beeline straight to Terrance's side of the firm and find Greg leaving the break room with a cup of coffee in his hands. When he sees me, he stops and smiles,

"Morning."

"Good morning," I smile back.

"You look great," he gave me a once over and a thumbs up sign with his spare hand,

"Thanks, I figured if I was about to be fired then I may as well look good."

"Fired?" Greg frowns at me. "He's not going to fire you. He's going to apologize, he said he felt like a jackass and needed to make amends."

I don't know if I believe Greg, after all, this is Terrance.

"Shocked me too," Greg laughs. "Maybe he's changed his tone? You did nab him McFadden, so he owes you."

I had forgotten about that.

"How is that going?"

"Pretty well, so far. Future ex-McFadden says she has evidence of him cheating though, so we have to deal with that," Greg says with a shrug. "Your other boss is in there right now."

"Porter?" I frown.

"He showed up about ten minutes ago."

"Why is Porter here?" I look from Greg to the closed office door a few feet away.

"I don't know."

"He wants to sell the company!"

Edie's shriek vibrates down the hallway.

She appears in front of me, her face tightened and beet red. Her usual delicate strawberry blond hair is a frizzy mess, and she's in a purple house coat. It takes me a moment to breathe her in, having never seen her without a hair out of place.

"There's no will and Merida will get the entire company!" Edie yells at me, her hands in the air. "She's been hounding Porter to sell it to her and to start the auction; did you know that the auction is next Thursday? I could just kill that Scottish hussy. Porter feels pressured without the will to make a decision and he's tired of feeling stressed out."

Relax Edie; we have time to think about how to stop the auction.

"You have to go straight into storage and search every single piece of furniture when you get back to the house," Edie orders pointing through Greg. "Ask him about the investigator. Ask him."

"Greg, has Terrance used his investigator recently?"

Greg's brow scrunches and he slowly shakes his head, "I don't think so. Oh! A few months back he did. On a perspective client, why?" he slowly frowns and his eyes dart around my face.

"No reason, just curious."

"This man is an idiot," Edie swats Greg away with her hands and turns her back on him, "get in that office and stop that sale!"

How exactly, do I do that?

"I don't know!" Edie screams back.

The ceiling light above Greg and I flickers, and he looks up cautiously.

"Get rid of him," Edie orders gesturing at Greg, "I have a plan."

"Greg can you get me a cup of tea, please?"

"Sure" he smiles, "milk and one sugar right?"

"Perfect."

He backs away into the break room and Edie scoffs at him then places her eyes on me,

"Get into that office and follow my lead."

I let my purse slide down my arm and hurry towards the office. I knock only once and walk in casually. I find Terrance behind his desk, in a dark green suit tailored against his stocky build. He looks up, slightly frowning at my intrusion. Porter stands opposite him, his attention drawn off of Terrance, in a pair of grey trousers, a matching vest and white dress shirt.

"Sorry," I say looking from Porter to Terrance. "I thought you were alone."

I see Terrance's brow twitch, and I can tell that his first instinct is to scream at me to leave, but instead he clears his throat forcing a wobbly smile over his greying goatee. "Come in Ms. Mercer. Mr. Burroughs and I are just finishing up."

Edie, where are you?

Porter looks back at Terrance, "So, as I was saying. I'd need to review the contract before we hand it over to Merida. To make sure the children's charity stays on as a benefactor."

"Of course, of course," Terrance nods. "I've written down all your requests. Merida is very keen on buying out your aunt's half of the company so I don't see a problem with anything."

"And she intends to keep her promise about not liquidating?"

"Absolutely," Terrance nods.

Fat chance.

I stand awkwardly, looking around the room for Edie.

"I would also like a copy of the investor's bill. I intend to sell my shares, and have some interested buyers on the sidelines."

"Very good," Terrance stands slowly and puts a hand forward so Porter may shake it. "It feels good to be working together again Porter. I sympathize with you about your aunt's mistake in destroying the only copy of her will. Everything would have gone much simpler if she hadn't."

Where the hell are you, Edie?

"Indeed, very unlike her to do so but there is nothing I can do about. I'm sure Merida will be pleased, owning the last sixty percent of the company," Porter shook Terrance's hand and quickly pulled back. "She can rebrand it as she wishes."

"Wait, I thought she was interested in retiring and handing it to her kids?" I blurt out.

Both Porter and Terrance look over at me, but only Terrance eyes me warily.

"At least that's what Edie told me..." I look from Terrance to Porter, who slides both hands into his pockets and frowns at me.

"Phoebe," Terrance clears his throat, "I'm sure Mr. Burroughs isn't comfortable discussing—"

"—Its fine," Porter gives him a cool glance and then looks back over at me. From the corner of my eye I can see Terrance stiffen, as he pretends to be distracted by something on his desk. "Merida has no plans to sell it; she plans to bring it further into the modern times, which my aunt was never comfortable in doing. With the money Merida received from her late husband's life insurance, she's able to invest in it."

That doesn't make sense; Edie told me Merida's husband left her none of his life insurance. He left it all to their children.

She's lying to Porter.

"I'll have the contracts printed right away," Terrance walks around his desk and reaches Porter. "Then have them sent straight over to the house."

"You can't sell Lavish Looks!" I don't mean to yell but I do, and my voice echoes around the room as Porter and Terrance look at me.

With an annoyed breath and eye roll, Terrance opens his mouth, "Ms. Mercer—"

"—Edie didn't want Merida to have it all."

"Phoebe," Terrance exhales, "this is business and—"

"—I know where the will is."

Why-*Why* did I say that?!

Terrance freezes and Porter frowns at me before speaking. "How did you know it was missing?"

My mind draws a blank as I try to think of a viable explanation. I obviously can't tell them Edie's ghost told me it was missing can I?

"Where is it?" the urgency in Terrance's voice is profuse and he even takes a step forward.

"I'd rather not say." I look from Terrance to Porter, back to Terrance, "just in case I'm wrong."

Terrance drops his head and rubs his forehead with two fingers. "I'm sorry, Porter. I don't think Ms. Mercer has any idea the importance of this situation—"

"—I do too know the importance," I shoot back with a glare.

It's silent in the room as the three of us stare at each other and after a few awkward seconds Porter turns around, gathering his things on Terrance's desk. "I suppose I should give you both a moment. I'll send the contracts back tomorrow morning."

"Very good," Terrance walks with him to the door and I move out of their way, watching as Terrance places a hand on Porter's back ever so lightly, to hurry him from the room. "I'll be waiting for your call, fantastic doing business with you again, Porter."

Part of me knows I should slip out after Porter, but Terrance is now blocking the door so I could never sneak out without shoving him aside. As soon as Porter's gone, Terrance shuts his office door and spins on his heel to face me.

Gone is any bearing of an apology and kind attitude. He's back to his old self, scary bushy eyebrows and all. "Where's the will Phoebe?"

"I told you I won't say," I repeat glaring back at him, my feet are glued to the carpet, "and what's it any of your business anyway? You *aren't* her lawyer. She fired you."

His face releases quickly and he cocks an eyebrow, "So you do know more than I thought. What did you find when you broke into my office?"

"I don't have time for this," I move around his words as my grasp tightens around my purse strap. "You called me in for a meeting. I heard it was supposed to be a good one but now I have the feeling you're about to fire me."

"If you don't tell me where the will is I'll more than fire you," his voice deepens as he walks closer to me. "I'll fax a letter to every firm in this city depicting you as the most useless, laziest legal aid I have ever had the displeasure of working with. Your career will be over before it can even begin. Taking the bar will be meaningless because nobody will hire you."

Well, it looks as if my day *can* get worse.

There's a knock at the door and it slowly opens. Terrance keeps his back turned but from behind him, I can see Greg shuffle in with a mug in his hand, and he slowly extends his arm to me.

"Thank you Greg," I master my feet to finally move and hurry around Terrance. "But I have to get going."

I bolt down the hall as fast as my heels can carry me.

I'm pretty sure that was the last time I will ever go back into Meyers and Brant. I'm certain Terrance is drafting that horrible letter as I leave the building.

My God, I've fought with almost everyone today haven't I?

Edie, the cause of all of this, is nowhere to be found. I can't believe she just abandoned me in that office. She just let me waltz in with no idea what to say or do. What became of it? A huge lie, again. I have no idea where the will is, I don't even have a clue as to where it *could* be. Edie just keeps feeding me suggestions after suggestions, which are getting me nowhere.

Have I ruined my life because of a ghost?

I'm standing on the edge of the sidewalk, hailing a cab, as my mind races.

I spot a cab from the distance, and throw up my hand, when a grey sports car pulls up next to me. I stumble backwards as the driver's side window rolls down, and see Porter looking out at me, "Please get in. We need to talk."

I'm about to tell him politely, that I don't have the time. I should be heading over to talk to Riley, attempt to fix that part of my cascading life. Porter must sense my apprehension because he runs a hand through his hair, "I need to speak with you about my aunt."

I bite my lip, "I guess I have a few minutes to spare. As long as you could give me a ride?"

"I can," he nods motioning for me to hurry.

I run along the front of the car and towards the passenger side door. I open it and slide into the leather seat next to him. The car was tight, and as I glance over my shoulder I notice there was no backseat, just a small gap between the two front seats and the trunk. The gap was covered in file folders taped shut, two briefcases, and a few bags of fast food. The car jerks forward and I turn around, letting my purse fall between my feet.

"You have no idea where my aunt's will is, do you?" Porter asks me, as he swerves into the next lane to pass a slow cab. He looks at me only briefly, choosing to keep his focus on the road. "Where am I taking you?"

"Off King Street, north end of town, and I don't know *exactly* where the will is but I may have an idea." I answer him truthfully and place a hand on the dashboard as he slams the breaks to a fading yellow light. "You're not used to driving here, are you?"

"Not really," he keeps one hand on the wheel as his blue eyes dart my way. For a moment, I think I catch something mischievous about them. "Where do you think her will is?"

"In her room?" I'm grasping at straws here and Porter frowns at me,

"I've checked her room countless times."

"Under the mattress?"

"Now why would you think it would be there?" he watches me as I give him a shrug and then looks back at the road. "You're troubled that Merida will get Lavish Looks, but she's the only one who seems to care about it as much as Edie did."

I wonder if he's telling this to me or if he's saying it to himself; to ease the guilt of being unable to take over the company.

"I have a feeling Edie wouldn't want Merida to own Lavish Looks. I certainly wouldn't trust her with it," I shift in my seat as the light turns green and he slowly rolls across the intersection. "I mean she lost a chunk of her own money being irresponsible. Who knows what she'll do with the company once she's the CEO. It's just my opinion."

"I see," he slowly nods, "I have to ask, were you on her case when Terrance constructed her will?"

"No," I answer quickly, "he didn't have Greg or me on it with him."

"Her missing will is a serious situation; because of it I have to do what I think is best for the company, the house and her money. Aunt Edie fired Terrance and destroyed her will without even writing up a new one. That was irresponsible of her, and now it's thrown my life in a loop."

I want to tell him that Edie is just as stressed, that she's torn my life upside down because of it too. That there is in fact another will and its missing as well, but God, he'd think I was crazy for sure. And a liar. "Merida is the irresponsible one, the shady one."

"I don't think Terrance would have enjoyed you calling his client shady."

"Merida is his client?" I stare at Porter as he drives,

"She is."

I look back at the busy road in front of us.

This changes *everything*. Edie has no idea Terrance is Merida's lawyer otherwise she would have mentioned it to me. Merida hid that from her when she was alive.

"How long have you known Merida?" I ask,

"All my life I suppose."

"Do you like her?"

"She isn't someone I would spend my free time with, no."

"Do you trust her? I mean after the whole debacle with her money?"

He eyes me guardedly as he pulls up to another red light, "I don't suppose I would."

"So why would you sell Lavish Looks to her?"

"Who else would be interested?" Porter sighs as he grabs the wheel with both hands. "The only other parties are companies that plan to shut it down. I don't know anything about beauty products; I don't have the time or the energy to deal with a company like this. Merida will have the help of the board and creative directors."

"Couldn't you hire someone to take over managing?"

"I could, yes," Porter makes a left turn towards the large bridge, "but everyone qualified would need a large salary. My aunt and Merida took less than they should of when it came to their payday."

"I think you should hold back on signing the papers," I say. "I know it's a huge favor to ask, but I think you should really reconsider all of this. Give it a few days then sign things if you can't find the will."

He sighs, and from the way he looks at me I can tell his answer is going to be a swift no.

"For Aunt Edie's sake?" I push, "Just have one more look around."

We reach the next intersection and stop at the red light. He takes his hands off the wheel and reaches over to his smartphone which rests between us in a cup holder. "I suppose I could check under the mattress…"

I smile as he taps away at his phone and fall back into my seat; my mind buzzing like crazy. One thought after another pops in, none with an answer. Does Merida know about the missing will? Of course she does, she has to. Terrance is using her just like he's using Marta isn't he? Why use both of them? Isn't that a lot of work for one man? Marta is worth such a small sum, it would make sense to put his focus on Merida.

I glance back over at Porter and catch sight of his phone. He's emailing Terrance and I can see the words 'extension', 'more time' , and 'cautious' in the email text. My chest relaxes.

Now we have some time, let's hope it's enough.

"Are you alright? You look a bit pale."

I touch my face feeling no difference in touch and reach up to flip down the mirror. I hold in a gasp as I peek at myself. I do look ghastly; the bags under my eyes have returned and I've lost the rosy complexion on my cheeks that I began to notice after Faye mentioned it.

"I'm okay," I flip the mirror back up, "it's probably because I haven't eaten today."

"I haven't eaten either," he says. "Would you like to get a bite to eat before I drop you off?"

I don't suppose I should have this talk with Riley on an empty stomach, especially if he ends up getting angry at me again. I'll have more strength to calm him down if I eat beforehand.

"That would be nice."

Chapter Fourteen

There was a little eatery near the water that Porter suggested. It was an Italian run restaurant, and the food he claimed was outstanding. They had a deck in the back overlooking the river which gave a beautiful view in the evening, he said. It was called Olivia's, after the grandmother in the family who originally opened the small bistro. Her son and his wife ran it now with their children.

It was located between a butcher shop and a pastry shop, in a long red brick building only a few stories high. On the outside it was nothing to look at, a simple large window with the name printed in cursive across it, and a glass door tinted so you couldn't see inside. However, inside it was magnificent; exposed brick throughout, and pictures of beautiful country sides I only assume where in Italy. Hanging brass chandeliers came down from the ceiling; each table was square and possessed the cliché red and white checkered table cloth. There was a beautiful wooden archway in the back leading to the patio and you could see the skyline across the river.

We are led to the back of the restaurant through the archway, out the open doors and onto the patio by a female matradee. It only housed seven tables being so small, but the patio was exquisite with an iron railing sitting three feet high, as to not block the view of the skyline or water. String lights twisted through them and came down from the west and east side like waterfalls. Above our heads was a red, cloth dome tent. We are given a table in the corner of the patio where there are two waiting menus on the plates.

"You must eat here a lot," I say after we sit, "she led you straight to this table."

"I eat here once a week," Porter says as he picks up his menu, "I took aunt Edie here once."

I can't help but smirk as I think of the two of them dining together, "How did she like it?"

"The restaurant she approved of," Porter looked up at me from his menu, "my girlfriend she did not."

"Oh," I laugh as I imagine Edie glancing her way, with eye rolls and critical remarks, about her posture or her views on fashion or politics. "She was something wasn't she?"

"That she was," Porter sets down his menu. "Although she was right about that girl, dull as a doornail I believe were her words. It wasn't till she said it that I realized how boring Evelyn was. She had a knack for waking people up from their disillusions."

"She doesn't like my fiancé either," I tell him truthfully.

"What did she think of him?"

"I believe she called him an…" I crinkle my brow as I try to remember her exact words, "space cadet."

"And what did he say?"

"Nothing, he's never met her."

A round but short woman with an olive complexion and shaggy red hair appears at our table. She's in a long red dress with a white apron overtop of it and she clasps her hands at Porter,

"Two times in one week Porter!" her Italian accent is thick, "What a treat. I don't believe we have had you for brunch ever."

"Hello Lusia, how are you today?" Porter smiles up at her and for a moment I'm thrown by the sight of it. It's bright and broad, if I had just met him I would have assumed all he did was smile. It was natural and infectious. My heart skipped a hard beat and I looked down as my cheeks reddened.

"Better than yesterday," she gave him a pat on the back and looked my way. Her dark eyes ran all over me and she smiled crookedly at me. "And who is this?" Suddenly she gasps and lunges at my hand, removing it from the menu and staring at my engagement ring. "You didn't tell us you were betrothed Porter, congratulations! She's very pretty!"

I feel myself flush again, and Porter shifts uneasily in his seat as he clears his throat. "No Lusia. I'm just her employer."

"Oh," Lusia's entire attitude halts and she slowly lets go of my hand, "well I apologize for the mistake." Graciously she looks back at me and smiles again, "a congratulations to you my dear, it is a lovely ring."

165

"Thank you," I give it a quick glance wondering if she even meant it as I look back into the menu. "Everything looks so good here."

"No," she snaps the menu from my hands, "no menu for you two. I know just what to make you. It's a new recipe and I would love for the two of you to try it out for me. I promise it will be spectacular!"

"Oh, um does this plate have any meat on it by chance?" I ask, raising a finger at her slowly. Her posture falls a little bit and she frowns at me,

"You don't eat meat?"

It's then that I remember I'm sitting with Porter, and not Riley. Nobody will yell if I eat meat.

As I look back at Lusia, I feel instant guilt. She looks like she's about to cry, her mouth dips in the corners. It's as if I disappointed my grandmother.

"Of course I eat meat," I laugh too loudly, "I was just kidding."

Lusia then laughs herself, "That was a good one. Okay I will be back in a few minutes."

After she leaves us, the Matradee reappears with water in a beautiful glass jug. She fills our glasses and leaves us quickly, all the while glancing at Porter as she pours. I find Porter hiding a smile when I look back at him.

"You don't eat meat do you?" He's stifling a laugh, and I find myself grinning because of it. It's like I'm sitting with a completely different person. His whole demeanour is open, charming, his laugh lines are prominent around his mouth.

Finally I answer him, afraid he'll catch me staring at his smile. "No I do, it's just that, I'm not supposed to."

"Because of your accident?" he wonders leaning forward in his seat.

I shake my head as I reach for the water in my glass. "No, because Riley is going vegan for the wedding and wants me to, too."

"But you've been eating Rosanne's food and most of it contains some kind of meat," Porter frowns at me as he lays his hands on the table casually.

"I know," I make a face; "it's horrible isn't it? Riley thinks I'm sticking to the whole vegan thing. Edie hates it; she laughed when she heard about it."

Slowly, Porter smiles a little at me and dips his head.

"What?" I take a drink of my water as he looks back at me,

"You talk about her as if she is still around."

"Oh," I set down my glass and watch some water spill over the edge, "I don't mean to. It just sort of slips out I guess."

"How long have you been engaged?" Porter asks motioning to the ring on my finger.

"I got engaged the day of my accident, believe it or not," I play with the ring on my finger.

"And his advertising firm? Is he doing well?" Porter then asks.

I forgot that Riley had pitched to them, and I hadn't even asked Riley how it went either. Oh God, maybe I have been selfish?

"I suppose so, he doesn't talk about it much really," I shrug. "He's been pitching to a lot of clients though."

"Oh," Porter leans back into his seat and nods, "That's good."

His tone is less than optimistic, however, and I just can't help but ask what I do. "I know its conflict of interest but how did he do? Pitching to you?"

"I'm going to be honest with you," Porter's voice is serious again and he clears his throat. "I have never been presented to by someone who knows absolutely nothing about advertising, and yet is so egotistical."

With his answer I feel embarrassed, uncomfortable. I can picture Riley presenting and everything I picture matches with what Porter said. He must have looked like such a fool. Did he even research anything?

"I shouldn't have said that," Porter suddenly says looking down at the table.

I look up from the ring, "No. It's alright. I'm glad you were truthful."

It doesn't look like he believes me; he nods slow at my answer anyway and leans back into his seat, looking out over the railing at the city view. The sun was at high noon already and it beat off his dirty blond hair, producing shadows across his stern face. He looked effortlessly at ease, something I deduced never happened for him.

From the corner of my eye, I could see the matradee standing in the archway, pretending to shine the wood and using any opportunity to look over at him.

I was suddenly aware of just how good looking he was to me and it made me nervous. It had been a while since I was around someone who drew me in with his magnetic charm. My stomach began to turn in that exciting way it did whenever I had a school boy crush.

Had I even felt this with Riley? I must have, at one point, at the beginning of our relationship of course. I knew he was attractive from the moment I set eyes on him. He walked into his parents' house from the pool yard shirtless, and tanned, with beads of water dripping down his chest. I remember flirting with him after Terrance left me alone in the kitchen.

"I was engaged once," Porter breaks my thoughts as he looks away from the skyline and back at me.

"What happened?"

"We started quickly, my parents and her parents disapproved for different reasons. We wanted to throw our relationship in their faces, I suppose. I proposed and we were engaged only a month before I realized it was a mistake."

"I'm taking it didn't end well?"

"I thought it had, turns out I was wrong," Porter answers. "She went ahead and married my best friend out of spite. It appeared that he had been harboring strong feelings for her ever since I introduced them."

"That must be awkward."

"It was yes, but we don't communicate with each other anymore,"

"You don't speak?" I feel myself become deflated at the thought of losing a best friend. I couldn't imagine losing Clara, Faye or Satine.

"We tried to keep in touch but there was hostility. One evening we exchanged some choice words, and never spoke again."

168

Porter looks back at me, and I feel as if he's about to tell me more to the story when his cell phone rings. I watch him remove it from his jacket and place it to his ear saying,

"Porter here."

His eyes are focused on the plate in front of him now and slowly, he begins to frown. I watch him lean forward and place his elbow on the table before rubbing his forehead with his spare hand.

"Alright, alright. Give me thirty minutes, and I'll be right over."

With a drawn in breath, he hangs up the call and looks up at me,

"I'm sorry Phoebe but I have to head over to Lavish Looks. Merida has called a board meeting that I was uninformed of. I'll have to get our meal to go." Slowly he pulls away from the table and stands up, but before he walks away he glances down at me, "Would you like to go with me? Have a look inside of Lavish Looks?"

I bite my lip and look down at the watch on my wrist. It's already after twelve and I'm supposed to be in Riley's office, although he hasn't responded to my earlier message. If Edie where here she'd want me to head into Lavish Looks and deal with Riley later this evening. She'd tell me Riley clearly didn't want to see me yet, if he hadn't responded to my earlier message, that maybe he needed more time. She'd probably call me a fool too, wouldn't she?

I look up at Porter and smile, "Sure, I'd love to come along."

We drove back to Cedar Springs, but our destination was set on the other side of town; Behind its quaint downtown core, Festival Park, past its colorful campground and the town's only public beach. We drove up a large dirt path, the ten feet high gates to the road had been propped open and we approached an old-fashioned brown bricked building the length of a football field. It was only one story high and to the left, it extended to a large steel building several stories high, with square glass windows only at the very top where the roof met the wall.

169

A parking lot stretched out across the whole building and most spaces where occupied except for one right in front of the building doors. Porter slide into the space and turned off the engine. He gestures at the old building,

"This is the main office of Lavish Looks. It used to be a coffee factory for a local brew house before Aunt Edie bought it from them. It houses all of the company's departments, marketing, sales, public relations, even design. Further down," he motions to the left with his head, "is the factory that produces and packages the products. Shipping and Receiving comes in on a road on the other side."

"It's impressive."

We exit the car and head towards the generic glass doors, coming into a round lobby with dark hard wood floors and extraordinary vintage 1930's panel walls. There's a reception desk shaped as a circle in the centre of the room, and the older woman behind it just gives us both a nod as we cross the room. There are two doors behind her desk, about ten feet apart from each other, and in between them sits a security guard whose head is down in his crossword puzzle.

Porter leads me to the door to the left and pulls it open for me.

"These are the main offices at the factory, Merida and Edie's office are this way, and so is our managing C.O.O, Vanessa Terzis. We also have boardrooms this way and a product testing room."

The hallway we venture down is long but wide, with grey carpets and white walls. We pass doors marked for their purpose. When we reach a divide in the hallway Porter pointed to the right where I noticed a single glass door frosted over,

"That door way leads to our other divisions, and the working floors."

"Is it always this empty?" I ask, and follow him away from the other door.

"No, not usually. But everyone is either in the board room already or on lunch."

Porter stops abruptly at a door to our left and I see that it's marked Board Room One. He turns the door handle and pushes the door, waltzing in with no regard. I follow him in quickly and enter a room full of commotion.

It's a general board room with grey carpet and white walls, two ferns in the corner of the room. There was a long table in the centre, with a total of twelve chairs beneath it. There was a set of windows across the room, white blinds cast over them and standing before that window was a short round man dressed in a very tacky red and blue suit. He had a bow tie fastened around his collar with prints of dog paws all over it. His wispy brown hair was greying and thin. His face was contorted however with a shade of exasperated pink from frustration as he stood with his hands on his hips.

Merida stood across from him, in black heels that made her nearly six feet tall. She was in a pale tight skirt and a matching frilly top with a plunging neckline.

"You are a cheap dictator," the man spat her way. "I don't know how Edie put up with you!"

"How dare you speak to me like that, I could squish you like the fat fruit fly you are," Merida stomps one foot as she places her hands on her hips, "pack your desk Henry. Today is your last day."

"Just a moment," Porter raises his voice and the two of them take their eyes off each other. They clearly hadn't heard us enter the room because they both suddenly fix their demeanour and posture. "What is going on here?"

"Mr. Rubano thinks it's *his* business that I call this emergency board meeting. I'm trying to remind him he is nothing but our managing accountant and book keeper. What goes on in the commercial end is none of his concern," Merida's voice screams with aggravation.

"It *is* my business as a shareholder!" He glares back at her, "I have a right to protest any change of leadership within the company."

"Be quiet, you fat man," Merida hisses down at him. Henry lets out a drawn out gasp and his faces begins to flush again, as he twists his head back at Porter.

"Do you really intend to hand this company over to this vile, greedy woman—"

"—What is the maid doing here?" Merida throws her arm out and points at me, cutting Henry off in the process.

"Ms. Mercer was with me at lunch," Porter explains. "Merida? Firstly you cannot fire Henry; it falls outside of your responsibilities. Secondly, Henry is right, he does have the ability to protest any change of leadership, along with the other stakeholders."

"Then I shall simply remove him as a stakeholder under Clause 7.8 in the contract," Merida lets out a stiff laugh, "the moment I have complete control of the company."

"Merida, I have the contracts to sign from Terrance," Porter tells her, "I just need some time—"

"—You've had time! Over a month's worth of time," Merida counters. "I thought this was all going to be dealt with by tonight, I thought you had enough sense to sign that contract but no…Since you have been teetering on the decision of whether or not to sell the company to me, our stocks have fallen, and our sales are following suit. The delay of our next scent line has caused concern and disappointment. The launch of our organic make up line has now been halted because of your lack of decisiveness. I have rallied several board members against you and today we vote on removing you as acting CEO. Enough is enough. That is, unless you sign the papers we agreed on."

This woman is evil.

"Outrageous!" Henry bursts moving from behind her. "You are a despicable woman. Don't sign anything Porter."

I wish I could see Porter's face, but I can only imagine it from standing behind him.

"Move along Mr. Rubano," Merida shoos him away as if he was indeed a fruit fly. "In a few hours you'll be leaving Lavish Looks for good."

There's a drawn out silence in the room, heavy and painful, twirling around the four of us. Merida breaks it, her eyes never leaving Porter, "You're welcome to join us Porter for the vote but sadly, your maid is not." Her eyes dart my way for only a moment.

"Phoebe!"

Glancing behind me, I see Edie, standing through the doors, completely changed from this morning. A big yellow floppy hat over her strawberry curls. She's gesturing for me to approach her, "I need to speak with you."

Where have you been! Do you have any idea what has been going on? Porter was about to give Merida the company, contracts sealed and now she's planning to vote him out because he emailed Terrance that he needed more time. She'll get the company for free. Do you understand that? While you have been fixing yourself up everything has—

"—Just excuse yourself and come with me! That hussy won't be voting anyone out today."

Swallowing and trusting her, I speak to the room. "I should leave. This seems like a private matter."

I back myself up to the door and reach for the handle behind me, as Merida watches, eyes into me like daggers. I quickly pull the door open and hurry outside, shutting it behind me. I can hear them begin to speak again, but Merida's boasting squeals overpower Porter and Henry.

Poor Porter, he must feel so backed into a corner. All he wanted to do was help with everything. Sure, he can seem intimidating and cool to everyone, but really he—

Edie clearing her throat cuts through my thoughts, "Are we finished gushing?"

"I wasn't gushing," I spin on my heels to face her and instantly feel annoyed. "How could you just leave me at the firm? You told me you had a plan and you threw me in with nothing."

"Forgive me," her tone is less than merciful as she swats her hand at me. "I had nothing planned but you're quick on your feet, so I knew you would do something."

"I did do something!" I snap as she begins to glide down the hallway. "I stupidly told them I thought I knew where your will was!"

"*You what?*" Edie spins around dramatically, "Why? Phoebe, must you always run amuck when I leave you alone?"

"I was trying to stop Porter from selling Lavish Looks, which obviously you care little about anyway to have disappeared and left me—"

"—Where did you tell them you think it is?" Edie's voice is strangely calm.

173

"I told Porter it may be under the mattress. The Mattress! Can you believe that?"

Edie smirks and shrugs as we hurry down the hallway, "Mobsters keep money under their mattresses, so it's not too farfetched. Although, I know I would never hide it there. I couldn't lift my mattress."

She moves around the corner and I rush to follow her. As I turn it, I find her a few feet away from me gesturing at the fire alarm as if she's Vanna White. "I found this."

She wants me to commit another felony.

"I am not doing that," I tell her, hands on my hips, "no way."

"Then let the rest of the board members get here and vote Porter out. Let me down, and poor Henry, and every other employee in here that is intent on leaving should Merida be appointed CEO," she casually shrugs and folds her arms over her chest. "I personally couldn't live with that on my conscious."

I raise my eyebrows at her, "I'm sure you could live with a lot more, knowing you."

"Just pull it!" Edie orders with a shriek.

It really was the easiest way to stop the board meeting, and I hated that Edie was, once again right. With a loud breath I walk over to her and shut my eyes as I reach up to the alarm. I feel the cool metal handle and grip my fingers around it. I cannot believe I'm doing this.

I tug once and the handle comes down easily, within seconds the alarm goes off. It's deafening and I have to cover my ears with my hand. Edie disappears and I find myself running down the hall, out the door into the lobby.

As I wait by Porter's car, I watch the employee's file out from different entrances and all gather in the parking lot. Edie is gone and for that I'm glad, I needed the moment to be alone without her badgering. My cellphone is in my hands, with missed calls from Clara. There was nothing from Riley.

He hadn't even replied to my text from this morning, and as I glance at the time I realise its well after one o'clock now. Perhaps he had no intention of speaking with me today? Maybe it really was over? I mean, if he had second thoughts wouldn't he have reached out to see what was taking me so long?

"Phoebe."

I look up to see Porter rushing towards me and his car, buttoning up his suit jacket, "I have to head back to the house and make some phone calls. I can send a car to take you back to the city."

I push up from the hood and look down at my phone.

I suppose it really is over.

A mass of feelings come over me; there's a bout of sorrow from being severed from Riley that causes my heart to ache heavily against my warm chest. Then there's the spell of irritation from the man not having the decency to reach out to me in. Is it normal that the latter is the feeling more dominant?

I can't go back to the loft right now. I don't want to go back to it.

"No, it's alright," I slip the phone back into my bag and hurry towards the passenger side, "I'll just come back to the house with you. See if Rosanne needs any help."

Chapter Fifteen

"We'll look in my room later tonight when everyone is asleep, after midnight. Yes, that's what we'll do. I'm sure we'll find the will in there."

When we got back to the house Porter ran straight into the library upstairs and shut the door. Rosanne had me cleaning the guest rooms today so she could focus on cooking meals for Porter, since it was supposed to be her weekend off. The only time I saw her leave the kitchen was whenever she brought Porter his coffee or something to eat. Anytime I had returned down to my room, I impulsively checked my phone; nobody else had reached out to me.

Part of me was relieved, another part was let down by it. What could I expect though really? They could only hound me so long until giving up.

I took a long supper in the kitchen with Rosanne, who spoke little to me but would occasionally glance my way whenever she thought I wasn't aware. Marta left before dinner, barely saying a word to me but complaining to Rosanne about having to work the next day.

It was now nine p.m. and I had hit a level of exhaustion I hadn't felt in years. I was laying on the bed in my small room, with only the dim lighting from the lamp on my nightstand on. I was still in my uniform, staring up at the white ceiling as Edie paced the floor next to me.

"Oh for goodness sake, enough with the melodrama," Edie sighs standing over the bed now and looking down at me. "I'm positive you'll find a man ten times better than that vegan."

"Edie, please. I don't want to discuss my personal life with you."

"Well that's your problem! You never want to discuss it with anyone," Edie says. "Maybe if you talked about things with someone, you would feel better. You would get some perspective."

"I had planned to do that with Riley earlier today."

"Not Riley, I mean a friend. Someone outside of the situation."

"That's what Satine, Clara and Faye are for."

"Mmmm…yes," Edie murmurs, "and exactly how did that go for you? How open had you been, how vulnerable to their suggestions and opinions?"

Well played Edie.

"I thought so," Edie smirks.

"Never the less, I don't want to talk about it."

Slowly I shut my eyes hoping she'll get the hint but she keeps talking.

"You did well today. I don't applaud the part where you told Porter and Terrance you thought you knew where the will could be, but you could have said worse. And at least it has Terrance on his toes."

I pry my eyes up and look over to her, "Did you know he is Merida's lawyer?"

"Oh he's more than her lawyer," Edie's face twists in disgust and I feel my jaw drop,

"No!"

"Oh yes. Apparently there is no level that man won't stoop to for money."

"How long?" I push myself up and bring my knees into my chest.

"Almost a year, right after her husband had his heart attack and died," Edie answers, "He's promised to leave his wife for her."

I can't help but laugh, "She cannot believe that he's serious? His wife is heir to a fortune! I doubt even with Lavish Looks Merida would have that kind of money."

"You should have seen Merida after the two of you left Lavish Looks. The Fire Marshall told her he had to do an investigation throughout the weekend just in case, so the building would be on lock down. I've only seen that shade of red on her once, and it wasn't complementary back then, either. Porter's been on the phone with some board members. Turns out, Merida wouldn't have secured enough votes to take the reins from Porter as she so previously thought," Edie explains. "I haven't heard him say a word about the contract though, but I have a feeling he's going ahead with it if he doesn't find the will soon. This whole mess has given him quite the headache. I've never known him to give up on anything before, but this could be the one time. Henry has been calling him nonstop, I assume about what happened today in the boardroom but he hasn't taken his call."

"Henry is an old friend of yours?" I prop the pillow up behind me so I can lean into it.

"An old beau actually," Edie declares nonchalantly. "We dated decades ago, before I married. It was a brief and fun affair."

"So that's why he's so loyal to you." I begin to joke, raising my eyebrows, "he's probably still in love with you, heartbroken over your death and the treatment your beloved company is getting."

"Oh please," Edie rolls her eyes at me.

"I bet he is, or, at least still harbors feelings."

"Speaking of feelings," Edie's eyebrows rise now as she places her hands delicately at her hips, her yellow garden dress ruffling a bit. "I saw you and Porter today, at lunch."

"So?"

"So…" she moves closer to the bed, "did I detect a little chemistry between the two of you?"

I let out a bellowing laugh, "Edie. Please."

"I'm just saying it like I saw it," she nods, "and that, is what I saw."

"I am not interested in your nephew," I tell her firmly. "Please don't get any ideas. I'm not in the right frame of mind to bother with any romances, new or old."

"It's not like you're taken," Edie tells me with a breath. "You're newly single. And Porter is a great catch and he's also single."

"Edie, no."

We're silent for a while merely looking around the room and at each other.

"He likes you."

I frown at her, "who?"

"The Pope!" Edie jokes as she rolls her eyes at me. "Porter, who else?"

"He doesn't like me," I sit up slowly. I suddenly feel very watched under Edie's eye as I adjust the two pillows behind my back. I'm careful not to think anything remotely incriminating, since she can interject herself inside my thoughts.

"I know my nephew."

"Edie, I need to get some sleep, alright? Wake me up at midnight."

I lean into the pillows quickly and shut my eyes. After a moment I turn my back on her to prove my point and hear her let out a frustrated sigh.

"Fine. I'll be back in two hours."

I open my eyes a second later and look over my shoulder, finding the room empty. I toss myself on my back and place my hands under my head, looking up at the ceiling again.

Porter likes me?

I might have been able to stop myself from thinking about Edie's claim but I wasn't able to stop the feeling that popped up when she said those three words. A mild curiosity, a slight euphoric bubbling that made me feel a whole lot better. How could she really know though? He was always so stone faced. Except I mean, when he smiled at lunch for a brief moment. He did have a great smile.

My phone begins to vibrate next to me, and I reach for it. The screen is lit up and I can see that its Tom calling. I think twice about answering it but my arm has a mind of its own and it places the phone to my ear.

"Hi."

There is silence for a moment, *"Sorry. I assumed that I would be leaving voicemail number 100."*

"Very funny. I'm sorry I haven't returned any of your calls, I have been a tad busy."

"So I've heard, from Clara, and your fiancé."

"You've talked to Riley?" I pull myself up and bring my knees to my chest, "When? Today?"

"Not today. A few days ago, is something wrong?" Tom clearly caught the urgency in my voice.

"No, nothing," I don't feel like getting into the problem of Riley. "Why did you talk to Riley?"

179

"He called me a few days ago. He was concerned about you. It was all I could do to stop him from calling mom."

"He never told me he called you."

"He thinks that you are a bit—"

"—Distracted?"

"Not yourself. He said you can't shut your mind off and relax. I told him I didn't see the problem. It's how you've always been."

"No I haven't."

"Why do you think mom calls you Jitterbug? You never sit still. When have you ever been able to relax? Remember Yoga? You lasted ten minutes into our first session."

"That was over five years ago! I could last now if I wanted to."

Tom laughs, *"I think not."*

I can't help but feel a little bit irritated. "Obviously that is not me, Tom, because it has Riley concerned. Obviously I've changed and become a bit more grounded. Obviously what you think of me hasn't been me in years and frankly—"

"—Phoebe, relax. I was just giving my observation. Clearly you know you better, you are almost thirty and I have noticed you changed since getting into Meyers and Brant. And being with Riley."

"That's right, I have matured." I state with a stern nod, "I've grown; Riley's helped me change and grow."

"Right..." Tom doesn't sound convinced.

Why should he? I suddenly realize. I don't sound convinced myself. Look at me, talking as if I still have a job at Meyers and Brant. As if Riley and I have a future. As if things haven't changed so quickly. There's a tickle in the back of my throat.

Don't cry Phoebe. Don't cry.

I'm grateful for the beep I hear through our line, and when I pull my phone from my ear I see that its Clara calling.

"Tom, I have to go, that's Clara. Could be important."

I hang up before he can say goodbye and switch calls, "Hello?"

"I wasn't sure you would answer after today."

"Me neither."

In drifts that awkward silence which Clara breaks almost instantly, *"I'm sorry. I shouldn't have said those things to you. Phoebs...it's just that you seem so unhappy lately. Maybe I just noticed now because Mark and I are over again or maybe—I don't know. I'm just sorry. You were right; I shouldn't have given you any advice about relationships."*

"No, I'm sorry," I jump upright, "I shouldn't have been so defensive. It's this whole Edie thing. Things are getting more and more complicated, and I don't know what to do."

"That's why I called," Clara's tone becomes animated, *"tomorrow afternoon, cancel your plans. Faye and I are taking you to a medium."*

I don't dare tell Edie my conversation with Clara. There's no need to guess her reaction if I told her that were going to see a medium tomorrow.

Right at midnight, Edie appeared and awoke me from my sleep. She told me Rosanne had decided to stay the night, and Porter had just retired to his room. I snuck upstairs slowly, with the light from my cellphone leading the way as Edie made sure Porter had indeed gone to bed. I met her upstairs in the dark hallway, in front of the white French doors of her bedroom.

I've never been in your room, Edie.

"It's nothing special," Edie declares with a shrug, "now hurry up and get inside."

I push open the doors and scurry into the darkness, as Edie waltzes through the wood.

"The light switch is to your left, along the wall."

I feel for the wall behind me, cold and smooth then run my hand along it. In no time, I feel the plastic outlet and flick the switch up. The lights gradually twinkle on above us.

The room I stand in is smaller than I imagined it would be, for some reason I pictured Edie in a grand room the size of my entire loft. Don't get me wrong, this room is enormous but it's far more cluttered. The walls around me are painted a light blue, almost light teal shade. There are three bay windows to my immediate left, lace curtains cover them elegantly. A gorgeous white 1930's desk sits near the windows, jumbled with large books and small boxes.

The carpet beneath our feet is a dark grey. I spot a seven foot mirror hanging near me on the wall; the frame is vintage and carved white wood. Above it, two directional lamps casting light upon the mirror in an attempt to aid the reflection. A white nightstand sits in the corner, with a vintage 1930's lamp and a stack of books.

The bed before me houses a giant canopy, the fabric coming down the posts and overhead, sheer and grey. The bed has been stripped of its bedding and on top of it are several empty boxes for packing. There are nightstands against it, like the one across the room, and both are cluttered with odds and ends. A large snowy armoire sits on the right side of the room, neatly against the wall near a narrow white door. However it was the glistening grey curtains against the right wall that drew my attention the most. What were they covering?

Her room was definitely impressive, and from the glowing look that had transpired over Edie's face, I was sure she knew it.

"Nice room."

"Isn't it?" Edie leaves my side and walks into the centre of it. Slowly she sniffs the air and makes a face, "Smells funny though."

"That's must," I let her know. "I take it nobody has really cleaned this room in a while, or opened a window."

"For which I am thankful," Edie nods strictly, coasting her arm up, pointing at her desk near the windows. "Check the drawers. There's only three so it shouldn't take you long."

"What's beyond that door?" I ask as I motion to the narrow white door,

"The bathroom."

I reach the desk and slide my phone into the pocket of the maid's uniform. The books on her desk are photo albums, and as I pick up the stack, I notice the weight they hold. They smell stale, and from the design I would guess most of them where from the late seventies and early eighties. I turn and move quickly to place them on the bed behind me, when one of them slips from the top landing with a clunk on the floor at my feet.

"What was that?" Edie has glided over, "Don't be so loud!"

"Go make sure no one heard," I motion with my head at the closed door. I step over the fallen photo album and plop the rest of the pile between the boxes. Slowly I kneel down to collect the one that fell on its side, and as I lift it a few old pictures skid out. I grab one of them, staring down at a black and weight photo of a very young woman in a tie dye blouse and a white peasant skirt. Her hair chutes down her back in beautiful spiral curls and she's laughing as she touches a flower crown placed upon her head. There are no wrinkles and no laugh lines, her blue eyes bright even in the black and white. "This is you, Edie?"

I stay on my knees and lift the picture in the air so Edie can see it, she squints once then nods, "Yes. In the summer of 72 or 73. I can't remember."

"You look really happy," I smile at the picture.

"I was young, I had no wrinkles and nothing sagged. Of course I was happy."

I roll my eyes at her as I watch her pull her head back through the door. "I don't think anybody heard, but just to be safe let me check in on them."

When she's gone, I place the photo back into the front page of the album and pick up the last photo that fell on the ground. On the back, in pen, is written 'Edie & Merida 89'. I pluck up the picture and give it a good look. There they are, in perfect eighties clothing. Edie in a bright power suit, her hair tossed up in massive curls. Merida is on her right, a tight black skirt and a rainbow colored blouse with a square neckline. Her blond hair, severely straight, resting down her long arms. They stand over a desk, upon the desk are empty plastic containers and I recognize the lavender symbol on the label.

This must be them at Lavish Looks when they were about to open it.

"Porter is working away on his laptop, with headphones, and Rosanne is asleep."

I look up to find Edie coming towards me; her face twists at the sight of the photo in my hand, "Ugh. Throw that entire album away. It's of Merida and I when we use to summer together."

"This is the album Merida mentioned at the auction," I suddenly realize as I look down at the washed up brown leather. "She made a comment—"

"—that I didn't even leave her this album after being friends for so long."

We both look at each other. I watch Edie's thin lips spread open and something around her lights up. She gestures at me,

"Well, open it up! Quickly!"

The will has to be in here! Otherwise why would Merida mention it at the auction?

I set the album down, letting go of the picture as I open the first page. Edie kneels down across from me and watches as I start flipping through the pages. They are heavy; a metal lining holds down the corners.

"It is genius," Edie says, "for me to hide the will, or both wills, in this album."

"Right because nobody would look for them in here," I nod as I continue. Dust races off the pages and up at us but I keep flipping. I catch sight of a few photos, there's one with young Edie sunbathing on the roof of a vintage Chevy, and one of Edie in the early nineties, dressed in an apron, covered in something dark purple. From the corner of my eye Edie is motioning for me to flip faster.

I can't believe it; after all this time we will have the wills.

I'll be free. Free to fix my relationship with Riley, free of Edie and free to go back to work—Oh right. I forgot.

No matter! If I find the wills maybe I can blackmail Terrance into keeping me on?

"That's a terrible idea sugar pie," Edie states as she watches me. "I would think you'd be happy to be done with that place."

I keep flipping.

The will is in here, or both of them, I can feel it. In my fingertips, in my bones, in my—

Hold on a second.

184

That's the last page.

That couldn't have been the last page.

I flip back, pause, and flip again. I'm frowning, and as I look up at Edie I see she shares my same expression. "That's it?"

"I guess so."

The gusto has vanished from the room, and we both have slumped down. It was exciting for a moment to think we were so close to victory. I liked the feeling.

"Look through the rest!" Edie points at the bed behind me, "Maybe this wasn't the album Merida wanted. Maybe it's one of the others."

Five minutes later, we've looked through the six other albums, and found nothing.

"It is possible that Merida really just wanted the album for the memories?"

"Horse dung," Edie remarks placing her hands on her hips. "Where else could that stupid thing be?" She bites her lip and slowly turns around the room as I place the albums back on the desk neatly. I haven't told her that I slipped the black and white photo of her into the pocket of my uniform. I don't even know why I did it, I just did.

"I'll have a quick look in the drawers," I suggest.

From the corner of my eye I see Edie move through the grey shimmering curtains against the right wall. I find nothing in the desk drawers and think maybe peeking inside her fancy armoire across the room would be a good idea.

Plus, I wanted to see her designer clothes.

I'm just making my way around the bed when it happens.

The bedroom door creeks open quickly and I freeze in place.

There's nowhere to hide.

I have no choice but to turn and look at Porter, who stands in the doorway running his eyes over me in confusion. He's in a pair of grey sweat pants and a loose t-shirt; his hair tussled from its usual kept style. "Phoebe?"

"Oh, uh hi," I wave lamely and grimace a little at the same time.

Quick Phoebe, think.

"What are you doing in here?" he asks without missing a beat. He takes his eyes off of me and starts scanning the room apprehensively. I feel my nerves shoot up my back.

"I heard a noise," I answer squeamishly. Could I have come up with an even bigger cliché of an answer?

"A noise?" his frown deepens.

"Yes," I put on a formal tone, realizing I have no choice but to sell it now. "I wasn't going to come up and investigate but I figured since you had your headphones in you might not have heard it."

His hands leave his sides and slide into the pockets of his sweatpants, "How did you know I had my headphones in?"

Damn it.

"Good job Sherlock." Edie scuffles as she leaves the curtain she vanished into earlier, "I wonder, how *did* you know that?"

"Rosanne mentioned you have them in when you're working sometimes." I shrug at Porter making sure to keep my eyes off of Edie. "I just assumed when I didn't hear any walking around that maybe you had gone to sleep already."

He blinks at me, "What was the noise?"

"One of her albums fell." I point to the desk I was just at, "They were stacked too high on her desk I guess, so I moved them on the bed and was just leaving."

To my horror Porter enters the room and looks from me to the desk against the window, "That desk?"

"Err, yes."

"I never left the albums there."

"But that's where they were when I got here, honest," I put my hands in the air.

"I believe you," he says, "but I never put them there. I left them in her closet." He motions at the curtain Edie stands in front of. I turn back to face the desk, feeling my eyebrows come together,

"But they were on the desk when I got here."

Porter walks up next to me, his eyes also on the empty desk. "Strange. I gave Rosanne strict orders to leave Edie's room alone, that nobody was allowed to go inside."

Edie gasps behind me and before I can turn around, she appears a foot away from my face. She snaps her fingers on both hands, "Marta! When you told her to come in here to clean, she went through my things!"

But albums?

"Terrance must have given her the idea."

"Why didn't you want anyone in this room?" I ask Porter curiously.

"I hadn't gone through it all yet so I wanted to keep everyone out," Porter explains walking in front of Edie and towards her bed. "That was until tonight. I flipped over her mattress and there was nothing there, by the way."

"Oh, sorry."

He says nothing but stops in front of the albums and opens the top one, the one full of pictures of Merida and Edie summering together. "It's so strange that they were once great friends and progressively drifted apart."

"Because she's two faced," Edie snaps. "Greedy and a back stabber."

"It happens," I shrug, "people move on and they change."

"Did you look at them?" Porter suddenly asks me and he meets my eye. I feel caught off guard, as if he might already know the answer. I don't know whether I should lie or not.

"Of course you should lie!" Edie exclaims, "You can't risk him thinking you are a snooper!"

"Uh…" Something in me can't lie, and maybe it's because of the way his intense eyes hold my stare. "Yes I did. I'm sorry, I know I shouldn't have but I peeked when I picked it up."

"You've done it now, haven't you?" Edie sucks in some air and shakes her head.

"It's alright," he looks away from me and grins, as if he found my penitent tone amusing. "No harm done in looking." It's only then I notice that again, he isn't in his usual formal demeanour. It could be because he's in a pair of PJ's and out of his suits, but it's evident he's relaxed. I watch as he glances down at a picture on the first page, squinting at first then allowing his mouth to twitch into a semi-smile.

187

"There's one of Edie sunbathing on the roof of a car," I suddenly can't help but tell him. "She looks like a model."

"Why thank you," Edie clears her throat behind me and I just imagine her face. "You know I could have been? I was begged by a few agents but my mother wouldn't—"

"—And there's one with her covered in something sticky and purple," I don't mean to cut her off but when Porter suddenly smiles at a picture I feel like I had to. It's that warm and soft smile I caught a glimpse of at lunch. "She looks *so* angry, it's very funny."

Edie makes a noise behind me, "it most definitely is not funny. How dare you."

Porter takes hold of the album in his hands and lifts it at me, "This one?"

I catch sight of the picture and laugh a little, "Yes, that one."

Porter holds the album in his hands as he looks down at it. He holds his smile, "She was my favorite aunt."

"How many do you have?"

"Four, five with aunt Edie," Porter sets the album down and turns the page. "My father says I inherited her business sense but not her people skills, or her hysterics."

"I'm sure she'd be happy to know that," I sneak a peek at Edie from the corner of my eye but realize she's gone. My remark about her picture must have annoyed her.

Slowly Porter closes the album and takes a step back from the bed. I gather from the drop of his smile and the proper posture he's collected up, it was time to leave the room.

Once in the hallway, Porter shuts the door slowly.

"Have a good night," I tell him as I begin to leave.

"Just a minute," Porter looks away from the bedrooms doors as I turn around. "I wasn't aware you would be staying overnight. If you're staying overnight tomorrow, then I'll get Rosanne to change the sheets in your room. I'm afraid they aren't the best—"

"—No its okay, they're fine but thank you."

"Why are you staying here?" he suddenly enquires, his eyes seem to be X-raying my face, from my forehead to my mouth. It's so easy to get lost in his eyes and stare at them forever; in the low lighting they go from blue to a hazel, but it's the golden undertones that pull you in.

Oh God, Phoebe, stop.

My cheeks flush a little as I look away casually, "Oh it's…I had a small fight with Riley and I thought some space would be good." What good would it be to lie anyway? There wasn't one I could come up with this fast that would make sense anyway. Besides, I had a feeling he wouldn't inquire beyond this.

"Ah," he nods slowly and places his hands in the pockets of his sweatpants, "I see." He clears his throat, "you're obviously welcome to stay whenever you'd like. You are still under employment so the room is yours."

He gives me a small smile and turns to walk away.

It's like I suddenly hear Edie's voice in my head, her allegations of me never talking about things, claiming I could get perspective if I shared even a little bit…

"Porter?"

I watch him stop and twist back around.

"After you became engaged, did you go through a behaviour change?"

Slowly he frowns at me. I suddenly feel foolish, knowing that of course, he never went through a change. That I probably haven't either, I've just been distracted by Edie's mess.

I shake my head at him, "It's just that people have told me I'm acting, different."

I suddenly feel very on display as he stares at me. I shouldn't be talking about this with him for God's sake. "Never mind, I don't know where I'm going with this. It's not like you knew me before this," I attempt a humorous tone to lighten the heaviness I've created. "Let's call it a night."

"I don't mind answering," he tells me as I move to leave, "it's a fair question. I think it's common for some people to react strangely after becoming engaged; it's a big commitment. I don't recall it myself, but I suppose I always knew I was doing it to rebel."

That doesn't really help me out.

Still he steps up to me and I catch a whiff of the fresh scent that exudes from him. His five o'clock shadow was growing in and I found myself wondering how he would look if he let it grow in completely. I had a feeling it would suit him better than the clean shaven look, although it may not bode well with his work style. "May I ask just how differently you have been accused of acting?"

"Scatter brained, all over the place, distracted."

The air around us suddenly feels dense, tight, and hot. I have to look away from him, but when my eyes fall upon his chest, I feel myself warming up anyway.

This is so not an appropriate feeling, Phoebe!

"Ah," Porter nods once and clasps his hands behind his back, "out of character for you?"

"I thought so but," I answer as I think back on my conversation with Tom, "I don't know anymore." I put my hands to my face and rub my temples. This was all starting to give me a headache. "Maybe working at Meyers and Brant changed me a bit, and I never noticed?"

"I see," I hear Porter say. "This fight with your fiancé was because of this change of character?"

"Mostly yes," I take my hands off my face and fold them over my chest, "there are some other things as well. We're both starting to get on each other's nerves."

He makes a face, and unlike his usual unreadable expression this one I can read. It's a 'that isn't a good sign' type of face. He thinks this engagement is a bad idea.

"I love him," I say quickly, watching as he looks into my eyes, "I mean obviously."

Why doesn't that sound reassuring? I sound so deadpanned, like I just gave an answer to a verbal pop quiz in History class.

"There are two types of love," Porter's voice fall's a decimal. "There are the people we love, and the people we are *in* love with. It's very easy to confuse the two."

"That's what my friend Clara said," I tell him.

"Smart woman."

There's undeniably something happening here. How did I get so close to him? I'm looking up at him now, if I reach out slightly I would be able to place a hand on his chest. And he smells *so* good. A slight tingling surges up my legs and into my

190

stomach. The butterfly effect begins to take place and it feels lovely. Every aspect of him suddenly overwhelms me and I wonder what it would be like to kiss him, or to have him touch me—

Phoebe. Stop it now.

I manage to shake whatever spell I was under off and take a step away from him.

"It's getting late. I should head to bed."

"Right," everything about his posture changes back to its usual stiffness, "same."

I take a few steps back clumsily, "Thanks for talking about this stuff."

"Of course."

Chapter Sixteen

I'm awoken the next day by shouting in my ear.

"Get up Phoebe! Get up!"

By the time I actually open my eyes it's whirled into shrieking.

I find Edie by my bedside in a frantic state. Her hair is pinned neatly though, and she's in a grey blouse with a high neckline and long sleeves that puffed up at her shoulders. The skirt she is in in simple and black, a triangle shaped belt buckle at the front. She looks perfectly eighties and I know it's because the albums rubbed off on her yesterday.

"Edie," my voice is groggy as I slowly pull myself up from my side, "stop."

"I can't stop! Merida is at the front door. She's demanding to grab the photo albums and she's in tears," Edie tells me. "I can't figure out how either, her eyelids are practically sealed with Botox."

"Edie, what's it matter if she takes them?" I ask with a yawn, "The wills aren't inside."

I watch Edie pause and think deeply for a moment.

"I think she just wants the excuse to snoop through my room. So get up and go out there."

"Fine. Let me get ready."

In five minutes I manage to make myself look somewhat decent. I have touched up my make up with the few pieces of product I keep in my purse, pulled my hair into a ponytail and gurgled some mouthwash of Roseanne's I found in our shared bathroom. The door to Rosanne's bedroom was closed and I heard shuffling through it.

"I thought she had the day off?"

Edie rolled her eyes and shrugged at me, before motioning for me to hurry.

I leave the corridor with Edie behind me and come into the empty kitchen. As I near the kitchen door I can hear voices on the other side. It's no doubt that they belong to Porter and Merida. Next to me Edie shuffles,

"What are we going to do?"

"If I can get upstairs unseen then I can hide the photo albums," I whisper.

Edie snaps her fingers, catching my attention, "Come with me."

She leads me back through the maid's hallway and towards the end of the hall. I find myself standing opposite of her, a triumphed look over her asymmetrical face.

"What?"

"Push against the wall."

I raise my eyebrows at her, but her look urges me to do what she says. I place my hands against the cool wood and press only a little, feeling the weight of the wall beneath me. Something creeks and suddenly the wall dislodges from place, sliding back a little, as I jump back in surprise.

Holy hell!

"It's a secret staircase!" Edie beams proudly behind me. "Don't you just love it? I'll meet you at the top."

I don't believe it; she had a secret passageway installed!

I watch her fade away slowly, and I turn back to the mismatched wall before me. Slowly I set my hands against it again and give another push. The wall moves swiftly behind with no problem, and as I let go it swings completely open. I can see a tiny wooden staircase before me, leading up into darkness. It smells stale and old as I walk into it, my shoulder brushing against the white wooden wall I had just moved.

I'm standing in a secret passage way!

I don't know what overcomes me but suddenly I get incredibly giddy. I turn quickly and shut the wall behind me, engulfing myself into darkness as I bolt up the stairs. For a moment I fear that I'll land flat on my face by missing a step, so I throw my hands out in front of me. Soon I feel them slam against a cool wall, and realize I have come to the top. I feel around for a handle but nothing pops out for me. Setting my hands against the dry wall before me, I give a small push and feel the wall shift from its place. I push it hard with both hands, and tumble out as the wall swings open.

Edie stands before me, hands at her sides and a smile over her face, "Fancy bumping into you up here."

My face is brimming with a grin as I shut the wall door, "Edie that was so cool!"

"Clinton had it installed about ten years ago. In case of an intruder, we had another way to get downstairs and out the door," she tells me. "One of his *only* genius ideas."

"Do you have a secret room off a bookcase too?"

"Don't be absurd," she frowns at me now, "I'm not cliché."

I notice we are standing on the other end of the hallway, away from Edie's room and the main guest rooms, including the one that Porter was staying in. It's dark; the velvet curtains are still drawn over the windows behind us. There are two armours in this end of the hallway, which Roseanne told me house the guest linens.

I move from my place and can feel the gust of Edie behind me, as we cross the hall, making sure to remain silent so nothing creeks under my feet. As we near the staircase we can hear Porter and Merida below, I pause at the top of the staircase leaning into the white banister to eavesdrop.

"I'm appealing to your human decency Porter," I hear Merida practically cry. *"She was my friend. All I want is our photo albums for God's sake."*

"Merida I cannot give them to you, she may have left them to someone else in her will."

"Her will, her will, her will! Face it Porter, there is no will. If there was, you would have found it already," Merida's voice hits a new high. *"Even if she had a will, why would the albums be left to someone else? They are pictures of her, me and our husbands! Nobody wants those pictures."*

"He doesn't want her in the room either," Edie says behind me, "maybe he thinks the wills are in the photo albums as well."

"Maybe," I whisper with a shrug, "but they aren't."

I push away from the bannister and walk across to Edie's bedroom. I stop when I find the door ajar. I exchange a glance at Edie who gives me a small nod, and vanishes through the door. I wait and a second later her figure comes roaring through the bedroom door.

"They're gone!"

I grimace at Edie keeping my voice low, "Porter must have moved them."

"Merida!"

"I'm sorry to be so abrupt but I want some reminder of my dear friend whether you like it or not!"

Edie and I freeze, the sound of stomping feet begin to echo up the stairs.

"She's gotten by Porter!" Edie exclaims, "Go hide!"

I run back down the hall, deciding to throw myself around the last armoire at the end of the hall. It's dark enough down that portion of the hall that they won't see me, unless they really look. As my back hits the wall, Edie appears before me, her focus on Merida and Porter as they reach the top of the stairs.

"Merida please don't touch anything in the room," I hear Porter beg her in a rough tone. "I haven't went through it all yet." She doesn't respond, but I hear the door to Edie's room open frantically.

"That's odd…" Porters voice trickles out of the room, and Edie and I place our eyes on each other. I freeze against the wall again, my sweaty palms against the cool paint. "They were here last night, all of her albums."

"You better get downstairs before Merida sees you and accuses you of stealing them," Edie ushers me away with her hands. "I'll go watch."

I decide to leave the house as soon as I get downstairs, hanging up my uniform in my room and washing myself up properly. Once out from the empty kitchen, I pause and listen for any voices. I hear nothing from Merida or Porter upstairs, so I figure Porter must have gotten Merida out of the house. With my purse on my shoulder I rush across the main hallway towards the grand doors.

"You."

I stop at the doors and slowly turn around to find Merida in the doorway of the living room. She has a cocktail glass in her hands, but it holds only ice. She's in a pair of skinny jeans and a tight white t-shirt with a sequin G over the chest. Her face is caked with bright blush and pink eyeshadow, to match her pink lipstick. Her mascara has smudged off her lashes and come onto her cheek bones though, and I wonder if she faked it to look as if she was in distress.

"Were you here last night?" she asks, the ice in her glass rocking as she pushes herself away from the doorway.

"Um, yes I was."

"Did you go into Edie's room, unattended?" Merida's eyebrows rise as she demands an answer from me.

"Merida, please," Porter comes up around her and his eyes fall upon me. Today he's in dark jeans and a grey sweater, his hair out of place, I assume from the frustration Merida's presence brings him. "There isn't a need to be so confrontational."

"Why not?" she snaps looking up at him, "We don't know her. Nobody knows her. She appears out of the blue and claims she's related to our poor Edie. I have yet to see any real evidence. What if she's just fishing for some kind of fortune?"

How dare she! She's the one who's trying to scoop the company out from under Porter. She's the one who can't be trusted.

"I don't want anything," I say to her.

"Where are the albums?" Merida suddenly insists, her hands fall to her side and a few ice cubes roll out of the glass. "Porter says they are missing."

"I don't know anything about any missing albums."

"I don't trust her Porter," Merida shoots a look his way and Porter looks away from me, "Something about her is off."

I open my mouth to retaliate when there comes a knock behind me. All three of us look at each other; Porter goes to make a move when Merida's hand comes against his hard chest. "She's the *help*, let her open it."

I glare at her before turning around and pulling the door open slowly. My mouth drops a little bit as I find myself gazing at Faye and Clara. Faye smiles at me, in a pair of white slacks and a black off the shoulder tunic, her black hair gleaming from the bright sun behind her. Clara adjusts her ponytail behind me, in a pair of dark jeans and a black t-shirt with an bejeweled neckline.

"Surprise!" they say in unison.

This is so not the right time.

I half wish that they would get that from the expression on my face, but instead Faye pushes against the door I'm holding half shut. Clara follows her in.

"We thought we would pick you up before we went to see the…" Faye's voice trails off when she sees Porter and Merida looking back at them. "Oh, hi."

"Faye, Clara," I shut the door behind them and inhale quickly, "this is Porter. Edie's nephew. And this is Merida, Edie's er, friend."

What I really want to saw is 'Edie's backstabbing, two faced ex-friend' but I would sound a little too much like Edie for my liking.

"Hi," both Faye and Clara give an awkward wave at the two of them. Clearly the snarly glare that Merida has placed over her tight face is making them uncomfortable. Porter doesn't look any more welcoming; he simply gives them a small nod. An unsurprising edgy silence is coming over the room, as the five of us standing looking at each other.

"Merida, let me call the car around," Porter finally looks back at her, "to take you home."

"No, I texted my daughter to retrieve me," Merida's sour demeanour rapidly softens, "Amanda. Perhaps you'll join us for lunch? I know she is dying to see you after all these months."

I watch Porter glance down on his watch and his brow comes together. He's trying to think of a way out of the lunch date, I can see it. I wonder if Merida has any idea of it. Another silence sweeps through the room, and I can't stand it.

"Okay," I step in front of Faye and Clara, making sure to place my eyes only on Porter. "I'll just be on my way then. If you need anything then you can call me."

I knew my mistake the moment it left my lips,

"He has Rosanne," Merida snaps frowning, "why would he need to call *you*?"

"I was—it was just a—never-mind," I turn away quickly, my cheeks flushing as I motion for Clara and Faye to hurry out the door. Astonishingly they don't even bat an eye and follow my lead, Clara pulling the door open quickly. We scurry outside and down the pathway of the house, towards the iron fence in silence, behind it I can see Clara's SUV parked against the curb.

"So who do you think took the albums?" Faye sits in the front, her head twisted over her shoulder and a look of curiosity over her face. "You sure it wasn't Porter?"

"Maybe, but I doubt he would think the will was in there. It's obvious Merida has a feeling they're in there as well."

"This is so crazy, two missing wills, a murder," Clara exhales as she shakes her head, gripping the steering wheel. "It's like a Nancy Drew Mystery."

Faye glances back at me from the front seat. "What about the other maid?"

"My money is on Marta, yes" I answer Faye confidently.

Faye frowns at me, "Didn't you say she went home on the weekends though?"

"Not this weekend," I remember Marta's attitude yesterday.

"Phoebs," Clara suddenly gasps, "You should have told us your boss is that hot."

"Clara," my reply is shallow, "he's not *that* good looking."

"On a scale of one to ten he's a nine or maybe even a ten," Clara giggled from the driver's seat. I watch as she looks over at Faye. "Right?"

"I guess so" Faye shrugs, "Maybe more of an eight." I see that her focus is mostly on the phone in her hands.

"Is he single?" Clara gives me a quick look over her shoulder as we stop at a traffic light.

"Yes he is, although probably not for long…"

I can't help but wonder if Porter went along for the lunch date with Amanda and I was curious as to what she looks like. I think back at the pictures from the album of Merida, and when she was younger she was quite the looker. Amanda can't look much different.

"So where is this medium?" I ask before I put myself in more of a bad mood.

"Actually she's here," Faye answers, "in Cedar Springs."

It's then I notice that we actually haven't gotten on the highway, and instead are driving through the busy tourist filled Main Street of Cedar Springs. Women in floppy hats and designer sundresses case the pavement, with well-dressed men on their arms.

"When I was googling some mediums the other day I found one here, she has a lot of five star reviews" Faye explained with a shrug. "Did you tell Satine any of this?"

"No," I lean into my seat as I answer. "She'd tell me I should go see a shrink, and she'd be right."

"By the way," Clara gives me a look in her rear-view mirror, "Is *she* around you?"

"Uh no," I answer quickly; despite Faye and Clara acting as if they are okay with Edie, I still feel they think I've completely lost my marbles deep down inside, and they're only doing this because they know I'd fight off any suggestion of therapy. The less we actually mention her, the better.

"So, have you spoken to Riley?" Clara makes a sharp left turn that sends me into the side of the door. After I reposition myself, I answer her,

"Not since our fight. I was supposed to see him yesterday but I didn't."

"I'm sure you guys will get over this," Faye nods optimistically as she smiles at Clara.

I know what they're doing; they're going to be more supportive because of my small argument with Clara and Satine.

Clara begins to slow the car down, "I think this is the place."

She pulls to the side of the road and we find ourselves looking down a grey dirt driveway that leads to a small drab, shack of a house. It's only one story and made from faded grey wood, a crotchety old porch wraps around it, with a few potted planets sitting on the ledge of the banisters. Beyond it, you can see the shores of the ocean, but the beach looks empty.

"Are you sure this is the place?" Faye leans forward,

"Yes, 38 Paulson street. This is it," Clara turns her car off and undoes her seatbelt.

A moment later we have left the SUV, and are making the trek down the long dirt driveway. Other than chirping birds we hear nothing except our footsteps against the grain. Its borderline eerie. Once we reach the house we look up at the porch, noting that the set of stairs up to the house were as lopsided as the porch.

Before we can make a move, the screen door swings open and the springs stop it from slamming against the wall. A woman walks out; I would guess she was in her fifties, dressed in a black peasant skirt and a brown suede shirt. She's a curvy woman with messy blonde hair resting down her back and a complexion almost brown from too much sun.

"You Clara?" her voice is hoarse. From the smoke that drifts out of the house behind her, I would guess it was that deep because of her smoking habit.

"Yeah, that's me," Clara then gestures over at me, "This is my friend. The one who needs to talk to you."

She surveys me with her green eyes for a moment, "Come on up."

Instead of letting us into the house, she lets the screen door swing shut and walks towards the left side of her porch as the three of us slowly climb her wobbly stairs. There's a small round table, a mosaic design over the top and two iron clad chairs tucked into it. She sits in one of the chairs, and points to the other one, "Sit down."

Clara and Faye move to the side of the porch but only Clara leans against the wooden railing. As I get to the table I notice that the woman has a deck of colorful cards out and a regular medium sized rock placed over them to keep them from drifting away with the wind. I pull the chair out slowly, hearing it squeal against the dated wood and quickly sit down.

"My name is Madame Amber, like the stone," she cups her hands over the table. "Your friend tells me you come to me for some guidance. To help do away with a negative energy?" Her thin eyebrows make her look menacing up close, and for a moment all I can focus on is the ashy smell protruding from her.

"Yes," my words catch in my throat, "sort of."

I'm starting to feel tormented, like I'm cheating on a test in high-school in my favorite teacher's class. I feel like I'm betraying Edie's trust or something...I mean, how would I feel if

I were a ghost and the person who promised to help me was trying to banish me?

"You have got to be joking," her voice slices through the air with amusement and I lift my eyes only briefly, to see Edie standing over Madame Amber. She's draped in a long blue dress, chiffon from the waist down and small plastic buttons making their way up from her stomach to the neck line. She looks rather done up and I wonder where she went off to.

"Give me your hand," Madame Amber reaches for my hand over my right one, watching as she clasps her hands over mine. Her skin is cold and rough. As I look back at her she exhales deeply three times and shuts her eyes.

"You know she is a fraud yes?" Edie sighs whisking herself to my side, "Everybody knows that here in Cedar Springs. Her only clients come from the city."

Before I can respond to Edie, Madame Amber squeezes my hand and her face tightens, "You have…a powerful energy surrounding you. A dark but powerful energy. This energy has taken over your life and you are not as happy as you can be. "

Edie gasps and I jump slightly, forcing Madame Amber to open her eyes at me briefly.

"I was wrong," Edie's voice is thick with sarcasm, "she is obviously the oracle."

"You are also in a committed relationship," Madame Amber then reveals, her eyes stay closed. "There is a communication problem."

Edie rolls her eyes, "But she foresees a long and happy life, with plenty of children."

"But I foresee a long and happy life for you, filled with the laughter of children."

"I can't believe you're wasting your time here when we should be looking for the wills. The house is empty you know?" Edie leans over to me and stops right at my ear. "Empty."

"If we could hurry this along," I break Madame Amber's concentration and she glares at me, "it's just that I have a busy day ahead of me." Instead of responding Madame Amber just shuts her eyes, shifts in her seat and exhales three times again.

"You are stressed, tense," she says breathing between the two words, "unhinged."

Well, she kind of nailed that.

"Oh please. Next she offers a cleansing with crystals at her discounted fee of three hundred dollars. If she was a true medium, she would be able to feel my presence." Edie stands up and walks down the porch looking at Clara and Faye. "Your friends dress very well, why don't you dress as well as they do?"

Edie—

"This powerful energy won't leave you anytime soon. Unless you do something about it," Madame Amber opens her eyes again, "you need a cleansing. I can do it for you for three hundred dollars, my discounted price. But you need to focus. This reading would have gone on much longer if you would relax."

She lets go of my hand and leans back into her seat, arms crossing over her chest. "You are difficult to read but that could be the negative energy that surrounds you. I have an opening this Monday evening for a Cleansing." She pauses, "that'll be twenty dollars."

Chapter Seventeen

"I'm really sorry about Madame Amber; I thought she was at least semi-legit."

"It's okay," I tell Faye as we trek towards the loft door, "you didn't know."

"We should have known," Clara chimes in, "I mean mediums really? They don't exist."

It's after supper time and Faye and Clara have decided to come up with me to the loft. After the failed reading with Madame Amber, Edie told me Porter had returned with the auctioneers from the auction house and that searching the house now would be useless. She gave me permission to spend the day with my friends as she busied herself. So the three of us went shopping in Cedar Springs, had a small lunch where I ordered a grilled chicken wrap and had to stop myself from ordering another, before returning to the city for more shopping. We had plans for supper, unless Riley was home, then Faye and Clara would leave.

I wouldn't know what to say to him now. He's been silent since the fight, and each time I open my contacts list to call him up, something stops me. Everything feels fragmented and I just can't feel as miserable as I should be.

All I think about now is Edie, Edie's wills, and Edie's house.

And Porter.

All day all I've thought about is Porter.

I'm in limbo with one man, while thinking about another.

"Phoebe? Are you alright?" Faye stops me at the door to the loft, "you look, well..."

"Sad," Clara jumps in, "she looks sad."

"I'm not sad," I sigh, "I'm just, conflicted."

Faye puts a hand on my shoulder. "Is this because of what Clara and Satine said about Riley? Because if it is, let me tell you it doesn't matter in the end what—"

"—No, no." I look at the two of them. "It's nothing to do with that, I swear. I'm over that. Actually I needed it; it was an eye opener, I think, to a few things..."

"What do you mean?" Clara steps up to my side.

"I think you and Satine are right, about me and Riley."

I turn and reach for the loft door handle when Faye grabs the fabric of my shirt. "Maybe we should just go straight to dinner?"

"I need to get a change of clothes," I wiggle from her grasp, "and shower, and talk to Riley if he is around."

They both step away from me as I unlock the door and begin to haul it open. It's completely dark in the loft, and I take it as a sign that Riley isn't home.

I shuffle inside with Faye and Clara behind me. As one of them starts to close the door, the rattling screeching echoing around us, the lights in the loft flick on and I stare into a room full of people.

"Surprise!"

I'm halted as I glance around the room. Huddled around the couches are my friends and family, a handful of strange faces as well. I see my brother and sister, my mother next to them, her face plastered with a smile. Stella and Maxwell stand in the small crowd, a few employee's from R&J including Jamie and James. I spot Greg as well.

Everyone looks dressed to the nines, in suits and dresses.

I catch sight of the fancy looking hor d'oeuvres on the coffee table, and look over to the kitchen where there stands a catering cart topped off with champagne glasses. There are three waiters in the kitchen, and as I lean over further I see them placing more pastries and hor d'oeuvres on serving trays. The smell in the loft is divine, and slowly someone turns on some instrumental music. There is a pile of gifts on a side table.

I watch Riley come over to me, immaculately dressed in a black suit with a blue dress shirt. His hair is quaffed stiffly to the side though, a style I have never see him in before. He's smiling at me, and takes my hands in his when he gets to me.

"Were you surprised?" he earnestly asks, his eyes sparkle at me.

"Um, yes. What is this?"

"It's your engagement party!" he throws a sturdy arm over my shoulder and pulls me up against him. "We did it everyone!" Riley calls out to the room as the guests begin to go back to their conversations, "We surprised her."

He lets me go abruptly then and motions towards our bedroom "Go on get changed and come join us."

A moment later I'm in the bedroom, hidden behind the large partitions with Clara and Faye, who had brought over their dresses for the party earlier this morning. It was Stella's idea they told me, to throw a surprise engagement party for me since Riley had told her I was stressed. The planning was done within the last few days and Riley never put a stop to it after our fight.

I felt out of place pulling up the navy dress up my body. I adjust the straps on my arms and waited for Faye to zip up the back of it. She looked elegant and simple, in a black dress with long sleeves and a graceful dip on the back. Across from me Clara smiled in a green wrap dress that complimented her tanned skin and showed off her toned arms. "You look great."

"Thanks Clara."

"So I guess that little fight meant nothing in the end," Faye says from behind me, "if it had, Riley would have stopped the party from happening."

That was true. I mean, anybody would, if they wanted to end the engagement. Riley obviously saw some hope for us, maybe my first initial thoughts where right. We could work on this.

"Are you sure you want to do this?" Faye then asks me, I watch her give me a comforting smile. I don't answer her; instead I give myself a once over, looking in the mirror.

"Your mom and Stella seem to be getting along," Clara points out; she's now standing near the partitions opening and looking out at the crowd. "Everyone is having a good time."

I leave Faye's side and walk towards Clara, overlooking everybody who seems to be mingling. My mother, in a black skirt and white frilly top sits next to Stella, who graces us with her presence in a smart black Armani suit. As usual Maxwell sits next to Stella, head down into his cell phone. Riley stands near the kitchen with a man in slacks and a grey sweater, he has a fancy camera in his hands and a strap around his neck. Greg stands with a few of Riley's co-workers, gabbing away. Our balcony door is half open and I can see a few guests gawking at our view and pointing at things down on the street. The usual strong breeze sweeps through their hair.

205

Tom stands with Reese, he gestures as he speaks to Porter and—

Wait, Porter?

"He invited Porter?" I ask Faye and Clara as Faye finally joins us.

"No, I did." A thin smile spreads over Clara's lips as she looks down at me, "What? I called him when you went into the bathroom at lunch. You said he was single."

I look over at him, the grey suit and black dress shirt he chose accents his eyes and hair. It's buttoned up above his navel and hugs his body suavely. Clara was right. Everything about the man gave off a prominent appeal even when he was solemn and serious. Suddenly I could feel it; the bubbling sensation of resentment in my gut as I think about Clara and him getting along.

I had no right to even feel that way for pity's sake! They were both single and I was still engaged.

Frankly I'm surprised he would accept Clara's invitation; Edie said he was busy with the upcoming auction.

"About that," Edie materializes before me in her blue dress. "I lied. There were no auctioneers at the house. I just remembered this party and felt that perhaps you could use the *fun*. That is, if this crowd is even capable of it, look how quiet and slow everything is..."

So you were in on this too?

"In my own ghostly way, but," she spins back at me and lifts a finger, "don't get drunk. We have to figure out a way to get you to sneak out early. The house is empty and it's the perfect time to search my room again, get into my safe."

Someone steps up from behind Porter with a cell phone to his ear, and his dark eyes fall straight to me. I suck in a breath; it's Terrance. He's in a dark suit, an orange dress shirt beneath it which was unbuttoned enough to show off the dark hair on his chest. He says something to his caller then ends the call, slipping his phone into his suit pocket and turning his back on me; rejoining the conversation with Porter and my siblings.

I get goosebumps, and wiggle them off.

"Why is he here?" Edie demands at me.

Riley must have invited him.

Edie grunts and glides away from me towards Terrance and Porter. As I look back at everyone, I see Riley coming my way and slowly leave Clara and Faye.

I need to talk to him. How can he pretend like we didn't fight the other day? Doesn't he want to talk about things?

He's smiling at me as we get to each other, and plants a kiss on my forehead.

"This was my mother's idea," he tells me shifting his eyes towards the couch; "she planned it all. She even had the caterer make the entire menu vegetarian for our benefit. The seaweed wraps are amazing, you need to try one." I watch him look from me and wave at someone coming in from the balcony.

Always the charmer I realize.

"Riley, don't you think this was—is a bit…" I can't think of the right word to say to him but I think my tone says it all. He's frowning at me, but after a second puts both hands on my shoulders firmly.

"Phoeb's," he sighs, "We had a fight. Couples fight all the time. It was nothing."

I make a face. "But Riley, you acted as if the engagement was over. You hung up on me."

He keeps his smile as he locks eyes with a guest, and only gives me a quick look. "I was angry. I got over it. Forget about the fight."

"You're not even mad about me not showing up yesterday?"

"I didn't even notice, I was busy with work," he smiles again at someone. "Now go mingle, and thank my mother for the party."

He lets me go and moves away from me quickly.

"I heard that you know," Edie's voice fills my space. "*I didn't even notice.*" She repeats his words as a waiter passes us with a tray of red wine. I scoop one up without a word and take a long drink. "Keep it minimal Madonna."

I'm not in the mood for your insults.

"I'm not insulting you," Edie states frowning, "I was *teasing*. There is a difference."

Just go stay near Terrance.

"Fine."

My mother, her jet black short hair pinned back with a glittery butterfly clip, is waving me over. I take a breath and make the short walk, smiling when I reach her and Stella.

"Stella, this was wonderful of you," I glance over at the woman who simply nods my way. "Thank you."

"Stella suggested brunch tomorrow morning, just us three. Isn't that nice?" my mother beams from me to Stella.

"Yes, I thought we could get down to this wedding business properly, and make sure everybody who would like to be involved, be rightfully so." As Stella finishes, she brings the champagne glass to her thin lips, "I was thinking Petite Jardin, they have a fantastic vegan menu for you, Phoebe. You know she is committing to veganism with Riley," Stella places a cool hand on my mother's arm. "She will look sensational at the wedding."

My mom blinks at her, impassive and quite possibly confused. Finally she turns to me, "You're a vegan?" To my mom, who adds meat to every meal of every day, this is unthinkable.

"Sort of," I tug at the side of my dress.

Stella frowns at me, "But Riley said that you and he are doing it together?"

I wouldn't wish this moment on my worst enemy. When I spot Jamie coming in from the balcony I decide to make my move, "Excuse me. I have to mingle."

I leave them quickly, reaching Jamie just as she makes her way towards our bathroom. She smiles largely when I come across her and leans in for a quick hug. All I can smell from her is patchouli and the earthiness of it makes my eyes sting. She's in a long sleeved woven dress with silk sleeves and a suede corset.

"How are you enjoying the party Phoebe?" she asks, "It's nice."

"The food is fantastic," she beams looking over at a nearby waiter; "James, Riley and I love it. Have you had a chance to try it? Oh here, try the seaweed wraps." She stops the female waiter and reaches down onto the silver tray. I watch her pick up two black wrapped objects with lettuce sticking out of them and hands me one with a napkin beneath it. Not any bit of this looks appetizing but I take it anyway,

"Wow yes, looks yummy."

I can tell she's waiting for me to taste it and slowly, with a small breath, I pop it into my mouth. I chew, expecting the worst, but it's not that bad. In fact, the lettuce is crispy and the salt from the seaweed tingles delightfully.

I knew Riley didn't know how to cook!

"How is it going anyway? Becoming a full fledge vegan is a hard transition," Jamie tells me. "I know I was just a wreck. I've handed Riley a few cookbooks to get you started." She pops the seaweed roll into her mouth and I watch her chew, her teeth becoming black from the residue.

Tom and Reese emerge behind her and I stand up alert, "Tom, Reese? This is Jamie. She is James's girlfriend."

"Yes we've already met," Tom nods at her as Jamie turns to them.

"Turns out your brother and sister have strong views on veganism," Jamie swallows her seaweed wrap and I watch a smile take over her wrinkle-less face. "Excuse me." She touches my arm slowly as she leaves and I look up at Tom and Reese, who both roll their eyes in unison.

"What did you say to her?" I frown.

"We told her that humans were meant to eat meat once in a while," Reese shrugs casually as she takes a sip of the black carbonated beverage in her wine glass. Her silver sweater sparkles beneath the dim lighting and is in great contrast with her black trouser pants.

"I believe she called us unsupportive," Tom slides a hand into the pocket of his khakis, "to which I responded with calling her a loon."

I grimace, "Tom!"

"I don't like her," he practically snarls my way.

"You two don't like anyone," I remind them as I look around the room, "except yourselves."

"Not true", Reese points a finger at me, "we like you."

Were interrupted by childlike laughter.

Strange, I don't know any children and I doubt Riley would have any over.

"My God," Reese sneers through her glass, "*who* are they?" she points behind me and I glance over my shoulder. I suddenly realize that wasn't a child's laughter, but the laughter of Riley's two cousins; Kennedy and Amelia. Neither look appropriately dressed for this party either. Amelia is in a skin tight pink body-con dress with an excessive amount of cleavage, and Kennedy is in some kind of orange running suit that is sleeveless to show off her butch arms.

"Riley's cousins," I groan, as I finish off the rest of my wine. "He's trying to get them to be my bridesmaids."

Tom lets out a chuckle and as I face him he loses it in his champagne glass. I open my mouth to retaliate when I see Porter and Clara. I don't know where Terrance has gone, but I wasn't going to worry unless Edie came to me in a hysterics. Porter and Clara stand facing each other, and I wish I could hear what they were saying. I watch Clara take a step closer to him, and my stomach turns with a grumble as he leans in closer to her.

I need some air.

"Take this," I force my empty wine glass into Tom's hand and escape towards the vacant balcony.

I slide through the open glass door and take a deep breath once I'm outside. The street lights up all around me, sirens are going off to my left, cars are honking at each other to my right. I can hear my guests behind me chatting away and the music drowning any dialogue out. The chilly breeze makes my skin crawl but it doesn't bother me much right now.

I really need to get myself together. For God's sake, I am engaged, at a wonderful engagement party thrown for me by my mother-in-law and fiancé. I should be more grateful.

I need a distraction. Where's Edie? I should get back to the house, look for the wills.

"Phoebe?"

I turn my head to see that Tom has pushed his head out and there is a look of concern over his pale face that not even his prim glasses can hide. "Are you alright?"

"I'm fine," I nod with a small smile. "A slight headache, I still get them from the accident."

"Do you want some water?"

"No, I'll be inside in a minute."

He stares at me for a moment and I think he's about to say something else. Finally he just nods, pulling his head back into the loft.

I lean back into the glass railing and slump. Why couldn't I put myself in a more festive mood? Did I even want to be in a festive mood? I need to talk to Riley. This isn't a normal feeling, people aren't supposed to feel this way when they've just been thrown a surprise engagement party.

"Phoebe?"

The voice is Porter's, and I immediately spin on my heel to face him. He comes onto the balcony alone, his one hand inside his jacket pocket. My posture changes and I can feel my heart flutter a few beats, which I feel instantaneously guilty for. I smile at him as he nears me, keeping my knees together and my hands clasped in front of me.

"Thanks so much for coming."

"I'm afraid I can't stay," he takes his hand from his pocket revealing a small black box tied with a red ribbon. He hands it to me, "This is for you. An engagement gift. I'm sorry it's not for you the both of you, or anything useful but it was short notice and I—"

"—No, no that's alright. This is very thoughtful of you," I take the box slowly, my fingertips playing with the ribbon; "you didn't even need to bring anything really."

I begin to pull the ribbon apart as he goes on,

"It may not even be your fancy. On second thought, give it back to me. Let me get you something more suitable," his hand reaches for the box but I pull it away, allowing our hands to brush against each other. The hair on my arms stands up as I smirk at him,

"I haven't even opened it yet."

With the ribbon undone, I flip the top of the box open and find myself staring down at a stunning piece of antique jewellery. It's a gold rose, dotted with rubies throughout and attached to a striking gold chain. A prominent feeling of familiarity hits as I touch the cold piece with my finger,

"It's beautiful."

211

"It belonged to Edie," he said after a moment. "It was to go up at auction; I had a very interested buyer at one point. When I saw it I thought of you."

I remember it now, or at least where I saw it. At the auction, its picture was on the table with the projector.

Porter goes on. "When your friend Clara called to invite me, I expressed concern I had no gift for you. I heard a thud behind me a moment later and there was this necklace laying on the floor. As if Aunt Edie wanted you to have it." There's a strange sentimentality in his expression that surprises me, and I believe he catches it too because he smiles largely, as he dips his head as if embarrassed. "Ridiculous, I know."

"No, not ridiculous" my tone is more serious then I intend it to be and I wait for him to look back at me, "I really like it. It's better than all the other gifts I got." As our eyes meet, I think about last night; the things I said to him, how he responded to my clear confusion. How close we got to one another...

"Porter." I clear my throat as I look from the necklace to him again, "about last night. I know I sounded confused and I'm sorry—"

"—Please don't apologize," he lifts a hand slowly; "being newly engaged can be a difficult time, especially if you've had an accident—"

"—But it shouldn't be, should it?" the thought hits me and I can't help but ask it out loud. "You should feel happy when you're engaged right? You shouldn't be feeling out of it and unsure. Pretending you don't eat meat, while eating it behind everyone's back, and being totally okay with a vegan wedding cake—"

"—A vegan what?" Porter frowns and I go on,

"—or be told that you would look better on the wedding day if you work out two hours a day, or get into the tanning booth, and have your wedding at the boring golf and country club. I mean what's next? Coloring my hair? Changing my clothes?"

Porter is staring at me, only his look is far from the judgemental one I would expect. He looks worried, a slight frown and dip of the lips make it adamant. I can't take my eyes off of him even though I want to, but something about him standing near me, at this moment, eases me.

We open our mouths at the same time; I drive to speak when someone else does first. It's shrill, and unfeeling,

"Phoebe."

We turn towards the door and find Riley, standing half way in, half way out of the balcony. His hands grip the doorway; he's looking only at me. Nothing about him looks congenial.

We watch him excuse himself, and march away from the door. My body caves a little.

"Damn it," I rub my forehead with the back of my hand as my eyes flutter shut for a second.

What is wrong with me?

"Sorry," I look up at Porter as I take a step away and motion at the door, "I have to go talk to him."

I turn away when his hand comes up and takes hold of my elbow, "Phoebe wait."

There it is the tingling up my back and around the rest of me, my heart beats in that longing way. I ease into his hold and I get the idea I could just wrap my arms around his body and cling to him. I hate but love the feeling.

A few seconds slip between us and Porter says nothing, instead he looks away from my eyes and lets go of my arm. "Nothing, never mind. Go, deal with your fiancé. I have to get going, myself."

I leave the balcony behind Porter, watching as he walks over to Terrance and Greg to say goodbye. My eyes scan the room for Riley and I don't see him anywhere; everybody else is acting normal. Slowly with the box in my hands, I cross the room around the guests and walk into the bedroom. My eyes are on the dresser where my jewellery stand sits and I drag my heels across the area rug towards it. What was happening to me? What the *hell* was I doing?

"We need to talk."

I turn to face the bed and find Riley sitting on the edge. His hands are placed at his sides and he grips the sheets. His charming demeanour has been replaced by a grim glare.

I swallow. "Riley, I'm sorry. I didn't mean for you to hear all that, that way."

"Clearly you didn't," he snaps. "You've been secretly eating meat? I can't believe you."

"Meat?" I frown at him. "Who cares about the meat…Look, I tried to talk to you," I go on. "I wanted to see you yesterday to talk. Things got in the way and you never called or texted either so I thought—"

"—I was busy. I was working. Building my career, you know what that is, yes?" He's on his feet now with his hands on his hips, "my job isn't as easy as your new one."

My hands drop to my sides and I frown at him, "Just hold on a second here. I told you I'm doing it because—"

"—I don't care anymore why you're doing it!" He throws a hand in the air as he turns away from me, "I hate it and I don't want to talk about that right now."

"You just said you wanted to talk," I step away from the dresser, watch him run his hand through his hair and seeing that frustration forces me to stop. "Riley, what are we doing? Who are we kidding here?"

He whips my way. "What do you mean?"

I look away from him, to the black kitten heels at my feet. "The other day on the phone, when we fought, you were right about us not getting married. We're not on the same page, we're fighting, and we're annoyed with each other—"

"—Couples fight Phoebe, they argue, it's how they show their love. Were just going through a rough patch, we'll get through it. We have a meeting with the therapist tomorrow at five. We're going to discuss things then; maybe she can suggest a support group for you about the vegan thing too." His tone changes into a normal octave; he adjusts his suit jacket and begins to pat down his hair. "Let's just get back out there, smile, mingle and act normal okay?"

Act normal? He cannot be serious right now.

I feel like I'm about to burst into tears.

He takes a long breath between his teeth then slowly looks at me, "*okay?*"

"Okay."

Chapter Eighteen

I don't know how I managed it but I did.

Late into the evening until the last guests left, Riley and I played nice; I was sure nobody suspected a thing. Though I went to bed bothered and spent half the night tossing and turning, as Riley slept soundly next to me. When I awoke after nine a.m. Riley was gone and so were his running shoes and gym bag. I was relieved to be alone in the loft as I got ready for brunch with my mother and Stella.

As I finished getting ready, choosing a black and white striped skirt with a plain black t-shirt, Edie appeared in the room, arms crossed over her chest. She was in brown slacks and a white blouse, a plain white headband in her strawberry blonde hair, and she looked less than pleased.

"Morning Edie."

"Is it?"

"Something happen?" I tuck my shirt into my skirt waist and am about to turn around when I spot the black box with Edie's necklace inside. I don't know if she knows I even have it.

"I know you have it," Edie says immediately, "and I don't care. You should own at least one decent pair of jewels. Anyway, I visited our dear friend Terrance this morning."

"What did you find out?"

"Only that he has drafted a letter to some lawyer bureau about your deceiving actions and manipulative tactics, and how he wishes to warn his good friends and colleagues about hiring you."

"Well," I let out a sigh as I turn around to face her, "I suppose I knew that was coming."

"He was also on the phone with his Private Investigator."

"Why?"

"He has him following Porter, but I'm not worried. He won't find anything important. Anyway, point is the house is empty. Marta and Rosanne won't be returning till the evening so chop chop. Let's get going, we have a full day of searching ahead of us. I'd like to go through the furniture from the auction again, and check the attic as well—"

"Edie, I can't. I have brunch with my mom and Stella."

Her hands drop to her side, "forgive me but didn't you and Riley end things last evening? You didn't think I noticed, did you?"

"We didn't exactly end things, alright?"

She raises her eyebrows at me, "I see. So you are still deluded enough to think your engagement is a good idea, despite the fact you have feelings for my nephew and Riley is an imbecile?"

I wasn't stunned to learn she had been watching Porter and me. The woman knows nothing of privacy, but to suggest I have actual feelings for Porter is ridiculous. I don't even know him; all I have is a *tiny* crush which is normal and healthy.

"I do not have any feelings for your nephew," I gawk at her, hoping to sell the reaction, but she merely rolls her eyes at me. "And furthermore Riley is not a moron, he's just unique."

"I won't be able to convince you to ditch this brunch, will I?"

"No," my jaw tightens as I snatch the black box from the dresser and cross the bedroom.

"Fine then. Fine indeed."

We meet at Petite Jardin, not too far from the loft. It's a quaint French bistro which serves overpriced dishes that taste mediocre at best, but happen to be very generous with their wine orders. We are seated in the middle of the bistro behind a round black table and leather dining chairs, a small pod light hanging from the ceiling above us. There isn't a table empty in the place, and even the art deco bar behind us is full of patrons.

I sit in between Stella and my mother, who couldn't look more drastically different from each other if they tried. My mother had her short black hair up in a ponytail, strands of her thick curls bounced out. She was in a pair of black pants and a red blouse that tied nicely around her neck. Stella sat in a white wrap dress with the Louis Vuitton symbol patterned throughout, her greying hair in its usual miniature beehive. As my mother reads the menu, her face tense with determination as she tries to decide what is safe enough to eat, Stella sits with her wedding binder on her plate before her.

216

"I was thinking we should have the bridal shower in a little less than three weeks. Beginning of June," Stella says looking from my mother to me. "I understand its quick but the wedding is only seven weeks away."

"That sounds great." My mother glances up from her menu and beams at Stella, "I already know the theme! I was thinking whimsical colors because when Phoebe was little she used to love going to fairs and carnivals—"

Stella lets out a small laugh as she picks up her glass of water, "as did all small children. I don't think that theme would work for a twenty eight year old woman. It should be sophisticated and classy; she works at a top law firm you know."

I grimace as my mother's face clenches; the thing about my mother is she never really gets her feelings hurt; she gets angry.

"Um, why don't we put the theme aside for a second," I suggest looking from Stella to my mom, "and think about the location? Maybe we could have it outside since it will most likely be nice weather—"

Stella waves me off, "I've already reserved Ballroom B at the country club for it."

My mom sets down her menu, "I was hoping the shower could be at—"

Edie surfaces right between Stella and my mom, arms drawn over her chest. "*So sorry,*" her tone is not the least apologetic, "I don't mean to interrupt this delightful meal but I come with news that may have you come to your senses."

And what is that?

"At a *hall?*" Stella frowns at my mother; her face contorts. "You cannot be serious."

"What's wrong with a hall?" my mother demands.

"It seems I was right to never trust that hippie," Edie exclaims over the raising voices.

What do you mean?

"I mean her and your space cadet, are dancing the tango behind your back. I gather it's for some time as well."

No that can't be. Riley would never—Jamie would never, it's not in her nature, she's good, she—

217

"—is a fake," Edie proudly interrupts. "If you don't believe me, why don't you hop on over to her apartment? They have conveniently ordered a vegan pizza set to arrive in about forty minutes."

"That is outrageous!" Stella has slammed her wedding binder closed as she leans over the table, "Goodie bags filled with popcorn, lollipops and lip-gloss? This isn't a child's birthday party! It doesn't go with the Parisian theme!"

"The theme," my mom's voice has now caught the attention of surrounding patrons, "is Whimsical. Not pretentious, boring Paris!"

I can't think with all this noise.

I place my elbow on the table in front of me and put my hands over my ears so I can hear myself think. I shut my eyes. Everything gets muffled and I can hear my heart pulsing against me, every second that passes. Thud, thud, thud.

Riley wouldn't do this, he would never do this. There must be something else going on, Edie. Maybe Jamie is teaching Riley to dance for the wedding?

"Oh for Hell's Fire stop this!" Edie stomps her foot next to me. "Stop making excuses! It's infuriating. Just own up to it Phoebe, own up to the fact that you don't even love him and that it's possible he's having an affair!"

I feel someone touch my shoulder gently and when I look over I see my mother has inched her chair closer to me. Stella bears a quizzical look my way.

"Phoebe? Are you alright?"

Dropping my hands I look into her mocha colored eyes and slowly smile, "I'm okay, just not feeling all that well."

"My God, could you be pregnant?" Stella's breath staggers, "If you are, it's no matter. We can tell everyone the baby was premature—"

"—I'm not pregnant!" I exclaim in horror,

"Oh," my mom slouches in her chair, disappointed.

"I'm sorry, but I have to be going," I push my chair back and look at Edie as I do. "I forgot I have something important to do. Please stay, and enjoy each other's company."

"But—but," Stella stutters as she watches me gather my purse, "the wedding—"

"—I'm sorry, bye."

Outside I've hailed a cab. Where Edie has gone, I'm not sure. Frankly I wasn't the least bit upset in her disappearance either; I don't want her there when I get to Jamie's apartment.

I feel numb as the cab pulls up and I slide inside, giving the cab driver Jamie's address in the west end.

What will I do if I find them together? I mean obviously this is the end, who wouldn't end things with their significant other over something like this?

I'm not in the cab for more than a few minutes when we stop at an intersection, and Edie appears next to me. She tries to put a hectic hand on my arm but it slides back through and gives me the chills.

"Forget the space cadet," her voice is full of concern. "You have to get back to the house. Terrance just pulled up. Nobody is home but Marta. She's going to let him search the place!"

She can't do that!

"She can when nobody is there! He's going to find the will. I overheard him tell her he knows where it may be based on simple elimination."

But if Riley is cheating—

"—Okay! I will be honest with you. All I saw was them doing some weird yoga moves," Edie puts both hands up. "But from where I stood I saw a lot of sexual tension so I know he's having an affair, I have a hunch!"

Edie I could kill you! You don't know anything, it's just a feeling and not even feasible because you hate the guy. Your judgement is clouded. How can you trust your intuition!

My hands are balled up into fists at my sides and my jaw clenches so hard I feel like I could break my teeth. I can't believe her, I can't believe she would lie—actually I do believe it.

"Big deal," Edie shoots back at me, "I don't even know why you're angry *if* he is cheating on you. You have feelings for someone else, and that is technically cheating as well. And it's not like you haven't spread a few white lies yourself."

"It's just a crush!" I scream.

The cab driver turns his head abruptly and frowns at me, "Miss? Are you alright?"

I slump back and put my head in my heads, embarrassed, infuriated and onus. "I'm fine. There's been a change in plans. I need you to take me to Cedar Springs, right away. As fast as you can."

"Okay, as fast as I can," he shrugs slowly, "will cost extra to go out there."

"That's fine."

"Should be there in under forty five minutes."

True to his word, the cab driver pulls up to the estate less than forty five minutes later, and I throw him a generous tip. I don't see Terrance's car in the driveway or Porter's, just a beat up rust bucket which I know is Marta's car. I skim the street to my left and then to my right, catching sight of a shiny designer car a block or so down wedged between two SUV's. Definitely Terrance's.

I race up the pathway of the house, letting the gate slam shut behind me and take the stairs to the porch two at a time. I'm not surprised to find the front door locked as I turn the handle a few times but I had a key. I begin fishing in my purse as Edie emerges through the front door.

"Thank goodness you're here," Edie flusters, "he's in the library with Marta. She's making a mess of the books on the selves, thinks I have it hidden behind one or something."

I get the keys out and quickly open the door, throwing my purse on the ground beneath the antique coat rack in the corner. As I hurry towards the stairs I freeze, suddenly realizing that I don't have a plan.

"What? What is it?" Edie pushes as she sees me stop.

I whisper, "What am I supposed to do?"

"You demand he leaves and inform Marta that you will be telling Porter of what she did. It's against house rules to allow anyone in when Porter isn't home."

"Okay..."

"Don't be scared of your boss," Edie seems to guess my thoughts before they even come to, "He can't do anything to you. He can just yell at you."

"I guess you're right," I start to climb the stairs quickly; "he's already ruined my career with that fax letter. Don't think

220

I've forgiven you for what you did back there either, it was rotten."

"My hunches," she snaps, "are never wrong!"

When I'm finally at the top of the stairs I can hear movement in the library, and tip toe against the hard wood to reach the door. Before opening it I place an ear to the door to listen. It's silent from voices; all I hear are muffled thuds and clunks for a few seconds.

"What if the wills are at the office?" Marta's voice comes through sounding panicky, *"What if she, like, hid it in there?"*

"Merida checked the offices," Terrance snaps. *"There is nothing there. It has to be in this house. I know Edie found the one I put in the desk, and moved it."*

"The only place we haven't looked is the attic, guest house and Porter's room."

"You're useless," Terrance grunts, *"Did you find the albums Merida wants?"*

"No, I looked before you got here," Marta answers gloomily. *"I don't know where they are."* Her voices quiver a bit now, *"And you don't have to be so mean."*

"Just keep looking."

"What does she want them for? The wills aren't in them."

"She doesn't want them for the wills. There's a delicate picture in there she wants destroyed before anybody gets their hands on it. Now shut up and keep looking. Finish that bookshelf," he orders loudly, *"then let's move to the attic."*

"They won't find anything in there," Edie whispers to me, "but Christmas boxes, tables and old clothes. I haven't been up there in years."

"Where is all the furniture up for auction?" I whisper, my hands rest against the library door. "And what picture is Terrance talking about?"

"In the guest house. Only Rosanna and Porter have the key."

"And the picture?"

Edie sighs loudly and rolls her eyes, "There's a picture in there of her in a rather compromising position from our last vacation together with our husbands. If the picture was published or seen by anyone other than us she'd have a lot of explaining to do. I suppose that's the one she wants."

"What is it?" I can't help but smile as my mind wonders. *What could she have done that was so bad? Did she commit a robbery? A murder?*

Edie laughs, "A murder? Please."

We hear a ringtone go off and freeze, immediate relief washes over the two of us when we realize it's coming from inside the library. All noise stops as we hear Terrance shout into his phone. A few seconds of silence go by before his voice booms through the closed door again. "I see. And the contracts? Did he sign them and fax them yet?"

I mouth the name 'Merida' to Edie, and she gives a serious nod.

"Fine," Terrance snarls. "I have to go."

It's silent; we hear nothing and slowly Edie puts her head through the door. I make a face at the sight. A second later she pulls it out, and narrows her eyes at me. "He's whispering something to her, I think he heard us or rather *you.*"

How? I was dead silent!

"Obviously not," Edie raises one eyebrow, "You better get in there."

I adjust my posture as I take my hands from the door and reach for the doorknob. Not even bothering to knock, I turn the knob and push the door open with my foot.

Both Terrance and Marta are looking at me as I enter; he is on one side of the desk and she's on the other. Her hands are placed on her hips and she gives me an unwelcoming glare. I can't help but make a face at what she's wearing. A pair of skinny jeans and a crop top with a giant flaming skull on the front. Giant gold hoops hang from her ears and her hair is a mess of curls around her.

I try not to giggle as I notice the contrast between her and Terrance, in his dark green polo sweater and khakis. He looks as if he just left the golf course.

"What the hell are you doing here?" Marta demands, the pile of cheap gold toned bracelets on her arms cling as she folds her arms over her chest.

"I work here," I remind her. "What is going on?"

"None of your business," Terrance's voice barely shakes at being caught.

"Really? Well then, you won't mind me calling up Porter and letting him know what I stumbled upon would you?" I watch Terrance smile; its smug and ugly. Next to him Marta's morose temperament turns into one of worry.

"Please do," Terrance slowly walks from around the desk. "I'm sure he'd love to know why you never mentioned being part of his Aunt's case."

Edie exclaims pointing at him. "Dirty liar."

"I was not on her case, he knows that," I try to keep my voice steady but the weight of his vicious stare makes my palms sweat. He wouldn't hit me, would he?

"I wouldn't count it out," Edie states.

"Oh but yes you were," Terrance smiles as he sets his hands into his pockets. "Your signature will be on every receiving document the firm obtained from Mrs. Edwards. I'm surprised he hasn't been wondering how convenient it is that you worked at my firm, and yet also claim to be related to Mrs. Edwards."

I shake my head confidently at him. "Doesn't matter, Porter trusts me. He doesn't trust you very much, does he?" I watch Marta roll her eyes at me, and I frown at her, "And you. You should be ashamed of yourself. Edie treated you well, you're betraying her."

"Whatever," Marta smirks running a hand through her thick luscious hair, "I hated that old bat. She was bossy and grumpy. She never tipped me, not even at Christmas. I had to steal her Lavish Look products from her inventory and sell them at discounted prices."

Edie gasps and stomps both her feet, "you hussy!"

"Come along Marta," Terrance grabs her arm and yanks her from her place. I slide out of the way of the door but stay close to it, in an attempt to hold my ground. Once they reach me Terrance shoves Marta outside and she stumbles a bit as to not lose her footing. He steps before me and looks down at me, "Ms. Mercer won't be telling anybody about this and I guarantee it."

"Oh yes she will, you beast," Edie snaps firmly.

No Edie, I can't.

"What? Why not!"

"You don't mind if I walk you both out do you?" I narrow my eyes at him and he grunts before leaving the room. I wrap my hand around the doorknob and pull it shut behind me. Neither Marta or Terrance say a word as they head down the stairs, Marta looks over her shoulder a few times at me, but I pretend not to notice her death stare. I stop at the bottom of the stairs, my eyes glued on the two of them as they slowly leave the house, slamming the door behind them.

"We need to start searching my belongings in the guest house," Edie breaks the silence a second after they've gone. "Let me see if either Porter or Rosanne have left their key here."

I'm standing on the stairs after she's gone. Both hands rested on the bannisters at my sides and I can't help but think of all the times Edie made her grand entrance on these stairs.

A ringing cuts the silence around me and I look over at my purse. I move off the stairs and cross the front lobby quickly. Once at my bag, I pluck out my phone, seeing the name *Riley* flickering across the screen.

After everything that just happened I had forgotten about Edie's accusation.

"Hi" I say into the cold metal against my ear.

"Phoebe. What went on during brunch today?" He's asking calmly.

"Oh right, that. Well…it didn't go too well."

"So I heard. You rushed out of there, on our mothers, without an explanation."

Edie said there was sexual tension…

"Riley? Are you alone?"

There's a sharp pause from him. *"Yes I'm alone. I'm at our loft. Where are you?"*

Is he telling the truth? I mean, if Edie *says* he saw him at Jamie's apartment then she must have seen him. Why would she lie about that?

"In Cedar Springs. Where you with Jamie today?"

"Yes, I was at her apartment. I met James there after his run, and she's teaching me some new Yoga positions. They're a

224

*bit challenging but my back feels wonderful. I'll teach you.
Why?"*

Edie did say she saw them doing Yoga.

"Er, never mind. Look I have to stay here tonight; I have an early day tomorrow."

I can't accuse him over the phone, that's ridiculous. Besides his story matches up with Edie's and she didn't see any kissing or fondling or—

"Is something wrong? Are you angry at me?"

"Are you cheating on me?" The words slip out just as I'm about to say, 'no I'm not.'

"Excuse me? Phoebe, are you serious?"

I swallow a lump in my throat, "Someone saw you with Jamie today—"

"Who saw me?" he's snarky now.

"Never mind who."

"And do you believe this person? Jamie who is madly in love with James? Jamie who asks about you every day and considers you a friend? That is the Jamie I'm cheating on you with?"

Oh God, it is stupid sounding. It's not in Jamie's nature to do something like this. I knew this.

"I'm sorry, you're right," I shake my head as I slump to my knees.

"It's fine, this is just something we can bring up tomorrow at our first session. Don't forget it's at five thirty. I'll text you the address."

The couple's therapist. I had forgot.

Chapter Nineteen

I couldn't sleep half the night. My mind was racing; where the hell was Edie's will? How could a pile of papers be so damned hard to find? Why did Riley seem so calm yesterday? Shouldn't he have freaked out when I asked him if he was cheating?

By the time three a.m. rolled around I had exhausted myself with my thoughts and passed right out, only to awake at seven a.m. to start the day's chores. I showered in our shared bathroom, hearing neither Marta nor Rosanne as I got ready. Around seven thirty, I slipped my phone into the pocket of my uniform and headed down the hall towards the kitchen. I stopped shy of pushing the swinging door open when I heard voices in the kitchen.

"I don't trust her Aunt Rosie. She's sneaky. She appeared out of the blue, says she's related to Edie with no real proof," I hear Marta wail.

"It's none of our business."

"Oh come on, you know she's shifty. You know. She's always sneaking around the house as if she's looking for something. She's probably stealing out from under us!"

"Marta."

"If you tell Porter, he'll listen to you, he trusts you."

There's silence.

"You better get in there," comes Edie's voice behind me. "Marta can be pretty convincing and she's right about Porter trusting Rosanne. If she says anything he may just fire you…" I glance at her over my shoulder. She's playing with the frilly sleeves of her red top and shrugs. "Or maybe not, since you and he have chemistry—"

We have nothing.

"Have you dumped that man-child of yours yet?" Edie demands with a sigh, "Or are you wasting more time?"

I ignore her and straighten up before I push the kitchen door open loudly. I enter casually, stopping when I see Marta and Rosanne around the counter. Rosanne's preparing something on the stove behind her, which smells divinely cheesy, and Marta stands with her arms crossed near her. Her massive curly hair pulled up in a big bun, signature hoops glistening from the light of the sun that streams through the bay windows.

"Morning," I smile nonchalantly.

"Good morning," Rosanne turns from me and goes back to the pans on the stove, "Do you want some breakfast before you start? I'm making eggs benedict."

"How fitting," Edie snaps as she settles next to Marta, and glares at her. I watch the ghost take a sniff of the young girl. "She smells odd, familiar…"

She's probably using your products.

"No I'm okay," I answer Rosanne, "What's on the agenda today?"

"I don't have a product that smells like vanilla and rose," Edie keeps sniffing and I have to stop myself from smirking. Edie gasps and turns to me, "She's stolen the prototype perfume for our new scent line!"

How could she have done that Edie?

"I don't know, but I bet Merida has something to do with it."

Rosanne looks at me and I turn my attention to her. "Mr. Burroughs has the auction to get ready for, it's in three days so that's what we focus on."

"Oh my God, it *is* in three days!" Edie shouts.

The door to the dining room opens and we all watch as Porter enters the dining room. He's in a dark suit and dark green shirt, and looking rather stressed. There are bags under his eyes, and his stubble has gotten thicker.

"Morning," he says looking at me only briefly before putting his attention on Rosanne. "Since the auction has been moved up I need all three of you to forsake the regular household chores and focus on that. There has been a growing interest in Aunt Edie's belongings and I plan to make a few new additions. There are quite a few objects in the attic that I need found, cleaned and—"

"—I'll take the attic!" Marta practically leaps out from her own skin and I watch Rosanne and Porter frown at her.

"Let her have it. There's nothing up there," Edie swats a hand at Marta.

227

"Very well," Porter slowly nods, "I'll give you a list. Most of it is seasonal décor that my aunt hasn't used in decades. Some are very old, worth quite a lot so please be careful."

Marta smiles at him, "I will."

I would roll my eyes if I knew nobody would see me.

"Rosanne, if you and Phoebe could get everything ready in the guest house?" Porter asks. "I have the list with me and if you could oil up the armoires and steam press any clothing."

"As soon as I'm done I will go right over there," Rosanne nods.

"Good. I'll let Phoebe get a head start," he looks at me. "Give me a moment to get the key."

Five minutes later I'm following Porter to the guest house as he fumbles to find the key to the guest house on a ring of keys. He juggles a clipboard underneath his other arm. I'm clutching a plastic bucket full of oils for wood. We don't say anything to one another until we get to the guest house and he finally unlocks it.

It was incredibly musty in the room; the air was dull and heavy. When was the last time someone cracked a window open in here?

The lights come on around me and I get a better look at the room. Everything in the guest room is modernized compared to the rest of Edie's house. The lights on the wall are sleek and slender in the form of a 'U'. The walls are painted a grey-blue and there is a grey carpet beneath our feet leading into a glamourous looking white wooden floor. Behind all the armoires and boxes, I can see a small kitchen and a door off of it.

"Everything in the boxes will be sold together," Porter says as he steps up next to me. "I spent most of last night looking through the boxes for Aunt Edie's will."

"Did you find it?" I feel my heart stop.

"No, and I've decided that was it. I've had enough," he runs a hand through his hair, "so I'll be dividing off and selling everything, as planned. I sign the contracts Thursday."

Edie is going to lose it.

Why was she such a crazy, paranoid lady? If she only had one extra copy lying around somewhere, or even at her lawyer's office then none of this would have happened.

"If you see a box with sketches of boats in it, let me know," Porter addresses. "Somehow I mixed them in with the boxes for the auction."

"I thought you sold Edie's boat?"

"I did yes. But those are my sketches," he steps up to a box and opens it up, the clipboard underneath his armpit.

"You draw?" I'm surprised, and slowly I watch him smile at me.

"Not well, I'm afraid. The sketches are private, for my boats."

Still in awe I smile as I ask him, "You build boats?"

"Small ones, yes."

Something moves from the corner of my eye and as I turn I see Edie, standing over an opened box near Porter. Looking down at its contents and making a face.

Where have you been? Porter has given up looking for your will—

"—I know," she sighs. "I was watching him last night as he looked through this junk. I know the will is in here, in this house," she clenches her fists, "I can feel it."

You're a ghost, you can't feel anything.

"Yes I can. I can feel happiness, anger, annoyance and even pity; which is what I feel for you right now," her eyes dart my way and I frown on her.

Why?

She draws in a breath and puts a hand on her forehead, "Don't get mad."

Why would I get—what did you do?

"Nothing," she throws her hands up blandly. "I just...I followed your space cadet to a hotel downtown this morning. The Stratacone Hotel. I guessed he checked in last night after you told him you planned to stay here. Room 108."

I suddenly feel as if I ate bad curry. Or bad tofu. My stomach grumbles and I turn my back on both Edie and Porter.

"She was—is there with him now. I overheard them planning to spend until lunch together."

I can feel Edie's presence next to me, and I bend down to the bucket, feeling the carpet against my knees. "Did you hear me?"

So he is—he is with her then, and has been for who knows how long. How could he do this? How could *she* do this to James?

Porter's voice breaks through Edie and me, "Are you alright?"

"I'm fine," my mouth soothes with dryness, "I'm good."

"Are you sure?"

"You look sick," Edie whispers loudly down at me, "use that bucket."

I grip the sides of the bucket for a moment, "I need to go do something important. It won't take long. I should be back by lunchtime."

I push myself up, letting the bucket tip on its side and look over to find Porter dropping his arms to the sides, impatience washing over his face. "Phoebe, I know you are busy with your engagement and wedding, but I hired you to do this job."

"I know," I tell him, "and if it wasn't important then I'd—"

"—Unless its life or death," Porter interrupts, "then it has to wait."

"It is life or death!" Edie practically shouts. "Tell him being in that relationship is sucking the life out of you, and you need to end it." She disappears instantly, her gusto leaving us behind.

I suppose it could wait, I tell myself, I could ask Riley about it at the session tonight. I could say that I have proof that he was cheating, with Jamie. He would ask for it though, or he would come up with some excuse as to why they were there? What is wrong with me? Why can't I just call him up and tell him it's over? Why can't I stand my ground on *anything*?

Oh God no, I'm tearing up.

It's so pathetic.

I turn away quickly, blinking away the tears in my eyes so Porter doesn't see me.

"Phoebe?"

"I'm alright," I clear my throat and take a deep breath, "I'm a little bit overwhelmed."

"With the cleaning?" Porter's tone was critical, and it more than upset me. In fact, it bothered me to a maddening degree and I felt my face tighten.

"No, not with the cleaning," I snap, "with everything. My fiancé is cheating on me but I'm sure it's my fault," I spat as I turn to face him. "I should have ended things with him a while ago when I knew we weren't working. I no longer have a career, but let's be honest, I probably never really had one. No, the cleaning doesn't bother me, which I'll take as a good sign because after today it may be my new career path. A maid. Forever."

Porter blinks at me and I watch as he opens his mouth to say something, but he promptly shuts it. I feel like a fool, for more than one reason. My insides burn with embarrassment and I hate it. "I'm sorry, but I have to go talk to Riley."

I make a beeline for the open door, and don't dare meet Porter's eyes as I do.

Inside the house I don't answer Rosanne, who asks me if somethings the matter as I race through the kitchen. I undress from my uniform into my clothes from yesterday.

What will I say to them? How do I confront them?

There's a tapping at my closed bedroom door and I know its Rosanne,

"I will be back in a few hours Rosanne, I promise."

"It's not Rosanne."

The sound of Porter's voice freezes me.

The door budges a few inches, enough for me to see Porter standing in the doorway. His hands are in the pockets of his pants and he looks from the floor to me slowly, "I'd like to apologise. I shouldn't have been so coarse a few minutes ago."

"It's alright," I shrug him off as I throw my purse strap over my shoulder, "really it's fine. I do have to leave now, he's at a hotel right now and I need to get there."

"Let me take you," he offers softly.

"No, thank you but I have to go alone. It could turn out to be nothing."

I reach the door and he speaks again, "Please let me take you. It'll save you the cab fare and the time."

The entire ride to the city is silent; apart from Porter taking several calls on his bluetooth about the auction, and some client meetings in London. It came to my knowledge that I never asked what he did for a living.

"What do you do, exactly?"

"I run a direct marketing and branding agency in London," he answers looking at me briefly. "We're opening up a division here, towards the end of next year."

"So that's why Riley presented to you?"

"We've been hiring outside advertising firms for clients we have in other countries. I was looking for a firm here to handle the advertising for our new client based in the city," he explains making a sharp left onto the busy city street.

I don't say anything else as he slows down the car until it finally stops against the sidewalk. I peer out the window before me and see the Stratacone Hotel. A grand hotel that looks like every other sky scraper around it, with only a dazzling red and gold marque establishing its name. There are guests buzzing in and out of the revolving doors.

I feel a warm sensation come over my left hand, and look down to see that Porter has placed his over it. "Do you want me to come with you?"

"No," the word barely escapes my lips as I look away from his eyes, back at the building.

"May I just say," he pauses and glances down for a second. As he looks back a moment later, his eyes square into mine, "That he is a fool."

My heart takes little time to rush against my ribcage and my breath is caught as we look at each other. He gazes at me with light admiration that it makes me bashful. Riley never looked at me this way.

I force myself to leave his car without a word, fearing I'll lose my nerve in confronting Riley, and possibly give in to my desire to have Porter's lips touch mine.

The lobby of the Stratacone is beautiful, warm and bright. The Check In desk sits in bright marble between two large digital machines designed for Self-Check In. I spot the golden elevator doors behind them and the crowd of people waiting for them to open so I hurry over, not to miss the next ride.

I don't have a game plan really, and as the doors open seconds later, I realize that maybe the best thing would be to just to slide my ring, with a note, under the door.

I nestle between the groups of people and hit the button '1', just as the elevator doors close. The ride up is short and the doors 'bing' open in no time. I find myself standing in a luxurious hallway as bright as the lobby below, with gold wallpaper and giant clear vases that stand three feet off the floor filled with real flowers.

I see the gold plated sign against the wall pointing left to room numbers 100-150 and right to numbers 150-199.

"Room 108," Edie's voice drifts into my ears and I see her step up.

"Go away," I tell her as I make the turn down the hall, "I don't need an audience."

She says nothing and just vanishes.

It's not long until I reach the white wooden door with the golden 108 number plated on it.

This is it.

I knock with my knuckle and wait.

I need to see for myself that he was in there with her, though slipping a note underneath the door would be ideal, I couldn't risk the room being occupied by someone else.

Finally the door opens and I take a long deep breath, preparing myself for her face or his but the door opens to an unknown blond woman in a light blue uniform. "Can I help you?"

"I'm looking for a man who—"

"—The tenant checked out," the woman tells me, "I'm cleaning the room now."

She shuts the door in my face and I'm left staring at it.

I drag myself back down the hall towards the elevator.

What was I expecting to find honestly? Riley and Jamie in a heap of passion? For God's sake this is reality. And the reality is...

I don't want to be engaged.

I ride the elevator down in silence, grateful that I'm alone on the short trip.

I don't want to be with Riley anymore; we aren't working and I don't know if we ever truly did. I leave the elevator with a heavy stride and begin to make my way past the check in/out desk when I'm stopped by what I see across from me.

Near the revolving doors, stands Riley. He's in a track suit, running a hand through his hair but he's standing alone.

Then, a woman pops up out of nowhere. In a tight black skirt and an off the shoulder crème toned blouse. She kisses him quickly on the cheek, her long black wavy hair sashaying around her. Riley pulls away, saying something to her that makes her frown at him.

She turns around and sees me, her expression whitens a little. When Riley sees her face he spins, his body stiffening as he sees me. I watch him swallow a few times.

Edie was wrong. He isn't cheating with Jamie. He's cheating with a stranger.

I feel my breathing slow, and suddenly I'm weightless. My stomach spasms in rage, and I can feel my brow come together tightly.

Finally Riley moves towards me, his arms out, as the woman turns her back on us and drops her head. "Phoebe. I can explain."

I don't know what I feel anymore as he comes up to me, panicked and white. A wave of emotions comes over me; my fists clench from anger and my stomach twists as if I'm about to be sick. I don't believe he would do this, after everything he's accused me of, of not caring or—

"This isn't what you think it is," he interrupts my thoughts as he gets to me. He grabs my hands in his and pulls them to his chest.

I try to pull from him but he holds my hands firmly. "I can't believe you would do this, Riley! You made me feel stupid, and the bad guy the last few weeks but *you're* the one who is cheating!"

"She's nobody, just an intern we hired last month. It doesn't matter," he suddenly shakes his head at me. "It was nothing. A stupid onetime thing, and I've been stressed Phoebs. I've been *so* stressed. With what is going on with you, with the firm not doing well, with the wedding—"

"—don't use me as an excuse!" I yank my hands away, and a few people look our way.

"Sshh," Riley snaps. "Don't make a scene. Just let me explain."

I gape at him; he looks so concerned, flustered and hurt. His hair is dull, falling from its usually savvy style and there is paleness over his usual tanned tone. His eyebrows have dipped in sadness, and his whole posture is weak.

"I don't think there is anything left to explain," I look down on my finger; at the ring that has felt alien to me for the last few days. "I don't even blame you for this. I mean I *blame* you," I awkwardly backtrack, "but it's not all your fault. I should have done this days ago." I look up to find him frowning at me. "I don't think we're a good match, I don't think we ever were," I shrug at him as I slide the ring off my finger. Forcing it into his hands, I take a step back as he speaks,

"No Phoebe, we're fine. This is just a rough—"

"—No," I cut him off firmly, "it's not a rough patch Riley. This is over."

Chapter Twenty

I was able to convince Porter to drop me off at the loft to collect some things. I hadn't needed to tell him anything; he immediately glanced down at my hand and noticed the missing ring. The short ride to the loft was quiet and when he offered to wait for me downstairs I declined.

Now I stood in the loft alone and empty; I had packed a duffle bag worth of clothes along with some toiletries. I had showered, ignoring every beep or vibration that came from my phone.

My eyes strung with tears but none of them ever ran. Riley and I had been together for over a year. We had spent holidays together, went to funerals with each other, and talked about a future. This was the only true, serious relationship I had ever been in, so why wasn't I more in a heaping mess?

There's a knock on the door, a soft banging that gets louder, and one that I don't recognize. Sincerely hoping it isn't Riley, I move towards the door and use my strength to slowly slide the heavy door wide open. Luckily it's not Riley, but Greg staring at me with a half-hearted smile in his navy blue pin stripped suit which oddly enough only makes him look shorter.

"Hey. Thought I'd stop by and see how you're doing."

"You didn't have to Greg."

In truth I wasn't in the mood to see anyone, but I couldn't be rude to someone who didn't deserve it. I let him in and shut the door behind him slowly.

"It wasn't any trouble. The other day, when Terrance sent off that awful fax I figured when I had a minute to spare I should check up on you. Tell you that the world isn't over just yet," he gives me a crooked smile and shrugs.

So it had been done then, just as Terrance promised it would be. When Edie told me he had drafted the letter, I had some hope he wouldn't really send it. Now I'm a fool in every legal firm in this glorious city.

Greg clears his throat, "Can I have a glass of water?"

"Oh yeah, sure," I leave his side. "I appreciate it Greg, but I think I can successfully say my career at any law firm in the city is over."

"There are always other cities," Greg jokes.

I get the water slowly and think about it. I could move, really what's stopping me now? I don't have a fiancé anymore or any career prospects. Nothing is tying me down; as soon as I find Edie's stupid will I can get myself a new life. I just wish I felt optimistic about it.

I carry the water back over to Greg who is looking down my purse and my duffle bag. When he sees me he shy's away, guilt washing over his face as he looks down at his feet. "Sorry, I didn't mean to be nosey. I just saw the bag and, well…"

"It's okay," I shrug as I hand him the glass, "it's not like I was trying to hide it."

He glances at my left hand, noticing no ring, "Sorry about that, when did it happen?"

"An hour ago, I was just leaving."

"Man, Phoebe, I am really sorry. You don't deserve any of this," his face scrunches up as he looks at the glass of water in his hands. "Was it because of the fax or…?"

"It wasn't the fax. I doubt Riley even knows about it. We were just a bad match from the start. I couldn't see it past—"

"—His good looks?" Greg guesses as he drinks his water slowly.

"You could say that."

Or you could say my own *delusion* as to how perfect he was.

"If there is anything I can do for you," Greg goes on, placing a hand on my shoulder, "please let me know. A reference, or if you need a place to stay, I can talk to my roommate."

"No, that's alright but thank you," I add quickly with a small smile. "I still have my other job."

For the time being, anyway.

"Let me help you with these," he bends over and retrieves the duffle bag, setting the empty glass on the mail table next to the door. He begins to open the loft door as I turn around to face the empty place. My eyes fall to my old vintage roll top desk which always looked so perfect against the exposed brick wall.

When I get back go Edie's house with my duffle bag in tow, I spot an empty driveway. I'm grateful of Porter's absence, and only hope that Rosanne and Marta are too busy to notice my return. I manage to sneak into my room, deciding against unpacking when I notice that I've missed a total of seven calls on my cell phone, and have fifteen unanswered text messages. Before I can scroll through the notifications my phone rings, and Faye's name appears in bold.

"Hello?"

"Oh my God, how are you? Are you okay? We've been trying to reach you for the last hour. Your brother even offered to stop by your loft after he was done work to check up on you."

"Wait, how did you even find out?" I ask frowning, "I haven't told anybody yet."

"Riley reached out to us. Turns out his father found out from someone on his legal team about the fax. So Riley called us all, said he was worried about what you may do."

She's talking about the fax?

"Not that your suicidal or anything, but he said you've worked so hard at that firm and put in all these hours and maybe this would cause you to have a nervous breakdown or something."

"So he didn't tell you?" I frown as I sit down on the bed behind me, staring at the dull white wall and mundane white dresser.

"Tell me what?"

I open my mouth to tell her about Riley, about the hotel, about everything when Edie suddenly appears. She's in a purple frock with a matching 1930's sequin headband around her forehead, her strawberry blond curls however in a frizzy mess.

The temperature drops in the room and I can't help but shiver. It comes like a wave from where Edie stands, and somehow darkens the room at the same time.

"You have to get to Lavish Looks right now. Right away. Merida is meeting with the board in fifteen minutes to vote Porter out. Those old buffoons are convinced by her claim that Porter is disorganized and reckless with my estate. They don't trust him any more to make decisions with the company and are willing to hand over every aspect of it to her. He'll lose his shares, and won't get a dime."

Damn it. Merida and Terrance must be getting tired of waiting for Porter to sign everything over to them.

"Phoebe? Hello?"

"Sorry Faye, I have to call you back," I drop the call quickly and look over at the ghost. "Edie, there is no way I can stop this meeting. I have nothing to go by. What do you expect me to do?"

"Go in there and say you have the will!"

"I don't have the will. I don't have either wills."

"Do you have another suggestion?" Edie spits at me. "It's not like you can call in a fire or something. Nobody will believe you. If you say that you found the will then meeting will stop."

"And then what will happen when they demand it from me?" I jump to my feet and glare at her. "Once they realize I don't have the will then the meeting will start up again and I'll be thrown out. Porter too."

"I think I know where the will is."

We look at each other. Beneath the sudden darkness that erodes around the woman, there's a sparkle in her eye and the hairs stand up in the back of my neck. "You do?"

"I found the old will, the one Terrance hid in the desk the day of my birthday celebration right?"

My eyes dart over her as she begins to pace.

"Remember I told you how glamourous my dress was, how I didn't have time to really hide my will so I could have put it into one of the fireplaces to burn since I had soot over the sleeves of my dress?"

"I remember."

"But we didn't find it in any fireplace?"

"Edie, the point?" I push her along.

"I hid it in my dress! The dress I wore. It had deep pockets on the side. I was in a rush, when I went to hide it in the fireplace, I realized how dirty I would get. I must have just folded it and put it into the pocket of my dress!"

She shimmers with pride. Her hair turns back into its soft waves, any frizz that once was, is gone now. Even the purple shade of her dress seems to sparkle brighter as she smiles at me.

But I can't help and frown at her, "Edie even if we find that will, it doesn't help us. It's the old will; the will Terrance is looking for. The one that leaves quite a bit of money to Marta and the company to Merida. We hand it over to Porter, they win."

"My dear girl," Edie sighs as a feather fan appears in her right hand. She swats it at her face once before speaking, "that old will was dated just days before my birthday."

"Okay?"

"It proves that the will was reprinted *without* my permission, and that Terrance lied about destroying all copies. It will put enough doubt in Porter's mind to rethink signing the company over, and possibly the boards too. It would look suspicious that this man was Merida's lawyer."

I'm either having trouble following, or she's having trouble understanding. It's probably the later.

"Edie," I sigh, "as great as that sounds you're forgetting something important. There are no documents that prove that you had a new lawyer or wrote a new will. Porter may have some doubt when we show him the old will but I believe him when he says he is done with everything. Despite it all he may still hand over the company to Merida."

Edie snaps her fingers at me, "I have a cheque book. The amount to retain my new lawyer was two hundred dollars; the payment of the new will was also paid by cheque as I preferred to do business that way."

"Alright?" I frown at her.

"There are dates on that cheque. Names and payments that match up with the cost of consultation fees and the fees of drawing up a new will. Honestly Phoebe, must I put the pieces together for you? You're the lawyer for heaven's sake."

"I thought I was just an assistant?" I raise my eyebrows at her. I bite my lip and look at her; her hopeful expression, her buoyant stance has warmed the room.

I breathe in and exhale dramatically, "Do you know where the cheque book is?"

"In the desk in my room," she nods as if she's on stand herself, "I checked just before I came in here."

"And the secretary, at your lawyers office? I suppose we could call her and she would vouch seeing you again. Do you think Rosanne could as well?"

Edie frowns at me, "I told you. I don't trust her as far as I can throw her."

"Fine, forget Rosanne. I just thought it may be good to have someone else on our side, but I suppose the check book and the secretary will do for now. This isn't a trial, but this circumstantial evidence just may cast enough doubt on things to get the board to postpone handing anything over to Merida."

Edie tosses her fan in the air, "Call Porter now!"

"Okay, we have less than twenty minutes before he gets here," I race up the stairs with Edie at my side. "I want to have the cheque book in hand and the old will. Merida will probably be with him, so I want to have everything ready for when she tries to discredit me as crazy."

"What did he sound like?" Edie badgers, "When you told him. I couldn't hear."

"He sounded, I don't know," I get to the top of the stairs and shrug at her, "stressed. Where's Rosanne?"

"In the guest house, getting things ready for the auction. She won't be a bother."

Once in Edie's room, she orders me back to the desk where the stack of the albums use to be. I cross the magnificent room to the old desk, my stomach is in knots and I find myself smiling ear to ear.

I feel excited.

I yank open the top drawer, and there it is. A black cheque book with the name Edie Edwards painted on it with golden cursive. I take it and flip it open, after only a few pages I can see the second copy of a cheque written to a Mr. Herman Puckett for the amount of two hundred dollars. After that page is an amount written to him for five hundred dollars. All signed by Edie. All dated well within two months of her birthday.

"See? I told you!" Edie squeals in my ear. "Now the dress, it's the one made of yellow satin. Ruffles at the sleeve and neckline, you can't miss it. Sunshine gold."

With the check book in my hand, I march back across the room to the grey shimmery curtain that covers the wall on the opposite side. Gracefully I pull the curtain apart and find myself staring into an abyss of colorful material. This section of the wall had to be at least twenty feet long, with racks of clothing and glass shelves stocked with hats, shoes and headbands. There were two yellow ottomans in the middle of the room, and a three part mirror against the wall in the back so you had a look at yourself in whole.

"Jesus, Edie. This is—"

"—Remarkable, no? It's my pride and joy, along with Lavish Looks," Edie waltz into the closet and stands through the first ottoman with a smile. "I don't only have designers in here; I have vintage pieces from way back into the twenties. Pieces of my clothing alone are worth more than Terrance's salary."

That I believed.

I saw the dress almost instantly as my eyes moved from the right side to the left side of the room. There was a yellow satin gown hanging against the wall, it had silk ruffles at the neckline and sleeves, but it wasn't sunshine gold. It was dingy and murky. It hung on that hanger like a beaten rag. It was a really depressing sight. Even the flower shaped sequin black headband with golden beads, looked trashed.

"That's it?" I make a face as I walk over to it slowly,

"Yes that's it."

I can see Edie frown from the corner of my eye, "But that…that isn't what it should look like. It's supposed to be bright and vibrant and…and…not like that."

We both get to the dress at the same time but when Edie reaches for it her fingers slide right through. She looks startled, then brings her hand back against her chest and looks away from me. As if tending a burn on her thin finger.

I can see the pockets of the dress so I slowly reach into the right one. The soft fabric is hard and unwelcoming. That pocket is empty. With hesitance I move my hand into the left one, and it brushes against something.

I gasp, and Edie spins back around.

Whatever I grasp is harder than fabric but softer than wood. I can feel creases and indents. When my hand emerges, it's holding a folded piece of paper that's mighty thick one.

"That's it's," Edie whispers sharply. "Open it!"

I unfold the paper with shaky hands and fail to stifle the smile spreading over my lips. This is it. I can see half the logo of Meyers and Brant at the top of the page!

"Edie," I exclaim, "This is it! This is the old—"

Wait. What?

I stiffen as my eyes jump across the page. It's clearly a document from the firm; I mean anyone who works there would recognize it. Or the half that's left of it that is. It's run off the page, and it's not the only thing. Whatever else was written on this page, and the stapled page behind it is smudged. Blue and black ink runs amuck on the pages. Nothing is legible.

My stomach turns violently.

"What?" Edie demands. "What is it?"

I glance over at the dress. Now I notice the smell. The mold, the dirt.

"Edie," I swallow the lump in my throat, "this dress…you wore it on your birthday?"

"Yes, I have only mentioned it a hundred times," Edie snaps, her hands at her hips.

"So you were wearing it when you fell into the water right? When you, you know, almost drowned?"

She freezes, her scowl vanishes and her peachy complexion turns grey. In it she looks hideous, even the purple shade of her dress turns black. She isn't looking at me anymore; she's looking at the dress hanging against the wall, staring at it with her deep green eyes.

"Edie? I'm sorry," I whisper. "Everything on here is smudged. There isn't anything decipherable."

She doesn't look at me; she keeps her eyes on the dress. "I think he pushed me in."

This again.

"Edie, you can't just assume that Terrance was the one—"

243

"—I don't assume," she cracks angrily as she looks at me. Her bottom lip quivers. "I know. I know it, God damn it. I remember us fighting on the deck. I remember falling into the water and him leaving me in when he realized I couldn't swim. I remember him rushing off before anybody could see him, as I bobbed under the murky water."

"See? You fell. You just said you fell. He didn't push you…"

I can feel it; her anger, it pulses like ice around us. My skin is cold, my face woeful, but I don't have the heart to move from my place. So I just watch her. Watch her as she relives that day, that moment Terrance may or may not have pushed her into the water, realizing his good fortune when she couldn't swim. I didn't need proof to believe it anymore.

"Edie—"

"—Come along; let's check the safe for my new will again," Edie interrupts. She disappears before me and I look back at the yellow dress one more time before leaving her fantastic closet.

Once in her room I find her standing to my right, in the corner of the room near her armoire. She points at the small three foot tall, three foot wide black safe. "Open it."

"Just put your head through," I gesture. She raises an eyebrow at me and I prepare for a snarky remark, but instead, she does what I say. After a moment, her head comes out from the armoire and she shakes her head at me,

"Empty."

"Okay, you also said that only you and Porter had the code to the safe. So that means someone else had the code without your knowledge, or you never put the will in there like you thought you had." She's giving the safe a funny look. "It's possible no?"

She sighs, "I suppose."

"Back to square one" I say.

Edie lets out a sigh, "With only ten minutes before Porter gets here."

"We haven't checked the attic," I recall, "Would there be any possibility that you hid it up there?" Edie makes a face that tells me the answer to that question is a definite no. "Okay. On the day of your party you found Terrance's reprinted will, you stuffed it into your pocket and made a dash to get rid of it. Did you think that maybe Terrance would know where you stashed the new will?"

"No, he would never," Edie scoffs but her demeanour changes a second later. "But Marta would. She's a maid! They say maids know the darkest secrets of their masters."

"*Masters?* Edie," I give her a look.

"Hush up," she orders, "if Marta knew my hiding places then it would make sense to hide the new will somewhere I didn't think she would ever go."

"Which was?"

"My car!"

I flicked the lights on in the garage to find Edie standing proudly in front of a bright red, antique but well-kept two door car. The vehicle definitely stuck out in the dismal garage, which was cluttered with boxes from the floor to the ceiling behind it. There was only enough space to walk around the car and get inside comfortably. To my left was a series of old work benches, with tools laid out and hanging on the wall in an orderly fashion. If the dust didn't give it away then the smell sure did; it was clear the garage hadn't been open in months.

"Isn't it glamorous?" Edie stands up against the car, her hands placed on the hood of it behind her with a proud smile on her face. "It's from the 50's. It's a Chevy Bel Air. It was my fathers. I've kept it in mint condition all these years."

I creep down the creaky wooden steps onto the cold concrete as I look back at the car. It really was extraordinary. Shiny, bright red with wheels that kept it low to the ground, and rims as glossy as the color. The headlights where round, popping out gracefully, and the roof of the car indicated that it was a convertible. I neared the car and could see inside, noticing the seats where a tacky leather.

"It really is nice," I agree.

"*Nice,*" Edie repeats, "*nice?* Do you even know cars?"

"Do you?" I shoot back raising my eyebrows at her.

245

"Just get inside and look in the dashboard. Nobody is allowed to touch the car," Edie explains, "except for me and my mechanic. Nobody is allowed in the garage in fact."

I reach down for the thin steel handle and pull it lightly; it's enough to get the passenger's side door to open. Sliding in I suddenly find as tacky as the seats look, they are actually comfortable and warm. The car inside is in perfect condition. The seats shiny, not a speck of dust sits on the steering wheel or the dashboard. The old radio in between the two front seats is smudge less.

I see the dashboard compartment before me, and pull the red handle down so that it pops open. A chaos of papers come rushing out at me, and litter themselves at my feet and on my lap.

"Whoops, sorry about that," Edie laughs.

I begin to rummage through the papers that are on my lap, most of them are receipts or warranties for a part in the car. I'm about to snap at Edie for this mess, when I hear someone call my name.

When I look up, Edie is gone, and I find Porter standing in the doorway to the garage, his hand on the light switch and garage door opener. He doesn't look very happy; in fact he looks enraged. "What the hell are you doing?"

Chapter Twenty-One

I exit the car quickly, not just because Porter is charging down the stairs towards me but because I have a strong feeling that the will isn't in Edie's car either. I leave the paper on the seat and on the floor, as I shut the door behind me.

"I can explain," I say as Porter gets to me.

"I don't care. Give me the will," he puts out his hand and I feel my face scrunch up.

"The thing is..."

His eyes scour my face and he seems unmoved by my defeated expression. My hand slides into the back pocket of my jeans and I pull out the folded up paper I found in Edie's dress. "It's not the right will."

"What?" he takes the paper from me and begins to walk away. I glance around the dark garage for Edie, but I don't find her anywhere so I run after Porter who's already at the door of the garage. I panic,

"Porter, there's another will. Don't ask me how I know but I do. Edie had it made after she fired Terrance and had him destroy the old will. Only he didn't, he lied to her. That will is missing too."

His back is to me so I can't see the expression on his face as we enter the house. I follow him through the unused den, and can see him flipping the pages of what I gave him as he enters the kitchen.

Merida stands near the counter, tapping away angrily at her phone. She's in a tight black suit with a low cut that leaves little to the imagination.

"You," she practically snarls when she sees me. "You are unbelievable. You do nothing but cause trouble."

I ignore her and move around Porter, to stand in front of him just as he looks up from the murky papers he took from me. The look he gives is not one of amusement. "This is the will?"

"No it's not," I begin, "well no, I mean it is, but it's the old one. The one that Edie wanted destroyed. I found it in the dress she wore on her birthday, when she fell into the water."

"It's the will?" Merida's heels click against the tile as if they were hooves. Her shoulder brushes mine violently and she snatches the papers from Porter. Her tight face falling when she flips through the pages. "What in the...there is nothing here but running ink!"

Her scream ricochets around the empty kitchen and Porter takes back the papers from her, his glare set on her, one of suspicion. "It's not even the correct will. According to Phoebe, there are two wills."

"According to..." she snaps her head my way, "according to this *maid*? This *stranger* who claims she was related to Edie? This idiot?" she shrieks and my mouth parts, but she's quicker than me. "For God's sake Porter, there is *no* other will. Don't you think if there was Edie would have told you? This tramp is lying about a second will, god knows for whatever reason!"

"At least I'm smart enough to know how to dress for my age!"

"How dare you!" she repels her eyebrows arching high. "I would sue you if I thought it was worth my time, and you had the money!"

"She's nothing but a money hungry drone." I point at her as I look at Porter, "She doesn't care about Lavish Looks or you or Edie. It was all about the money for her. That's why Edie made another will, because she didn't trust Merida to do anything right!"

"She didn't trust—you are an evil manipulator," Merida's hands hit her hips, "Edie was my friend. We may have had our share of problems but what friendship doesn't? The company means the world to me, it always has. I have never had anything but its best interests at heart."

"You're a fraud!" I accuse.

Porter runs a hand through his hair and shouts, "Stop!"

It echoes around the room, and Merida and I look over at him. He turns his back to us and hangs his head for a moment as he looks back at the papers in his hands.

"The check book Phoebe!" Edie's scream makes me jump, and I look to my right. She's standing behind Merida, hands clasped together. "Show him the book!"

"Wait, hold on. I have proof that there is another will," the words rush out of my mouth and Porter slowly turns around. Merida takes a silent step towards me,

"What proof?"

"Here," I pull the check book from my front pocket and hand it over to Porter. "Edie wrote two cheques to Herman Puckett, a lawyer here in Cedar Springs. For the amount of a consultation fee and for the amount of a new will." Slowly Porter takes it from me, "And if you talk to his secretary, she will tell you that Edie went to see him a few times."

I can see Merida. Her entire position has changed. She's on her toes and stiff as a board, biting her lower lip. Next to her Edie stands triumphantly, with her arms crossed over her chest.

Slowly Porter looks through the book, "There are cheques made out to Mr. Puckett in here."

We hear a beep from Merida's phone and instantly she glances down at it. She mutters an 'excuse me' and makes her way for some privacy in the maid's hallway. I let out a sigh of relief as she leaves, and so does Edie.

I don't say anything as I watch Porter close the check book and fling it on the counter next to us. He rans another hand through his hair and looks up at me; I expect him to say something but he's silent for a few seconds.

"How did you know about the cheque book?" he finally asks.

"It was just a hunch," I shrug, "Edie always liked to pay with checks."

"And why where you in her car?" Porter takes a step towards the counter and sets his hands down on the marble, turning his head to look at me. "She didn't like anybody touching it, including me."

"That's because when he was twenty one he smashed it into a telephone pole," Edie remarks with a tone. "I better check on that hussy, I'll be right back."

After she's gone I look back at Porter and smile, "She didn't want you near it because you wrapped it around a telephone pole."

He lets out a smirk and rubs his eyebrows with one hand as he looks away from me. "That I did, yes." He pauses but continues rubbing his eyebrows. "I take it you'll be staying in the house with us for a while? Rosanne spotted you with extra bags when you returned."

"Oh," I cross my arms over my chest and look down at my feet quickly, "um yeah. I know the auction is in two days so it made sense to just stay here instead of check into a hotel. If you don't mind."

"I don't mind no," He rubs the back of his neck and looks ahead. "After I send away Merida perhaps you can join me for a drink. I think we both need it."

"That sounds great," the thought of a stiff drink or even a tall glass of wine sounded like a cure all at this moment. It only then dawned on me that maybe this qualified as a date, but that would be ridiculous. I doubt he was the type of guy to ask a girl out who ended her engagement hours before. Still, the thought of having a private drink with him made me warm inside, and it was hard to hide my creeping smile.

Get a grip Phoebe.

Porter looks down at the cheque book. "I suppose I should be calling Mr. Puckett to ask about the new will, he'd obviously have a copy of it on him."

"Actually…no," I squint as he looks over at me and frowns. "I called him. Last week. He's not in the country till the end of the month and his secretary says doesn't have any records of Edie but she will confirm that Edie was there."

"You knew about this last week?" he's standing up right now, whatever softness had crept up over him is now gone and replaced by the hardness that was only moments ago with Merida and me.

"Um, yes…"

"Why wouldn't you tell me about this?" he kept a hand on his forehead as he stared at me in bewilderment. "You knew this wasn't something to keep from me."

"Uhhh…"

"How did you know where to find the cheque book? Or to look in the car for this new will?" he asks quickly.

I had really hoped we dropped that.

"I had a hunch that the new will could be in there," I repeat, "Edie loved that car."

"You had a hunch? *Another hunch?*"

He doesn't believe me. Hell, would I even believe me in his place?

"Phoebe," he gestures at me with both of his hands, "I asked you once not to lie to me remember? I was on your side when Terrance accused you of breaking into his office. You promised that you would be truthful."

I feel my face go red and I wonder if it shows.

I did promise it. And I lied.

I have been lying.

My insides grumble and I suddenly feel nauseous, like anytime my mother would catch me lying about skipping class in high school. I hear Porter take a step towards me and when I look up I find him staring down at me, he's that close.

"Phoebe," he repeats my name quietly but with authority.

"I can't tell you!" I practically shout under the pressure of his shadow. He frowns startled, as I move against the counter. "You're going to think I'm crazy, I mean, I even think I'm crazy."

"It's too late, I already think you're crazy." There's a humorous tone to his remark and it takes me off guard. I look up to find a half smile over his face, and bite my lower lip.

"It was Edie," I blurt out, taking my eyes off him. "Edie told me where to look. She's been telling me where to look for her other will the entire time I have been employed here. It's how I know everything about Lavish Looks, the wills, everything."

"I'm sorry?" he shakes his head slightly, *"what?"*

"The ghost of your Aunt Edie," I clarify, I cover my face with my hands now. Just saying the words out loud to him does not in fact, make me feel any better. It makes me feel worse. Infinitely worse.

"The ghost of my aunt?" he repeats the words like they are poison.

"Oh God, Phoebe, no," Edie appears across from me, standing half way into the marble counter. "Please, tell me you didn't tell him!" I cover my face with my hands again as she lets out a scream. "Everything is about to get so much worse!"

251

"Have you gone mad?" Porter suddenly bellows demanding my attention. "The ghost of my aunt!"

The door from the maid's hallway swings open aggressively, and we both turn around to see Merida stomping out with my purse in her hand. There's a meek smile over her plastic face and she stands upright, looking from me to Porter.

"I too, have stumbled upon something interesting in this house," she tells us coolly.

"That's my purse," I sneer without control, "did you go through my things?"

"This is the worse part," Edie mutters behind me.

"When I was on the phone in your room, needing privacy, something caught my eye poking out from your purse." Merida opens my purse and yanks out pieces of folded paper that I have never seen before. "What I found was *very* interesting."

She plods at us with the papers in her left hand, thrusting them towards Porter but keeping her eyes only on me. I watch Porter's eyes scan the pages and I catch a glimpse of what they are.

Photographs. Black and white photographs of Edie. Date marked.

On the street. In the kitchen with her husband.

A handful of Porter as well.

The pictures from the files in Terrance's office.

"Those aren't mine!" I exclaim, "She put them in my purse!"

"How could I have placed them in your purse? Did you see them on me before I went away to take my phone call?" Merida throws my purse at my feet and wags a finger at me. "No, because I couldn't have hid them in this outfit, or on this tight body. If I had your physique then maybe I would have gotten away with sticking them somewhere."

"She is not fat!" Edie shrieks, "She's curvy!"

I'm perfectly proportionate Edie! 135 pounds is not over weight.

"Don't yell at me!" Edie shouts, "I'm on your side!"

"I am not fat," I snap at Merida then I look back at Porter, "and those are not mine. I swear they aren't mine. Terrance took them, not me."

Merida lets out a practiced chuckle, "Now you're blaming my lawyer? Edie's lawyer? Your boss? Oh please. The truth is Porter, that your *trusted* maid here hired a Private Investigator a year ago to trail Edie, your late uncle and you. She isn't related to Edie at all. I bet if you call this Private Investigator, whose name is on the back of the photographs that he will tell you she was a client of his and hired him. I bet after he hears how she so obviously concocted this plan for money, he will give her up in a heartbeat."

"That's a lie!"

This isn't happening. Please tell me this isn't happening.

"And another thing, hold your opinion of Terrance whichever way you want but he had to fire her," Merida goes on her voice at a reasonable decimal now. "When Terrance learned how she wanted to use his late client, and you, he fired her and warned every other respectable firm in this city about her actions. He couldn't believe she did that."

"Edie wasn't my client," I defend, 'I never knew Terrance was working on her case, he hid that from Greg and me."

"Then explain how your signature is on the fax sheets sent to Edie and back, or how your name wound up on the witness section underneath Terrance's signature?" Merida requests, her voice shakes the space between us. "Terrance says he can email proof of everything.

"That's not true! You two forged my signature," I look from her to Porter who now glimpses up from the photos in his hands at me. "He's the impostor who sent out a fax full of lies about me. Terrance was angry that I wouldn't back away from finding Edie's real will which cut out Marta."

"Marta?" Porter frowned.

"Terrance and Marta are having an affair, and it's because Terrance knew Marta would inherit money when Edie passed. When Edie found out about his unprofessional behaviour she fired him and cut Marta out. That's one reason that Terrance is after Edie's new will, to get rid of it so there is no copy of it!"

Merida lets out another laugh, "What a ridiculous story. Terrance having an affair with a girl young enough to be his daughter? I have it under good authority that you are the one who had the affair my dear."

"Excuse me?"

"Phoebe, stop talking," Edie's panicked voice raises over us, "you're going to make things worse." She covers her face with her ghostly hands.

"Terrance almost had to fire her partner. Greg or Gary, or whatever his name is", Merida says to Porter, "when he found out she was sleeping with him. If Greg wasn't an exceptional lawyer, he would have sacked him then and there."

"That's a lie! I never slept with Greg. Not ever! I was engaged to a man I loved. I would never cheat!" I'm shouting so much that my voice fractures. I've started to sweat in panic. "Greg would never lie, he's my friend."

"He's the one who came clean to Terrance a few days ago about your affair," Merida shoots me a stern look before looking back at Porter. "If you don't believe me, then call him. Call him, Porter, and I know he'll tell you the truth."

This isn't happening.

Greg would never do that. He always looks out for me, and even when I drunkenly kissed him years back he remained professional.

"Face it. Porter. There never was a second will. She created this lie to get closer to you," Merida takes advantage of my silence and places a steady hand on Porter's arm. "It's obvious all she ever wanted was money."

"I don't want money," I say ignoring her and looking at Porter, "why would I need money? I don't need it!"

"That's what Terrance thought as well," Merida told me, "he said that he couldn't believe that you would risk your career to tail this client. He tried to convince himself that there had to be a good reason behind it. So he did some digging of his own." We watch as she taps on her smart phone and after a few seconds she shoves the screen in my face, holding it steady. "Guess what he found out?"

It's my bank statement.

Oh no. No, no, no!

I have zero in savings, and a couple thousand in checking. There is one account below that is in the deep negatives. Twenty thousand dollars negative to be exact.

Merida swipes the phone towards Porter's face, and gives me a heinous glare.

"I think that explains everything," Merida says after she gives Porter a few seconds to look at the screen. "She needed the money. And what better way to get it, plus more, than to convince everyone she was Edie's relative. She played to your kind heart Porter; she knew even if she wasn't in the will you would give her something. Shameful. It's probably why she even began dating her fiancé, Terrance suspects. He's from a wealthy family."

"I can explain that debt," I look to Porter who already has his impassive eyes upon me. "I was really stupid four years ago. I was dating this guy and he had this stupid idea to invest in—it doesn't matter. I thought I loved him, I was young and stupid so I took out the money for him."

"The reason doesn't matter," Porter tells me. He throws the photographs next to the cheque book on the counter. "Merida, I'd like you to leave please."

Her face falls, "but I have more to—"

"—Get out!" he shouts.

We both jump at his tone and I watch Merida. Collecting her composure, she pats the back of her golden hair and clears her throat. Turning on her heels, she throws me one last look and trudges her way out of the kitchen. We can hear her heels in the front lobby and after a minute the door to the house slams shut.

We're left in total silence, and Edie evaporates from my view.

Please let this mean that he doesn't believe Merida and Terrance.

Please.

I don't know who I'm praying to.

Porter looks over at me, and with a deep sigh he runs a hand through his already stressed hair, then he rubs the space between his eyebrows.

"Porter, I know—"

"—I'd like you to retrieve your belongings," he cuts me off brutishly. "I would like to know that you're gone from this house before I come back into the kitchen. I have a few calls to make now, excuse me."

He walks away leaving the cheque book and the photographs on the counter.

"Porter wait. If you would just listen to me—"

"—Have a nice life Ms. Mercer."

I know I had at least two other places I could go stay at after I left Edie's house.

But for some reason, I went back to the city and back on the West side.

The cab ride back to the city felt longer than normal, or maybe that was because I felt completely numb as I kept my head slumped against the glass window in the back.

Now I was here. Riding the old elevator up to the third floor and pulling myself along the renovated hallway, a faint smell of drying paint in the air.

I reach the dark metal door, and kick it with my right foot three times.

It wasn't long before I could hear footsteps on the other side and the door began to slide open for me. He let out a soft breath when he saw me; his dark hair falling slightly over his pale forehead. He was in a big navy blue robe and matching slippers, looking very content yet tiny in it.

"Phoebe," he sighs with relief.

"I need a place to stay."

Chapter Twenty-Two

The good thing about staying with Tom is that he has a never ending supply of wine. He never drinks alone as a personal rule, and he rarely has people over. So after he let me settle into his guest bedroom, he told me I had free reign over his wine rack in the kitchen. He never asked any questions, he just gave me a wine glass and told me there were left over quiches in the fridge then excused himself.

I called for Edie several times, whenever Tom was locked away in his bedroom, and she never appeared. Maybe it was for the better. I did screw everything up for her anyway. I would probably never see her again.

When I awoke the next morning I felt instantly relieved about drinking three bottles of water after that bottle and a half of wine. Although my bladder felt ready to burst and I was groggy, I had no headache or desire to vomit.

Tom's guest room looked as if Martha Stewart had decorated it. The walls where painted a pale blue, the queen sized bed was four posted white wood with matching nautical side tables. There was a white four drawer dresser directly across from the bed with a hanging fifty inch TV over it. My duffle bag and purse lay in the corner of the room directly under the loft sized windows with blue drapes.

I muscled myself out of the bed and dragged my bare feet across the floor, hearing muffled voices in the apartment. I knew it was Reese without seeing her. I left my room and scurried across the small hallway to use the bathroom.

I should have showered, but only washed up. It's not like I had a job to go to this Tuesday morning, or a man to look good for.

I threw my auburn hair in a messy bun, and left the bathroom.

Part of me wanted to call out to Edie again, once in the bedroom. To see if she was okay after yesterday, but when I pushed the door to the guest room open I found someone sitting on my bed.

In a black pencil skirt and a grey suit jacket, matched with a dragonfly brooch over her chest, greying hair in its usual

257

beehive style was Stella. She sat perfectly still with her ankles crossed and her hands on her lap, her designer Chanel bag hanging off her boney wrist.

Now I felt the headache.

I rub both eyes, as if it would make her go away and when I drop them back at my sides she's giving me a condemning stare. "Good Morning, Phoebe."

"What are you doing here?"

"Isn't it obvious?" Stella pats down her skirt as if it wasn't already perfectly aligned. "I'm here to discuss Riley with you."

I tap the bedroom door shut behind me with my foot and let out a tired breath, "Stella. There isn't anything left to say. I think it's great that you love your son enough to come over here and convince me to forgive him, even though you hate me. But the truth is—"

"—Just a moment," Stella raises a hand as her beady eyes focus on me hard, "let me clarify something. I did not come over here to beg you to forgive my son. On the contrary, I came over here to ask you to never return to him."

I scoff and shake my head at her. "Obviously, I am not surprised."

"Secondly? I never said I hated you. My behavior, at times, may have implied it but I never have, *hated* you," she throws back righteously. "In fact I am, well, I am slightly fond of you." She clears her throat and shifts uneasily in her seat, avoiding my eyes.

I don't think I heard her right.

"I'm sorry?"

"I don't hate you," Stella answers acting exasperated at my slow keep up. "I never have hated you. Do I need to repeat it a third time?"

Seconds pass in a dreadful, awkward silence that starts to give me goosebumps. It may be all the wine that I drank last night, and lack of food I ate, but I'm suddenly feeling woozy.

I somehow make it to the bed, and drop down next to Stella, who hurdles elegantly away from me as we sit together side by side. "That doesn't make sense. You've always been so rude to me, judgemental, and nasty to my mother. I can't believe that you ever liked me."

Stella sighs and her shoulders slump as she unclasps her hands from her lap. "I love my son with all my heart, but I will not pretend that he is the apple of my eye. He is selfish and lazy and frankly, a bit of a dreamer." She gives a shrug when she sees my dazed look, "believe it or not, it's the truth. And you my dear, are fiancée number eight. My mother's ring has seen seven fingers before it saw yours."

Riley's been engaged seven times?

"Each time I sat in silence waiting for the inevitable doom of his relationships. His father told me he would eventually grow out of this behaviour. It shouldn't come as a shock to you that commitment isn't my son's strong suit. Of course he enjoys talking about marriage and children but it is the *idea* of it he relishes; not the reality. In the last five years he pursued a career as a police officer, a fire fighter, a personal trainer, a sports agent and now an advertising representative."

It suddenly dawned on me as her words rang out around me; Riley *did* have a problem with commitment. He wasn't a vegetarian for more than six months before he moved on to veganism. I met him when he was leaving his personal training career behind him, and his career as a sports agent was so short lived. His attitude changed after our engagement became real, he was suddenly so overbearing and short.

All the signs where there.

I watch Stella as she lets out a breath and goes on. "The second I met you six months ago, I knew it was only a matter of time, but you were different from the other girls. They were all the same. Beautiful, well dressed, slim, health driven like Riley, ambitious—"

"—The point, Stella?" I interrupt trying to keep myself from feeling offended.

"My point, Phoebe," she looks me in the eye now. "Is that you *became* all those things that my boy wanted. You gave more selflessly than the others. You gave up meat for him, *meat.* I wouldn't do that if my husband paid me a million dollars."

I should tell her I faked that, I *so* should tell her…

259

"I knew you were different and I knew you didn't deserve the fate that my neglectful son would eventually drop on you," Stella goes on. "So I was rude, and judgemental, and unpleasant to your mother in hopes you would come to your senses and leave him. That's the truth."

She looks away from me and unclasps her vintage Chanel purse, reaching inside. "I know about the fax."

I grimace. Like I need reminding of that. I don't even want to know what was on it; I just want to forget it ever existed.

"Never you mind that fax," she goes on, and when I drop my hands from my face she gives me a quick glance. "I will give you a spectacular recommendation letter, and I can pull some strings in several firms in the city who think Terrance Meyers is a greedy moron."

"Really?"

"Yes," she nods formally at me and then finally takes whatever she was searching for out. It's a ball of tissue and I watch her unwrap it with her hands, she produces the ring. The ring that was on my finger only yesterday. "I would like you to have it. I don't have a daughter, and I don't believe I will ever receive a daughter in law. If I do, I know it won't be one that I like so I would rather the ring sit in your hands. Please take it, and please don't play coy with me about it."

I open my lips to tell her she must be insane. Never in my right mind could I take a ring I know costs more than—, I don't know exactly what but I know it's worth a lot. She must see my hesitation because she forces the ring into my hand and puts the tissue back into her purse. "Now I have to be on my way. I wish you the best, and hope you'll consider my offer of recommendation. Please, give my apologies to your mother."

The ring feels out of place in the palm of my hand but I go against my first thought of refusing it. I say bye to Stella as she leaves the room shutting the door gently behind her. I felt like I owed her, and in a strange way, I did.

So I'm keeping the ring.

I dressed quickly in a pair of dark jeans and a white tank top. I left my hair the mess it was and went out with minimal makeup. I turned the small hallway into the living room and kitchen. It was modest tiny apartment in the heart of downtown. The ceilings housed old industrial vents from when the building was a shoe factory. The living room was carpeted a shade of grey that looked comfortably medieval and Tom's modern blue square sofa set matched it well. He had shelves installed against the entire back wall of the apartment that were filled to the brim with books. It was very sophisticated.

The dining room bled into the living room, and he had a gorgeous dark vintage table for six with King Arthur chairs. Underneath the loft style window was a vintage record player, softly spinning a record by some folksy singer I have never heard of.

The kitchen was dark blue and light grey. Specks of silver lined the granite counter tops and all his appliances were shiny metal, including the four cup espresso machine which sat in the corner of the kitchen, barely used. He was a tea person.

In his kitchen is where I found Tom and Reese. They stood around the island counter, uniquely circle shaped, with cups of tea in their hands. Tom's in a pair of grey sweatpants I saw David Beckham wearing on a billboard, and a blue t-shirt. Next to him Reese stands in a pair of orange pants and an oversized bohemian black sweater that slipped off her pale shoulder.

"Morning," they say in unison when they see me.

"I have tea, and coffee. Which would you like?" Tom gestures to his tea brewer behind him and then the fancy espresso machine in the corner.

"Tea is fine, do you have anything fruity?" I pull out one of the stools at the counter.

"I have several fruit teas," Tom turns as he begins to look through his cupboard.

"Surprise me," I yawn as I slide onto the stool.

"So," Reese takes a long drink of her tea, "what did she want?"

"To apologize, I suppose."

"For her rudeness?" Reese guesses.

"She was actually very pleasant on the phone," Tom tells me, "she called you nonstop this morning, I had to pick up your phone. It's charging in the dining room by the way."

261

"Thanks, and yes, she apologized for Riley. And for her behavior," I tell Reese and Tom as I slump into the counter. "Then told me Riley was engaged seven times before."

Tom turns with his black eyebrows arched, and Reese gapes at me. "Seriously?"

"Apparently," I sigh, "she's been rude to me hoping I would call things off myself."

"There's a twist nobody saw coming," Tom says as he turns back around to make my tea.

"I, for one, am glad that he's gone from our lives." Reese declares with a smile, "I don't trust anybody who doesn't eat meat." I master a small smile at her as Tom hands me a white mug with a strawberry aroma escaping it.

"I don't worry about your love life," Tom tells me with a matter of fact tone. "What I worry about, is the ridiculous accusations against you from your former employer."

"I don't even know what they are."

"You don't want to know," Reese quickly says.

"You read it?" I make a face at her,

"We both have," Reese motions towards Tom. "Your friend Satine was able to get a copy forwarded to us."

I drop my head into arms, hiding. "What did it say?"

"Never mind." Tom dismisses.

"Just tell me."

Why did I want to know? I knew it would only make the wounds deeper.

"You're greedy, a thief, an exploiter, a slut..." Reese's voice trails off and I groan.

"I think it's time," Tom's voice echoes around us, "that you tell Reese and I just what the hell has been going on with you. I know very well from Clara that you've been dealing with something, un-natural."

I could kill Clara.

"Don't be mad at her," Reese jumps in as she sees my expression. "She only mentioned it because she was worried about you when she heard about the fax."

If telling Porter didn't go over well then telling two atheists wouldn't go any better.

"Let's go, Phoebe," Tom orders with a sigh.

I pull my head up and cup the warm mug of tea that sits before me. I look up at the two of them, their eyes drawn over me like blankets as they wait for me to speak.

"Alright," I sigh, "but this is going to sound insane..."

It took forty five minutes to tell the story. Forty five minutes and two more cups of tea each. They listened; they sat on the stools across from me, and listened without taking their eyes off of me. They didn't speak, or show signs of cynicism.

"So he fired me, which I don't blame him for," I go on as I push away the empty mug. "I mean, wouldn't you? I had no proof of Edie's second will except a cheque book. The private investigator basically told me to scram. The lawyer is gone till the end of the month. Greg betrayed me, and the P.I. sided with Terrance probably because he pays him well. Edie is gone. She usually appears when I call her, if not right away then soon after."

Now they both frown at me, and slowly exchange a look with each other.

I knew it. *I knew it.*

"Right," I exhale as I set my elbows on the counter. I grab the sides of my head. "I need to be committed."

"No, we didn't say that," Reese proclaimed. I catch it, the look they give each other which tells me they definitely think I'm bonkers for claiming to see a ghost. Tom and Reese aren't ones to believe in, well, unscientific manias. They need proof.

"Regardless of my opinion of you claiming to see a 'ghost'," Tom air quotes with a sigh, "this is quite a situation you've gotten yourself in."

"The worst part? I feel horrible for lying to Porter. I promised him I wouldn't lie about anything when he hired me, and when I promised I knew I was lying." I contort as I think back to that time in the dining room where he stood up for me against Terrance. "I'm such a loser."

"How in the world did you end up owing over twenty thousand dollars on a line of credit?" Tom asks breaking up my pity party.

"Dylan."

"Dylan?" he frowns, "Dylan who?"

"Wait, as in your last boyfriend Dylan?" Reese recalls.

"Yes," I exhale air that darts across my forehead.

"Oh Phoebe," Tom shakes his head at me, "that clown?"

"Not my finest hour, I know."

The three of us are silent, and when I realize there isn't anything left to say or do, I shake off the feeling of hopelessness that I was bathed in. "I guess I have to get the rest of my stuff out from Riley's. There isn't a point in dragging it out any longer."

"I'll get you the number to my moving company," Reese offers, "they can get your stuff out within twenty-four hours."

"Thanks," I slide off the stool, "but all I really have is a desk. And clothes."

"I can't believe you just stood there and took it!" Clara exclaims, "Phoebe, this woman is atrocious. I mean everything she and Terrance planned was a lie to get you out of the house!"

"I know that Clara, but I couldn't do anything about it. They had 'proof'," I air quote the words before going back to my martini. "I had nothing but a cheque book."

"Maybe he called the secretary," Faye suggests, "after you left."

"No I don't think so. I think he was convinced by Merida that I was the devil."

"Such bull," Clara exclaims again, as she throws down her menu.

It's nearly six p.m. and I'm having dinner with Faye and Clara in a Thai restaurant near my brother's house. They've both just come from work so next to Clara's grey Saks blazer and matching grey trousers, Faye's trendy aquamarine blouse and pleather leggings, I look stark.

"And what about, you know?" Faye leans over her cosmo. "Your ghost?"

"She's gone. I tried calling her all last night and again this afternoon. I think she's moved on. I think she realized she lost."

I catch the croak in my throat before I can let it out.

All afternoon I thought about Edie, I even thought about getting an Ouija board and maybe channeling her through it. How could she just disappear like that after yesterday? You would think she would feel bad that I was crucified that way on her behalf.

It's ironic really, here I am missing this loud, in your face woman that I've only known for a few weeks and always wished away. Now I wished she was here.

"You miss her," Faye says her face breaking into a small smile. "I can tell."

"It doesn't matter," I say picking up my apple martini and taking a drag. "Everything is over and done with. Technically, the one thing I wanted has come true and I can move along with my life."

"It's a shame about Porter," Clara tells me, "he was really nice."

"Right," I say as I think back on their flirtation. "Well, now he's out of both of our lives."

"He was never in my life," Clara pops the straw from her drink into her mouth. "He was in yours."

"Yeah, but you had your eyes on him," I set my drink down and lean back into my seat. "Trust me when I say that he isn't your type. He's too hard, and a workaholic."

"Me?" Clara frowns at Faye, "I wasn't interested in him."

I make a face at her. "But you said he was good looking and wondered if he was single."

"I asked if he was single for you."

"What?"

"I had a feeling the two of you could hit it off," Clara leans over the table and I see her give Faye a brief look. "That's why I invited him to your surprise engagement party. Right Faye?"

"Yeah," Faye nods, "we thought that maybe if you got to know him better you would dump Riley. It was a long shot but we had nothing to lose. We noticed right away that you had some chemistry."

I can't be a fool and ignore that. I remember how I felt whenever I stood close to him, or when I touched his hand that time on the balcony. My heart drops the same way it does when I think about Edie. I'm missing Porter.

It can't be this possible to miss a man you barely knew, could it?

"Guess it wasn't meant to be." Clara drinks through her straw again as her eyes scan the restaurant. "Where is the waiter? I'm getting—" She gasps mid-way and both Faye and I throw her a look. She points across the restaurant and I follow her direction, "Look who it is!"

Now it's my turn to gasp.

Across the restaurant from us, is Greg. He's sitting at a table for two against the wall, but his only company is a stack of papers and his laptop. He's clicking away at something with one hand as his other works with chopsticks in a bowl of Pho.

"You get over there Phoebe," Clara orders me sternly, "and you confront that loser."

"No," Faye shakes her head at me as I turn to them, "nothing can be done by causing a scene Phoebe. And what if he tells Terrance? You already have half the lawyers in the city thinking you're terrible. I say just leave it."

Clara looks appalled as her eyes whiz from Faye to me, "You most definitely do not leave it. If the lawyers in the city already think you're terrible then confronting him here and potentially causing a scene won't hurt you any more than that fax did."

"Oh," Faye looks over at Clara, "actually yes, that makes more sense. Forget what I said. I say get over there and confront him."

"Right," I push my chair back, "right, absolutely."

"I have your back," Clara shuffles in her seat and picks up her purse. I hurry from the table before the courage inside of me disappears like Edie.

I stalk across the restaurant and around the tables until I get closer to where Greg sits. I don't even need to get to his table before he casually glances up, with a stick full of noodles half way to his mouth. He drops the noodles back in the bowl, splashing broth on his green tie.

"Phoebe," he stammers when I get to his table, "I didn't expect—what are you doing here?"

"You mean, why am I not in hiding?" I shoot back as I cross my arms. "Is that what you mean, you backstabbing coward?"

Backstabbing coward? Yikes. You would think I'd be able to do better.

"Phoebe," Greg gazes away briefly, "look I'm sorry. I really am, but I had no choice. If I didn't lie, then Terrance would have fired me too. I'm disposable, he said. You know how hard this was for me to do, to betray you like that?"

"Oh it was hard for *you?*" I gawk at his suffering stance. "Are you serious? You where my friend! We helped each other with stuff. You did a really mean thing!"

"I was backed into a corner," Greg keeps his voice down but his tone sharpens. "I had no choice. I couldn't have that kind of fax floating around about me. It didn't matter how I felt about you at that moment in time, Terrance made things perfectly clear. I mean, Meyers and Brant is one of the top law firms in the city! I had to put my feelings for you to the side."

"If you think that after this, Terrance is going to promote you or—wait a second," I pull back my pointed finger and look down at him. "Feelings for me?"

"Yes," awkwardly Greg throws down the napkin he had set on his lap. "Feelings, I have feelings for you. Ever since that time you tried to kiss me. I kicked myself every day from then on about backing away from you."

Edie was right.

I stand uncomfortably now, looking down at him and when he masters enough courage to look up at me, I have to look away. Well, this is beyond awkward. As I gaze back at him I can't help but frown. How in the world did I ever think kissing this man was a good idea? Now, he is good looking, in an over-worked frat boy kind of way but what possessed me to ever think I was sexually attracted to this man? He's a doormat. To me, to Terrance, to everybody.

"I'm sorry, Phoebe. I knew putting the photos in your purse was the wrong thing to do, and I knew agreeing to that horrendous lie for Terrance was worse…"

So that's how the Private Investigator's pictures got into my bag. Greg. He must have thrown them in there when he stopped by to 'check' on me.

"I suppose you want to hit me or something," Greg places both hands on the table as he looks me in the eyes.

He looks so derelict, so hopeless. I can't feel any anger towards him anymore, all I feel is pity.

"No," I shake my head slowly, "I wanted to earlier, but now I don't. I feel sorry for you. You're a spineless weasel, and you'll fit into Meyers and Brant well. Good luck Greg, you're going to need it."

I turn to walk away when I find Clara behind me. She gives me a smile and places a hand on my shoulder, "Good job. Be the better person." As I pass her I do hear what she says behind my back to Greg however, "Ass-wipe."

When I get home three hours later, whatever victory I felt when dealing with Greg was gone. I found Tom's apartment empty and to that I was grateful. I just wanted to run into my room with another bottle of his wine and drink to whatever sitcom rerun was on at this hour.

I was settling onto the bed with the open bottle of wine and an empty glass when a shadow swings around behind me. I let out a shout and jump to my feet spinning around to the window.

It's Edie.

She's still in that purple dress of hers from yesterday but there isn't a headband. Her hair lies flat on her shoulders as well. It's not in its usual curly up do. She stands with her hands cupped together in front of her. Like a three year girl ready to apologize. I get instantly comforted by her presence, a reprieve launders over me and I can feel myself relax.

"Edie. Where have you been? I've been calling for you."

"I know," she cuts me off raising one hand in the air. "I'm sorry but I was busy. I had to do my usual thing."

"Spy on people?" I guess and I even manage to crack a small smile.

She returns one but I feel it's forced.

"I saw Greg at dinner today," I tell her as I set the wine bottle and empty wine glass down on the night stand. "You were right about him having feelings for me. He also admitted to lying, but there isn't anything that can be done about it now I suppose."

"No, there isn't" she agrees.

"Stella came to see me too," I say, "she told me Riley was engaged seven times before me. She told me she was rude to me so I would break things off with him, because she liked me. She wanted to spare me the heart ache of Riley leaving me right before the wedding. I have the ring back too; she wanted me to keep it."

"You can use it to pay off that debt," Edie suggests.

"I thought that," I tell her, "but I don't feel right pawning it off to pay for my mistake—"

"—Phoebe, I'm sorry I have to stop you," Edie takes a step towards the bed and smiles at me again. It's a small one, but it ruptures with a sad kindness that makes my heart sink. "I've only come by to thank you. I know we failed but I still want to thank you for at least trying to save my company. My legacy. I pride myself on being a wise woman, and a wise woman knows when to claim defeat."

"But what—"

"—Now it's not all bad," she shrugs as she looks away from me. "I had some fun spying on my enemies, and ordering you around. Even if you drove me up the wall several times," she raises an eyebrow at me, "but you were a good friend when I needed it. So before I go I want to thank you—"

"—What do you mean go?" there's a panic in my voice that I don't try to hide. I walk around the bed quickly, "Where are you going?"

"Don't be dense, Phoebe. It doesn't suit you." Her eyebrows drop as she goes on, "You know very well what I mean. It's time I," she gestures with her one finger to the ceiling, "move on. A few spirits I came across the last few months told me it's really easy."

She's leaving?

I need to stop her.

"No," she throws a finger my way. "Absolutely not. Now," she adjusts her posture and smiles again at me, "I won't have you being upset about this. Understand? After all, we barely know each other and if I were alive I wouldn't bother dealing with you, we run in different circles."

"I guess so…"

"Excellent."

I shut my eyes for moment, and let out a breath. My eyes water underneath the lids and I bite my lip to stop them before Edie snaps at me. When I open my eyes a second later, she's gone.

Chapter Twenty-Three

Not many people can brag about crying over a ghost they lost.

Sure they cry over the person who died *before* they became a spirit, but only *I* would cry over losing a ghost. Drink an entire bottle of wine and cry, for a whole twenty four hours.

Over a ghost.

But not over an ex-fiancé who cheated on me.

What was wrong with me?

How long did I know Edie? Two weeks? I knew Riley for over a year and was engaged to him. My priorities are extremely messed up.

It's already Thursday morning; I spent all of yesterday in my pajama's watching TV, only moving from the living room to the bedroom. Tom left me alone, only occasionally sighing at my melodrama.

I haven't been awake for more than five minutes when there comes a tapping on the bedroom door. I don't move from my place.

"I'm up Tom," I call from the pillow I'm face down in.

"It's not Tom, jitterbug."

"Oh God," I groan loudly, "no…"

Anything but this.

"She forced her way in," I hear Tom call from the other side of the door. *"I couldn't keep our mother in the hallway."*

I moan loudly as the door opens, and pull the duvet cover over my head before she can see me. I listen as she forsakes shutting the door and makes a 'tsk, tsk' sound as she undoubtedly sees the empty wine bottle and glass on the ground.

"Phoebe," she says, "an entire bottle of wine, come on now."

"In case you haven't heard, my entire life has fallen apart."

"Don't be dramatic."

I feel her plump down on the bed and with one swift pull; the duvet comes off of me. I turn my head from the pillow and look over at my mother. She sits with her hands on her hips.

271

Her short black hair is a bob today and she's in a bright red sweater and blue jeans. "You should have called me."

"Who did call you? It was Reese wasn't it?" I sit half way up and rub my eyes.

"It was not!" I hear her shout from the kitchen.

"No, it wasn't," she reaches over and brushes the hair from my face, "it was Clara."

"Clara called you?"

"She told me everything," my mother cocks her head at me and raises her eyebrows, "why didn't you tell me what was happening?"

"I just found out about the fax a few days ago mom," I pull myself up and yank my knees to my chest. "I wasn't keen on telling the whole world. I haven't told many people about Riley either."

"I'm not talking about the fax or Riley," my mother huffs, "I'm talking about your ghost."

I make a mental note to kill Clara. She just can't keep her mouth shut, can she?

"Okay, I know you think I'm crazy—"

She swats her hand at me, "I'm your mother. If you say you see ghosts then you see ghosts. There are hundreds of people around the world who see ghosts."

I blink at her and watch as she smiles at me. "You believe that?"

"Jitterbug," she gives me a sigh, "I believe that a virgin gave birth to a son, and that son walked on water. What kind of person would that make me if I said I didn't believe in the afterlife?"

"Good point," I hang my head, "Tom and Reese don't believe me."

"Most people won't believe you," my mother shrugs. "Maybe it's best you don't tell anybody else, unless you absolutely trust them?" She then looks at my night stand and slightly scowls at the mess. She reaches over and picks something up, softly smiling at what she holds.

Edie's picture.

"Is this her?"

"When she was younger, yes," I nod. "I stole it from her room because I liked the picture."

"She looks very beautiful in it."

"Man would she have loved to hear you say that," I chuckle watching as my mother sets the picture back down on the night stand. "She'd probably yell at me for sleeping this late, and wallowing."

"Then get out of bed," she orders me. "Look what your make up did to your brother's sheets." As I stand up she pushes me away slightly and leans over the pillow case. "Now I have to wash this, and I didn't bring my stain remover."

I shake my head as I leave the room, "You are aware you don't live here right?"

I figured a shower was in the works and I took an extra-long one. I choose the teal colored halter jumper to wear for the day seeing as I had run out of clothes. In a few hours I would be heading over to the loft with Reese and Clara to pick up the rest of my belongings, and meet the movers. I only hoped Riley wouldn't be there.

When I get into the living room I find Tom, Reese and my mother behind the island counter. Tom and Reese are face first into the plates before them, and my mother is at the stove with a wooden spoon.

"You know I have to pay for water right?" Tom asks as I slide into the stool next to him.

"I'll pay you in hugs," I joke as I reach for the plate of pancakes before me.

"Are those returnable?" Tom jests back, remaining serious as he looks at his wristwatch.

"Exchangeable, maybe," I shrug.

There's a knock that interrupts our banter and Tom slips off his stool to answer it.

"Do you want some tea?" Reese asks as she gets off her stool as well and looks my way,

"Sure, Earl Grey please."

"Oh you have got to be kidding me," we hear Tom grumble loudly a few seconds later.

My mother turns away from the stove as Reese and I lean backwards to spot who's at the door. All we can see is Tom

273

though; his hand rests against the doorframe as if to prevent whoever it was from entering the apartment. He lowers his voice and all we hear now is mumbling.

"Tom," my mom calls out to him, "who is it?"

"Nobody," Tom gives us a quick glance, "don't worry about it."

I suddenly have a very sneaking suspicion of whom it might be, and force myself off the stool. I walk over to the door and hesitantly Tom drops his arm, "Be my guest" he says gesturing at the visitor.

I dip my head, and drop my shoulders when I see the blue track suit and wavy brown hair. It wasn't that I was expecting him to look like garbage. Perhaps a five o'clock shadow and dry lips from forsaking water, but hey, it would have been nice. Instead he looks as immaculate as he always does.

"Riley."

"Hey." His voice is low as he locks eyes with me. "I went to everyone's place looking for you, and I even went to Cedar Springs. For a while Clara had me convinced you were staying with her, but then my mother called."

"Stella ratted me out eh?"

"No, she didn't. She told me to leave you alone. She said you were with your family so I took a shot that you'd be at Tom's."

"What do you want Riley?" I step out of the apartment a little bit when I notice six eyes from the kitchen pierced on me.

"I just want to talk," he takes his hands from his pockets and runs one through the gel in his hair. "My original plan was to beg you to forgive me, to come back to me. I mean if there is still a chance that you would then I will do it right here, right now." He begins to kneel when I motion for him to stop,

"No Riley. Stop."

"Are you sure?"

I place my hands on the metal door frame at my sides. "I know about the engagements."

"That's bad luck" he declares defensively, "I had bad luck in love."

"Oh please," I can't help but smirk at him, "you don't believe in bad luck. If by chance you had any, it's because *you* created it. Bad luck didn't make you cheat on me."

"That," he takes a step towards me "was a onetime slip up. I swear."

I crinkle my nose, "No. It wasn't. It went on a while, and I know that."

Thanks to Edie.

"There has to be something I can do," his voice dips as his eyes cloud over with melancholy, "Phoebe, we love each other. Don't we?"

I bite my bottom lip. I could tell him about my debt, which could make him think I only dated him for his family's money. It would be a for sure way to get rid of him forever. Something stops me however, and maybe it's because as I look into his persuasive eyes I'm reminded of the fact that I did at one time, love him. Maybe I was never really *in* love with him, but I was fond for him. I did care about him.

"No, Riley," I shake my head at him, "I don't think we ever did. Not in that way at least. We wanted to; we even fooled ourselves into thinking it, but come on. If you ever really truly loved me with every bone in your body you wouldn't have cheated on me. Even if I was acting crazy and out of character."

I'm expecting him to get defensive again, to protest and be a Romeo but instead a small smile spreads over his lips. "I think losing you, is going to bite me in the ass."

"It's not like you have much fat on there anyway," I kid and he nods at me,

"That's true, I don't."

I take a step back into the apartment and find Tom leaning on the wall next to the door listening. He motions for me to shut the door and I look back at Riley,

"I think you should go, Riley."

He pounces forward again, "Unless you think that just maybe, maybe we could work something out—"

I feel Tom's hand on my arm and he jerks me backwards before reaching for the door that I hold open. "Goodbye Riley. Have a fantastic life, hope we never cross paths again."

He shuts the door with a bang and turns around to face me.

"Don't you think that was a bit rude?" I ask my brother.

"I don't care," he frowns back at me, "that man is an idiot. He knew I never liked him and now I never have to be kind to him again. Besides I'm expecting someone shortly."

"Your tea is ready," Reese calls out to me.

I leave Tom with a shake of my head, and just as I get to the island there's another knock on the door. I look over my shoulder as Tom exhales and spins back around, "What the hell does he want now?"

We watch him pull the door open but his annoyed expression instantly disappears. "Can I help you?"

"I need to speak to Phoebe Mercer, is she here?"

I snap my head towards the door at the sound of the voice.

It can't be...

Tom moves out of the doorway, "She's here."

I walk away from the counter, "Rosie?"

She hurries inside in full uniform. She's clenching a big leather brown book and I recognize it as one of Edie's albums. Her usual tidy hair is a lumped up mess and she's sweating down her wrinkled brow. When she sees me she lets out a sigh of relief.

"I'm so happy I found you."

"What are you doing here?"

"I know what's been going on," Rosanne tells me, she stays in place clasping the album as if losing it would cause her to lose her life.

"Porter told you," I guess.

"No," she shakes her head feverously. "I have known the entire time."

I frown at her and she nods her head, as if I'm supposed to guess her thoughts.

Tom's phone rings and both Rosanne and I look at him. He apologizes and hurries away from us, into the small hallway of bedrooms.

"What do you mean?" I ask Rosanne, "How did you know?"

"I saw Mrs. Edwards," Rosanne's voice gets hoarse so she clears her throat, "with you." She lets go of the album with one hand and gestures in the air. "You know, around the house. On the porch once and in the laundry room."

I don't think I follow this.

From the corner of my eye, Reese rolls her eyes and takes a drink of her tea.

I look back at Rosanne with my mouth slightly ajar as she gives me a slow nod.

"You *saw* Edie?"

"Mrs. Edwards," she corrects my usage of her name. "And yes, I saw her many times floating around the house spying on all of us. I heard her speaking with you."

Holy hell. I can feel my mouth dry as I gaze at her. Nothing about the way she looks or stands tells me she's lying; she looks so concerned I feel I could cry.

"Does Porter know?"

"No, please," she jerks her head back, "he would never believe. He would tell me I'm siding with you because I feel sorry for you. But I know about the missing will, I overheard you and Mrs. Edwards in the laundry room that one day."

"How is it you can see her?"

She shrugs casually. "It's something that runs in my family." She waves it off then. "It's not important."

"You came all this way to tell her you believe her and can see ghosts too?" Reese asks skeptically from the kitchen.

"No, I came because of Merida," Rosanne looks from Reese to me. "Today is the auction. She arrived at the house straight in the morning to help set everything up. Porter is to sign over all of Lavish Looks to her after the auction is over, his shares too. He told her he is finished with the company, the house, everything. He wants to go back home to England and forget about all of this."

Ouch.

"I can't do anything about it Rosie," as I say the words I feel immediate fault. "He fired me. He thinks I'm a liar and a gold digger—"

"—Here," she pushes the album at me and I fumble as I take hold of it. "I caught her searching through desks and cabinets and boxes meant to go up for auction. Then I followed her up to Mrs. Edwards' room. She was looking for this album. I moved them after I heard you and Mrs. Edwards talk about Merida's suspicious behaviour. I was the one who took them from Mrs. Edwards' room after you left her room Friday evening, and hid them behind my dresser."

"There isn't anything in this album," I tell Rosanne as I look down at it.

"Yes," Rosanne reaches at it and flips open the cover almost knocking me in the chin with it. I watch her reach to the first page and she lifts both sides of the stiff paper that holds the pictures on the first page and on the second. Sliding two fingers between the pages she pulls out a thin orange envelope. There's a stamp on it reading *Puckett Family Law*.

Oh. My. God.

No way, this cannot be—

"I found it last night. This morning, I went to show it to Mr. Burroughs when Mr. Meyers stopped me. He wanted to know what I held in my hand and I told him it was my termination papers, before running back to my room. I put it back in the album and hid the album. Merida comes into my room ordering to see my termination papers. This is after I saw her looking through Mrs. Edwards things. Then she told me she was going to get Mr. Meyers to escort me from the house, and after she went to get him I took the album and left. She knew the will was in the album, I don't know how, but she did."

Unbelievable. I knew she wasn't after some incriminating photo!

Rosanne suddenly smiles at me as she wraps her arms around herself. "This solves everything, yes?"

I open the envelope without answering her and pull out what feels like a thin contract. I can hear Reese and my mother shuffle up behind me as I pull the papers from the envelope. I know I shouldn't open it but I *needed* to.

There it is.

Dated two months prior to Edie's death.

In big bold, beautiful cursive.

Last Will and Testament of Mrs. Edie Doris Edwards.

"Oh my God," I giggle and catch Rosanne's look, "Edie's middle name is Doris."

"It's a respectable name," Rosanne frowns at me.

I skim the will quickly, my entire body ready to dance in elation.

Everything is as Edie stated it was.

Marta gets nothing.

She condemns selling her half of the company to Merida and requests that it is run by Porter or a 'trusted associate' of his.

Rosanne gets—oh my god. Wow. That's a lot of money.

But that doesn't make sense, Edie didn't trust Rosanne.

"Well?" my mother's tone is so eager that I give her a look over my shoulder. "It solves everything yes?" she repeats Rosanne's words with equal impatience as before.

I smile as I glance back down at it.

Yes it does. This is it. This fixes everything. Edie will be so happy when—

Wait.

"What's wrong?" Rosanne catches my worried form and steps up closer trying to get a better look at the will. "Is something wrong?"

"It doesn't matter anymore," I look up slowly from the paper to the maid, "it doesn't matter that these are Edie's wishes. In it she writes that she leaves Lavish Looks to Porter or a trusted associate of his choosing. He'll choose Merida, because he is through with everything. Merida will get the company either way."

It's over.

As quickly as it seemed fixed, it ends dispiritingly.

Edie was right; we did fail. We came close, again, but we still nose-dived.

I was miserable that she moved on, but now I was thankful. I couldn't bear to have given her false hope like this and seconds later swipe it out from under her feet.

"Actually," my brother rounds the corner of the hallway with his cell phone in his hand. He's grinning officiously as he looks at Rosanne and me, "I don't think she will."

Chapter Twenty-Four

"We only have one shot of pulling this off, Phoebe." Tom tells me again. "I doubt this Merida and Terrance will let you just walk through the front doors of the house."

"Well, too bad," I snap, "because that's what I'm going to do."

"No you won't," Reese slaps me on the knee and I glare at her, "they won't let you get to Porter that easily. Not you or Rosanne."

We were about fifteen minutes away from Cedar Springs and the tension in Tom's Jaguar has sky rocketed. When Tom told Rosanne and I, what he and Reese had done, we stood stunned.

I didn't think anybody anywhere would do what they did for me.

"When did the auction start?" Reese asks Rosanne, who sits up front with my brother.

"At two o'clock, an hour ago. It will be over at four o'clock."

"We'll be there before that," Tom says, "but you have to wait in the car. I will distract Terrance and Merida. Reese will text you when she manages to get Porter alone."

"How are you going to do that?" I look over at her as I clench the head rest in front of me, careful not to pull Rosanne's hair.

"Don't worry about it," Reese leans back in her seat and adjusts her seat belt. "Put your seat belt on. If we get pulled over because of you this whole thing is scheme is over before it can begin."

I do as she says, looking down at the album between the two of us and the orange envelope that rests above it.

I find myself praying that this works.

I even attempt to call out to Edie and scold myself for being disappointed when she doesn't show up in the car somewhere.

She's gone. Stop it.

It feels like hours before we pull onto Lundy Lane and I see Edie's house in the distance. The street is packed with cars, and Tom darts around looking for a good parking space. He manages to find one across the street, about a block down.

"Maybe you two should get out and wait nearer to the house," Tom turns around to look at me in the back. "Hide behind those tall trees in the neighbor's yard."

"Yes. We can do that," Rosanne nods at Tom as he looks at her, "they aren't home. They go away every spring and summer to Venice."

"Must be nice," Reese mutters as she exits the car.

Tom's phone rings as we begin to exit the car, so he stays in it to take the call. I lean against the car with Rosanne and we both look over at the house in the distance.

"He's crazy," I say to Rosanne, "Porter. For not wanting anything to do with the house. The house is gorgeous. I've never been to London but I would bet Cedar Springs is nicer than it is."

"Me too," Rosanne nudges me with a smile, "me too."

I look down at the maid and find myself debating telling her about Marta and Terrance.

"Rosie? I shouldn't tell you this but Edie left you a lot of money in the will," I admit.

"Did she?" she raises an eyebrow at me, "But I thought she didn't trust me as far as she could throw me, since I'm related to Marta."

I can't help but smirk. "I wish I could see Edie's face, knowing you heard her."

Rosanne chuckles; it's a hearty and warm laugh that has me smiling, "Me too" she then says. After a few seconds passes she speaks again. "Marta deserved to be cut out of the will. Sleeping with a married man..." Rosanne makes the sign of the cross twice and shakes her head.

"Yeah, that was pretty horrible of her," I agree.

"Alright, we have a small hitch."

Rosanne and I turn to watch Tom leave the car, slamming the door behind him. He and Reese walk around it towards us, and Tom has his phone in his hand. "There has been a slight delay." It takes less than a minute for Tom to tell Rosanne and me about the phone call.

And it takes one second for panic to set in.

"Oh God, we're not going to be able to do this," I place a hand to my forehead as I spin towards the house, "we have no chance." Next to me Rosanne holds her hands together and I think I hear her start to pray.

"No, that isn't true," Tom points my way, "it's just a hold-up. A five minute, ten minute hold up the most."

"A Five minute, ten minute hold up is enough to ruin everything!" I cry.

"Calm down," Reese orders, "Tom will just have to distract Merida and Terrance a bit longer than planned. We still go with the original plan okay?"

"Okay," Rosanne nods at her.

I realize I have no choice.

"Alright," I sigh, "okay."

"Now," Tom straightens up his blazer and clears his throat, "just wait for Reese's text."

Rosanne has been leaning against the tall willow tree in the next yard. We haven't said anything to each other the entire time we have been waiting, which feels like hours. Yet it's only been ten minutes. I pace back and forth, the orange envelope in my hands.

"Auction should be over in about an hour," Rosanne tells me.

I stop pacing and brush my hair from my face as I look down at my phone. No new notifications.

"What's taking so long? It shouldn't have taken this long to get Porter alone, or Merida and Terrance distracted." I stand on my toes and peer over the iron fence to catch a glimpse of the house.

"Maybe Reese and Tom are still waiting."

I put a hand to my mouth and bite down on my thumb nail.

I can't take this anymore.

I'm going crazy.

I have a better chance of getting Porter alone than Reese does anyway.

Come to think of it, this will is probably all I need to convince him that I am not a liar and that Merida and Terrance are the bad guys.

I'm going in there.

I clench my fists and hold firmly onto the envelope as I begin to walk away from Rosanne.

"Where are you going?" she calls frantically.

"I can't wait any longer!"

I hurry off the neighbor's yard and run along the sidewalk, turning the corner onto the driveway. I rush past Merida's Porsche and Porter's sports car, towards the stone pathway leading up to the front doors. My sandals click against the stone, I'm breathing heavily already.

I need to start working out.

I get to the front porch and grasp the handle to the front door. I turn it once and the door opens. I run inside the main foyer and find it empty. The entire house is silent as well, which makes sense as the auction is outside. Realizing that Porter is most likely outside watching the auction, I cross the foyer towards the kitchen when I hear voices upstairs. I freeze near the stairs and look up, waiting.

"Oh? Hello Porter."

It's a woman's voice, and it sounds like Merida's.

She's upstairs with Porter.

I take a step back and head up the stairs, taking them two at a time. One hand on the bannister. When I reach the top I find the entire hallway dark, except towards my right, towards the very end of it. The door to Porter's room is open, and there's a light coming from it.

I march towards the room, heading past the other closed doors. His room is right next to one of the broom closets and as I turn to storm into it, someone comes out at full speed taking hold of my arm.

I'm pushed backwards but not into the wall. Into a room of darkness, where I stumble and slam into hard sticks and wooden planks. I open my eyes just in time to see a familiar shade of golden hair, standing a few feet away from me.

Merida!

With both hands, she grabs hold of the door and closes it in front of me.

I can't see anything in front of me now, yet the smell is recognizable. I'm in the broom closet.

There comes a click sound as I push myself away from the shelves behind me.

I fumble towards the door knob with my spare hand, grateful that Merida hadn't noticed the orange envelope in my hands when she attacked me. Finally my hand wraps around the door knob but turning it is of no use. She's locked me in.

"Great," I mumble. "Perfect."

I kick at the door and bang on it with my fists. Somebody has to hear me.

Not everybody is outside, are they?

My phone!

I reach into the pocket of my jumper and feel around for it. It's empty.

I must have dropped it running to the house! Or maybe it's in here somewhere. I begin to scuffle against the floor with my wedges, hoping to kick something small, like my phone. With my other hand I bang upon the door again. "Hello! Somebody help me!"

I don't know how long I've been banging on the door, or shouting for help, but I know it's longer than five minutes. That's when I decide to give up. Everybody's outside, nobody can hear me. My phone isn't in here, its lost somewhere.

Why didn't I just stay outside like Tom planned?!

I drop against the door and put my hands to my eyes. The envelope rubs against my cheek. Now I've definitely blown it.

The door gives way behind me and I yelp as I find myself leaning backwards. I fall to the ground hard, my back seizing lightly as I hit the hard wood with my head. Looking up, I see Rosanne standing over me.

"Phoebe! You okay?" she reaches down to help me get to my feet, and I gladly take her warm hand.

"I'm alright. Merida locked me in the closet," I explain as I get to my feet and let go.

"You're bleeding," she reaches up and touches a spot near my widow's peak. At her touch I feel stinging and clench my jaw,

"Its fine," I push her hand away. "I'll be okay. Come on, we have to find Porter."

"I saw him outside."

We head towards the stairs together and I lead the way down when we hear Rosanne's name. We stop in the middle of the staircase and see Marta standing in the doorway of the living room. Her mouth is open and she looks from Rosanne to me, back to Rosanne.

"Porter is angry with you," she says to her, "you left with no word. If he sees that you brought her back with you he's going to flip out."

"Go find him," Rosanne whispers to me as she walks around me. I watch her throw her hands in the air and begin to shout something in spanish at Marta. Each time Marta tries to cut her off, Rosanne gets louder, and faster. Gesturing wildly as well.

As entertaining as it was to watch them, I didn't have the time. I headed down the stairs and gave them one last look as I push the swinging kitchen doors open.

I'm halted in my tracks almost immediately upon entering the kitchen.

Sitting at the island with a glass of what I assume is scotch, is Terrance. He's in a black suit, red dress shirt and matching black tie. What a perfect day for him to look like the devil.

"Good afternoon Phoebe," he says when he sees me, "I told Merida locking you in the closet wouldn't hold."

"I don't have anything to say to you." I eye the door across the room that leads to the back porch. "My business is with Porter."

"I assumed," he nods as he takes a drink of his scotch. The ice hitting the glass loudly in the empty room. "What do you have there?"

"None of your business," I say, swiping the envelope behind my back away from his reach in case he decided to jump at it.

"Phoebe, explain this to me." He sounds bored as he sets down his glass. "Why are you going through all this effort for somebody you never met? I mean, what is it to you what happens to Lavish Looks? This house? Her money?"

"She's my friend," I say,

"She's dead," he frowns.

"Did you kill her?" As the words leave my mouth I wish I could retrieve them. Terrance bursts out with laughter, and even rubs his stomach a second later.

"Oh Phoebe, come on now." He gives me an amused stare, "A murderer I am not. Did I watch her slip into the water and fail to recover her? Perhaps. But she shouldn't have been wearing those kinds of heels on such an unstable deck."

Son of a—Edie was right, mostly.

"So you did let her drown?" I realize, revulsion thick in my tone of voice. "You're a disgusting human being."

The amusement vanishes from his face, and he gets off the stool. I watch him button the bottom of his suit jacket and snap his fingers at me. "Give me that will."

"Screw you," I tighten my fingers around it.

"You are resourceful, I will give you that," Terrance wags a large finger at me, "I almost didn't recognize your brother and sister outside. I'm having them escorted off the property, in case you're wondering."

Damn.

I look over him to the bay windows, and I can see the garden abuzz with people attending the auction. I can't see Tom or Reese, and now my nervousness is growing.

"Phoebe, please," Terrance lets out an annoyed breath. "It's over. Porter is signing over the papers. Even with that will, you lose. The company will be Merida's, and everything here will be sold. Now if you give me the will I promise you I will give you a good referral to a top firm in the next state over. I did feel a tad bad about that fabricated fax I sent out."

"You don't seriously expect me to believe you do you?" I ask grimly.

"Give it to me," he demands ruthlessly. "*Now*."

"No, get out of my way," I'm firm in my place as I look at the door to my far right. "I have something to deliver."

"I don't think so!"

I'm not fast enough, again.

The envelope is torn from my hands and as I whirl around I see Merida walking away quickly to the other side of the island counter. She holds the envelope up in the air and exchanges a look with Terrance.

She must have been waiting in the maid's hallway for me. I watch her smile when she notices the panic in my eyes.

"What should we do with it?" she asks him,

"Get rid of it," Terrance shrugs without taking my eyes off me.

"No, don't," I can't help but beg her. As pathetic as it was, I had no choice. I was backed into a corner; I had nowhere to go and no way to get back that envelope. "Please Merida. Don't do this. You don't have to like me, but you did like Edie once, she was your friend. You built the company together."

She scoffs at me, "Don't play those cards with me darling. Edie means nothing to me. And Lavish Looks? It's just my piggy bank. I don't want anything to do with it. By the end of the year, I'll be free of it and a millionaire, again."

This woman has no soul.

"How did you know it was in the album?" my curiosity gets the better of me. Merida looks at me without moving and her eyebrows arch,

"By chance. I came over to meet with Edie about Lavish Looks, and caught her stuffing something into the album. After we found out the will was missing I guessed that was where she had hid it."

"Just get rid of it," Terrance orders again, he glares at her. "Hurry up. Stop wasting time."

"No Merida, don't," I plead.

She rolls her eyes at me and turns towards the stove. I watch her turn the knob nearest to her, and a burner lights up blue, green then red.

Behind me the kitchen door swings open and Rosanne enters. She gasps when she sees Merida and grabs onto my arm.

I don't know what she mutters in Spanish but I doubt that it's a prayer.

Merida lowers her hand quickly and sits the envelope over the flame. It catches instantly and next to me Rosanne makes a whimpering sound. I watch as the envelope slowly burns, and become anesthetized as the smell of burning paper fills the air.

There it goes.

Just like that.

There was nothing I could do to stop it.

The four of us are silent as we watch the flame consume the envelope. When it gets too close to Merida's fingers, she lets it go and it floats down into the burner, disappearing forever. Once it's gone, Merida turns off the burner and faces me with a proud smile.

"There," Terrance slides his hands into the pockets of his pants and looks at me, "now it's definitely over. Would you like to be escorted out Ms. Mercer or would you like to leave with the little dignity you have left?"

Rosanne still clenches my hand as I frown nastily at Terrance, who only chuckles.

The door to the back porch opens and we all turn to face it. Rosanne lets out an exultant shriek as Porter appears, stopping in his tracks when he spots Rosanne and I huddled together across the room. I'm trying not to notice how good he looks in his fit navy blue suit and grey dress shirt.

"What the hell is going on?" Porter asks as his eyes lock onto mine. He gestures towards his own forehead, "What happened to you?" He then makes a face and sniffs the air, "and what is that smell?"

"She burned the will!" Rosanne points a finger at Merida.

"Excuse me?" Porter frowns slowly, "The will?"

"She's a liar! She's obviously teamed up with Phoebe," Merida rolls her eyes at Rosanne as she looks to Porter.

"I believe it," Terrance says calmly. "I was here the whole time and I didn't see Merida burn anything."

"He's a liar too!" Rosanne screams.

"Sshh," I push her behind me.

"I don't have time for this," Porter looks at me, "I don't have time for any of this."

"Did you sign the company away?" I ask him, my voices shakes and I hate that it does because it makes Terrance snicker.

"I'm about to yes, I just need Terrance as a witness," Porter looks at the lawyer and motions at him to follow him.

"My pleasure," Terrance nods.

"Wait!" I leave Rosanne behind me and walk over to Porter, making sure to stay a good three feet away from Terrance.

"Ms. Mercer," Porter's tone is less than pleased when he faces me. "You are the very last person I want to see at this moment." His eyes drift back up to my tingling forehead though, and I hopelessly think I catch a trace of concern from him.

I force my eyes from his face and reach into my cleavage, much to his dismay. He looks away awkwardly, "what are you doing?"

"I think," I fish down deeper with my two fingers, "you should…" The second I feel it, I can't help but smile to myself, "read this before you sign anything." I pluck the paper out, relieved that I didn't give myself any paper cuts along the way.

I hand him the small square and look over at Rosanne, throwing her a casual smile in hopes she stops shaking in the corner. I then catch Terrance's face and he's still, fixated on Porter as he watches him un-wrap the square.

Once it's unfolded Porter scans the paper with his frazzled eyes and says nothing when he's finished. He just looks up at me.

"What is it?" Terrance practically snaps.

"It's the will," I tell him casually and with a shrug as I look from him to Merida. "Like you said, I'm resourceful. I took the will out of the envelope on the way over here."

Merida turns her back at us, but remains quiet.

"It appears that my aunt would have rather lost the company to pirates than to have you run things Merida," Porter announces, "but I have a feeling that you already knew this."

"Merida," Terrance looks over at her, "is this true?" I watch her twist to look at the lawyer, her brows so low they hide her eyes. "You deceived us all?"

289

I have to hand it to Terrance, he's a great actor. I almost believe his reverse game of surprise.

"Oh blow it out your rear end," I say glaring at him. "You're not innocent in this either. You reprinted Edie's old will in an attempt to pawn it off as the only one she had. Knowing very well that she wanted it destroyed. She found it in her desk and confronted you on the day she drowned."

"Don't be foolish," Terrance barks at me, "I would never betray a client like that. I'm not *you*. I have respect for them. I'm honest, if Edie wanted to destroy the will she made with me then I would have made sure it had been done."

Ugh, he's so good at acting honourable.

"You cannot believe her Porter," Terrance gestures at me, "Merida and I have showed you countless reasons as to why she cannot be trusted. If the woman deceived her own fiancé then of course she would deceive you, me, and your aunt Edie."

"Actually, she never deceived her fiancé."

I look around Porter and shake my head at the sight of Clara and Faye. They both stand in the doorway to the porch, dressed to the nines to blend in with the crowd, in gorgeous bright summer dresses that exposed just the right amount of skin. Clara comes around to where Porter and I stand, her orange dress swashing behind her as she walks. She has her cell phone in her hands and she stands on Porter's other side.

"Watch," she tells him.

What is she doing?

I step closer to Porter, standing on my toes so I can see what he and Clara are watching. I know the voices, they are slightly muffled from the background noise in the video but you can still make out the words.

"If I didn't lie then Terrance would have fired me too. I'm disposable he said...I had no choice. I couldn't have that kind of fax floating around about me. It didn't matter how I felt about you..."

It's from the other day; Greg and I at the Thai restaurant.

I could kiss Clara right now!

"That dumbass!" Terrance spun angrily, running both hands through his hair.

"I don't need to see anymore," Porter pushes Clara's hand away from him and he looks over at Terrance. "Your plan was to what? Pull the wool over my eyes?"

"No offense," Clara moved towards the breakfast nook with Faye, "but it almost worked."

Porter ignores her and Faye hushes her.

"Edie may have not trusted me," Merida panics, walking over to us, "but I never tried to truly deceive you. I love Lavish Looks. That company is like my third child. Edie was angry at me for the past but I had proved to her I was serious about what we created together—"

"—Merida," Porter cuts her off sternly, "You won't be getting the company, save your theatrics."

Edie! Did you hear that?!

Oh right.

"We'll see about that," Merida places her hands on her tiny hips, "don't forget that I've managed to convince the board to replace you. With one meeting I will have you removed, your shares stripped and your name completely trashed in the papers. I wonder what they'll think of you in England once they learn of your recklessness?"

I would hit her if I was certain she wouldn't sue me.

"I don't think they will be learning of anybody's recklessness, my dear."

How we missed the kitchen door being swung open was beyond me.

Tom and Reese stood together in front of the door as a short round man stood before them. His wispy hair blew from draft of the open terrace door, and just like the first time I saw him, he wore a bow tie imprinted with dog bones. He was glaring at Merida callously.

"Henry? What are you doing here?" Porter watches the man adjust his bow tie and then come towards us. He reaches into the pocket of his suit jacket and as he passes Terrance and Merida, he sticks his nose up to them.

"He tried to get a hold of you the last few days," Tom speaks up, "but you never returned his phone calls. Whenever he came to the house, your maid Marta turned him away."

"I thought you may be interested in having a look at this," from his suit jacket Henry takes out a folded sheet of paper. "There was a reason Edie didn't want Merida anywhere near the company and it isn't just because she is irresponsible with her *own* money. Have a look."

Porter takes the sheet of paper and since I'm still standing close to him I have a glance it at. I see nothing but numbers, and after a while I just look away.

"As you'll notice those are negatives from the advertising funds," Henry raises his hand and points on the paper Porter holds. "And you will observe the account number and name that the money had been transferred to the last six months..."

"You've been stealing from Lavish Looks?" Porter tears his eyes off the paper to Merida.

"That's why she was in a rush to take over," I say, remembering everything Tom told me this morning. "She had to get in there to fire everybody and wipe any evidence clean of her taking the money. Henry says Edie was suspicious for a while and asked him to investigate over the last six months."

"And I was not surprised as to what I found," Henry snaps giving Merida a glare. "She's also been stealing the prototype of the new launch line, and attempting to sell them to the competitors. This is enough to have her arrested."

Edie was right! Marta was wearing a stolen scent the other day; she must have received it from Terrance, who took it from Merida.

We did it, we actually did it.

We saved everything.

"What are you smiling at?" Terrance growls my way. I had almost forgotten that he was here.

"At your downfall," I shoot back.

I don't know if he would actually hit me, but he takes a single step towards me. His fists balled at his sides. He then stops short as he realizes what he's doing and Porter speaks. "I'd be careful if I were you, Mr. Meyers."

"Okay," Clara's voice cuts through the building tension, "I think our job is done. We should go."

"Yeah, okay," I agree glancing over at her and Faye, "go on home."

"Phoebe," Porter steps to the side with me, "go home with your friends. Henry and I need to discuss a few things with Terrance and Merida."

My heart sinks a little.

"But I want to stay," I look over at Terrance, who has his back to us now, his hands on the island counter. Merida's head hangs as she rubs her temples.

I look back at Porter when his hand touches my back lightly. I arch against it as my skin tingles, and find his eyes scanning my face.

"Phoebe. There isn't anything else you can do," his voice is a whisper. "We'll be in contact in a little while. I promise."

Chapter Twenty-Five

While I was out at dinner with Faye and Clara Tuesday evening, Tom and Reese had started to discuss my incident. They told me how much it bothered them that I had been bullied, despite whatever pretenses had come before Porter firing me. On a whim, Reese googled Merida's name and went through the articles she found on the internet. There was one article written two years ago in the Cedar Springs newsletter, a publication that was run by volunteers, that was pretty damning against her. It had something to do with her cheating at a dog show, and it was written by a Henry Rubano.

So Tom made a call, and received more than he had bargained for. He found out Henry had been the head accountant at Lavish Looks for over twenty years. Henry told Tom how he had been instructed six months ago by Edie to keep a look out for any suspicious activity in the accounts. She never told him the reasoning behind her request, until Henry stumbled onto a missing ten grand.

So Reese and Tom met up with Henry that night, in the offices of Lavish Looks, and hatched a plan. Henry was supposed to meet us when we pulled up at the house to stop the auction, but he had car trouble and was stuck dealing with a tow.

It was by sheer dumb luck that Clara texted Tom to tell him about running into Greg and the video she took, in hopes that maybe it could clear me of something. Reese had the idea to have them sneak in as regular auction goers, just in case confronting Terrance and Merida went badly. At least the video could shed some light that I wasn't a complete liar.

Porter had Rosanne escort us out quickly after the confrontation and as she shut the door she told me she would call me as soon as she could.

She called at midnight, but I was lying in bed wide awake.

Porter had threatened both Terrance and Merida with calling the authorities. When Terrance told Porter he could easily get rid of the support Henry had, Henry was quick to tell him he had emailed a copy to both Reese and Tom. Though Rosanne said she wished Porter had called the police on them, he decided not to.

In fact, he had given Merida the option to give up her half of the company and sell her shares; the opportunity to be done with Lavish Looks, to resign with dignity and to keep *her* name out of the papers. Or she could be arrested. Rosanne said she took less than ten seconds to decide. Porter told her he'd have the lawyers draw up the papers in the morning, and they were to be signed by noon that day.

He threatened to show Clara's video, and tell the entire story, to Terrance's partners. He told him that he had a feeling Greg would give him up in a heartbeat if it meant he could stay at Meyers and Brant. When Terrance asked Porter what he wanted, he demanded he send a new fax. Declaring the previous fax he sent about Legal Assistant Phoebe Mercer an error on his part, and that she is an exceptional future lawyer. Terrance agreed, realizing that taking a hit on his reputation was better than getting arrested.

Porter fired Marta, but it was Rosanne that kicked her out of the house.

The auction was stopped before it could end, and none of the bidders were given their purchases, which caused a riot, Rosanne explained.

Now it was Friday, and it was going by dreadfully slow. The high of catching Merida and Terrance had worn off by lunch time when Tom had to go into the publishing house and Reese had a meeting at a gallery. I was stuck alone with my mother, who had taken it upon herself to clean Tom's already sterile apartment. I sat on the couch flipping through the channels, settling on a television show for a mere five minutes before I was bored. I didn't even put effort in dressing today, settling with leggings and a sleeveless red tunic.

My phone sat next to me, and with each vibration I looked with anticipation. It was always Faye or Clara or Satine. It was never Porter. I don't know why I thought he would call me; he must have known Rosanne delivered the new to me last night.

I *wanted* him to call.

By three o'clock my mother had harped on me for not eating, and produced several sandwiches on the plate before me. My phone pinged with an email notification.

It was an email from Greg and I sat up to read it.

There was no subject line and only two sentences in the text box.

It was sent out this morning. He's getting flak from his partners, but he'll live.

I'm sorry. Again. ☹ Let me buy you dinner and apologize?

He has to be joking; he's asking me out after all of this?

I open the attachment and browse the copy of the fax. It was sent from the desk of Terrance Meyers and it was only a paragraph long, but to the point.

Phoebe Mercer is an exceptional legal assistant and always has been... A hard working, determined, resourceful, moral future lawyer...a fantastic addition to any firm she should get hired into...I was wrong to have sent that falsified fax without analysing all the facts, and take full responsibility...

I don't bother reading the rest of it. None of it makes me feel better, but I did reply to Greg.

I sent him a poop emoticon.

By the time Tom returned with Reese and Chinese take-out, it was after six and I hadn't removed myself from the couch except to use the bathroom. I tell them, and my mother about the email from Greg.

"Well," Tom pushes his glasses up his nose, "looks like everything has been cleaned up."

He continues to remove the take out containers from the paper bag as Reese and my mother gather plates and utensils. We sit around the kitchen island, the smell from the greasy take out starts making my mouth water.

"What about Porter?" Reese asks as she slides an empty plate my way, "has he called you?"

"No, but I suspect he's busy," I answer, "dealing with the aftermath of everything that happened. How he almost screwed everything up believing those two whack jobs." None of them respond, but I see the look Reese gives Tom and can't help but wail, "What?"

"Nothing," Reese shrugs, "I just thought—"

She's interrupted by a knock on the door, and we all freeze. My mother looks over at Reese and Tom, but avoids my eyes.

"I'll get it," I finally say as I leave the stool.

I know what they're thinking back there; they're thinking its Porter.

It must be Porter they think.

Please be Porter.

I get to the door and pull it open gently, my heart beating so fast I can hear it in my ears.

But it's not Porter, its Henry.

He stands there with a large white envelope in this hands, a large smile over his round face. He's in a pair of jeans and a bright Hawaiian shirt, no sign of paw prints anywhere on his attire. He brushes his thinning hair to the side and greets me, "Evening Ms. Mercer."

"Henry, come on in." I move to the side and he waltzes in quickly, giving me another smile as I begin to shut the door behind him. I take a quick look down the hallway, just in case, Porter is straggling after him, but it's empty.

"Hello all," Henry gives a wave at the kitchen when he spots them,

"Hello Henry." Tom nods, "we heard everything wrapped up nicely after we left yesterday."

"It did yes." Henry draws in a gratified breath, the kind you would take around a really good smelling meal. "It was a very satisfying to see Merida turn that shade and admit defeat. I've hated that woman for twenty years. And," he turns to face me now, "I heard about the new fax. That should clear the air on a few things for you, shouldn't it?"

"It was nice of Porter to get Terrance to do that; I can only imagine his face when he heard that request."

"You know," Henry gets serious on me, "I have never seen a man's stomach puff up the way his did. He looked like a circus bear."

I smirk and gesture towards the kitchen, "We're just about to eat, do you want to join us?"

"No, no my dear but thank you," he pats my arm gently; "I have to hurry home. The wife and I leave to Hawaii in a little over six hours, for seven days."

"That explains the shirt," I hear Tom mutter with a sneer at Reese.

"I've come on official business," Henry gets sombre again, and straightens up his posture. He pushes the large envelope at me. "This is for you. Please open it."

"What is it?" I take it slowly from him; the weight of it has me thinking it's something official and important. He gestures at me to quickly open it, and so, I pull apart the string that ties it together. Once the flap pops up I reach inside and find a stack of paper stapled together. Henry pulls the envelope from me so I can take the inside contents with both hands.

Good Lord. I'm holding a stack of paperwork about two hundred pages, if not more.

"Does anybody have a pen?" Henry steals my attention away from the papers as he begins to fiddle through the pockets of his tight jeans.

"I do," Tom says from the kitchen,

"Ah, thank you Thomas."

"What is this?" I can tell it's some sort of contract. As I hold it with one hand, using my other to flip through the pages I catch the sight of the words *Lavish Looks* scattered throughout the paragraphs.

"It's the company," Henry simply states, as he watches Tom cross the room with a metal pen in his hand. "Including thirty percent of Merida's shares, a handsome business account, parking space, and creative control."

"I'm sorry?"

Tom stops next to Henry and holds out the pen, which Henry takes with a smile. Even Tom stares at the papers in my hand with a perplexed brow.

"With Merida so *selflessly* stepping down from Lavish Looks", Henry quips with a roll of his big eyes, "and Porter unable to step up as CEO we have to go with an outside hire. We don't have the time to rummage through hundreds of resumes and take a chance on someone who may not have the company's best interest at heart. So he's giving it to you, if you'll take it, that is." He pushes the pen at me, "Now I've marked the places you're to sign, on the last three pages."

"Holy crap," Tom says looking up at me.

Me? Run Lavish Looks? This must be some kind of joke.

"Henry," I push the contract back at him, my face cool with surprise. "You have to be joking. I'm not CEO material here."

"On the contrary," Henry practically barks, offended. "You're determined, restless, clearly a hard worker, and you have fortitude. You had the best interests of the company at heart and even though you had your back to the wall, you never strayed off course. That's quite impressive."

"Well," I feel myself blush lightly, "I had some help in the end."

"*Some* help?" Reese repeats with a laugh, "*some?*"

"A lot of help," I correct but I look back at Henry seriously and change my tone. "Henry, I don't know the first thing about running a company. I went to school for Law, I was eventually going to take the bar—"

"—And if that's still what you plan to do, then let it be so." Henry throws up both hands, "we won't stop you from that. But I do think you could do some good running this company. I think you would be a natural at it. It will take some time to learn the ropes but I will be there to help you, so will our C.O.O. Vanessa."

"I don't mean to interfere here," my mother comes around the island but stops away from us. "This is certainly none of my business but my opinion...now my opinion is, jitterbug," she narrows her eyes at me, "is that this is a great opportunity. You're a fool to reject it."

"I agree," Reese chimes in as she opens a container of take out and picks up a set of wooden chopsticks. "I personally think you should give up on the lawyer dream. Not that you aren't good at it..." It's clear she doesn't think I'm good at it.

"This would suit you better," Tom simply shrugs.

They must be all mad. Me, run a multi-million dollar company?

I was barely able to run around and get Terrance's errands done properly! How the hell do they expect me to be able to run a company like Lavish Looks? How could Henry have convinced Porter that I would be a great candidate?

"Henry, I really appreciate it," I look down at the contract, "this is amazing and I'm grateful you told Porter I would be a great choice but I—"

Henry frowns at me as he rests his hands atop his belly, "I never told Porter anything. It was his idea. The second I asked him who he thought should take over, he said your name."

"He did?" I look back down at the contracts I hold.

I have to admit now, that I like looking at my name in print above the Lavish Looks logo. It feels lovely to hold this contract, to think about taking over Edie's office and making sure nobody like Merida steps into the company again. Is it that farfetched of an idea to try my hand at this?

I see the pen slide slowly across the top of the page and as I look up I see Henry focusing on pushing the pen towards my hands.

"You'd have to move to Cedar Springs," Tom breaks the silence as he puts his hands into the pockets of his brown trousers. "The commute from the city to there every day could break you."

I didn't even think about that. Cedar Springs is such an expansive place to live, or to rent in, especially in the summer. Tourists flood the beach and the motels are always packed with families and young partiers. "I'm sure I could find an affordable place."

"Not necessary," Henry shakes his head at me and reaches for the contract. He pulls the pages up and flips past the orange marker. "The deed of the house has been transferred to your name, legal fees paid courtesy of Porter. There is no mortgage, but there are your amenities and the payment of the help if you choose to keep Rosanne on. He's leaving you Edie's car to do as you want; sell it, keep it or donate it, as well as her other things that had been put to auction. All yours."

"He's leaving me the house?" I don't believe the words as they roll from my mouth. *The house?"*

"Yes, well," Henry looks at the contract and sighs. "Rosanne mentioned how much you loved the house, and Porter lives in London. There's no other family and instead of dealing with the mess of trying to sell it, you seemed like the perfect option."

"That house must be worth a million dollars," Tom grabs the deed from my hands and brings it up to his eyes, "Easily."

"A little over actually," I remark silently.

I have to sit down.

The couch is only a few feet away from me so I make a beeline to it and drop down. The contract to Lavish Looks drops on my lap. Lavish Looks? Edie's house? It's all mine?

"I think she's going to have a stroke," I hear Reese whisper.

"I'm not...I'm fine." I manage to say. "I'm just a little, shocked."

"Naturally," Henry bellows with laughter like Saint Nick, "anybody would be. A mere fifteen minutes ago you were unemployed and homeless." He chuckles and it echoes around the group of us. "Does this mean you'll take it?"

"Of course she will," Tom answers for me quickly, "I can't let her turn this down."

He gave me the house. The house that has stayed in Edie's family for generations? That monster of a house?

I need to see him.

"Where's Porter?" I clench the contract again and look up at Henry, "I should thank him for this. This is—it's incredible."

"Well you'd have to do it via email, I'm afraid," Henry lets me know. "He's on his way back home. I believe his flight leaves in an hour or two. He has important things to attend to back home he says, but will be available via email if you need him, if you have any questions."

"He's leaving?"

"At the airport as we speak."

Of course he's leaving. He has a life back there; this was only a temporary thing. He has a job to get back to, an apartment, friends, his parents, maybe even a girlfriend. A pretty, skinny, posh British girlfriend.

I have no real right to feel this way! I barely knew him. So we had a few moments? So what? I lost Riley too, and I don't feel so heartbroken, disappointed, and wretched.

There's a brass banging on the door and I look up as everyone turns towards it. Tom moves to the door without missing a beat and pulls it open, "Oh hi."

"Hey."

It's Clara. She drives her way around Tom and makes a face when she sees the seriousness in the room. As she looks at me, her blond hair in a neat French braid, she smiles and clasps her hands together. "Satine is coming back next week!"

I smile, "that's great."

The grin drops off her face, her perfect teeth disappearing behind her lips that are dressed in a light pink shade. "What's going on? Why aren't you more excited?"

"Porter gave Phoebe the company," Tom explains as he scratches the back of his neck, "he also left her the house and everything in it."

Clara turns my way, her jaw plummets and her eyes widen. "No way."

"Yes way," Henry tells her, "She just has to sign everything."

"Sign it!" Clara orders me, "sign it all right now. Phoebe that is amazing." She walks over and sits down next to me, lifting the contract from my hands. "I can't believe he did that. What did you say when he told you?"

"He didn't tell me," I say and motion at Henry, "Henry told me. Porter didn't have time, he's leaving."

"*Leaving*?" she says the word harshly. "What do you mean leaving?"

"To London," I tell her, "where he lives. He's at the airport now."

"But he can't leave," Clara frowns at me, "like obviously, you know…"

"It's alright." I suddenly feel foolish as everyone stares at me. My crush on Porter, now known broadly around the apartment. "I'll thank him via email. Maybe I'll send him a basket or something next week…"

"Splendid idea." Henry agrees. "I happen to know he's a fan of those caramel chocolate pecan things."

"Hurry up and sign those," Clara picks up the pen that has rolled between us and hands it to me, "then get your coat."

Chapter Twenty-Six

"Clara, this is insane."

"I'm not saying you have to tell him you're *in love* with him, I'm just saying—"

"—I am not in love with him!" I look at her in horror, "I barely know him."

"But you have *feelings* for him yes?" She glances in her rear-view mirror as she changes lanes. "And I know he has feelings for you. We all saw it yesterday."

I can't believe that I let her convince me to go to the airport; I must be the insane one. I signed the papers, handed them to Henry and ran out the door. Now I was driving through the city in Clara's SUV as she tried best to avoid traffic jams, on my way to catch Porter before he got on his plane.

What was I even going to say? 'Hi. I like you, do you really have to go back home? Maybe you could stay a while and we can date?' Just thinking about it has me feeling nutty.

Clara gets onto the highway, and sprints her SUV into the express lane, I bounce as she maneuvers to avoid hitting any cars. "Look, you don't have to tell him how you feel. You can just thank him. Thanking him via email for giving you a million dollar home and a million dollar company is not something you should do. It should be face to face."

"You have a point."

"And if he says something to you, or you say something to him, well then it happens."

"I'm not going to do that Clara."

I reach over to her radio and turn it on.

"You broke up with Riley five days ago, and I know you weren't as crushed as you looked back there when you told me Porter was leaving. That doesn't make you a bad person; it just means that you and Riley weren't meant to be. In my opinion any guy who tells you to stop eating meat needs to hit the road—"

"—Clara."

"No offense," she states, gripping the steering wheel with her hand as she spots the exit for the airport. "My point is that if you haven't felt this way about a man in a very long time *or ever*, you ought to do something about it. Even if it means just saying 'I like you.' Things are different when you're with someone who you have chemistry with. I know it sounds cliché, but it's true. I mean sometimes it doesn't work out and you break up and you get some space but sometimes that can be a good thing."

I side-eye her, "You're with Mark again aren't you?"

"He asked me to move in with him."

Well, that's new.

"Wow."

"I know," Clara smirks, "I almost fell off the chair at the restaurant."

"Will you?"

"I haven't decided yet."

I have a feeling that's a yes, but I keep it to myself.

Twenty minutes later, she pulls off the exit and within ten minutes we see the domes of the airport ahead of us. My fingers are gripping into my knees at my jeans. I haven't been this nervous since my finals in university, maybe not even then.

She glides into a space between two taxies on the loading dock and near the departure doors. I watch them slide open and close, people going in and out with luggage.

"Okay, I'm staying here, parking is too expensive."

"You're making me go alone?" I wince looking over my shoulder at her,

"Do you actually want an audience?"

I make a face and decide I don't.

How is it I'm more nervous about doing this then I was confronting Terrance and Merida?

Because you're about to put yourself out there that's why, Edie's voice floats through my head and a ping of longing surfaces for her.

Okay, if I don't just force myself to do it, I'll never master enough valour to do it.

I grab the handle to the door, and pull it towards me so the door pushes outward. For the middle of May it's a rather cool night, and a harsh wind brushes against my cheeks as I leave Clara's car.

"Good luck," she smiles as I turn to shut the door.

After it slams shut, I turn around to the long sliding doors and hurry towards them, zig zagging around crowds of people exiting the airport. I excuse myself to a group of older women holding Welcome Home signs that I cut in front of who are moving too slow to the doors.

I've only been to the airport a few times, and rarely inside. I was usually the one waiting outside on the curb in the taxi.

The area I stood in was incredibly large; I couldn't see any walls in front of me except the doors and windows behind me. Large flat screens hung from the ceiling giving you the time and gate of the arrivals. They hung from every angle and the entire room was abuzz with venders in kiosks selling tourist merchandise. I spotted a Starbucks booth, a famous donut eatery, even a Hershey's chocolate store to my far right. The nearest screen was only a few feet away. It hung over a set of trendy steel benches that where occupied by a family with suitcases.

I stepped up as close as I could without invading the personal space of the family, then I realized I didn't have Porter's flight number.

"Damn," I mutter as my eyes frantically scan the screen.

But luck was on my side; there was only one flight leaving to London, England this evening, and it was at gate thirty three. It was boarding in less than ten minutes.

Okay, maybe luck wasn't totally on my side.

Where the hell was gate thirty three?!

I step back and look up at the ceiling, catching plastic hanging signs with lathe numbers imprinted on them. Gate numbers.

Gate twenty five to thirty five was to my left, according to the arrow and the sign hanging over top.

I realize I would have to run to make it before anybody starts boarding that plane, I had a feeling Porter would be one of the very first people on that plane. So I begin my sprint, careful to avoid anybody slow before me, and cautious not to knock anybody over at the same time.

My heart has never raced this much in my entire life, and I knew it wasn't just because I was running. What if I missed it? Or couldn't find him, and lose him as people start boarding?

At this point I don't think I could stand the disappointment.

I end up passing the doors that led into Gate twenty five, twenty six and twenty seven's waiting area. Each door had a warning sign for passengers to make sure they had their tickets and passports on them.

Oh God, how far away is Gate thirty three anyway?

The next door is marked Gate twenty eight.

I'm nearly there.

But I can feel myself gassing out, and cramping at my right side.

Ow. Damn it...

Ow.

I stop and bend over a little bit, feeling my lungs burning a little bit. I inhale bouts of air that I hope will make the sharp cramps go away.

That's it, beginning Monday I start going to the gym. I'm only twenty eight years old; there isn't an excuse to be this out of shape.

I spot Gate Thirty One to my left, and unbend.

I don't have much time, how long have I been running?

I draw in a deep breath and force my feet to move from their place, dashing down the wide hallway, narrowly missing a couple too engrossed in each other to notice anyone else.

The cramping has returned but I don't have any time to stop and let it settle. I'm passing right in front of Gate Thirty Two, which means the next gate is the one I need.

There it is. There's the hanging sign pointing to the frosted sliding doors that have Gate Thirty Three painted onto them, and the general warning sign.

Holy hell, I made it.

I hurry towards the door and it slides open immediately.

The room is gigantic. More TV screens hang from the ceiling but most of them are playing a news station. There are over fifty pews of plastic blue chairs running along the room and my guess was, I was staring at nearly two hundred people gathered.

How in the hell am I supposed to find him in this crowd?

The back wall is all windows, showcasing the impressive tarmac and a jumbo jet just outside ready to take passengers. I spot the blue and white desk across the room with several flight attendants behind it. A line of passengers had already formed, and I watch as one of the flight attendants reaches for a microphone on the desk.

"Attention passengers, please have your ticket and your passport on hand. We are starting to board. Anyone without a ticket is not allowed beyond this point. Thank you."

Slowly, people start to gather their things and I panic.

I find myself spotting the line that's formed at the Check In desk, and decide to head to the front of it. I pass by everyone in my way, knocking over luggage and shouldering innocent bystanders shouting an apology as I do. I start to skim the line as I near it but not one face is familiar. The people I pass give me a strange look, when I stare at them longer than needed.

He's not here. He's not in line.

I stop and ready myself to turn, when I hear his voice sharply in my right ear.

"Thank you."

He's near the front of the line, an attendant hands him back a passport and scans his ticket. When she returns them with a flirty smile and batting of the eyes, he goes to put them in the brown leather carry on he holds in his left hand.

Call his name!

I open my mouth but nothing comes out, and I don't know why.

He's in a black t-shirt and a pair of faded jeans. It takes a moment for me to take in his casual appearance. His hair is un-brushed and his five o'clock shadow has grown into a full scruff that, if I'm to be honest, has my breath taken. I hadn't really noticed it yesterday.

Before I could chastise myself for chickening out, he looks up nonchalantly after he zips up his bag. His eyes collapse on me and he stands up right, blinking a few times at me as if he isn't sure that I was truly standing there.

"Excuse me sir? You can't hold up the line," the flight attendant gives me a mere glance as she speaks to him, running a hand through her shiny brown hair as what I can only assume is a flirtation tactic.

He steps out of the line, giving her a small glance and then looks back over at me. I watch as he moves to the window a few feet away from the line, and I take the indication to follow him.

He drops his bag to the floor at his feet and watches as I step in front of him.

"Phoebe."

"Hi."

Hi? That's all you can say? I feel like shrinking away as I watch him frown at me.

"I uh, I wanted to thank you," I manage to come up with the words, "in person. For everything."

His eyebrows lift and he half nods, "It was nothing, the least I could do."

"You gave me everything," I say.

"It seemed wrong if I didn't at least extend the option," he explains, "I think it's what my aunt would have wanted."

I can see the flight attendant glance over at us as she scans a couple's tickets.

"Maybe," I look back at him and find him skimming my face.

"It was considerate of you to come all the way down to tell me this," Porter tells me, "but it wasn't necessary. A simple email would have sufficed."

"Right, I knew that," I state with a small smile.

Now we stare at each other, awkwardly and tense. This was such a bad idea. I can feel my fingers ice over and my nerves play havoc on my stomach. Despite those feelings, my heart batters against my rib cage in a way it never did with Riley.

I can feel Edie's voice trickle into my mind again. *If you don't tell him you will regret it. Maybe not now, maybe not next week or month but you will. Just friggin' do it Phoebe.*

"I just wanted…uh I just wanted to tell you that, I like you." It finally slips and Porter remains impassive as he looks into my eyes. "I like you, and I think that you like me. Or not, I don't know. Maybe we could get that drink?"

I run a hand through my hair nervously and look back at him, hoping my embarrassment slides off my shoulders but it doesn't. I still feel mortified as his expression remains unchanged.

"I have to catch my flight," he points over his shoulder.

"Of course," I pull an aloof smile over my sunken face and laugh gracelessly, pretending I don't feel my heart stab in pain, "duh."

"Perhaps next time I'm here?"

I can tell from his tone he doesn't mean it.

"Sure, yes," I fold my hands tightly over my chest and nod, "that would be great."

Finally he smiles, but it's tight and unwavering. He gives me a quick nod and bends over to pick up his bag, "till then."

"Right," the forced smile is starting to pain me, "have a safe flight."

Why in the bloody hell did I listen to Clara?

What did I *actually* think was going to happen? Did I think he'd wrap me in his arms and declare his undying love for me?

I'm such an idiot.

I stare at myself in the mirror.

After Porter walked away from me, I avoided the eye of the attendant as she allowed him to cut in line. I left the room as quick as I could, and found the nearest bathroom.

I was in it alone, and for that I was ever grateful. Alone, staring at my image in the long clean, mirror before me; my cheeks still red, the effects of humiliation lingering.

I hope I never see him again.

"Now I would have *never* done that, how embarrassing."

I freeze for only a moment and then turn slowly, leaving my hands on the white sink counter in front of me.

She's standing in front of the nearest blue stall, leaning into it, careful not to escape through the metal door. Her strawberry blonde hair is tight against her head, and the red dress she's in ends at her ankles, hugging her torso and arms in a very flattering way.

"Edie?"

310

"But that aside," she pushes herself away from the stall, folding her arms over her chest and piercing her lips at me. "I think he's a colossal fool and am forever disappointed in him." A thin smile graciously spreads over her.

"I thought you had, moved on?"

"I almost did," she states, "but something told me to do one last check on everything. Imagine my surprise, when I stumbled into your brother's apartment the morning of the auction as he was telling you how he had contacted Henry."

"Why didn't you come when I called you then?" I demand. "We could have used you yesterday!"

"You didn't need me," Edie's face falls, "for goodness sakes Phoebe, you and your people put all the ducks in the row. And I was there." She points a finger in my face, "I was just hiding. In case you messed up, not that I thought you would but you know. It's you, your track record needs improving."

I gawk at her, but can't pretend to be offended for long.

I was just happy to see her.

"I'm happy to see you too," Edie shrugs casually, as she looks at me from the corner of her eye, examining her nails. I smirk at her, knowing she isn't the sentimental one.

"Does this mean you're ready to move on?" I suddenly realize, her wish had been granted. I had helped her save her company and punish the people who tried to tear everything apart.

"I suppose I could stay a little while longer," Edie drops her arms and looks over at me, "you may need help running my company, after all."

I smile.

That wasn't the reason she was staying, but I couldn't admit to her that I had the feeling she was lying to save face. So instead, I cross my arms over my chest and smile, "Okay."

"You like having me around?" she questions, clearing her throat and glancing around the bathroom, avoiding eye contact until I answer her.

"I wouldn't mind you around, no."

"Great!" she claps her hands together and moves towards me, "Because we have to zip back to Cedar Springs in the morning right away."

"Why?" I eye her suspiciously as her green eyes sparkle with an enthusiasm that is worrying.

"Because," she grins, "we have to find Rebecca's killer."

Oh God.

To be continued...

Acknowledgements

This book couldn't have been completed without these individuals, and I thank them to the moon and back;

Kassie Wright, who was not only my editor but my writing coach during the entire process.

Monica Kim and Josemine Singson, who as usual, serve as my first beta readers and critics.

Keelan Fiorillo, whose adventures remind me to never lose sight of what is truly important.

My Nanowrimo writing group, and the weekly write in's that kept me on track in November.

My father-in-law, for being my number one customer.

My parents, and in-laws, who babysat on the weekends.

My sister Margaret Banas, whose creative handmade soaps inspired the foundation of Lavish Looks.

Niki Browning, of Peculiar Perspective Designs, for my lovely cover.

To my amazing Beta Readers who are honest, straight-forward and delightfully quirky.

To Laura Tait and the fantastic review crew at Books, Chocolate and Wine. Reviewing with you all is always a blast.

To all the wonderful fellow author's and bloggers I've met the last few years who consistently give me advice, and laughs, when I need it. You know who you are.

To my fellow Leaguers, I owe my discovered passion for writing to the both of you.

And finally, to my readers. Thank you so very much.

About the Author

Nikki LeClair lives in Canada with her loving husband and their two rambunctious daughters. When she isn't ordering her children to behave or begging her Border Terrier to listen to her, she sits behind her lap-top plotting out the next adventure for her new characters. She loves a good glass of Pinot Noir, and a steaming cup of her favorite tea blends. This is her first series. She also writes under a pen name, Vivian Brooks, and enjoys hearing from readers. You can find her on twitter at @NikkiL_Books, and on her Facebook Fanpage Nikki LeClair.

Made in the USA
Charleston, SC
02 May 2016